Catherine King was born in Rotherham, South Yorkshire. A search for her roots – her father, grandfather and great-grandfather all worked with coal, steel or iron – and an interest in local industrial history provided inspiration for her stories. Catherine wrote ten novels, including *A Sister's Courage* and *Her Mother's Secret*. Her second novel, *Silk and Steel*, was shortlisted for the Romantic Novel of the Year award.

Catherine sadly passed away in 2015.

Also by Catherine King

Women of Iron
Silk and Steel
Without a Mother's Love
A Mother's Sacrifice
The Orphan Child
The Lost and Found Girl
A Sister's Courage
Her Mother's Secret
A Daughter's Love

Digital-exclusive short stories

Stolen Passion

The
Secret
Daughter

Catherine King

sphere

SPHERE

First published in Great Britain in 2012 by Sphere
This paperback edition published in 2012 by Sphere

7 9 10 8

A CIP catalogue record for this book
is available from the British Library.

ISBN 978-0-7515-4807-5

Typeset in Bembo by Palimpsest Book Production Limited,
Falkirk, Stirlingshire
Printed and bound in Great Britain by
Clays Ltd, Elcograf S.p.A

Papers used by Sphere are from well-managed forests
and other responsible sources.

MIX
Paper from
responsible sources
FSC® C104740

Sphere
An imprint of
Little, Brown Book Group
Carmelite House
50 Victoria Embankment
London EC4Y 0DZ

An Hachette UK Company
www.hachette.co.uk

www.littlebrown.co.uk

This book is dedicated to my mother, who, as a young woman, worked 'in service'.

Acknowledgements

I should like to thank Jean Grantham for telling me about Stansted Park, which gave me a model for Melton Hall, and the helpful volunteers and staff there who answered my questions about upstairs-downstairs life in a stately home.

Redfern Abbey is inspired by Wentworth Woodhouse in Yorkshire, hopefully soon to be restored to its former glory. I am grateful to Jacqueline Piper for her updates over the years on the continuing saga of this once magnificent building.

As always, I am indebted to my agent Judith Murdoch, and to the wonderfully hard-working team at Little, Brown for ensuring this book is finished on time. It is my second title out this year and a special mention is due to my editor, Manpreet Grewal for 'stepping up to the plate'. Thank you, Manpreet.

Catherine King

PART ONE

PHYLLIS

Prologue

1888 South Riding, Yorkshire

Phyllis Kimber whimpered as her mother gently took her from her husband's sinewy arms. 'She's so pretty, isn't she? Don't you think she's the bonniest baby you've ever seen?'

Her pink and white skin, silky fair hair and large blue eyes gave the infant an angelic appearance that melted the stoniest of hearts.

Jack Kimber's features barely moved. 'Aye, she is. You make sure you take good care of her.'

'As if I wouldn't! I'm her mother.'

Jack looked away and the ensuing silence was broken only by Phyllis's snuffles as she rooted for a breast. Ellen took a deep breath. 'I know I wasn't your choice of bride but I've given up as much as you, Jack Kimber!'

'He would never have wed you, he didn't want to.'

'He did! He couldn't, that's all.'

'Well, what's done is done,' Jack replied.

'Yes it is, and you are my husband now, and – and my baby's father.'

'Don't fret yourself. I'll do my duty by you and the bairn. You'll have food on the table and she'll have her penny a week for the board school.'

'She needs more than that.'

An impatient expression passed across her husband's weathered face and Ellen swallowed back the words *she needs your love as well*. This marriage had to work for Phyllis's sake.

'We might grow to love each other if,' she added, 'if we have more children.'

She watched his mouth turn down at the corners. 'Don't ask that of me,' he said. Ellen thought he was about to leave but he stopped and added, 'You'll sleep with the bairn in the second bedroom.'

'Not for ever, surely?'

'As soon as she is old enough, I'll put a window in the gable end of the box room to make a bedroom for her.'

A tear welled in Ellen's eye and she blinked it back. 'You'll have to ask the land steward for permission. People will talk.'

'How we live is none of their business!'

'You did agree to marry me, Jack,' she protested.

'You should be grateful for that so we'll say no more about it,' he retaliated. 'But make no mistake, I don't care for you in that way and never shall.'

4

'No, all you care about is that woman! Well *she* didn't want you and *I* am your wife!' Phyllis's whimper rose to a wail and she squirmed in her mother's arms.

Jack Kimber stood up abruptly. 'Didn't you hear me, woman? I won't have another word said on the matter in my house!' He collected his cap from a peg by the back door and added, 'I'm to be made up from stable hand to one of His Lordship's grooms. You and the bairn won't want for anything from me.'

He closed the door behind him. 'Except love,' she whispered to the empty room. Ellen licked her finger and placed it between the baby's tiny lips where she sucked on it hungrily.

Chapter 1

Summer, 1898

'Ta-ra, then,' Phyllis said.

A straggling group of children dawdled down the street outside the board school in town and a shopkeeper sweeping her front step called, 'Get off home you lot before I tell your teacher.'

The girls ignored her but the boys pulled grotesque faces and she shook her broom at them.

A girl from her class asked, 'Are you coming to the canal for a swim?'

It was a boiling hot day and a cooling dip would have been welcome. She frowned. 'I have to go straight home.' She had a long walk to her father's isolated cottage on the edge of Redfern estate. It used to be in the hunting chase years ago, but Sheffield factories and houses had spread and gobbled up most of the land.

One of the lads shouted after her, 'Scaredy-cat! Scaredy-cat!'

'No I'm not! I'm not frightened of you lot. Anyroad, I'm leaving this rotten school soon, so there.'

The lads laughed and ran off, leaving the girls to absorb this new information. Phyllis picked up a stick and thrashed at the long grass growing beside the dusty path, glad to be free from sitting still all day chanting times tables and spellings. But she daren't dawdle too long or Mother might come looking for her and the other kids would call her a big baby if they found out.

The biggest of the girls stopped and turned. 'You can't leave. You're not ten yet.'

'I am in September.'

'Oh.' The girl thought for a second and added, 'Well I'm ten already. That makes me the eldest here so I get to say what we do and I say we go and watch the lads swimming.'

Phyllis lifted her chin. 'I've told you I can't. I've got too much sewing to do before I go—' She stopped abruptly. Oh lord, she mustn't say! Father would be furious with her!

'Go where? You're not going to the bottle factory, are you? My dad says it's the only place taking on girls this year.'

'I'm not working in any factory,' Phyllis stated. She said it in the same haughty tone that she had heard her mother use about anything regarded as 'common', and regretted it immediately. Most girls from this school went into factories. Fortunately, none of them teased her about it. They were too curious.

'Have you got a place already, then?'

Another girl became interested. 'I bet she has. Her dad works on t'Redfern estate. I bet her dad has got her into service at the Abbey. She's allus been little Miss Lah-de-dah.'

'Well,' the bossy girl said, 'my dad says going into service is beneath any decent person and he wouldn't let me do it. He said none of his lasses should have to kow-tow to anybody just because he's rich. My dad says you ought to be able to speak your mind if you want.' She stopped her tirade and demanded, 'Have you then? Have you got a place at the Abbey?'

'No I haven't! Anyroad, I can't go before I've been to training school.'

'What training school?'

Phyllis had said too much and muttered, 'I – I don't know.'

'Yes you do and I'll pull your hair if you don't tell.' The leader scanned the gathering group of interested onlookers triumphantly and added, 'Won't we?'

The others were smaller but there were several of them and they nodded with glee.

'Tell us then.'

'It's – it's like an industrial school that the lads have so they can learn a trade. Only it's for girls.'

'Where is it, then? What's it called?'

'I – I don't know.'

'*I don't know,*' the older girl mimicked and grasped her long plaits. 'Tell or I'll string you up by these and leave you to the crows.'

Another girl added, 'They peck your eyes out first.'

Phyllis's head jerked backwards and she yelped. But she'd had her fill of this constant tormenting because she wasn't one of them and elbowed her assailant in the stomach while kicking back with her boot. The older girl was caught off guard and loosened her grip. Phyllis whirled around and kicked her again, hard on the shin, making her squeal. She doubled over to rub her shin and yelled at the little ones, 'Get her!'

Phyllis took one look at the advancing group and realised her legs were longer than theirs. She swished her stick backwards and forwards a couple of times until they backed off then turned and fled, running as fast as she could until her breath was coming in rasps and her heart was thumping in her ears. Eventually she realised that they weren't coming after her and slowed. The river and the lads, who took off all their clothes to swim, held more attraction than she did.

She was glad to be leaving. She hated it here. She hated the tormenting kids at school only marginally more than she hated going home to her stiff and starchy mother and father who hardly said two words to each other. Being home was as boring as being in school and she got the cane from her father and teacher alike if she misbehaved. At least at home it was across her backside with her clothes on. Mr Green gave you strokes across the palms of your hands and still expected you to write neatly afterwards. She breathed in so deeply that her throat rattled but her heart began to slow.

Phyllis knew she was different from the town kids because Mother and Father had brought her up not to mix with them outside of school. They called their parents 'Mam' and 'Dad' and she was often the butt of their jokes. Although she liked the learning, and the teacher when he wasn't caning her, she was pleased to be getting away from the constant teasing. She turned her back on the town and began the long trudge home, thrashing harder and harder at the grass as she walked.

She would have been happier at the village school with other children from the estate. But Redfern village was further away from home. You couldn't live much further from the Abbey and still be on the Redfern estate. Mother and Father had argued about it when she started school. She remembered the raised voices as she darned her stockings by her bedroom window overlooking the garden. Chase Cottage was a pretty stone-built house, but it was a mile away from its nearest neighbour and down a long muddy lane. However, anybody could tell it was on Redfern land because its woodwork was painted in the same green as all the other properties owned by the Earl.

Her father was head groom and His Lordship kept a stable of hunters as well as his carriage horses so he was well enough off to afford her the training she needed to go into service. Mother thought it was a good idea. Phyllis wasn't that keen but her father insisted and he was old-fashioned. He was ten years older than Mother and expected unquestioning obedience from his wife and daughter. He was dutiful and loyal to the Earl and spent long hours at his work even in winter. Phyllis's younger memories were of coming home from school to a well-ordered but joyless home.

Yet she knew her parents cared for her in their own way. She never doubted her mother's love, but her father was a different kettle of fish altogether. She wasn't sure that he really loved her. And she was certainly never convinced he loved her mother, or that she loved him. She heard other girls talking in the playground and giggling about creaking bedsprings through cottage walls. She listened for them at home, but her nights were silent. One day, when the house was empty, she crept into her mother's room and bounced up and down on the bed. Sure enough, it creaked. Her father's bed was noisy too, but he slept alone in the big bedroom and she knew instinctively that her mother and father were different and she ought not to talk about them.

Mother was waiting at the front gate for her and as soon as she was in sight, she waved and called, 'Tea's ready!' Phyllis was hungry and quickened her step. Tea would be laid out on the kitchen table, on a fresh cloth with pretty china and a clean napkin. It was always a slice of bread and butter and a drink of tea from a pot that was kept warm from a brew Mother had made for herself earlier. If Phyllis was really hungry and asked for more Mother always refused, telling her not to spoil her proper tea, which she would eat at the table with Father when he came in from work. Father's days at the Abbey stables were long and he walked there and back every day so he needed a lot of feeding. But his quarter acre of garden around Chase Cottage grew most of the vegetables they needed for the whole year.

'Goodness me, what have you been doing? Look at the

state of your pinafore. That will never do for Lady Maude's. Find a clean one straightaway, then wash your hands and sit to the table. I have Father's tea to see to.'

It was always Father's tea. Never *your* tea or even *our* tea, but Father's tea as if no one else in the house would be eating it. She obeyed her mother without question, washed in the scullery and returned to the warm kitchen. It was cosy and comfortable, with a cooking range and dresser, and gingham curtains at the window. But the kids at school had unsettled her and she felt irritable.

'Do you have to watch me all the time, Mother?' Phyllis couldn't stop herself sounding ungrateful and felt guilty.

'I want to be sure you know your table manners. Besides, we can talk.'

'What about?' *There I go again!* Phyllis thought.

Her mother looked cross and replied. 'Father is right, it's high time you got away from those town children, you're beginning to sound just like them.'

'You sent me there.'

'It was your father's decision, not mine.'

'Well, they say I'm lah-de-dah in town because Father works at the Abbey, but their dads get paid more down the pit so I've no call to put on airs.'

'I've told you to take no notice of them! I don't know why children need all this schooling anyway. I only went to Sunday school until I did my two years at Lady Maude's.'

'Everybody has to go to board school now. It's the law. Mr Green told us.' She liked Mr Green except when he used his cane that he kept in the corner of the classroom.

13

She wondered if they used the cane at training school and guessed they would. As well, the other girls would be older than she was and bossy like the girl in her class. Lady Maude's was probably going to be worse than the board school.

'Do I have to go to Lady Maude's?'

Her mother's face took on an expression of pained shock. 'Oh Phyllis, it's an honour for you to be given a place there! Father will have to pay a lot more than a penny a week for you.'

'But it means I'll have to go into service. None of the other girls at school are, they're going straight to the bottle factory.'

'Well, more fool them. None of the other girls at school live on the Redfern estate and their fathers have to pay rent for their houses. I was in service and so was my mother. In fact, your grandmother was a parlour maid at the Abbey before she wed.'

'Did she go to Lady Maude's?' she persisted.

'She was one of the first. You can't get a good position in a titled household without proper training. You have to know how to carry on in front of your betters.'

'Kow-towing, you mean?'

'You've picked that up from town, haven't you? I knew I should have insisted you went to the village school, but your father wouldn't have it. Thank goodness he isn't home to hear you! He'd give you a caning for saying that. The sooner you leave that school the better. Lady Maude's might cost more to send you there but you'll mix with a better class of girls.'

By that, Mother meant the daughters of shopkeepers and clerks instead of the coal miners and steelworkers whose children populated the town school. But at least, Phyllis thought, the town girls came from big families that could stick together in the playground. Her parents' families didn't have much to do with her. She once met a great-aunt at a funeral in Redfern and thought she put on airs. She had been Head Laundress at the Abbey, her mother explained, and Phyllis had wondered what was so special about that.

Phyllis said, 'How can they be a better class if they're going to be servants just like me?'

'Don't argue. When you're fourteen, you'll get a respectable place in a titled household.'

'You mean I'll work at the Abbey like you and Father.'

'No, you can't work there.'

'Why can't I? They have loads of servants.'

Phyllis remembered her visit to Redfern Abbey last year for the Queen's Jubilee. She sat at a long table on the lawn in front of the grand house with a lot of other children. It was a hot day and she wore her best dress with ribbons in her fair hair. Mother and Father walked to Redfern village then travelled with other families in a farm cart to the Abbey where the kitchen servants gave them tea. They had potted meat and jam sandwiches, lemon curd tarts and butterfly buns washed down with lemon barley water.

'Because you can't,' her mother replied.

'Why not?'

'Because – because – because Father says you can't.

15

Now stop answering back. I want you to finish that smocking on your nightgowns before you go to bed tonight.'

Three of them, Phyllis sighed, three new nightgowns, three new of everything. Each piece of linen had to have her initials embroidered in a corner and there were six handkerchiefs and those special monthly towels that her mother had told about. She didn't need them yet, of course, but would one day and had to take them just in case. Mother was making her brown uniform dresses as the cloth was too dear to let her loose on it, but Phyllis made the pinafores because she had learned how to in sewing lessons at school.

Phyllis sat by the window where the light was good and she would be able to see Father come in through the back door. Everything had to be put away for when he came home from work and his tea had to be on the table as soon as he had washed at the stone sink in the scullery. It was toad-in-the-hole today and Phyllis could smell the sausages cooking and hear her mother beating the Yorkshire pudding batter to pour over them. When she was little Father used to come home for his dinner in the middle of the day but he didn't do that any more. He took bread and cheese and a bottle of cold tea and stayed with his horses. In the cold weather, the stable master's wife made broth and brought it out for all her husband's men. Mother always said Father was 'well-placed' at the Abbey stables, and they were better off than many a family in town or village.

Phyllis put away her sewing, brushed down her pinafore

with her hands and went to set Father's place at the table. She mashed the tea, put a knitted tea cosy over the pot and placed her father's pint mug beside it. Not a word was said as he sat at the table and waited for her to pour, add milk and sugar and stir it round. Mother placed a plate of steaming food in front of him and he picked up his knife and fork straightaway. Phyllis waited quietly for Mother to sit down with their dinner plates. When Father had finished he nodded in the direction of his pint mug and mother refilled it silently, rose to add hot water to the teapot and brought it back. Phyllis took the rice pudding out of the oven and Mother dished it up at the table, passing the pot of jam first to Father. He always did the same, plopped the jam in the middle and heaped the creamy pudding over the top with his spoon. She preferred to swirl it around making patterns in the bowl. When he had finished eating, Phyllis got up to clear the table. If Mother made a start before she did, Father said, 'Leave it to the lass. I've told you before about spoiling her. She has to learn her place.' Then he scraped back his chair and went out to the garden behind the cottage to pass the hours before bedtime.

Father's productive vegetable patch was helped by cart-loads of horse manure from the stables. Sometimes he brought home a brace of pheasant or partridge that the Abbey gamekeeper gave him and Mother kept a few laying hens so they never went hungry. In fact, when she listened to the town kids going on about their lives with only bread and dripping to eat on some days, Phyllis realised how comfortable she was. Father had a secure position and they lived in a proper house. Mother excelled at all her domestic tasks and won prizes for her baking and preserves at the village show. Even though they didn't live anywhere near the village she was allowed to enter because Father was employed by the Abbey.

Phyllis washed up the pots and returned to her sewing. When Father came in from the garden he drank beer that Mother had brewed in the scullery. It made Father's eyes go shiny very quickly and if Mother heard him slur his speech she sent Phyllis to bed whatever time it was. It was worse in winter because daylight faded early and so did her lamp as Father was mean with the oil. She had to lie awake for hours sometimes with nothing to do but think. Mother followed soon after but often Phyllis was asleep before Father lumbered up the stairs crashing and banging enough to wake her. Very early on Phyllis realised that she didn't want to be like them when she grew up. I want to be different, she thought.

But she didn't want to be a town kid with hand-me-down boots and sleeping six to a bed. She knew that was true because one of the little ones had told her in the playground. It was a big bed, she had said, and with three at the top and three at the bottom there was plenty of space. Phyllis reflected on this, alone in her tiny bedroom with its window in the end gable. It was a pretty room. Father had painted it and Mother had furnished it with print cotton curtains, bedcovers and made her nightgowns to match. But she so wished she was sharing it with a sister. Even a brother was better than nothing. Although she really didn't want to go into

18

service she did consider that going to Lady Maude's might not be so bad after all. At least there would be other girls to talk to.

Chapter 2

1900 Redfern Abbey, Yorkshire

Edward Redfern sat opposite his father across the mahogany desk. He could see his face in the high gloss of its polished surface. He was still a handsome fellow in spite of his wrinkles. 'You're working too hard, Father,' he commented.

'Redfern Abbey demands it.'

'Then let me take some of the burden from you. Give me the coalfields to manage.'

'There'll be time enough for that when I'm gone. You have your hands full looking after the farmland and tenants. Besides, I have an important task for you.'

Edward brightened and waited. His father rolled a pen around in his fingers looking pensive. It was one of the new designs, with its own reservoir of ink so you didn't have to keep dipping it in the inkwell. Nonetheless, his father's desk displayed a fine mahogany and cut-glass writing set. 'How are you getting on with the Marshall-Kemp girl?' his father asked.

'What? Oh Lucy.' She was pleasant enough, Edward thought, but she didn't fire his passion. 'I am taking her to the races next week. Why do you ask?'

'You will be thirty next year. It's high time you settled down and raised a family.'

Not that again! He bristled and replied, 'You didn't marry until you were thirty-three. Mother told me.'

'It was different for me. It took someone as wonderful as your mother to show me—' his face softened, '—to show me the way.'

Edward's mother was older than his father and she had told him that everyone was against the match because of her years. But she had given him an heir, a cause for much celebration at Redfern Abbey, and although they had hoped for more children, it was not to be.

Edward tried not to show his impatience with his father. Why should it be any different for him? 'I simply haven't met the right girl yet,' he said.

'Not Lucy Marshall-Kemp then?'

Edward would have laughed at the notion if it wouldn't have sounded rude. 'No. Is that why you asked to see me?'

'Partly. A good woman is always helpful in these situations and I really don't wish to worry your mother more than necessary. She is very upset about her brother's death.'

'So was I, Father. It was unexpected. What is it you want of me?'

21

'It's her nephew,' he ruminated. 'Mine too, I know, but he's her blood.'

Edward had enjoyed his cousin Melton's company when they were at Oxford together. But that was nearly ten years ago. He had returned to Redfern Abbey to help his father run his estate. But Melton had continued to enjoy life in the same way that he had as an undergraduate. 'Is Mama worried about him?'

'Yes she is, and I understand how she feels. I felt the same about you ten years ago.'

Lord, Father had a good memory. His father had caught him with . . . with . . . He heaved a sigh. Well, she was one of the maids and they couldn't hide what they were doing. It hadn't been the first time either. Edward gazed out of the window. It was over ten years ago and had been his first experience of passionate love. He truly believed he had loved the girl, and in the rebelliousness of his youth, hadn't seen anything amiss with falling in love with a maid.

'I was eighteen, Father,' he said by way of explanation. 'And I learned my lesson.'

It was a hard lesson, too, for she had been dismissed and he wasn't allowed to know where she had gone. But, maid or not, his heart had been broken. His father had given him a thrashing and sent him up to Oxford where he'd had extra tuition to keep him out of mischief. He had not needed to be distracted in this way, Edward reflected, because it had been a long time before he had even attempted to kiss a girl again. And it wasn't the same as in his father's time when a lady was closely chaperoned. These days, some were forward with their desires.

He said, 'I'm sure if you could remember what it's like to be that age you'd be more understanding.'

Pain showed in his father's face as he recollected old memories and Edward watched with interest. He didn't speak of it much except to say he barely knew his own father. Edward's Aunt Daisy, of whom both were very fond, had chosen not to live on the Redfern estate. Aunt Daisy was Father's twin and she and Uncle Boyd were travelling, visiting their children in America. They had left their beloved Dales farm in the capable hands of their younger half-brother, Edward's Uncle Albert.

'I inherited at eighteen!' his father exclaimed and spread his arms. 'I became head of all of this. I had good stewards but every decision was mine.'

'You are not complaining about being Earl Redfern, are you?'

'No, of course I'm not.' His father, who was not one to dwell on the past, stood up to walk around the desk. He stopped beside Edward and placed a hand on his shoulder, giving it a firm squeeze. 'I am very proud of you, Edward, and so is your mother.'

Edward placed the palm of his own hand over his father's. 'Thank you, Father.'

'But your cousin Melton . . .' Earl Redfern shook his head. 'Amelia is worried about him without his father there to hold the reins and she – we – hoped you might help.'

Edward's spirits sank. 'What has he done now?'

'He's getting through his money far too fast.'

'Well he's just like his father was with his extravagant ways.'

'But he can't afford it! He hasn't got coalfields to finance his lifestyle and he cannot continue selling off his farms as his father did.'

Edward saw the sense in what his father was saying. If his cousin invested his income in modern machinery and proper management, his estate farms would turn him a tidy profit. But as long as his gamekeeper kept the streams and forests well stocked for sport, Melton was satisfied. Melton Hall shooting and fishing were legendary and invitations keenly sought after.

'Your mother is thinking of giving back her dowry.'

'No! You can't let her do that. Mama uses her money for charitable works. Be honest, Father, you wouldn't have let her keep it if she had been a spendthrift like her brother.' Edward stopped and chewed his lips. 'I'm not speaking ill of the dead. Uncle Mel was great fun, but he was what he was and my cousin is from the same mould.'

His father ran his fingers through his hair. 'Your mother is so worried that he will fritter his wealth away on cards and horses and whatever new craze takes his fancy.'

'He's irresponsible, Father. He was not ready to inherit.'

His father raised his eyebrows. 'He was twelve years older than I was.'

'But he isn't you and times have changed.'

'Quite so. And he isn't giving his estate the attention it needs. He's fallen in with a group of like-minded drinkers and gamblers and Amelia and I want you to distract him. Bring him back into the fold, as it were.'

'How am I supposed to do that? Melton is a law unto himself. He makes his own rules.'

'He may be Viscount Melton but he's not above the law. Did you know he was at Tranby Croft when the baccarat scandal happened?'

Edward was shocked. 'No I didn't. Did Mama?'

'Yes, and between us we managed to keep his name out of the papers. That's more than can be said for the Prince of Wales.'

'Well, HRH doesn't exactly set a good example himself, does he? It's the second time he's been called to give evidence in court over a scandal.'

'That is enough, Edward. He is your future king and you are named after him.'

Edward tapped his hands impatiently on the arms of his leather chair. 'What exactly do you want me to do?'

'Melton needs to marry; settle down and produce heirs. He might start taking an interest in their inheritance then.'

Edward thought privately that as far as Melton Hall was concerned it was too late. Most of it was already sold off and that didn't make Melton a particularly attractive marriage prospect in spite of being a viscount. Besides, he'd not shown any inclination to marry. Edward was wondering how he could influence his cousin in this respect when his father went on, 'There are plenty of eligible girls in the country and your mother and I have agreed to keep open house at our hunting lodge when the shooting starts.'

Edward considered this an excellent prospect. He enjoyed shooting and the more relaxed routines of their moorland retreat. However, the task remained a difficult one. 'No self-respecting debutante will go near him.'

'Amelia will find him one.'

'She'll have to be rich,' Edward warned.

'Your mother knows what she is doing.' His father smiled. 'Why do you think she married me?'

Edward grinned back fondly. His father's land sat on coal, making him one of the richest men in England and at some time in the future, he would inherit that fortune. But he, and others who knew his parents well, were in no doubt that James and Amelia's match had been one of passion, based on a genuine, deep-rooted and enduring love that Edward wanted for himself and his own wife, whenever he met her.

His cousin Melton, however, was a different animal altogether.

Amelia, Countess Redfern, decided to hold a summer ball in honour of her nephew's birthday in the Great Hall of the Abbey. Its marble floor was perfect for dancing and it had wonderful glazed French doors that allowed dancers to escape easily into the cooling night air. The estate carpenters built a platform for the orchestra and gardeners prepared hothouse plants for decoration. The kitchens began preparing a cold table for supper days beforehand. The Countess invited over two hundred guests, many of whom stayed at the Abbey with their personal servants. There was a good sprinkling of marriageable young ladies to tempt Edward's cousin including, to his annoyance, his long-term friend Lucy, who was quite taken by Melton's handsome appearance. Mel was at his best when he was the centre of everyone's attention.

'Don't go near him, Lucy, I beg of you.' Edward held on to her arm and half-dragged her out on to the terrace.

She was very cross with him. 'Just because you don't want me, you don't want anyone else to! Is that it?'

'No!' he anguished. 'Please don't be angry with me.'

'But I know you like me, Edward.' She sidled towards him. 'This is the twentieth century. You can get to know me better, if you wish.'

'You are a dear friend and I wouldn't dream of taking advantage of you in that way. That's my point. Melton wouldn't give two hoots about your reputation.'

'He might fall in love with me.'

Edward agreed. Lucy was an attractive and charming girl from a good Dorset family with acres of fertile farmland. But that was all. 'He won't marry you,' he said gently.

She looked hurt, then affronted and stepped back. 'Thank you for the compliment, My Lord.'

'Don't take this the wrong way. You're too intelligent for that. He can't marry you. He has to marry into money.'

'More than my father has?'

'I'm sorry, Lucy, he needs a lot more. But please keep that to yourself.'

'Of course. How much more does he need?'

'Ashby Shipping more,' he answered and watched her absorb this information.

Lucy gave a short, good humoured laugh. 'Clara Ashby! She is such a mouse and he is so – so *alive*.'

'She is the only daughter of a successful shipbuilder and that makes her a very rich mouse.'

'I see.'

Edward realised that she understood fully. It was one of the things he admired about Lucy. She really was a very nice girl and would have made him a very good wife. Sometimes he wished that he did feel a strong passion for her, akin to the searing love he had experienced in his youth. But he didn't and for the first time considered that he might never again love any woman with such strength.

'Don't say anything to anybody. My parents approve and so does her father.' He pulled Lucy towards him and gave her a hug. She didn't resist but she didn't respond. He knew their relationship was coming to an end and that she had only accepted this invitation to please her parents – and his.

Edward's friendly hug was brief and as Lucy straightened her dress she murmured, 'You're not like that – that Oscar Wilde fellow, are you Edward?'

'Good God, no! Whatever makes you think that?'

'Do you have to ask? I'm told I am an attractive girl.'

'You are a dear friend and I love you as I would a sister.'

She held his eyes and nodded. She sounded tired. 'Yes, I believe you do. I don't want to be your sister, Edward. I think we should stop seeing each other.'

He was genuinely hurt by her suggestion until she

added, 'I love you in a different way but if there is no future for us then I shall leave your field clear for another.'

'Lucy!' It came out as a groan, but she hadn't finished.

'Has it occurred to you how selfish it was to allow your mother to invite me here? I believed you wished to further our relationship but in truth, all you wanted was a comfortable trouble-free partner for another season. Just because you will be an earl one day doesn't give you leave to be lazy as well as selfish.'

Surprised at her outburst, he murmured, 'Ouch!'

'I turned down Scotland to come here.'

He blew out his cheeks hard. There was a stinging truth in what she said. Her way with words that he so admired had come home to roost. He deserved her rebuke.

'Perhaps your parents ought to be considering *your* future, as well as their nephew's.' Then she gave him a smile that he thought was genuine. 'I enjoy your company, Edward, but I shall make my excuses to your mother and catch the midday train tomorrow. Goodnight.'

She left him alone on the terrace before he had time to word his response. He was angry at first and didn't go after her. But the more he thought about it the more he realised that she had a point. He had used her. And that was unforgiveable of him. He resolved to mend his ways.

Chapter 3

1902

Lady Maude's School for Servants was 'down south'. It was considered to be a first class opportunity for Phyllis four years ago, and mother was right about mixing with 'nicer girls'. She was ten at the time, but not the youngest. There was a girl of eight, although the girl's elder sister of twelve was there too. Their father had died suddenly. He had been a footman at a titled house in Derbyshire. His employer had paid for both girls' schooling until they were fourteen and their mother was taken back as a housemaid.

Daily life, for Phyllis, was very different from the board school. The girls here didn't chew with their mouths open and nobody got the cane. Instead, the teachers gave you black marks on a wall chart for others to see. They were totted up at the end of the week and those who had them against their name were given extra menial tasks while others took recreation. Black marks also went on reports to fathers and guardians.

The school was organised and run in the same way as the household of any English aristocratic family, with the teachers behaving as Master and Mistress and being waited on hand and foot while the older girls acted as Housekeeper and Head Housemaid or Cook and Head Kitchenmaid. They had classroom lessons in the quiet time of the afternoon and these were about how a large household was run and who took orders from whom. Phyllis was expected to take copious notes in a rough book which she had to copy neatly into a stiff backed exercise book and told this was her bible for the future.

The teachers had all worked in very grand houses and seemed to know a lot about them and their occupants. Phyllis was aware that her father answered to a stable master who answered to a land steward at Redfern Abbey but was surprised to learn that Earl Redfern had a house steward as well to oversee his butler and housekeeper. It was the house steward who sent word to Lady Maude's if they needed another female servant.

The School Principal was Miss Fanshaw, a stout old lady who resembled the pictures Phyllis had seen of the late Queen Victoria. She came into the classroom at the end of every lesson and tested her pupils on their learning. She stood in front of the rows of desks with a pair of spectacles perched on her nose and selected victims for her questions at random. It was a black mark if you got the answer wrong. Three black marks meant you had to do extra laundry or scrub the floors, so Phyllis concentrated hard.

For two years Phyllis was shown how to do housework, basic cooking and looking after young children as well as how to behave invisibly when 'above stairs'. Then she did it under the watchful eye of her teachers, day in and day out for another year after which she was sent out to big houses in the local county to work with real servants and see how she fared.

It didn't take long for Phyllis to decide that if she had to go into service – which unfortunately she did – she wanted to be a lady's maid. She excelled at dressing hair and looking after clothes. The older girls laughed at her ambition and said you couldn't do that until you were much older and she would have to make do with parlourmaid or chambermaid for a few years. Maybe, she shrugged. They were ranked above housemaids and earned twenty pounds a year. Also, they wore the prettiest aprons and caps and worked in the grandest rooms.

Every year she had a week off to go home. It had to be taken in the summer, after the season went quiet and before the shooting got underway. The school had its own horse-drawn omnibus to take them to the railway station and Father met her at the other end in a pony and trap borrowed from the Abbey. Mother was always keen to hear all about Lady Maude's and to fill in the gaps between her letters; and Father, she acknowledged, seemed genuinely proud of her achievements.

Her allocated week to go home drew close and Phyllis

was copying notes from her rough book into neat when one of the teachers called her.

'Kimber!'

'Yes, Miss.'

'Miss Fanshaw wants to see you in her office right away. What have you done?'

'Nothing, Miss. Honest.'

'Run up to the dormitory for a clean cap and apron.'

Phyllis racked her brain for anything she might have inadvertently done to warrant an interview with Miss Fanshaw but could think of nothing. She straightened her back and knocked firmly on the door. Inside, Miss Fanshaw stood up and walked around her large oak desk to offer her a chair. Normally she would stand in the presence of Miss Fanshaw. The Principal's face was frowning but not in a cross way and Phyllis experienced a peculiar sense of dread.

'Something's wrong,' she muttered as she sank onto the hard wooden chair.

'I fear so, Kimber. Your father has suffered an accident.'

A shiver travelled over her body and head as she took in this information. 'Oh no! Is he hurt bad, Miss?' she asked.

'Your mother needs you at home with her.'

'He's – he's not dead, is he?'

'No Kimber, he is not dead. He has been injured while exercising Lord Redfern's hunter.'

'B–but he's a good rider! Mother says he's the best they've got.'

'Lord Redfern believes that something scared his horse. It reared and bolted, unseating your father and – and he was dragged by his stirrup for a considerable distance.'

This dreadful image ran through her mind and tears sprang into her eyes. 'Oh dear Lord,' she uttered. 'Poor Father.'

The normally severe Miss Fanshaw placed her hand on Phyllis's shoulder and gripped it lightly. 'Bear up, Kimber. You must be strong for your mother's sake.'

An icy shiver tingled across her back and scalp. 'I – I should be with her.' She half rose and saw the opened letter on Miss Fanshaw's desk, with Lord Redfern's crest on it.

Miss Fanshaw noticed and said, 'Your father is held in high regard by Lord Redfern. His Lordship wrote to me personally and his steward has arranged for you to go home immediately.'

'Yes. Yes.' Phyllis became anxious to be on her way and added, 'May I go and pack now, Miss Fanshaw?'

'You will find that Miss Brown has made a start for you.'

'Th-thank you, Miss Fanshaw.'

Miss Fanshaw acknowledged her with a sympathetic nod and went back to her desk.

'Are you young Phyllis?'

'Yes.' She stood beside her luggage waiting for the steam to clear on the railway station platform.

'Ee, lass, they said you'd grown bonny and they were right. I'm right sorry about your father.' He helped her into the trap and stowed her bag beside her feet.

'You're the sexton from Redfern Church, aren't you?' she realised.

'That's right.' He climbed into the driver's seat and took up the reins.

'How is my father?' she asked.

'I don't rightly know. Gee-up there, girl.' He cracked his whip and the horse broke into a trot so Phyllis had to hold on tight as they sped along the roadway and then the lanes towards home. She was hot with anxiety and wished she could let go to pull off her Lady Maude's felt hat and heavy buttoned coat. She gazed enviously at the women gleaning in the fields in their summer frocks and straw hats. They stopped work and straightened their backs to stare, no doubt wondering who was in such a hurry.

'Whoa, girl.' The driver eased the pony to a walk in the lane leading to Chase Cottage and stopped outside her front gate. 'Get yourself indoors, lass. I'll see to t'luggage.'

'Is that you, dear?' Mother's voice floated down the stairs.

'Mother?' Phyllis crept up the stairs to Father's bedroom.

He was lying with his eyes closed and he had a blood-stained bandage around his head. His face was covered with angry red cuts and grazes and purple bruises. Phyllis suppressed a cry of shock. Her mother was sitting on a kitchen chair beside the bed. She was holding one of his hands between hers. There a stuffy fetid smell even though the window was open.

'Is he asleep?' Phyllis asked.

Mother's pallid face turned towards her. She had a vacant look in her eyes. Her lips barely moved. 'Whatever shall I do?' she whispered.

Alarmed, Phyllis crouched beside her and put her arm across her shoulders. 'What do you mean, Mother? Has the doctor been to see him?'

Her mother nodded and chewed her lips. 'Lord Redfern had his own physician to look at him where they found him on the estate. They brought him home on a stretcher in His Lordship's motor car. The chauffeur drove very slowly because the doors wouldn't close properly.'

How typical of her mother to think about practicalities. 'What did the doctor say, Mother?'

'He hasn't opened his eyes since he got here.'

'How long have you been sitting there, Mother?'

'I don't know. I was dusting the front parlour and I saw His Lordship's motor car come down the lane. The vicar's wife was here yesterday.'

'Would you like a cup of tea, Mother?'

'Oh yes please, dear. I'm so glad you're here. I don't know what I'm going to do without your father.'

Oh dear Lord! Mother was talking as though Father were dead. Phyllis went downstairs and opened the damper to coax the fire. Someone must have seen to it because the coals sprang into life. She picked up the kettle, shook it to see if there was water inside, and placed it in the centre of the hotplate. There was a piece of cold boiled bacon in the meat safe and a sponge cake on the pantry shelf. Neither was her mother's baking. The vicar's wife must have brought them and both were untouched.

Phyllis laid a tray with a clean cloth, picked a single rose from the garden and placed it in a small vase. She cut the cake and when the tea was ready picked up the tray. Then changed her mind, put it down on the kitchen table and went upstairs without it.

'Mother, why don't you go down to the kitchen for your tea?'

'Your father might wake up, dear.'

'I'll stay with him.'

'Will you? The doctor said not to leave him.'

'Let me sit there for a while.'

'Very well, dear.' Mother rose to her feet. She gave a sharp cry and frowned as she tried to straighten up. 'I've been sitting for too long,' she muttered.

Phyllis took her place. 'Go for a walk in the fresh air while you're downstairs,' she suggested. Her father's hand was limp and cold. The only sign that he was alive was the slight movement of his chest as he breathed.

After about ten minutes she heard the sound of a motor car in the lane and went to the window. Lord Redfern was here! His chauffeur held open the motor car door for His Lordship and another gentleman to climb out. The other gentleman carried a leather Gladstone bag. She heard voices drifting upstairs and then heavy footsteps on the treads.

Her mother came into the room first. 'His Lordship is here, Phyllis, with the doctor.'

She rose immediately and turned. She had not met Lord Redfern face to face before but had seen grainy photographs of him occasionally in the newspaper. He was much older than his pictures, she thought.

'Please don't get up,' he said. He smiled at her but his eyes were sad. 'You are Mr Kimber's daughter.'

'Yes, My Lord. I arrived home from Lady Maude's an hour or so ago.'

'Quite so. Your mother will need you.'

They stood looking at each for a few seconds then Phyllis sat down again. She thought that he looked sorry for her and realised that he knew more than she about her father's condition.

'Has he woken at any time, or moved?' the doctor asked.

'None at all.' Her mother's voice was squeaky.

'Miss Kimber?'

She shook her head. 'Nothing, sir, not even the flicker of an eyelid.'

'May I?' The doctor took her father's hand and took out his pocket watch. Then he lifted his eyelids one by one and looked at his eyes. Phyllis moved to her mother's side and linked arms with her.

'Shall we go downstairs?' the doctor said.

'I'll stay with Father,' Phyllis volunteered.

'You can leave him for a few minutes,' the doctor went on. 'I want to talk to you both.'

Mother led the way into the front parlour. She had hardly said a word since the doctor arrived. Her feather duster lay across the armchair where she had left it. Normally she would have whisked it out of sight but it was Phyllis who picked it up and asked, 'Would you like some tea, My Lord?'

'Thank you, no. Come and sit next to your mother. This is a difficult time for both of you.'

Phyllis placed the duster in the hearth and sat on the couch. 'Father will get better, won't he?' she said.

The doctor replied. 'I am sorry, my dear. He has not been conscious since his accident and he has no signs of reflexes. It is only a matter of time.'

Her father was going to die! She searched for her mother's hand. 'How much time, sir?'

'His heart is very weak now, it may only be hours. You must prepare yourselves.'

Her mother gazed out of the window. 'What shall I do without him? Where shall I go?' she whispered.

Phyllis shared her mother's concern. Father may not have shown either of them any love, but he had given them a good home and better standard of living than most in their position. The cottage, however, was tied to Father's position at the Abbey stables and – oh dear heaven, His Lordship would want it for Father's replacement! She looked from one gentleman to the other. 'Wh-what will happen to us, My Lord?' The doctor's face was expressionless.

Lord Redfern replied. 'Please try not to worry, Miss Kimber. Your mother may live here for as long as she wishes.'

'I may?' Mother seemed relieved. 'Thank you, My Lord.'

Phyllis hoped he meant it. It was a lovely little house and Father had taken good care of it. Mother, too, had made it comfortable and pretty using her skills as a needlewoman. But, Phyllis wondered, how would Mother pay the rent? Or buy meat for the table? And without Father's wage there would be no money for her school fees. She said, 'Don't worry, Mother. I shall be fourteen soon and old enough to earn a proper wage.'

The empty look in her mother's eyes told her she wasn't taking in much of the conversation. 'I'll find a position,' Phyllis added. She sounded more confident than she felt.

Her mother responded absently. 'In a titled household, dear.'

It was Mother's stock phrase when Phyllis talked of her future. It had been drummed into her from an early age that she had to start off in a good family to be well placed for the best positions. Phyllis stared at her mother and realised that she was not herself. The shock of Father's accident had drained all her energy and she had hardly eaten since yesterday. The tea had revived her colour but she was behaving like a clockwork toy. She needed some proper nourishment and a good night's sleep. 'Let's not fret about that now, Mother,' she went on.

Lord Redfern stood up to leave. 'I shall speak to Her Ladyship on the matter. My vicar's wife will call again tomorrow.'

Mrs Kimber began to rise awkwardly and Phyllis jumped to her feet. 'Stay where you are, Mother. I'll show His Lordship out.'

'Thank you, miss.'

'It is very kind of you to take the trouble to come over here, My Lord.' He followed her down the stairs and she opened the front door for him.

'Your father was one of my most loyal servants.' He said as he bid her good day. He walked down the path to the front gate where his chauffeur stood to attention. 'Look after your mother, Miss Kimber.'

As if I wouldn't, she thought, but said, 'I shall, My Lord.' The doctor followed and as he walked past her said, 'I can do no more for him, miss. It won't be long now.'

Her father stopped breathing in the early hours of the next day. She and Mother were both by his bed and had dozed. The oil in the lamp had burned out when Phyllis woke and stared through the gloom. She got up to fetch a looking glass and held it near his mouth in case she was mistaken but there was no sign of misting on its cold surface. Mother stirred and then opened her eyes in alarm.

'Has he gone?'

'Yes. I'll wash him and lay him out.'

Mother stood up stiffly. 'No, dear, I'll do it when it's daylight. I don't want you to see his bruised body.' She seemed more relaxed than yesterday.

They sat watching the grey streaks of dawn lighten the room. 'Did you love him, Mother?' Phyllis asked.

'He was my husband.'

'He didn't love you though, or me for that matter.'

'He took care of us both. We had a decent home and never wanted for anything.'

'He was such a stickler, Mother! Why did you marry him?'

'Phyllis! Your father has just passed away! He was not a perfect husband but he was steadfast and loyal. You will respect his memory, my girl.'

Phyllis deserved the rebuke and in some ways it cheered her because this was more like the mother she knew. She believed Mother agreed with her about Father but would never dream of saying it. Phyllis guessed that Mother would be just as loyal to Father's memory as she had been when he was alive. But she knew it was all pretence for appearances' sake and she determined she would never put up with such a marriage for herself. She'd rather be a spinster! She said, 'Yes, of course, Mother. I'm sorry.'

'So you should be! Your father's loyalty to Lord Redfern means we still have a home to live in so don't you forget it!' Her mother began to weep which upset Phyllis even more and she began to sob as well. 'Come here,' her mother took her hands and pulled her close, wrapped her arms around Phyllis and held her tight. Through her tears, Mother went on, 'It was all for you, my love. You are all I have left now and I love you more than life itself.' She sniffled and choked. 'I – I'm so – so proud of you, my darling, so very proud.'

Phyllis cried with her. 'I love you, Mother. I'll get a good position, in a titled household, and work hard so you'll always be proud of me. I promise.' She meant it. She never wanted to go into service but now she was more determined than ever to *do well* in whatever she did. She knew she would have to start off in a position that used her training. But it wouldn't be for ever. There was a rich and vibrant world outside the South Riding that beckoned her and Phyllis wanted to be a part of it.

Chapter 4

James, Earl Redfern was feeling his age. He climbed the wide stone steps at the front of the Abbey and the door opened. His butler stood back as he entered, then took his straw boater. 'Where is Lady Amelia?' James enquired.

'Her Ladyship is in her boudoir, My Lord.'

'Does she have a visitor?'

'No, My Lord, I believe she is attending to her correspondence.'

The metal ferrule on his cane rang on the mosaic marble floor as he crossed to Lady Amelia's private room and tapped lightly on the door. 'It's me, Amelia.'

His wife glanced up from her French ormolu and gilt desk as he entered. 'How timely, darling. I am just finishing a letter to our niece at Melton Hall.'

'Give her my good wishes for her health. When is the baby due?'

'The birth is expected in October.'

'I do hope it's a boy this time. She doesn't seem to be a very strong girl.'

'Clara has a nervous disposition. Melton's behaviour does not help. He is inclined to go off and leave her for days on end.'

James agreed, though he was grateful that his wife had made that comment and not he. Amelia held no illusions about her nephew, but James tried not to criticise him unduly. He said, 'I thought he would settle down more when he married.'

'I did, too. Perhaps we should ask Clara to come and stay with us for a few weeks.'

'I think it is wisest not to interfere between husband and wife, don't you? A second child is bound to slow him down. Will you ring for tea? I want to talk to you of another matter.'

Amelia put down her pen, and went to sit by the open French door that looked out over the park. The ormolu carriage clock on her desk chimed delicately. 'Tea will be here shortly. What is on your mind?'

'My head groom.'

His wife looked contrite. 'Oh, of course, darling. How is he?'

'I'm afraid he is dying.'

Amelia's hand went to her throat. 'You didn't tell me the accident was so serious! I am very sorry to hear that. Would you like me to visit?'

'You are far too busy with our miners' welfare work.'

'You must send your steward's wife, then. Someone should be with his family.'

'I've asked the vicar's wife. Kimber lives way over in the Chase. You don't hunt so you won't know that area well. The terrain is rough and the Rectory is nearer to their cottage than we are.'

'I don't believe I have ever set eyes on Mrs Kimber or her children. But I ought to visit them, dearest.'

'You are a very busy lady, my dear, and their cottage is isolated. The track is not suitable for the motor car.' He bent to kiss the top of her head. 'Leave the visiting to the vicar's wife this time.'

'Certainly, if that is your wish, dearest. Is there anything else I can do to help?'

'I believe there is. Kimber has been a very loyal servant all his life. He has one child, a girl who has done four years at Lady Maude's.'

His wife raised her eyebrows. 'You must reward your head groom well.'

'He deserves it. My hunters are admired across the county. The daughter will have to leave Lady Maude's now, of course. But she will be fourteen in the autumn and able to look for a position.'

'Do you want her to work at the Abbey?'

'I think she will fare better elsewhere. She has wits and Lady Maude's has given her confidence.'

'You seem to know a lot about her.'

James considered telling her more. Amelia was a ninteenth-century woman who had embraced twentieth-century

45

ideas. But she had an independent mind so he could not be sure what she might do. Best to let sleeping dogs lie. He said, 'Her father always spoke of her progress with pride and to lose one's father so young is a devastating tragedy for any young person. It is my duty to help. It occurs to me that Clara might take her.'

Lord Redfern watched his wife as she considered this notion and saw a light come into her eyes. 'We-e-ell,' she said. 'I have been trying to persuade her to take on a young nursemaid. Melton has insisted on bringing his old nanny out of retirement for his children.'

James grinned. 'I remember her. She was a true Victorian if ever there was one.'

'Precisely. She is getting on in years and two infants will be far too much for her. But Nanny Byrne is a proud woman and wouldn't dream of even hinting that she needed help.'

'A nursemaid,' Lord Redfern mused and nodded thoughtfully. 'That might work. She will receive excellent training from Nanny Byrne. Will you put the notion to Clara in your letter today?'

'More than that, if she is from Lady Maude's, I shall recommend her.'

Afternoon tea arrived and Lady Redfern offered the plate of scones to James then leaned forward to pour. 'What will happen to Kimber's wife when—' she stopped then added, '—the doctor is sure about his condition?'

'I'm afraid so. Mrs Kimber is not yet forty and her cottage is in an isolated spot. I've already suggested to the vicar that his wife asks her to help on the almshouse committee.'

'But that is charitable work. How will she support herself?'

'Her husband was fatally injured in my service. She will have her cottage rent free and an allowance from the welfare fund.'

'Edward has set up a similar arrangement for our miners' widows.'

'When I attended the party meeting the other day our esteemed Member of Parliament told me the government is considering introducing a pension for all old people.'

'Really? I hadn't heard, but I think it is an excellent idea. When will it happen?'

'Not for a few years yet, and our taxes will go up to pay for it.'

'When I think of how much money my father and brother wasted when they could have put it to much better use, as you and Edward do, then paying taxes seems quite sensible to me.'

Her husband gave a dry laugh. 'You sound like one of our trade union fellows.'

'Some of what they say makes sense. I feel the same about the suffragists. I don't agree with some of their more radical ideas but I listen to what they say.'

'So do I.'

'Don't you agree that they have a point?'

'Girls don't have the same education as boys,' he commented.

'Well, their fathers won't pay for it and no one bothers because they are supposed to marry and have children instead!' She noticed her husband's bland, patient expression

47

and added. 'I wish the government would listen more to what these women say.'

'Then you ought to be a politician yourself.'

'Heavens no, I have far too much to do here.'

'I'm relieved you see it that way. I couldn't run Redfern without you and Edward. He is making a first rate job of managing the coal mines. Although, considering that is what he always asked for, he doesn't seem as happy as he used to be.'

'I wish he'd find a nice girl. He hasn't brought anyone home to meet us since Lucy. He seems to have lost interest.'

'No, I don't think so. He hasn't met the right one yet.'

'He's taking his time.'

'I was still single at his age,' James remarked. 'But I'll talk to him on Sunday.'

Phyllis was surprised to see so many people at her father's funeral in the village church. Lord Redfern was there with his land steward and two pews full of estate workers, mainly from the stables, she guessed. Father's cousin from Doncaster came and the warden of the orphanage where Mother had been brought up.

After the burial, both gentlemen offered Mother their condolences and confirmed that she was provided for then left for the Redfern Arms where a barrel of ale and a cold table had been provided for refreshment. Phyllis and her mother spoke with the vicar's wife and she invited them for tea the following week.

* * *

Father had insisted that they went to church every Sunday, even though it was a very long walk. Often Mother and Phyllis would be offered a ride in a dog cart for the last mile which was most welcome when it rained. This time they walked all the way to the Rectory and Mother sat with her hostess in the dark old-fashioned drawing room while Phyllis was sent to help the housemaid prepare tea. They had cucumber sandwiches and a Victoria sponge cake with a jam filling that looked as good as Mother's own. When she helped carry it into the parlour, her mother seemed quite excited by her discussions and Phyllis wondered why. She guessed she would hear all about it after tea.

'Ah, Phyllis, do sit down with your dear mama. She has important news for you.'

'Mother?' Phyllis handed out plates and napkins while the maid offered sandwiches.

The vicar's wife answered. 'We have news of a wonderful opportunity for you.'

'It's all settled, dear.' Her mother was beaming.

Phyllis finished her sandwich. 'What is all settled?'

Again the vicar's wife responded. 'You have done so very well in your training that Lady Redfern has secured the position for you.'

Phyllis's eyes rounded. 'Lady Redfern? She doesn't know me.'

Mother interrupted. 'Don't be awkward, dear, not today.'

'Am I going to work at the Abbey?'

Her mother's smile became an impatient frown. 'Will you be quiet and let me tell you?' She glanced hastily at the vicar's wife who was sitting absolutely still with her hands folded in her lap. 'I'm sorry, ma'am. It is a difficult time for her.'

The vicar's wife smiled weakly. 'Lady Redfern has obtained a position for you in her nephew's household.'

Mother could not contain herself any longer. 'He's a viscount, dear, Viscount Melton of Melton Hall. It's all arranged.'

The vicar's wife continued, 'Lord Melton has not been married long and his wife is expecting her second child. Her nanny needs a nursemaid.'

'Nursemaid?' This was a surprise. It was an honour to be sure but Lady Maude's had never considered her suitable for nursemaid duties. She was inclined to ask too many questions.

'You'll be looking after a viscount's children,' her mother added.

'But I don't want to be a nursemaid! I want to be a lady's maid.' If the truth were known, Phyllis didn't want to be that either but she knew she had to go somewhere as a servant or her time at Lady Maude's would be wasted.

'You are far too young for that,' the vicar's wife said. 'Do well with the children and then when you are older and they are older, your wish may be granted. Lady Melton's first child is a daughter. As soon as she is out she will need her own maid.'

Sixteen years as a nursemaid, and then she might be given her reward. Heavens, she'll be old herself by then! She couldn't think of anything pleasing to say and remembered to keep her mouth shut.

'This is a valuable start for any young girl,' the vicar's wife added. 'You are so lucky, my dear, and you have two weeks to get your uniforms ready. Lord and Lady Melton live in the East Riding. You will take the railway train to Doncaster and from there catch another train to Melton Halt. A servent will meet you as the Halt is several miles away from the Hall.'

'Oh I'm so excited for you,' Mother exclaimed. 'You must write to me and tell me everything about Melton Hall. Lady Melton has an infant not yet one year old and she is due to have another baby very soon.'

Two babies, Phyllis thought and asked, 'Will I have to look after both infants on my own?'

'Goodness me, no dear,' the vicar's wife responded. 'Her Ladyship has a head nurse already. But she is getting on in years and one day you might be filling her shoes. Think of that!'

Phyllis did and wasn't happy with the notion. Nursemaids spent all their time in attic nurseries and didn't get the same time off as the other maids.

The vicar's wife waited for her to comment and, when she didn't, turned to her mother and said, 'Would you like some cake, Mrs Kimber?'

The maid came forward to serve them. She was very neatly turned out in a grey dress and white pinafore with a lace trim that matched the piece of lace in her hair. It was a very dainty apron and Phyllis thought she looked pretty. Nursemaids' pinnies were often as big as cooks' aprons. They covered everywhere and she'd probably have to wear a horrid plain cap over her hair as well. But she realised that she had no choice in this decision and it was quite clearly making Mother very happy. Phyllis accepted a piece of sponge cake with a smile and found a voice of sorts. 'Thank you, ma'am,' she said. 'I am very grateful. Should I write and thank Lady Redfern?'

'That won't be necessary. You will be busy with your sewing needle for the next two weeks.'

Mrs Kimber looked alarmed. 'Will I have to order the fabrics from Leeds?'

'It is the same that Lady Redfern used for her nurse-maids, so the draper has plenty in stock. Her Ladyship said that you may charge the cost to her estate account. If you order while you are in the village today he will deliver tomorrow.'

Phyllis's mother could hardly contain her joy and her eyes shone. Fortunately she sensed that their tea was at an end. The vicar's wife had done her duty and Mrs Kimber reacted accordingly. 'Yes, of course, we'll be on our way. Thank you for the tea, ma'am.'

'Oh, Phyllis, it is a lovely shade. You look nice in that pink, it suits your colouring. I didn't like you in Lady Maude's brown.' Neither did Phyllis. There was only one girl at Lady Maude's that favoured the brown and she had ginger hair and freckles.

Mrs Kimber scanned with a frown the list that the vicar's wife had given her. 'You will need a portmanteau for all this.'

Phyllis spent all of her two weeks at home sewing shifts, dresses and aprons. The sewing mistress from the

Abbey sent over one of her patented sewing machines. Phyllis had learned to use one at Lady Maude's and she showed her mother, who took to it as a duckling does to water. Those two weeks, Phyllis thought, spent sewing, pressing and folding were the happiest they had ever been. For the first time, Phyllis was sorry to be leaving Chase Cottage. But nothing could detract from the absolute joy her mother felt about Phyllis's future and Phyllis was careful not to allow her to think otherwise.

Before everything was folded carefully in her travelling trunk, Mother insisted that she tried everything on to show her. Phyllis stood in front of the long mirror in her mother's bedroom and stared.

Her mother smiled at her image and murmured, 'You're growing up, my dear.'

It's true, Phyllis thought. Her skinny frame was filling out and she was becoming a young woman, with proper breasts and rounded hips. Her monthly visits confirmed it. She had her mother's abundant fair hair and skin but had inherited blue eyes with dark lashes from her father, except that his were small and close together whereas hers were large and set well apart so she looked much more like her mother than she did her father. Her brow and nose were different from both, though.

She twisted and twirled, surprised that she appeared so grown-up in her uniform dress that stopped above her ankles to reveal new black leather lace-ups over black stockings. Her snow-white bibbed apron hid most of the dress and had, to her delight, pretty lace cap sleeves that spread across her shoulders. She had pinned up her long hair in a coil at the back and tried on her nursemaid's cap, a disappointingly plain cotton affair that had to be fixed with hairpins. There was also a maroon overcoat and felt hat for winter walks, and a maroon woollen cape lined with special pink flannel for indoors. These outdoor garments had been delivered from a Leeds store and must have cost a small fortune.

In the mirror, Mother's eyes met hers. 'Oh you do look nice. Pretty, but somehow much more mature and capable,' she said.

Phyllis grinned at her mother's face peeping over her shoulder and commented, 'You could be my older sister.'

'You flatter me, dear.'

'Who paid for the things from Leeds, Mother?' she wondered.

'Apparently Nanny Byrne was insistent. The children's father is a viscount, you see. You must not be mistaken for an ordinary domestic servant.'

'Well yes I understand that, but you can't afford all this?'

'The vicar's wife said the account would go to Lady Redfern. She – well she said it was from the estate welfare fund.'

'But isn't that for folk who are really hard-up, to keep them out of the workhouse?'

Her mother sighed. 'Don't look a gift horse in the mouth, dear. Your father gave his life to His Lordship's service.'

Phyllis thought that Mother was being a little over-dramatic. Father's death had been caused by an accident but it wasn't quite the same as a coal mine disaster. Nonetheless he had died in His Lordship's service so she supposed he felt responsible. She decided not to spoil the moment by asking any more of her awkward questions. For the first time in her young life, Phyllis thought she looked attractive and Mother definitely approved.

'You'll do,' her mother nodded. 'You make sure you do everything you're told and don't you dare let me down.'

'No, Mother. I won't. I promise.'

Her mother hesitated. 'I don't mean about your duties, I'm mean when you have time off.'

'Well I suppose I'll be allowed to talk to the other servants.'

Mother sighed and looked worried. 'You will wear your corsets every day, won't you?'

'Yes,' Phyllis was puzzled. Wearing corsets was part of being properly grown up.

'It's only that, some of these young things these days don't wear corsets and it's asking for trouble.'

'Well, I can stand up straight without them.'

'It's not that, dear.' Mother closed her eyes and took a deep breath. She seemed at a loss for the words but eventually went on, 'You have to be careful with the male servants. Now you're growing up and look so, well, so pretty in your uniform,' Phyllis saw her mother's face colour as she went on, 'one of the footmen might ask if he can kiss you. You mustn't let him. Not ever.' She finished in a rush. 'You'll have a baby if you do and be sent away in disgrace.'

It was obviously something her mother found difficult to say to her and Phyllis suppressed an impatient gasp. 'It takes more than a kiss.' She'd learned all about that from the school playground and Lady Maude's dormitory. 'You mean he'll want to do what mothers and fathers do in bed at night?'

She said it without thinking because some of the girls had been aware of everything their parents did and had described it in detail to anyone who would listen. But as she watched her mother's blush deepen she regretted her words. Phyllis's mother and father hadn't even slept in the same room, let alone the same bed. But they must have done so once together otherwise she wouldn't be here.

She wondered for the umpteenth time why they had never got on but Mother looked so uncomfortable that Phyllis rushed on, 'Don't worry about me, Mother. We had lessons in "Decorum" at Lady Maude's. They taught us how to behave with male servants and put the fear of God into us if we misbehaved.'

She didn't say that the dormitory conversation after lights-out had been more about the behaviour of the young masters of the house rather than his footmen. Or that it was considered a way out of service if you fell for a baby and he married you. It didn't happen often but it wasn't unheard of either, so maybe Mother was right to be concerned because if the young master didn't marry you, you would be in real trouble.

Anyway, Melton Hall had no such young master as Viscount Melton was recently married so there'd be none

56

of those shenanigans there. She wondered if there used to be goings-on like that at the Abbey and was acutely disappointed that Mother would never speak of such things and she'd never dared ask her father. Well, she wasn't going to stay in service for ever. She couldn't say that to Mother now so she added, 'Don't worry, Mother, I'm not going to walk out with any footman. I think I might turn out to be one of those suffragists instead.'

This was absolutely the wrong thing to say and Mother looked horrified. 'Oh I don't want you to be like them, dear. Politics is for men. Eventually, you will want to settle down with a nice respectable fellow who has a good position. He won't want his wife getting into all sorts of bother with opinions of her own, will he?'

Phyllis didn't argue but several of the teachers at Lady Maude's had never married and they seemed to have a happier time than her mother ever had as a wife. Mother's life had been controlled by an inflexible and unloving husband and Phyllis certainly didn't want that for herself.

Chapter 5

Phyllis's curiosity mounted as the railway train neared its destination. Melton Hall was in the middle of Yorkshire, surrounded by farms and forests. It was small compared with Redfern but, since Viscount Melton's marriage, he had had renovations to the Hall for his Viscountess. She was not from the aristocracy but her father was extremely wealthy. He had made his fortune from building ships that crossed the world's oceans and it was his generosity that had paid for modernisation of the Hall as a part of his daughter's marriage settlement. Phyllis learned this from a gossipy lady who shared her carriage compartment and who was pleased to have a willing listener.

But Phyllis's head was beginning to throb. In the rush to catch her train, she had taken little to eat and drink that morning. The noise and smoke of the railway did not help and she welcomed the end of her journey. Phyllis was met at Melton Halt by a man as old as her father had been who loaded her and her travelling trunk into a dog cart and set off for the Hall. She sat beside him clutching her small travelling bag and marvelled at the beauty of the estate parkland.

'Oh! Is that Melton Hall?'

'Aye.'

Her first sight was of a redbrick house with stone-dressed corners of Georgian proportions. It had an impressive flight of marble steps leading up to a pillared entrance. The cart turned off the main drive around a lake and trundled into a rear courtyard surrounded by stabling and storage buildings. The driver heaved her trunk onto the cobbles and muttered. 'Down yon steps and tell Mr Haddon to send two of his men for your trunk.'

'Where shall I find Mr Haddon?'

'He's the butler.' Her driver sounded weary so she didn't question him further.

Phyllis straightened her back and headed for the steps to the servants' quarters in the basement. An unpainted wooden door led her into a large square kitchen with a high ceiling and windows just beneath it that let in the daylight. A young maid was sitting at the scrubbed deal table cutting bread and butter and piling it onto an oval platter. Phyllis cleared her throat and the girl looked up.

'Who are you?' she asked.

'Kimber, the new nursemaid.'

'Oh yes, you'll be wanting Nanny Byrne. She'll be

wanting you an' all.' The girl jerked her head. 'Go through there. You're just in time for tea.'

Phyllis walked though an open door at the other side of the room into a dark passageway with a narrow flight of stone steps that disappeared upwards. She followed voices to a large room with a table in the middle and benches either side of it. Two older maids in grey dresses were sitting by an upright piano and talking with their heads close together. They had their shoes off and white lace aprons and caps in their hands. They were obviously housemaids so she raised her voice and said, 'Good afternoon, I'm looking for Nanny Byrne.'

'She's upstairs with Her Ladyship.' One of the maids threw this comment over her shoulder but when she caught sight of Phyllis in her maroon coat and felt hat, she turned fully round and said, 'Who are you?'

Both servants stared at her, taking in her appearance.

'I'm the new nursemaid.'

The maids exchanged glances that Phyllis could only describe as smirks. 'Nanny Byrne doesn't come down here much,' one commented. 'She's too lah-de-dah for us.'

Phyllis's heart sank. The servants here sounded no different from the girls she'd known at the board school, except that one of them had a very lovely face with startling pale blue eyes.

'My letter says I have to report to Mrs Phipps, the housekeeper, first.'

'She'll be in for her tea soon.' They went back to their hushed conversation.

Phyllis sat down on a wooden settle by the wall and waited. As she did she watched the other servants come in, cast a curious glance in her direction and then wander off into a corner to chat or take their places at the table. They didn't appear to be half as disciplined as Lady Maude's had led her to believe. But she supposed they were off duty until their evening work got underway. The footmen were in their shirtsleeves and waistcoats and two of them came over to speak with her. They were joined by three other maids so Phyllis did not notice when the tea came in followed by the housekeeper and butler.

A deep voice boomed, 'What have we here?'

A footman replied, 'It's the new girl, Mr Haddon.'

'Oh here you are.'

The housekeeper, recognisable by her greying hair and black silk dress with tiny matching pleated apron, loomed into view as the other servants melted away. Mrs Phipps stared at her, chewed her lip and frowned.

'Is something wrong, ma'am?' Phyllis asked.

Mrs Phipps shook her head and turned away. Phyllis raised her eyebrows at the footman who leaned forward and whispered, 'She doesn't like pretty female servants. She says they get above themselves and cause trouble.'

'Oh!' Phyllis wouldn't have described herself as pretty despite her mother's opinion. Mothers were biased, although she had been aware of interested glances from a young man on the railway train. One of the maids chatting by the piano was very pretty by any standard. She had round rosy cheeks, curling fair hair and the lightest, brightest blue eyes Phyllis had ever seen. Her skin was unblemished and underneath her plain grey dress she had rounded hips and a full bosom. Nonetheless, as they took their places at the tea table, Phyllis learned that prettiness didn't count for anything in the servants' hierarchy at Melton Hall. She realised very quickly that there was as much of a pecking order here as there had been at Lady Maude's.

The footmen sat on one bench and the maids were opposite on the other. The butler presided in his armchair at the top end of the table and the housekeeper took the other end. She motioned Phyllis to sit saying, 'Cook is next to me, and head footman next to Mr Haddon. The rest of you sit where you can unless the nanny is down and she sits next to Mr Haddon opposite his head footman.'

When everyone had taken their fill of meat paste sandwiches followed by Yorkshire tea bread, Mr Haddon sat back in his chair and said, 'Well now, Kimber, what do you think of us so far?'

Phyllis coughed on her crumbs and took a gulp of tea from her cup. 'I thought there would be more of you.'

'We're very modern here. We have the electric, you see.'

'Lady Melton's father paid to have it put in when she married His Lordship.'

The butler cast a disapproving glance at this informant. Phyllis noticed it was the pretty housemaid she had interrupted earlier. Phyllis didn't know much about electric because Lady Maude's didn't have it. She frowned; some people said it was dangerous.

'I had a dozen footmen when the old Viscount was alive and could have used more,' the butler explained. 'We have over fifty rooms here, you know, and every occupied room had a footman posted nearby to wait on the family needs.' Mr Haddon appeared to be proud of this achievement and his face fell when he added, 'I had to let some good lads go when the electric came.'

The housekeeper interrupted. 'A few went before then, Mr Haddon. We had a mechanical bell panel down here before the electric.' She turned to Phyllis. 'It's in the passage that goes from Mr Haddon's quarters to my housekeeping room. It means we can be getting on with our jobs down here instead of waiting around upstairs just in case they want something. Nanny Byrne did ask for a bell push in the nursery, but she doesn't need it now she has you.'

Phyllis was aware that her main task as nursemaid would be to fetch and carry for the nursery so that Nanny was free to devote all her time to her infants, and that the rest of her time would be spent keeping the nursery spotlessly clean.

Mrs Phipps continued, 'Nanny Byrne won't have her baby linen go to the wash house. You'll be doing it from now on in the small scullery so I can have my scullery maid back. I'll take you up to the nursery after tea. It's on the third floor just under the attics.'

'That's where we sleep,' a young maid added. 'In the attics.'

Phyllis expected this and her training at Lady Maude's had ensured that she was well used to stairs. 'Oh yes, that reminds me,' she said. 'The driver who brought me from the station told me to ask Mr Haddon for a couple of men to take my luggage upstairs.'

'I'll do it!' Two footmen volunteered together and the maids giggled.

'I shall choose and I shall supervise,' Mr Haddon replied, and sparked a banter of exchange between the butler and his footmen.

Phyllis felt a nudge on her left and the maid sitting next to her whispered, 'Male servants are not allowed to go up to the attics.'

'Where do they sleep, then?'

'Some have rooms through the other side of the butler's quarters. Others are over the stables and coach houses.'

'Kimber will be sleeping in the nursery,' Mr Haddon interrupted, 'just in case Nanny Byrne needs her during the night.'

'You'll have your meals up there, too, with the children,' the housekeeper added.

'Nanny Byrne doesn't want you to mix with us riff-raff,' one of the maids muttered.

'Who said that?' the housekeeper demanded, and explained to Phyllis, 'We have not had a nursemaid before, let alone one from Lady Maude's.'

Phyllis didn't want to be thought of as being aloof and explained, 'My mother was in service at Redfern Abbey before she married and my – my father was head groom for Lord Redfern. He used to have a dozen carriage horses.'

A young man opposite her heard and leaned forward,

'We don't have many horses here now. His Lordship only keeps two for Her Ladyship's carriage now and she hardly ever goes out.'

'How does His Lordship get about then?' she wondered.

'He has a motor car,' he grinned. Phyllis thought he had a handsome face. His hair was brown and he had dark eyes. 'I'm Aaron Wilson, His Lordship's chauffeur and engineer. I keep the generator going for the electric as well.' His former grin broadened into a smile and, impressed by his importance, she smiled back, only faltering when the footman by his side commented, 'You only have to look at his fingernails to see that.' Aaron grimaced and slid his hands out of sight.

Phyllis remembered that her mother had had a similar problem after she black-leaded the kitchen range on a Sunday afternoon, in spite of scrubbing them with soap. She had sent her a recipe for rubbing-in cream from Lady Maude's that used lamp oil and beeswax. It was smelly but it worked on ingrained dirt.

'Haven't you got a cream that your scullery maid uses, Mr Phipps?' she asked.

The cook replied. 'She doesn't need one. Her hands are always in hot water and soda.'

Phyllis reflected that this part of Yorkshire was farming country and they didn't have coal mines and steelworks so they didn't really know what sticky ingrained dirt was. 'I can make one up for you,' she suggested to Aaron, glanced nervously at Mr Haddon and added, 'if I can have the ingredients.'

The butler was prevented from replying by a penetrating

ring of the electric bell. He jerked his head at the bootboy who rose to his feet immediately and hurried into the passage.

'Her Ladyship's bedroom,' he called.

'That'll be the hired nurse or Nanny Byrne.' Mr Haddon stood up. 'Regan, get yourself up there sharpish.'

The pretty housemaid rose to her feet and reached for her apron and cap that she had discarded on the piano. She took her time putting them on in front of an old and spotty cheval glass in the corner of the room until the housekeeper got up as well and spoke to her firmly.

'Get a move on, Regan, and take that pile of linen in my room with you.'

'No time. Mrs Phipps,' Regan replied and skipped off.

The housekeeper tutted, shook her head and turned her attention to Phyllis. 'Kimber, you come with me, if it is the baby starting you're going to be busy.' As Mrs Phipps walked passed the butler she said, 'Mr Haddon, she will need to unpack her uniform now.'

Phyllis scurried after the housekeeper's nimble form and followed her up the narrow back stairs. She was out of breath when she reached the third floor but was impressed by the size of the nursery which had several rooms stretched along the rear of the Hall, just under the eaves. A door from a long narrow landing opened into a spacious day nursery with barred windows overlooking formal gardens at the back of the Hall.

Mrs Phipps stood in the middle of the room and waved her arms around as she spoke. 'Miss Agnes is napping in the night nursery through there. You will sleep in the room next door. On the other side is the old schoolroom and washroom. That is now Nanny Byrne's sitting room and bedroom. She will explain how things work. It'll be different when there are two babies to look after.'

'Shall I check on Miss Agnes now?'

'If you wish. She cries if she needs attention, then you go and fetch Nanny Byrne if she's not already here. She is with Her Ladyship at present. Now where is your luggage?' Mrs Phipps went out onto the landing to listen and returned immediately. 'It's on its way. Wash your hands and face and put your uniform on straightaway. You'll find a sink with water cans and slop buckets through that door.'

'Yes, Mrs Phipps.'

While Phyllis was investigating this small scullery next to the day nursery, her travelling trunk arrived. Mrs Phipps ushered away the footmen to find the butler waiting in the corridor. 'Mr Haddon? Why are you up here? Is it the baby?'

He replied, 'The hired nurse has asked to send for the doctor. I've told Wilson to fetch him in the motor car.'

'Where is His Lordship?'

'I have no idea. He went off to the races a couple of days ago with the Marquess of Branbury in the Marquess's new Rolls Royce and he hasn't been home since.'

'He must be aware that the baby is due. Have you asked Her Ladyship?'

The butler shook his head. 'No point. He doesn't tell her where he is going either. I've asked Wilson to make enquiries from the telephone in the postal office.'

67

'We ought to have one of those telephones here.'

'His Lordship has ordered one to be put in as soon as we have the poles and wires from the village.'

'Did you ask Wilson to send for Her Ladyship's father? She hasn't any other family to be with her.'

Their voices faded as Phyllis went through to her bedroom and set about unpacking her uniform. She stowed it in one of the three cream painted wooden cupboards and chest of drawers in the nursemaids' bedroom. There were three bedsteads but only one of them had a mattress with folded sheets and blankets on top. She found a pillow in the cupboard. As she was making up her bed she heard Miss Agnes whimpering and went to check on her.

Mrs Phipps heard too and called from the corridor, 'Go down and get that linen from my room and take it up to Her Ladyship's bedroom when you go for Nanny Byrne.'

'Yes Mrs Phipps,' Phyllis answered automatically and wondered why she hadn't insisted that Regan go back for the linen.

Chapter 6

Phyllis stood in the doorway of Her Ladyship's elegant cream and gilt bedroom. She had never seen anything quite so luxurious, furnished with heavy white silk bed-hangings and window curtains and a thick carpet covering most of the floor.

'Try and keep calm, My Lady. It could be hours away.' A nurse in a starched white dress and veil, black stockings and boots was standing by the bed holding Lady Melton's hand. Another nurse wearing a maroon dress similar to the housekeeper's stood by like a sentry and said, 'Miss Agnes took more than twenty-four hours to arrive.'

'First babies often take longer.'

Lady Melton's features screwed up and her voice squeaked, 'I want Mama.'

Phyllis was surprised at how young she seemed to be.

She was probably pretty when her flushed face wasn't screwed up with pain. Her long dark hair was awry and she wore a crumpled, white, lace-edged nightgown. Her bedlinen was tumbled and creased. The nurses exchanged glances and one said, 'Your father has been sent for, My Lady.'

'Daddy?' Her Ladyship cried as though she were calling him in from the landing. Then she gripped a handful of her white and gold silk bedcover and squealed, 'The pains are starting again!'

The nurse in white commented, 'This one may be quicker than the last.'

Phyllis stood with the bale of clean linen that she had carried upstairs from the housekeeper's room. She hoped her cap was straight as she had had little time to check her own appearance before she had obeyed the house-keeper's instructions. The linen was heavy in her arms. Her legs were aching but she guessed she'd soon get used to all the stairs. She wasn't wholly sure which of these two women was Nanny Byrne so she ventured, 'Where shall I put the linen?'

The younger of the two nurses answered with a jerk of her head, 'In the bathroom. The older, taller woman in maroon glanced in her direction and demanded, 'Who are you?'

'Kimber, ma'am, the new nursemaid.'

'Oh. What are you doing in here?'

'The housekeeper asked me to bring the linen and tell you that Miss Agnes is awake.'

'Where is Regan?'

Phyllis realised that this must be Nanny Byrne. The maroon dress should have told her. Her own dresses were pink but her cape, outdoor cloak and felt hat were maroon. Nanny Byrne did not seem to expect a reply, which was fortunate because Phyllis couldn't answer her. She looked around the bedroom curiously. There were two doors and she guessed that one was a dressing room and the other a bathroom. If she couldn't put the linen down soon she would drop it. She walked towards one of the doors.

Nanny Byrne stopped her. 'You should not be in here. Give that to me and go back to the nursery immediately.' Nanny Byrne wrenched the linen from her and dropped it on an upholstered blanket box at the foot of the bed. The pile toppled and Phyllis dashed forward to stop it falling to the polished floor. However, the neat stack of towels and face cloths ended up in disarray.

'Clumsy girl!' Nanny Byrne snapped.

It was not her fault but Phyllis said, 'I'm sorry, Nanny.'

'Nanny Byrne. I am Nanny Byrne or ma'am.'

'Yes, ma'am.'

'Leave the towels to Regan and go.' Nanny Byrne pressed the bell push on the wall by the bed.

Phyllis escaped thankfully and headed for the back stairs where she collided with Regan as she sauntered through the small door cut into the wooden panelling that lined the landing walls. 'Oh there you are. I've taken the towels into Her Ladyship.'

Regan looked mildly offended by this information. 'Shouldn't you be in the nursery? I could hear Miss Agnes

71

crying from the back stairs. Shall I tell Nanny Byrne for you?'

'She knows already, thank you,' Phyllis muttered and hurried past her, not sure what to make of her casual behaviour.

She reached the nursery quickly and followed the cries through the day nursery to where the one-year-old had been fast asleep when she had left her. She picked her out of her cot and sniffed. Poor mite, she needed changing. Phyllis had only done this on a doll before and a real child was as wriggly and slippery as a fish! She placed her back in the cot and searched for a clean baby napkin and towel. There was hot water in the kettle on the hob behind the fireguard in the day nursery and she found a bowl and some soap. When she was ready, she lifted the child out and tried to calm her before placing her on the changing table in the night nursery.

'What do you think you are doing?'

Startled, Phyllis jumped, unsettling the child and causing her to start crying again. 'Miss Agnes needs a clean nappy, ma'am.'

'Then I shall do it. Stand aside at once. You do not touch Miss Agnes. She is my responsibility.' Nanny Byrne took over and Phyllis watched as she changed and washed the child with slightly shaky hands.

'I am sorry, Nanny Byrne, but Miss Agnes was crying.'

'I shall give you your duties later.' Her task finished, she picked up the child, took her through to the day nursery and placed her on a rug inside a wooden pen containing wooden toys. 'Clear away for now. Take all the soiled napkins downstairs and wash them with boiling water and a rubbing board. Do not use soap on anything baby wears next to her skin and rinse at least three times. I shall know if you do not follow my directions.'

'Yes, ma'am.'

'Bring nursery tea as soon as Cook has prepared it, and we shall need more cans of water now you are here.'

'Yes, ma'am.' She poured the dirty washing water on top of the napkins in a nursery pail and made her way downstairs to the scullery. She chose the smallest of the three wooden sinks to wash the baby linen and found bowls and a washboard underneath it. Fortunately the sink had cold water from a brass tap in the wall above it and a proper drain to take away the dirty water.

The scullery maid came in with a wooden drying horse. 'If you leave your washing by the kitchen range overnight, it'll be nearly dry by morning. But you must be down to move it before Cook comes in to do the breakfasts or you'll be in trouble.'

'Thank you,' she said.

'Thank *you*,' she replied. 'I'm really pleased to see you. I've been fetching and carrying for Nanny Byrne as well my scullery work for the cook. Nanny Byrne is such an old fashioned stickler.' The maid put her hand to her mouth. 'Oooh, I shouldn't have said that.'

'I won't tell,' Phyllis smiled.

'Will we see you at supper in the servants' hall?'

'I don't know,' Phyllis answered honestly. At least, not until after she received her list of duties from Nanny Byrne, she thought.

'Well we eat at six in the servants' hall if you fancy a chat, so you'd better crack on. Cook said to tell you that nursery tea is ready to go up.'

'Thank you,' Phyllis repeated and went in search of the tray.

She hurried upstairs with the covered dishes. Cook had made scrambled eggs and stewed apples for Miss Agnes and a plate of cold meat with chutney for Phyllis and Nanny Byrne, who was dozing in a rocking chair by the nursery fire when Phyllis arrived. A kettle on the hob rattled as it bubbled. Miss Agnes was playing in her pen on the rug with a collection of dolls. Phyllis placed the tray carefully on a table and called, 'Tea is here, Nanny Byrne.'

Her superior roused and looked around with a bleary eye. She rose stiffly to her feet and lifted the covers to inspect the food. She made a soft grunting sound in her throat and picked at the meat on the platter but appeared to approve. 'Tableware is in the scullery cupboard,' she said.

'Shall I give Miss Agnes her tea, ma'am?' Phyllis suggested as she set out cutlery and crockery.

'Certainly not, I have told you that Miss Agnes is my responsibility. Make a pot of tea.'

Although Nanny Byrne appeared to be weary it did not seem to affect the care and attention she gave to her charge, who enjoyed sitting in her specially made high chair to be fed. She was a good-natured child and Phyllis found tea-time a pleasant experience. The food was tasty and there was plenty of it. After tea, Nanny Byrne entertained Miss Agnes with rhymes and games while Phyllis cleared away and washed up the nursery china in the scullery, made up the fire and refilled the kettles. She put the kitchen tray and a bucket of slops on the back stairs landing to take down later. When the day nursery was clean and tidy again Nanny Byrne sent her downstairs with another pail of laundry.

'Present yourself here again at seven and don't forget my night tray.'

'Yes, Nanny Byrne.' Phyllis realised that much of her time would be spent going up and down the narrow back stair carrying trays and buckets. But she was cheered by the prospect of joining the other servants at supper. She did not have much time and wasn't hungry after her nursery tea but it was a chance to talk to the other servants. She wondered if Aaron Wilson the chauffeur would be there. He had a lovely smile and dark mysterious eyes that intrigued her.

She managed ten minutes in the servants' hall at suppertime and enjoyed a slab of fruit cake with a piece of Wensleydale cheese. However, Aaron did not appear and Phyllis was disappointed. She heard Mr Haddon tell the housekeeper that he had been delayed with the motor car and to leave out his supper for when he returned.

Regan, too, only appeared at the end of the meal but she had news of Her Ladyship. 'False alarm,' she stated. 'Nurse says she won't leave her alone now and will you send up a tray. She wants the day bed made up in Her Ladyship's dressing room.' Regan took her seat as head housemaid next to the cook adding, 'The baby won't be long so His Lordship will have to come home now.'

Everyone welcomed this news, which Phyllis thought was a sign that His Lordship was popular with his servants.

'Well enjoy the peace and quiet while you can,' Mrs Phipps commented. 'We shall have a houseful when the new baby arrives.'

'That reminds me, Mr Haddon,' Cook added, 'the game larder is nearly empty and you know I must have my venison well hung.'

'It's in hand. The gamekeeper brought in a dozen brace of pheasant today and he is culling roe deer this week.'

Their conversation on meat supplies continued and Phyllis excused herself to see to her washing. The young scullery maid was occupied in the kitchen helping Cook with dinner for Her Ladyship to be served by Mr Haddon from a trolley in her bedroom, and a supper tray for the hired nurse. Finally Phyllis drew a can of fresh water from the tap in the scullery and began the first of her several climbs to the third floor.

She heard Nanny Byrne moving about in the night nursery when she arrived. Eventually, the older woman came in and said, 'Fetch a can of hot water from the downstairs boiler to scrub the table.'

Phyllis obeyed and Nanny Byrne watched her from the rocking chair as she washed and dried the nursery table. When she had finished, her superior launched into a long list of her duties from six in the morning until eight at night, essentially outlining that her task was to be the housemaid for the nursery and personal servant to Nanny Byrne.

'I shall soon have two infants in my care,' Nanny Byrne said, 'and you will make sure that the nursery is scrupulously clean at all times and that I have everything I need. You will not touch either child without my express instruction. Is that clear?'

'Yes, ma'am.'

Nanny Byrne nodded. 'Good. Take the slop buckets downstairs, make my nightcap and damp down the fire. Then you may go to bed.'

'Thank you, ma'am.' She hesitated before asking, 'How is Her Ladyship?'

'That is none of your business. If I hear that you have been gossiping about any of His Lordship's family you will be dismissed.'

Phyllis wondered when she would have the time to even see any of the other servants let alone gossip with them. The nursery would be her home for the foreseeable future, and, while it was spacious and reasonably comfortable, it had five coal fires to be laid, lit and kept in during the winter. And it was her task to bring in buckets of coal and take out the ashes. The under-footmen and bootboy, who helped the housemaids with these tasks, were not allowed to set foot in Nanny Byrne's nursery.

It was eight-thirty by the time Phyllis had finished her nursery chores to Nanny Byrne's satisfaction and her head was splitting. The throbbing had started earlier on in the day on her railway train and made worse by the gritty smoke and noisy carriage wheels. She unpinned her cap, peeled off her apron and drank a cup of water but the pain did not go. 'I should like to take a walk in the fresh air before bed,' she asked.

'At this hour?'

'If I may, ma'am. It is a pleasant evening. At Lady Maude's, we were encouraged to take an hour's recreation out of doors when our duties allowed.'

Nanny Byrne continued to frown at her until she added, 'I have a headache, ma'am.'

'Very well, but see Mr Haddon first.'

'Thank you, ma'am.'

'While you are there, ask him for more lamp oil.'

'Has His Lordship considered electric light in the nursery?' she queried.

'I did not recommend it! It is far too bright for the children's eyes. Lady Maude's was remiss if it did not teach you that.'

Phyllis could have defended Lady Maude's views on good light for reading but Nanny Byrne's word was law in this nursery. 'Yes, ma'am,' she responded and escaped to the landing.

The basement was quiet. Mrs Phipps had retired to her sitting room and a few footmen were in the servants' hall playing cards. She went down the passage to the butler's quarters and tapped on the door.

'Enter.'

Mr Haddon was sitting in his shirtsleeves at a battered desk, poring over an open ledger. He glanced up and rose to his feet immediately. 'Heavens, Kimber, what are you doing here?'

'I am looking for you, sir.'

'Then send a message with one of the footmen. Female servants are not allowed in my quarters. What do you want?'

'The nursery needs more lamp oil, sir.'

'My bootboy will leave it on the back stairs by the nursery.'

'Oh, thank you, sir.' She smiled with relief.

'Is that all, Kimber? I am very busy.'

'Nanny Byrne said I must tell you that I am going for a walk.'

'What, now?'

'The railway train gave me a headache and it hasn't gone away.'

'Very well, but keep to the cart track past the stables and be back within thirty minutes. You'll hear the coach house clock chime the hour.'

'Yes, sir.' She let herself out of the back door near the pantries by the kitchen. The leaves were beginning to fall and some had blown down the outside steps. More were on the cart track used for deliveries. She walked briskly until her head had cleared and then retraced her steps. As she passed the stables she slowed, hesitated and when curiosity got the better of her she turned off the track towards the archway beneath the clock tower.

The moon was low in the sky so that the cobbled courtyard behind the Hall was dark. One or two lamps were burning in upstairs windows and a brighter light escaped through an open door of one of the coach houses.

She walked in the opposite direction then noticed the glow of a cigarette and stilled in her tracks. A male servant was leaning against a mounting stone. She decided that this was not a good idea after all.

'Do you want a smoke, Miss?' a voice called through the darkness.

'No – no thank you,' she replied and retraced her steps towards the archway.

The coach house door opened further and a man emerged carrying a lamp. 'Who's there?' he said. He strode towards her holding his lamp high. 'Oh, I thought it was one of the garden boys up to no good. Are you looking for someone?'

'I – I was – just walking.'

'At this hour?' He moved closer. 'Oh, it's you.' Aaron Wilson held his lamp higher. 'Does Mr Haddon know you're here?'

'Yes.'

'In the courtyard, after dark?'

'Well no. I – I needed some fresh air, that's all.'

'I'll take you back to the kitchen.'

'There is no need,' she said.

But she was grateful that he ignored her protest and added, 'Wait while I lock up the garage.'

'Thank you.' She watched him close up the wide wooden doors and pocket a large iron key.

When he rejoined her he said, 'His Lordship would never forgive me if anything happened to his Daimler.'

'You weren't in for supper,' she commented.

'I was at the railway station, waiting for His Lordship.'

'Oh good, Her Ladyship will be pleased he is home.'

'He isn't. He wasn't on the train as expected, or the one after that.'

'Isn't anybody worried about him?'

He laughed, 'Why should they? He isn't answerable to anyone. He is master of his own life. Besides, he told me that, after the races, he was going with Lord Branbury to see how a motor car is made. Mr Haddon sent a telegraph message about Her Ladyship, but I don't know whether it reached him.' He stopped at the top of the outside steps to the basement. 'Here we are.'

She stood for a few seconds wanting to prolong their conversation. She wanted him to have a favourable impression of her but could not think of anything interesting to say. It was unusual for her to be tongue-tied. She waited for Aaron to speak but he didn't. He just stared at her in the darkness. The clock chimed the quarter hour and she said, 'I have to go.'

'Don't upset Nanny Byrne on your first night,' he advised with a nod. He showed no inclination to walk away but eventually added, 'Goodnight, then,' and gave her a very gentle push towards the steps.

'Goodnight,' she responded. She walked carefully down the dark steps and opened the door, turning to glance back at him. He was still on the top step and he gave her a friendly wave. She waved back before disappearing inside, thinking what a kind man he was and how she wanted to get to know more about him. Her headache had gone and she felt better. She skipped up the stairs and was delighted to see a can of lamp oil and bucket of coal on the back stairs by the door to the third floor. Cheered by the outcome of her first evening, she picked them up and took them into the nursery.

Chapter 7

Over the next few days Phyllis became more accustomed to Nanny Byrne's routine. She worked hard and Nanny Byrne did not chastise her. This, she understood from a kitchen maid, meant that Nanny Byrne approved of her. Phyllis found that the scullery and kitchen maids were her allies. The housemaids were not so helpful, especially Regan, who as head housemaid was responsible for Lord and Lady Melton's bedrooms.

'I shall be relieving the hired nurse this morning while she goes into the chemists in town,' Nanny Byrne informed her one morning.

'Does Her Ladyship not have her own lady's maid?' she asked.

'She left.'

'Oh.' Phyllis thought that personal maid to Lady

Melton would be a desirable post. 'Did she find a better position?'

'I doubt it.' Nanny Byrne's disapproving tone made Phyllis wonder what had gone wrong. If only she were older she might have been eligible to be Lady Melton's maid and she would have liked that. But she had no time to dwell on it as her superior went on, 'As soon as you have finished cleaning the nursery, you may occupy Miss Agnes with her new farmyard toys then bring her down to see her mother for half an hour before nursery dinner.'

'Yes, ma'am.'

It was her most enjoyable morning since her arrival. With the fireguard securely in position, Phyllis arranged a whole farmyard of wooden animals on the rug in front of the nursery fire. Miss Agnes's little fingers stretched for her favourite sheep, which had thick woolly backs that hid her tiny fingernails. Phyllis washed and changed her then sat her with her sheep in the wooden pen while she tidied her own appearance to take Miss Agnes down to her mother via the main staircase. From the nursery floor it was not much wider than the back stairs, but its banister rails were highly polished and the treads had patterned carpet held in place by brass stair rods.

Miss Agnes began to grizzle in her arms. She was not happy to be parted from her wooden sheep and, Phyllis guessed, she was hungry for her dinner. However, her attention was diverted by the gilt and cream decor of her mother's bedroom and she was fascinated by the ornate crystal chandelier lit by electricity. Nanny Byrne was too occupied with Her Ladyship to worry about

Miss Agnes's eyes. She was standing beside Lady Melton's bed trying to persuade Her Ladyship to get dressed and go downstairs for luncheon.

'I'm too tired.' Her Ladyship sounded tearful. 'I look hideous and I don't want anything to eat. Where is my husband?'

'His Lordship is with Lord Branbury, my lady.'

'Why doesn't he come home?' Her Ladyship whined.

'Your Ladyship's father will be here soon.'

At the mention of her father, Lady Melton's face distorted into a sob. 'I don't want Papa, I want Mama,' she cried.

Nanny Byrne appeared relieved to see Phyllis. 'Miss Agnes is here, My Lady.'

Lady Melton's face was very miserable. Her pregnancy bulged under the bedclothes and she didn't even look pleased to see her daughter.

'I'm too exhausted to hold her,' she moaned. 'She doesn't like me anyway.'

'Of course she does, My Lady.' But when Phyllis leaned forward to present Miss Agnes to her reluctant mother, the child's face creased up in distress and Nanny Byrne whisked her from Phyllis's arms before the infant began to wail and beckoned her away from the bed. 'Kimber, have you seen Regan?' she demanded.

'No, ma'am.'

'You'll have to do it then. Gather the used linen from the bathroom and dressing room and take it outside to the laundry. You will have to take Miss Agnes back to the nursery and give her dinner. I shall follow you as soon as Regan makes an appearance. If you see her, tell her to buck up.'

'Yes, ma'am.' Phyllis hurried into the adjoining bathroom, which clearly had not been touched by a housemaid today.

Phyllis left the linen on the back stairs hoping no one would fall over it while she returned to Her Ladyship's bedroom and took Miss Agnes back to the nursery. She was becoming fractious and Phyllis was loath to leave her in the pen to take down the laundry but the child quietened at the sight of her farmyard sheep. Her Ladyship was certainly in a sorry state. But her new baby was overdue and she had to have someone with her day and night. Perhaps Regan was on an errand for Mrs Phipps. Phyllis found the laundry easily without having to ask. It was through the courtyard at the back of the Hall and recognisable by its tall brick chimney that took the smoke away from the boiler fire.

On her way back someone called her name from an open door in the one of the courtyard buildings. She twisted around and saw Aaron waving at her from the garage. 'Come and see His Lordship's motor car,' he said. He was in shirtsleeves and smiling and she would have liked nothing more than to exchange a few words with him, but Miss Agnes was hungry and waiting for her. 'I can't stop now,' she called and hurried on. Then she halted and turned, 'You haven't seen Regan, have you?'

'Regan? Yes, she was out here half an hour ago sitting in His Lordship's motor car. Why do you ask?'

'Her Ladyship wants her.'

He raised his eyebrows but didn't question her. 'She said she had an hour off. Try the housekeeper's room.'

She wasn't there either and Mrs Phipps was cross because she thought Regan *was* with Her Ladyship. Phyllis ran to the kitchen where her nursery tray was waiting and hurried upstairs to find a distressed Miss Agnes sitting in the corner of her pen and sucking on a woolly sheep. She suppressed her anger so as not to upset the child further. This would never have happened if Regan had been at her post!

Phyllis picked up Miss Agnes to comfort her. She quietened for a moment but when she focused her watery eyes on Phyllis's face she began her weeping all over again and wouldn't be pacified until she had been given her shepherd's pie and mashed carrots. She was a pretty child, taking after her mother in hair colour and eyes. Phyllis hoped she had not inherited Lady Melton's temperament. Her Ladyship did seem unduly miserable for one who led a such comfortable life being waited on by others. Perhaps she would be more cheerful when her new baby arrived.

Phyllis had not long to wait as Lady Melton went into labour two days later and gave birth in the middle of the following night. Lord Melton still had not returned home but had sent a telegram to announce his imminent arrival. Lady Melton's father visited to see his new grandchild and left the same day for his shipyard on the east coast. Nanny Byrne took over care of both infants but as she was reluctant to hand over Miss Agnes to Phyllis she became more exhausted in the process. The new baby was only a few days old before poor Miss Agnes became bored, spending hours alone in her pen while Phyllis completed her nursery housemaid duties.

Phyllis asked Nanny Byrne if she might take the toddler out for an afternoon walk in the perambulator, allowing the older woman to take a nap in the nursery where she would be on hand if the new baby woke up and needed her.

'Very well,' Nanny Byrne agreed readily.

'Shall I make you a pot of tea before I go?'

'Leave it in my sitting room.' She yawned and went to lie down.

Phyllis dressed Miss Agnes in a bottle green outdoor coat and hat and put on her own maroon woollen cloak and felt hat. She carried Miss Agnes down the main staircase and asked a footman to bring round the perambulator to the front door. The perambulator was housed in a basement luggage lobby at the front of the house. A small door emerged underneath and to one side of the marble entrance steps and a sloping path camouflaged by shrubs emerged at ground level some fifty yards away from the Hall front door. Phyllis waited at the top of the slope while a footman wheeled up the perambulator. She sat Miss Agnes up in the carriage so that she may see what a beautiful place she lived in.

Phyllis had not seen the park from this side of the Hall before and marvelled at its rolling grassland and majestic trees. Miss Agnes, a naturally inquisitive child, looked about with interest, pointed and burbled and Phyllis did her best to respond. She was on her way back when the sound of a raucous klaxon alarmed her and, curious, she followed the sound to the main drive. A motor car was rolling up the drive towards the wide expanse of gravel in front of the Hall. The driver squeezed the rubber bulb of his klaxon again to announce his approach. The motor car was a huge shiny carriage on wheels and its speed made Phyllis nervous as she wasn't sure which direction it would take. She waited and watched until it had drawn to a halt at the foot of the marble steps.

As the motor neared the front door she noticed a male servant appearing from beneath the clock tower that led to the courtyard at the far side of the Hall. She recognised Aaron immediately. He already wore his chauffeur's hat and was buttoning his jacket. He pulled on his gauntlets and ran to take up a position by the front steps as the motor drew to a halt. She saw him salute smartly and open the driver's door. When the motor car's engine went quiet, Phyllis could hear their conversation.

'Good afternoon, My Lord.'

'Beauty, isn't she, Wilson?'

'She is indeed, My Lord.'

'She's a Silver Ghost, one of the first to be made. Her engine is much quieter than my Daimler and she has a hood for when it rains.' He leaned back into the leather upholstery. 'I was measured for the driver's seat, y'know.' He squeezed the klaxon bulb. Its ear splitting sound made Miss Agnes jump and she had to be reassured to stop her crying. But Lord Melton hadn't noticed. He laughed and squeezed it again.

'I have prepared the large coach house for her, My Lord.'

'Excellent, Excellent. Unload my bags and then clean her up.'

The front door opened and Mr Haddon came outside and walked sedately down the steps. 'Welcome home, My Lord,' he said.

'See to my luggage, Haddon. Who's that over there?'

'It's Miss Agnes, My Lord.'

'Not the child, man, the maid with her.'

'Kimber is your new nursemaid, My Lord. You may recall that Lady Redfern recommended her.'

'Aunt Amelia? Did she, by Jove?' He walked towards Miss Agnes, glanced at his daughter then stared at Phyllis before moving away. Phyllis dipped a curtsy but felt uncomfortable as he scrutinised her appearance. Miss Agnes gazed curiously at her father and Phyllis wasn't at all sure that she recognised him.

Mr Haddon said, 'Her Ladyship would like to see you immediately, My Lord.'

Lord Melton grunted. 'She's given me another girl, Haddon, another girl, dammit.' He did not sound at all pleased.

Phyllis waited until Lord Melton had disappeared into the Hall before lifting Miss Agnes out of her perambulator. She put her down to walk a few steps, holding firmly onto both her hands and called, 'Mr Haddon, will you ask someone to put away the perambulator?'

He waved his hand in response and picked up two of His Lordship's valises. Aaron walked over to her. 'Did he say anything to you?' he said.

'No. Why should he?' she smiled. 'You look very smart in your livery.'

But Aaron didn't smile in return. 'He didn't speak to you directly?'

'No, why do you ask?'

'Well, he – he has something of a reputation with,' he began and she thought he was going to say more but decided against it, so she went on, 'If he wanted reports on his daughters he would ask Nanny Byrne, not me.'

'Yes, of course,' Aaron responded. 'Is this one of your regular duties?'

'Hopefully it will be, if Nanny Byrne agrees.'

'Do you know of the sunken garden at the back of the Hall?'

'I've seen it from the nursery windows.'

'It's ideal for Miss Agnes as it's sheltered from the wind and has grassy paths for her to walk on.'

'Thank you. I'll ask Nanny Byrne about it.'

'I'll look out for you.'

'Oh!' Her eyes widened. Was this an assignation?

'Don't be alarmed. I shan't intrude, not when Nanny Byrne might be watching you from the nursery windows.'

She did not know whether to be pleased that he was concerned or disappointed they would not be able to talk, but she was grateful and replied, 'Thank you.'

She watched him help Haddon with the bags and wondered if he was walking out with anybody. She realised with a jolt that he must be, and that she was Regan, who skipped her duties to spend time in the garage. It made sense that the prettiest housemaid and handsomest male servant were attracted to each other. Miss Agnes tugged at her hands and she carried her up the marble steps but set her down again to climb the first flight of carpeted main stairs to the nursery.

Nanny Byrne was asleep on her bed and her tea had gone cold in her sitting room. Phyllis heard the new baby whimpering in the night nursery and went to check on her, picking up Miss Agnes to see her new sister. Baby was not distressed but it was nearly time for Miss Agnes to see her mother for an hour before nursery tea. She went to wake Nanny then sat Miss Agnes in her own cot while she laid out clean clothes for her and put the baby's bottle feed to warm over a pan of hot water near the fire.

'I saw His Lordship arrive in his new motor car while I was out with Miss Agnes,' she said.

'At last. Perhaps Her Ladyship will cheer up now. Put the flat irons to heat and take out one of Miss Agnes's new dresses. We shall take both his daughters to see His Lordship before tea.'

'Will that be in the drawing room with Her Ladyship?'

'Of course! You will supervise Miss Agnes.'

'She does know who he is, doesn't she? Miss Agnes didn't appear to recognise her father when he arrived and he seemed more interested in his new motor car than his elder daughter.' Phyllis thought she was making a helpful observation but the shocked expression on Nanny Byrne's face told her otherwise.

'How dare you comment on His Lordship's conduct?

He is the master of this house and he has come home to see Baby. If you cannot hold your tongue I shall not allow you to take charge of Miss Agnes.'

'I beg your pardon, ma'am.'

Nanny Byrne tutted and shook her head. 'What is Lady Maude's teaching young girls these days?'

But Baby's personal habits didn't fit in with nursery schedule and by the time they had reached the ground floor, a recognisable baby smell was coming from Nanny Byrne's arms.

'Shall I take her back to the nursery and change her?' Phyllis volunteered.

'Certainly not. Baby is my responsibility. Wait for me outside the drawing room.'

Phyllis sat with her charge for a while on an upholstered couch in the marble-pillared hall, but Miss Agnes became restless so she picked her up and wandered to the back of the hall to show her the portraits of her ancestors hung on the wood panelled walls. She heard footsteps on the stairs and saw Lord Melton stride through the drawing room door leaving it slightly ajar. The clock chimed the hour and normally Nanny would take in Miss Agnes on the dot. Phyllis carried her back to the seat and waited. The voices of Lord and Lady Melton drifted through the open door.

'Pull yourself together, Clara, and stop weeping all over the furniture, you are no longer your daddy's little girl.'

'No one would know that. Daddy spends more time with me than you do.'

'Not that again.'

93

'Why didn't you come home before our baby was born?'

'Why should I, for heaven's sake?'

'I needed you with me.'

'Good God! You have a houseful of servants.'

'You should have been here.'

'You are a viscountess for God's sake, so start behaving as one.'

'But I'm your wife, Melton,' she whined.

'Precisely. You have a duty to provide me with a son and you knew that before you married me. I won't have you putting off the next one as you did this one.'

'No, Melton, please! I'm too tired to have another child. It's so exhausting having a baby. I want time to recover.'

'Well you can't have it. Not until you give me a son. Why do you think I came home? Not to celebrate the birth of another girl, that's for sure. The sooner you are pregnant again, the better.'

'No, Melton, not yet.' Phyllis heard Her Ladyship sob softly.

'Dear God give me strength! Don't get upset all over again. I can't stand it. Look, you have to do something with yourself when I'm away.'

'Well I could look after my children if you'd let me.'

'That is out of the question. Nanny Byrne brought me up to be an aristocrat and she will do the same for my children. You haven't the breeding, you see. Your father has money, but not the blood.'

This comment seemed to silence Lady Melton. Phyllis stared directly ahead. She heard a few snuffling sobs from Her Ladyship and an exasperated curse from His Lordship.

'Look, as soon as you're on your feet again,' he said, 'you can have the Daimler and Wilson to get out and about. I have a new motor which I shall be driving myself for most of the time.'

'May I not go with you?'

'Don't be ridiculous!'

'But where shall I go on my own?'

'Why don't you take the children and stay with Aunt Amelia in the South Riding? She knows how to keep herself busy and you can learn from her.'

'She won't have time for me.'

'Yes she will. She adores children. I'll talk to Uncle James when he comes for the christening. They have agreed to be godparents again. I was going to ask Edward to be godfather if she'd been a boy. But the Branbury girl is going to marry him so she will be godmother instead. By the way, don't gossip about that because Edward doesn't know yet.'

'Very well,' Lady Melton answered in a small voice.

'But understand this, Clara, you don't go until you are pregnant again. I will have a son.' The clock chimed the quarter hour. 'Where are those blessed children?' His Lordship wrenched the door open wide and saw Phyllis sitting there with Lady Agnes on her lap. 'Here's one.' He glanced over Phyllis's neat appearance and added. 'Oh it's you, the new girl. What's your name again?'

'Kimber, My Lord.'

'Bring her in, Kimber.'

Lady Melton inhaled noisily as though she were suppressing a sob. She held out her arms to take Miss Agnes who squirmed and grizzled on her mother's lap until Phyllis handed her a woolly sheep. The child stuck out her lower lip defiantly but eventually sat still. Nanny Byrne hurried through the door with a sweet-smelling and gurgling infant.

'Here is Baby, My Lord.' She handed the soft white bundle to her father who glanced at her briefly, handed her back to Nanny and pressed the electric bell push on the wall.

Phyllis lifted Miss Agnes from her mother's lap while she took her new baby from Nanny. This did seem to cheer Lady Melton and for the next few minutes she cuddled and cooed at her while Nanny hovered behind her as though she didn't trust a mother with her own child.

'You rang for me, My Lord.' His butler stood to attention and waited for his orders.

'Yes, Haddon. The christening will be next month,' his lordship announced. 'Tell Phipps we shall have a celebration luncheon and house guests for the following week. It's a good time of year for shooting. How is the new gamekeeper getting along?'

'Very well, My Lord.'

'Excellent. Send him in to see me tomorrow and tell the head gardener I want to talk to him about the driveways, now we have motor cars using them.'

'Very good, My Lord.' He cleared his throat. 'May I enquire of the new infant's name?'

'She'll be Beatrice, after my mother.'

'Yes, My Lord. Will that be all?'

'I'll inspect the wine cellar tomorrow.'

'Very good, My Lord.' Haddon went out, closing the drawing room door behind him.

Lord Melton turned to his wife. 'The christening should keep you occupied for the next few weeks.'

Lady Melton's eyes widened for a moment.

'Oh don't panic, for God's sake. Phipps will know what to do.' He left the drawing room without another word.

'Is nursery tea ready yet, Cook?'

'You'll have to prepare it yourself, Kimber. I've dinner tonight for ten including the Earl and Countess of Redfern, and luncheon for more than twenty tomorrow. Your trays are over there and the dishes are in the hot cupboard.'

Phyllis ladled soup into a tureen and added flaked fish to warmed béchamel sauce on the hotplate. When it was ready she transferred everything to trays and peeped under the dessert cover to check that the junket was set before placing the trays in the dumb waiter to take it to the ground floor.

'Cook,' she called, 'May I have a scullery maid to help carry?'

'I'm afraid not, Kimber. You'll have to do for yourself today.' That meant two journeys up to the nursery as the soup tureen was heavy. It was often soup for nursery tea now that winter was approaching. But she actually enjoyed taking her meals with Nanny Byrne and Miss Agnes in the day nursery. Although Nanny Byrne was 'an old fashioned stickler' as the scullery maid had described her, she was consistent in her approach so that Phyllis quickly learned how to respond to her; or not as the case may be. And even strait-laced Nanny Byrne was excited about tomorrow's christening, helping Phyllis with the laundering, starching and pressing of their own and the children's outfits.

'Will you join the other servants' in their celebrations?' Phyllis asked. 'Mr Haddon has given the evening off to all those who can be spared. Cook has prepared a cold table for upstairs dinner and we are to have similar treats and dancing in the servants' hall.'

'I shall take sherry with Mr Haddon and Mrs Phipps to drink Miss Beatrice's health and then retire to the nursery with my supper tray as usual.'

'Then may I join the party when I have settled Miss Agnes for the night?'

'If you must, as long as you are back in the nursery by ten.'

'Of course, Nanny Byrne.'

Chapter 8

'Is Wilson back from Melton Halt yet, Haddon?'

'He is approaching the Hall as I speak, My Lord.'

The next morning, Phyllis bent down to speak to Miss Agnes whose little toddling legs were becoming stronger every day. 'Shall we go outside and see your father's new motor car?' The child nodded vigorously.

Lord and Lady Melton joined them to walk down the marble steps and welcome their remaining guests. A chattering crowd of Hall visitors followed them. Phyllis watched Aaron motor the Silver Ghost to a halt, climb out and open the door for his passengers. She thought that everyone had dressed very stylishly for Miss Beatrice's christening and vowed that one day when she was older she would wear a fashionable costume instead of her nursemaid's uniform. In the exchange of greetings that followed, Aaron moved away from the motor car and whispered in her ear. 'Will you be at the servants' party this evening?'

'If the children settle after all this excitement,' she answered.

'I can't be there until after I've taken His Lordship's guests back to Melton Halt, so be sure to save a dance for me, won't you.'

'I shall,' she smiled and looked forward to the end of the day.

Every servant who could be spared squeezed into the rear pews of Melton Hall's private chapel waiting for the procession of guests to walk the few hundred yards from the Hall. Nanny Byrne had never looked prouder when she stepped forward at the stone font with Miss Beatrice in her slightly yellowing christening gown. It was the most beautiful delicate lace, handmade in the nearby county of Nottingham and a Melton family heirloom. Phyllis held Miss Agnes's hand as she toddled beside her, lifting the child into her arms to watch the event. As the party left, Lord Redfern paused for a moment to pick up Miss Agnes's tiny hand.

'She is very well-behaved in your care.'

Phyllis wanted to tell him how bright and clever Miss Agnes was too, but this was not the time or place. She curtseyed and said, 'Thank you, My Lord.'

'You're Kimber, aren't you?'

'Yes, My Lord.'

'Are you happy at Melton Hall?'

100

'Yes, My Lord.' She meant it.

'Good.'

'James, you are holding up the other guests,' Lady Redfern whispered in his ear and he moved on.

His son Edward escorted the other godparent, Anne. She was the daughter of His Lordship's friend the Marquess of Branbury. Edward stopped and stared at her in the same way that Lord Melton had when he first saw her, but Anne tugged at his sleeve and murmured, 'Edward, your mother is beckoning you.'

Phyllis gazed after him, feeling sure she had met him before somewhere. Perhaps she had, when she was a child at Queen Victoria's Diamond Jubilee and not known who he was. She racked her brain to remember but could not recall and decided she was mistaken. Surely Mother would have pointed him out to her?

Miss Beatrice's christening luncheon was the grandest occasion held at Melton Hall since Phyllis had taken up her position. Nanny Byrne stood in pride of place with Miss Beatrice in the drawing room, clearly enjoying the celebrations. Her severe features lifted as she found a smile for everyone. Lord and Lady Melton's guests toasted the birth with champagne and crowded around her to press golden guineas into the infant's tiny palm. Nanny passed them to Phyllis who placed them in a small leather purse that she had to give to Nanny when the guests went through for luncheon. There were silver gifts, too, displayed on a side table; ceremonial mugs and spoons, tiny shoes and several thimbles. Lady Redfern had lifted Miss Agnes from Phyllis's arms and taken her to look at the display, leaving Edward alone with Miss Branbury and Phyllis waiting for Miss Agnes to be returned. Phyllis stepped away from the group and looked down at her feet.

'Isn't Miss Beatrice a little darling?' Miss Branbury commented brightly to Edward.

Edward agreed. 'She is indeed. Melton is a lucky man.' Melton had told him quite a lot about Anne Branbury. In fact, Edward had thought he had said far too much and most of it complimentary. Anne had been out for several years now and was still unmarried so he suspected that she might be dull. But she was prettier than he had anticipated and she had entertained him well enough at dinner last night. He guessed Lady Branbury had primed her well.

'I was thrilled to be asked to be her godmother,' she said. 'It's the first time I have taken on such a responsibility.'

'Then you have the advantage of me.'

'Oh gosh, I didn't mean to slight you.'

Edward was about to say that he was not slighted in the least when she went on, 'I suppose one has to be younger than the parents to be able to take over should the worst happen.'

Now he did feel slighted. If it wasn't bad enough his parents going on about finding a wife to produce an heir, now he had this flibbertigibbet telling him he was too old to be a godparent. He didn't know what to say to her so he stayed silent.

Her eyes darted from side to side for a moment as

though she was anxious to put things right and she went on, 'You would be perfect, of course, to be a godfather to a son because you are the same age as Melton.' She sighed and added, 'Mother told me you were cousins and at university together.'

Edward smiled inwardly. In the course of one short conversation he had been offended and then flattered by her.

'Yes, we were,' he replied.

'Oh you are so lucky to be able to do that. I should like to go to university. Girls can attend the lectures, you know, but Father won't hear of it. He doesn't believe in wasting money on education for girls.'

'He is not alone in that view.'

'Oh, but haven't you read what the suffragists have said about that?' She stopped and put her hand to her mouth. 'Mother said I shouldn't talk of it.'

'Please go on, I'm interested. After all, my young cousin will be growing up in the twentieth century and her existence will be very different from your mother's life.'

Phyllis was interested too but she felt a tug on her hand as Lady Redfern brought Miss Agnes back and set her down on her tired legs. Phyllis heard a whine from her charge.

'Not long now, Miss Agnes,' she whispered. 'You have been a very good little girl for me today and we are having jelly and ice cream later.'

But the child was hungry now and tears were threatening so she picked her up and carried her over to Nanny Byrne who was standing guard over Lady Melton holding

Miss Beatrice. 'Miss Agnes is ready for her dinner,' she whispered.

'We haven't had the photographs taken yet,' she responded. 'Give her a sweetmeat from the sidetable.'

Phyllis moved away from the crush of grown-ups to inspect several crystal bowls containing sugared almonds and boiled sweets. She chose a barley sugar twist that brought the smile back to Miss Agnes's face. Then she tidied her hair, wiped her mouth with a damp cloth from her pocket, and took her into the chilly entrance hall where the photographer had set up his equipment. The noise and flashes frightened Miss Beatrice and she began to cry whilst the smell from the light explosions made Miss Agnes feel sick. But it was soon over and Phyllis hurried thankfully to the nursery, leaving the adults to finish their champagne and canapés and take their seats in the dining room for luncheon.

After nursery dinner, Miss Agnes was tired and fractious until she fell asleep. Nanny Byrne fed Miss Beatrice and put her down, then slept herself. Phyllis cleared away and washed up then rested for half an hour before she got up to make Nanny her pot of tea and wake her. She had to knock loudly to rouse her and volunteered to give Miss Beatrice her next feed.

'I am quite capable, Kimber. Concentrate your attentions on Miss Agnes. Is she awake yet?'

'She is playing with her dolls until it is time for her hour with Her Ladyship.'

'I have advised against that for today. Lady Melton will have too many guests in the drawing room and the child has had enough excitement for one day. She may play with her doll's house instead.'

The doll's house was a new toy, bought for the nursery to celebrate the arrival of a new baby and already had taken over from the farmyard as Miss Agnes's favourite toy. It was kept in reserve for when she had been especially well behaved. Phyllis spent hours with her arranging the furniture. She had made a nursery crib from directions she had found in a journal and had ordered a tiny baby doll to put in it.

Nanny Byrne opened the front and inspected her addition. 'Miss Agnes seems very pleased about her new toy,' she commented.

'Yes, she has rearranged the doll's house nursery herself.'

'His Lordship's day visitors will have left by now. I shall join Mrs Phipps in her sitting room for an hour this evening. You will report to me there when you come down for the servants' party.'

'Yes, Nanny Byrne.'

Phyllis felt a ripple of excitement as she took off her nursemaid's uniform and replaced it with her best dress. It was blue silk with lace edgings and she loved wearing it. She changed her black stockings and boots for white stockings and shoes with heels. Then she sat in front of the mirror and fiddled with her hair, trying to do something different with it. But it was too long and heavy so she wound it higher than usual, into a topknot, and secured it with all her hairpins, covering them with blue-dyed feathers on a comb. She was pleased with the result for it made her appear older. She wondered if Aaron would notice. The seven o'clock dressing gong rang as she made her way down to the basement.

The noise of piano music came from the servants' hall as she tapped on Mrs Phipps' door. Mr Haddon opened it and beamed at her. 'Come in, Kimber. My goodness, you look a picture. Doesn't she look a picture, eh? Will you take a glass of sherry with us?'

'No, she will not,' Nanny Byrne replied for her. 'Kimber, you will have one glass only of ale or cider tonight.'

'There is lemon barley water as well,' Mrs Phipps explained to her. 'That's an uncommonly pretty dress, my dear.'

'My mother made it for me. She is very clever with a sewing needle.'

'Are both infants settled for the night, Kimber?' Nanny interrupted.

'They are sound asleep, ma'am. I have left a night light in a saucer of water in case Miss Agnes wakes.'

'Very good.' Nanny stood up awkwardly. 'Miss Beatrice will be wanting another feed soon,' she said. 'It has been a long day and my knees are creaking. They don't like this damp autumn weather.'

'What you want is a drop of His Lordship's good brandy for your nightcap, Nanny.'

'Thank you, I don't mind if I do, Mr Haddon. Don't be late, Kimber.'

Phyllis took her cue to leave and followed the sound of a Viennese waltz from the piano. The servants' hall was crowded as the eight guests who were staying had brought more than a dozen servants between them. The dining table had been moved to one end of the room and most of the servants were clustered round it, helping themselves to pork pie, pressed beef and pickles, and ale from a barrel set up at the far end. There were three couples whirling around the room to the music. The head footman still wore his livery, presumably because he had to help Mr Haddon serve the upstairs buffet. He was dancing with one of the housemaids, and the scullery maid was clearly enjoying herself partnered by a ruddy faced young man whom Phyllis did not recognise. The other couple were Aaron, wearing a dark shirt unbuttoned at his throat with trousers that were definitely not his livery and – and Regan in her grey afternoon dress and lace apron. Her dainty hat was slipping off but she didn't seem to mind. They were a talented pair as dancers, well-matched in their attractiveness and making such a handsome couple that Phyllis felt a pang of disappointment. She wished it were her twirling and smiling at Aaron, and was grateful when the music stopped and she didn't have to watch them together. She focused on the visiting servants, some of whom were in a dark green livery with brass buttons.

'*Did none of you hear the dressing gong?*' Mr Haddon boomed from the doorway. There was a moment of complete silence before a ripple of murmurings and the departure of several valets and maids, including Regan. Mr Haddon glared at Cook who was sitting in Mrs Phipps' chair by the fire.

'Everything is ready to go up, Mr Haddon,' Cook told him. 'I'm not having it drying out in the dining room before they come down.' She turned to her scullery maid. 'Go and move the soup to the middle of the hot plate.' The young girl got up at once and Mr Haddon nodded in response. He had a slight flush on his face and Phyllis wondered if he would be able to carve the ham and serve the dressed salmon with a steady hand. As she was considering this she noticed Aaron walking towards her. She fingered her topknot nervously.

'It's been a long day hasn't it?' he said. 'You look very nice in that dress.'

'Thank you.'

'Shall I get you something to eat?'

'I'm not hungry.' He raised his eyebrows and she explained, 'I have nursery tea upstairs.'

'Will you have a drink then?'

'Yes please, cider.' She had noticed the stoneware bottles next to the ale barrel.

He went off to join the throng around the table and returned with a glass in each hand. She thanked him, adding, 'Nanny Byrne has allowed me only one drink.'

'Well, you must savour it then. Come over by the piano, it'll be quiet for half an hour and we can talk.'

'Is Regan coming back?'

'You can call her Violet when Mr Haddon and Mrs Phipps are not around. We all do, so she won't mind. Anyway, she won't be back for a while. She told me she has to help one of the guests to dress after she had seen to Her Ladyship.

'She has to turn down all the beds as well. How many guests are staying?'

'Let me see, Lord and Lady Redfern and their son. They arrived by motor car with a chauffeur, valet and maid, the same as the Marquess of Branbury. He has three ladies in his party, his wife and daughter and the dowager Marchioness. Mr Ashby is staying, of course, and his brother with a single lady who nobody knows. I expect she is the extra guest that Violet has been given.'

'You seem to know as much as Mr Haddon.'

'I look after the guests' motor cars or drive them to and from their railway trains,' he explained. 'Poor Violet,' he grinned and gave a soft chuckle.

'Why is that funny?'

'The single lady has neither title nor money and Violet feels slighted. She wanted another maid to dress her but Mr Haddon would have none of that.'

'Well, she is the head housemaid.'

'With high aspirations,' he added lightly. 'I think we have talked enough about Violet. Have you remembered that you said you'll dance with me?'

'Oh, I cannot dance as well as Vi—' She floundered around for the name of another maid but eventually said with a shrug, 'As well as Violet.'

'Very few can,' he commented. 'But I know you can sing because I've heard you.'

'When?' she exclaimed, 'and where?'

'In the chapel, of course. And on fine Sundays you take Miss Agnes around the church yard and show her the wild flowers.'

'Have you been spying on us?'

'No.' He sounded indignant. 'I often have a long wait

for Lady Melton after the service whilst the vicar talks to her and it is a very pretty churchyard.'

'Yes it is.'

'The late Dowager had a hand in the planting as she thought the vaults and tombstones were gloomy and forbidding.'

'Well next time, show yourself properly. If Miss Agnes caught sight of you lurking in the bushes she might be frightened.'

He raised his eyebrows and she realised that her tone had been sharp. 'I don't lurk,' he protested gently. 'I had no wish to intrude on you.'

She felt rebuked, deservedly, looked away and commented. 'Our pianist is back.'

'Good. There's going to be singing until the others come down from their duties, then more dancing and Cook has made ice-creams for later.'

Phyllis's eyes lit up at the prospect and Aaron laughed. 'You like ices?'

'Ooh yes, don't you?'

'Yes,' he agreed, nodding his head enthusiastically. 'Here, hold my glass while I fetch a couple of chairs for us.'

'This is fun,' she said when he returned with the chairs. 'I do believe Nanny Byrne is enjoying herself, too, with Mr Haddon's brandy.'

'His Lordship knows how to host a party and he doesn't stint with his servants either. That's probably why he has no money.'

'No money? Nonsense! Who pays for all this?'

'Not him. He has Her Ladyship's dowry to keep the

Hall running and he uses her father as if he were his own private banker.'

'Ssshhh, someone might hear you.'

'Oh, it's common knowledge that Her Ladyship's father paid for the electricity and hot water geysers. He boasts about it to his business friends. His chauffeur told me Mr Ashby tells anyone who will listen to him that Melton Hall would be bankrupt if it weren't for his shipbuilding fortune.'

Phyllis was shocked. 'Servants oughtn't to talk about their employers with such disrespect.'

'Maybe not, but it's the truth.'

'Well, it's none of our business.'

'Yes it is. It's our livelihoods.' His reply was abrupt and Phyllis frowned. She was grateful that he picked up a sheaf of papers from the piano stool as the pianist approached. 'Let's choose some songs for the singers, shall we. What are your favourites?'

Cook was supposed to be in charge while Mrs Phipps and Mr Haddon were upstairs making sure Lord and Lady Melton and their guests had everything for their comfort. Violet came back first and dominated the gathering, grabbing Aaron, who happened to be the best dancer, for herself, and even taking the floor on her own to give a music hall turn when she recognised a piece.

She had a very good singing voice, Phyllis realised, and a supple body that she moved in a sinuous way suggested by the saucy words to the song. When Violet lifted her skirts to show off her dance steps and shapely legs she drew an appreciative whistle from one of the gardeners.

Phyllis glanced around for Mr Haddon's reprimand, but he was still upstairs in the dining room.

'She's good, isn't she?' Aaron whispered in her ear.

'I wish I could sing like that,' she replied.

'You sing beautifully.'

'Yes, you said, but hymns are not the same as music hall songs.'

'Or nursery rhymes.' His tone was light and a smile played around his lips.

'You haven't been up to the nursery, have you?'

'And risk the wrath of Nanny Byrne? I've seen you with the perambulator in the sunken garden. If Miss Agnes cries you lift her out and sing to her. You have the softest, sweetest voice.'

Disconcerted that he had been watching her with Miss Agnes without her knowledge she said, 'Were you eavesdropping on me?'

'No. I was going about my business. There's a path at the other side of the garden wall that links the old stable yard to the generator shed and I often use it. Oh, this is a waltz. Shall we have that dance now?'

'Yes. Thank you.'

He led her out into the middle of the floor and held her for a waltz. His left hand felt cool in her grasp yet the other seem to burn straight through her thin dress to the skin of her back, as he held her firmly and twirled her around the servants' hall. She stumbled once or twice but he didn't seem to mind. He smiled at her. He had a lovely smile, with even white teeth and intensely dark eyes. There was the faint dark shadow of a day's growth

112

of beard already showing on his chin which gave him a definite masculine appearance. Tentatively, she smiled back and commented, 'You dance very well.'

'Thank you kindly, ma'am,' he replied with a mock formality and she smiled again, relaxing in his arms. His right hand crept a little further around her back so she was obliged to move a little closer to him. He swirled at one point to avoid colliding with another couple and her body almost touched his, causing her to inhale sharply.

'I'm sorry,' he murmured. But he was still smiling and she liked the way his eyes crinkled at the corners. When the pianist stopped he led her back to a chair.

'What would you like to drink now, lemonade or ginger beer?'

'I have to get back to the nursery.'

'So soon?'

'Nanny Byrne will want me. It has been a tiring day for her.'

'That's a shame. I am just getting to know you. Look, if you have half an hour to spare in your day sometime, come round to the garage and I'll show you His Lordship's new motor car.'

'Thank you, I'd like that. And thank you for a lovely time.'

In spite of being quite tired from the excitement of her day, Phyllis had a spring in her step as she ensured that Nanny Byrne had everything she needed to hand for Miss Beatrice. She didn't seem to mind the infant disturbing her sleep for a night feed, telling her she was often awake anyway. Phyllis found that hard to understand as she was always dead to the world after her long days as nursemaid.

But not tonight. She lay awake going over and over the time she had spent with Aaron, reliving those few minutes in his arms and thinking he was the most wonderful boy she had ever met. Well, he wasn't a boy, he was one-and-twenty, someone said. He was a man, a beautiful man who was thoughtful and kind and she felt a thrill of anticipation that he had taken an interest in her. She plotted and planned to find a free half-hour in her day so that she could take up his invitation.

Then she opened her eyes and was suddenly wide awake. Isn't that what Violet did? Oh heavens, did he ask all the maids to sit in His Lordship's motor car? She didn't want to get a reputation. Maybe he had an understanding with Violet? They had made a very attractive couple on the dance-floor and it wouldn't do to get on the wrong side of Violet until she was more firmly established at Melton Hall.

Her excitement began to wane. She heard Nanny Byrne moving around next door and got up to stoke the fire and help her with Miss Beatrice.

Chapter 9

Earlier that evening, upstairs in the drawing room Lady Redfern was worried about her niece. 'How are you, my dear?' Amelia enquired, peering into Lady Melton's face. She looked, as her maids would say, 'peaky'. 'You have recovered from the birth, I hope.'

'Melton should have been there.'

'Goodness, did you want him to be?'

'He only came home for the christening.'

Amelia hesitated. Her nephew had his failings, as her late brother had, but Clara could be so middle class about him. 'His position makes demands on his time. He has responsibilities towards his estate.'

'Then why doesn't he spend his time here?'

James had told her of his nephew's ambitions. Indeed, Melton had wished for his uncle to finance his new idea.

Amelia hesitated. James had told her it was too expensive and his instincts were usually sound. But Melton was Clara's husband and she did not wish to be disloyal to her nephew. 'I believe he wishes to use his land near Melton Halt to build an industrial workshop.'

'Daddy says he doesn't know what he's talking about.'

Amelia's eyes widened. Mr Ashby was a self made man, a wealthy industrialist who had benefitted substantially at the end of the last century from Victorian enterprise and prosperity. It was probably true but unwise for his daughter to repeat it. 'Hush, my dear, someone might hear you.'

She noticed Clara glance around and see her husband deep in conversation with her father. 'He never talks to me,' she moaned. 'I don't know why he married me.' Her lower lip trembled and Amelia felt she had to raise her spirits somehow. 'You have given him two very beautiful daughters.' She was genuine in her praise for she would have loved to have a daughter herself. In fact, she felt a pang of envy for her niece.

'He wants a son.' Clara was dangerously close to tears.

Amelia, brought up the daughter of a viscount, understood the importance of a son where there was a title to pass on. She thanked God in church every Sunday for giving her Edward. As it turned out, he had been her last chance for a child. She said, 'You are young, my dear. There is plenty of time for more babies.'

'I don't want any more babies. I don't want to be fat and bloated for most of the year.'

This was news to Amelia and she imagined what her

nephew might think of that. He would be angry, of course. But Clara must have known what marriage to Viscount Melton would mean for her. Nonetheless, Amelia remained cheerful and responded, 'Oh, isn't it worth it? Children are such a joy.'

'Are they? How would I know? I only see them for an hour a day.'

'That will change when they are older. How is your new nursemaid getting on? She seemed very competent with Agnes in church earlier.'

'Oh, Kimber? Nanny Byrne approves so I must thank you for recommending her.'

'In my experience, servants from Lady Maude's never fail to please.'

'Yes, I wanted a lady's maid from there but Melton wouldn't hear of it. He said I had Regan.'

'Regan?'

'She is head housemaid and Melton says she must double as my personal maid.'

'Well my dear, many families have to economise on servants these days.'

'I don't like her.'

'You do not need to, my dear. She is a servant.'

'When it suits her.'

Amelia was beginning to feel that she could not say anything to cheer her niece. She worried, too, that Melton kept his involvement in household matters to a minimum and said, 'Clara, if any of your servants fall below the standard you expect you must speak to your butler. He will handle the matter for you.'

117

'Melton says I am not to interfere in servants' affairs, I must speak with him on such matters.'

'That is even better for you,' Amelia responded. 'You do not have to worry yourself about servants.'

But Amelia's uneasiness about the state of her nephew's marriage increased. Clara, she acknowledged, had not been brought up in a house with a brigade of servants and her mother, who had been the daughter of a baronet, died before Clara came out. But Clara's father was extremely wealthy. She had enjoyed a governess and chaperone and a lavish London season, even been presented as a debutante at court. Yet none of this had fully prepared her for life as Viscountess Melton and she appeared to be not wholly comfortable with her role as mistress of Melton Hall. Nevertheless, Melton ought not to neglect his wife. He had a duty to ensure her happiness.

Amelia resolved to have a word with James about her nephew's behaviour. Meanwhile she tried to encourage Clara to take an interest in her husband's latest passion. 'Have you ridden in Melton's new motor car yet?'

She shook her head. 'He has given me his Daimler for my own use. Wilson drives me everywhere.'

Amelia despaired and was relieved when the drawing room door opened and a flush-faced butler announced dinner.

Later, after dinner, when the gentlemen had joined the ladies for coffee in the drawing room, Edward came over to Amelia. 'What do you think of her, Mama?' he asked.

'What do I think of whom, my dear?'

'Anne Branbury, of course, I assume you are party to this conspiracy.'

Amelia ignored her son's accusation, but mindful of her earlier conversation with Clara, she answered, 'She has the right background and will understand the pressures of running Redfern.'

'So you think she is suitable to follow in your footsteps?'

'I did not say that, Edward, and there is no conspiracy. What do *you* think of her?'

'She is very young, twelve years younger than I.'

'She is also very beautiful, rather as her mother was at her age. A bit of a butterfly, I believe.'

'I thought she was similar to her mother in temperament when I was sitting between them at dinner.'

'The Marquess seems happy with his Marchioness.'

'I am not the Marquess.'

'No. You need a little more depth.'

'Someone like Lucy, you mean?'

'Well, yes, I thought you and she were well suited.'

'I didn't love her, Mama. She didn't fire my passion.'

'Does Anne fire your passion?'

'She might.'

'Well she needs to if you are serious about her. There, you have my answer.' Her son was pensive for a moment so she added, 'Is that not what you wanted to hear?'

'No, I mean yes, I agree with you but I – I was thinking of . . . Mama, I was thinking of going to Europe to spend Christmas this year.'

'Oh! Oh, do you have to? Your father and I shall miss you and Father wishes you to take over his role as Santa Claus for the estate children.'

'I've been invited to join a skiing party in the Alps and then travel on to Italy. I thought it might broaden my horizons, so to speak.'

'I see. What does your father think of the notion?'

'He is very keen. He did the grand tour after university. He was younger than I am now but he said it was the making of him.'

'As I recall you were eager to run Redfern for him as soon as you finished your education. Do you regret that now?'

'Not at all. But I have good men who can do what I do, and probably do it better. Mining is in their blood and they understand our miners.'

'Well, if it's what you want, my dear—'

'It is,' he interrupted. But my main concern is you and Father. I don't want you to feel that I am deserting you.'

'You are going to Europe, darling, not India. Good heavens, your cousin Melton talks of crossing the Atlantic as though it were as easy as a trip to France.'

Edward laughed. 'It is, Mama, in these new ocean liners. They are so fast. Melton's got a bee in his bonnet about building a motor car and he has heard of Mr Ford's factory in America.'

'Motor cars are all very well, but they are not as reliable as the railways.'

'But infinitely more exciting, Mama.'

'Maybe,' Amelia sighed. 'How long are you planning to be away?'

'I haven't decided. I shan't go if you don't wish it.'

'Of course you must! But I shall miss you.'

He bent to kiss her cheek. 'Thank you, Mama.'

'Promise me one thing.'

'Anything.'

'Promise me that you won't take a wife before you have brought her to Redfern to meet your father and me.'

He grinned. 'I promise.' He added as an afterthought. 'Actually, I might ask Anne Branbury to join our party in Italy.'

As the days shortened and autumn frosts nipped the air, Phyllis's fire-tending duties increased, as did the work for housemaids and footmen. This left them little time to help her with carrying heavy buckets of coal from the basement to the nursery, raking out and laying the fires and taking down the cold ashes. Fortunately, Mr Haddon gave her a couple of the bootboy's brown drill aprons to protect her dresses.

However, each fine day Phyllis took Miss Agnes for her afternoon airing in the perambulator. The child's little legs were getting stronger and she danced on the paths while Phyllis held her hands and sang nursery rhymes. She always chose a spot in the sunken garden where her seat was visible from one of the footpaths that surrounded the Hall. Her ears were constantly alert for the sound of a footstep on the gravel and, occasionally, she was not disappointed.

Aaron walked by carrying his heavy canvas bag of engineer's tools for the generator. He stopped, waved and watched for a few minutes. She regretted her earlier objection to his eavesdropping and worse still lurking, but she had not taken up his offer to sit in His Lordship's motor car. However, when she saw him she wished he would come over and talk. She believed that he wanted to as well. But when she glanced up at the house, although the path was close to the Hall and might be hidden from prying eyes, the sunken garden was in clear view of the second and third floor windows of the Hall. The second floor bedrooms were empty unless His Lordship had guests. Not so the third floor which housed the nursery and Nanny Byrne, and Phyllis dare not risk her disapproval. So she did not return his wave or call, she simply smiled in return and he walked on.

She decided to ask Nanny Byrne if she might join the other servants in the servants' hall for their evening recreation on a more regular basis, where she might have an opportunity to talk to Aaron when others were present. She believed that Nanny Byrne approved of her and trusted her to behave properly, as she expected of a servant from Lady Maude's. But Nanny Byrne had her own rules.

'Nannies are like governesses. They do not mix freely with lower servants,' she stated.

Phyllis was flattered to be considered in this role, but her life was very dull after Lady Maude's where at least she had conversation in the dormitory at night. However, there was one day of light relief for Phyllis, on a Wednesday when Nanny Byrne took a half day to journey to the nearest town, make purchases and have tea and cakes with a friend in the Grand Hotel. Phyllis, having been alone with the infants all afternoon, was allowed the whole evening to herself and given leave to go downstairs to the servants' hall where, sometimes, there was singing and dancing around the piano.

She cast aside her cap and apron and unbuttoned the collar of her dress as others did. Some who joined later wore their own clothes as they had been out themselves and had tales to tell or purchases to show off. The outdoor staff came along too and Phyllis always kept an eye out for Aaron if she knew the mistress had not gone out in her motor car. Then it was fun as one of the footmen played the piano well and knew the words to the latest music hall songs. He even made up more saucy versions if Mr Haddon was not present.

The butler went out on Wednesdays but he gave permission for the table to be pushed aside after tea so they might have their own tea dance. Mrs Phipps was absent too because she had a poorly sister that she visited as often as possible, leaving the lower servants without supervision to enjoy themselves.

Phyllis took her woollen cape for the draughty back stairs and went down to the basement. The servants' hall was quiet. A few were playing cards and asked her to join them.

'Thank you, no. Where is everybody?'

'His Lordship was out in his Silver Ghost until after dark so he's dining late and the upstairs maids and footmen won't finish until ten. Aaron couldn't get over for tea because the motor car was covered in mud.'

'Oh,' she groaned. She must have sounded disappointed because one of the footmen said, 'Why don't you go and keep him company? Tell him Cook is making hot chocolate for later.'

She thought about this for a moment. Aaron had suggested she might call on him in the garages. Despite her earlier doubts she would have taken up his offer if she could have found the time in her day. She wouldn't get another chance until next Wednesday and maybe not then either.

'Ought I to tell Mr Haddon?'

'He's not back yet. Cook's in charge. We'll tell her for you.'

'Thank you.' She went out into the foggy night.

As she expected, Aaron was still cleaning His Lordship's motor car in readiness for the morning. The former coach house doors stood open as he worked by lamplight.

She approached boldly. 'Good evening, Aaron.'

He looked up immediately. 'What are you doing here at this time of night?'

She had not expected such a disapproving tone and her boldness faded. 'I – I came to tell you that Cook is doing hot chocolate for everyone tonight.'

'That'll be very welcome. It's a dreadful night.' He must have been working hard for quite a while because his hair was untidy and his face was streaked with dirt. He continued polishing the shiny coachwork.

124

'It looks very nice,' she commented.

'Mmm,' he murmured. She thought he agreed as he stood up straight to stretch his back and examine his handiwork. 'You can't really tell in this light. I'll know in the morning.'

He didn't seem very pleased to see her. Perhaps she had been right about him and Violet? When he resumed his polishing she commented, 'You said I might come and look at His Lordship's motor car.'

'Sometime during the day, I said. It's not good form for you to come here after dark, Phyllis.'

'It's quite safe isn't it? I mean I won't be set upon and robbed on the way.'

'This is where the male servants live. You'll get a reputation.'

'Oh! Oh, but I'm not here for – I mean – you said, well, you always wave to me in the garden and I – thought—'

He concentrated on the cloth in his hand for a few seconds then put it down and walked towards her. 'Look, you're a lovely girl and very pretty but I don't want you to get the wrong idea about me.'

'What do you mean?'

'I mean that I liked you enough to speak to Mr Haddon. I thought you were sixteen or seventeen and he put me right. You are too young to be anything more than a friend.'

She felt the heat spread over her features and knowledge that she was blushing made it worse. Her mind raced as she struggled to save face. 'I thought we could be friends! Friends meet and talk, don't they?'

'Not a girl with a man after dark when no one else is around.' He gazed at her steadily. 'I am right, aren't I?'

He was, but she was so dreadfully embarrassed that he had seen straight through her behaviour she felt compelled to deny it and cried, 'Well really, I had no idea you had such an inflated opinion of yourself. I came to look at the motor car and, *perhaps*, get to know you better but you have told me all I wish to find out about you. I don't want to be friendly with someone who is so conceited. Good night.' She turned her back on him and walked away with her head high.

'Phyllis! Come back!' She heard him groan. 'I didn't mean it that way!'

He gave an exasperated sigh, but she didn't look back because she didn't know what else to do. What else did he mean? Her pride had been hurt and she had the sickening feeling that he was right. She had intended to flirt with him but she had no experience of walking out with beaux or sweethearts. She had messed up her first attempt with a man that she truly liked. Why couldn't she do better than that? Violet wouldn't have behaved in that way. Violet would have — what would Violet have done? She stomped angrily back to the kitchen. Perhaps she ought to make friends with Violet first and learn some of her ways? The chance would be a fine thing, she fumed. Where would Phyllis find time in her day to make friends with anyone?

As the shooting season progressed, Melton Hall became busier than ever with house parties and the nursery was, increasingly, at the end of everyone's agenda. Except Nanny Byrne's of course, Phyllis reflected. Lord and Lady Melton were lucky to have such a devoted nanny for their children.

'Have you been down for our tea tray yet?' Nanny Byrne came into the day nursery every day for six o'clock tea.

'I'm sorry, Nanny Byrne. Miss Agnes is not well and her crying has made the baby fractious. I think a doctor ought to take a look at her.'

'Do you indeed? When I need your opinion I shall ask for it. Actually, His Lordship's physician is out with him on the shoot today.'

'Will he be attending the banquet tonight?'

'I imagine so but I am sure he does not wish be called away for a mere snuffle.'

Both infants were fed and changed and were quietening as sleep overtook them. She placed Miss Beatrice in her crib and rocked it gently. The kettle bubbled over the fire and water hissed on the hot coals. But Phyllis thought that the elder child had a raised temperature and answered, 'Perhaps you would take a look at Miss Agnes, Nanny Byrne?'

Nanny's head shook with impatience. 'Not now, Kimber. Go and get the tea. And hurry, Her Ladyship has had another of her turns and His Lordship wishes me to attend to her dress tonight.'

This is too much, Phyllis thought. Nanny might be the most trusted servant on His Lordship's staff but she was sixty years old and couldn't be expected to discharge the duties of lady's maid as well as head nurse. She said, 'Surely Her Ladyship has Regan for that?'

'She does not like Regan.' Nanny Byrne clicked her tongue in disapproval. 'The late Dowager, God rest her soul, would not dream of having an opinion on her husband's servants. If she were alive today she would be horrified that His Lordship has chosen to marry down.' Nanny glanced sideways and must have noticed Phyllis's open mouth. Nanny Byrne indulging in gossip! She stopped speaking and appeared to pull herself together. After a pause, she added, 'However, in this instance I agree with Her Ladyship. Regan's ways are very common. I expect yours used to be but Lady Maude's put that right well enough.'

Phyllis almost dropped the teapot. This was the nearest thing to a compliment she was likely to get from Nanny Byrne. She said, 'I hope that my work with His Lordship's children is satisfactory.'

'It is no less than I expect from Lady Maude's. You will know if it does not meet my standards.'

'Thank you.' Praise indeed from Nanny Byrne! Phyllis saw an opportunity to ease both her and Nanny Byrne's daily routines. 'I wondered if, as His Lordship wishes you to take on personal duties for Her Ladyship and you give morning lessons to Miss Agnes, that you might ask Mrs Phipps for a housemaid to help with the nursery rough work, ma'am?'

'I do not have housemaids in the nursery. Their below-stairs ways are not suitable.'

It was worth a try, Phyllis thought. But she realised

that, in Viscount Melton's household, Nanny Byrne would not have the same control over a housemaid as she had over her nursemaid.

'The kettle is boiling, ma'am. Shall I make you a pot of tea before I go down for our tray?'

'I am perfectly capable of making tea. Go and fetch the nursery tray.'

Phyllis hurried away thankfully. She wished she had more time in her day. She was only human and others worked as hard as she did. But not Violet, she thought and wondered, not for the first time, why she hadn't been dismissed. The servants had finished their afternoon tea and were busy preparing for the evening dinner.

'We thought you weren't hungry today,' Cook called when she collected soup, sandwiches and cake. Phyllis smiled but did not comment. She was hungry herself and her mouth watered as she trudged upstairs to the third floor.

Nanny Byrne was sitting by the fire in the day nursery, staring at the flames. Phyllis placed a selection of sandwich triangles on a plate and took it over to her. She waved it away. 'I shall sit at the table. Example is everything in the nursery.'

'Yes, Nanny Byrne.' Phyllis unloaded the tray and set out the table for tea. She stood by patiently while Nanny got up stiffly from her fireside chair. Years of service were taking their toll on her. Now that she trusted Phyllis with both infants, her evenings were spent relaxing as Phyllis attended to the babies. A prolonged session dressing temperamental Lady Melton for dinner was not an inviting prospect for her at the end of her day.

Phyllis gazed longingly at the sandwiches and slipped next door to the night nursery to check on Miss Beatrice before she sat down. On Nanny Byrne's instructions, she did not wake Miss Agnes from her nap. Her flushed cheeks indicated a possible temperature. She slid into her chair opposite Nanny and said, 'Would you check on the babies before you go down to Lady Melton? Miss Agnes looks hot to me.'

'She will sleep it off. Give her some soup if she wakes. I don't intend to be longer than an hour, but with Her Ladyship as she is, you never can tell. It's so unfair on His Lordship. A gentleman expects his wife to be a proper hostess to his guests.'

Phyllis agreed but wisely did not comment. It was only because Nanny Byrne trusted her that she made such comments. Mr Haddon didn't allow gossip any more than Nanny Byrne, but all the servants knew how difficult Her Ladyship was. She moped around for much of her time and didn't seem to be interested in anything. Unfortunately, this didn't engender sympathy from her servants, who were often rushed off their feet. *Doesn't know she's born* was a muttering frequently heard below stairs.

'Can I do anything to help, ma'am?' Phyllis volunteered, pouring out their tea.

'It won't be forever. Her Ladyship is going on an extended visit to her aunt at Redfern Abbey. Lady Redfern will know what to do with her.' Nanny Byrne sipped her tea and added, 'I certainly hope so because Melton Hall at the end of its tether with her.'

James, Earl Redfern, walked across the park enjoying the weak winter sunshine. He did this every morning after breakfast but had noticed lately that it tired him. In fact he was tired before he started and ruefully acknowledged that he was getting old. He must rest before he returned for his daily meeting with his land steward. He changed direction towards the folly.

It was a mistake, he realised, as he sat on the curved stone bench. The interior had not changed and it brought back memories of his younger years when he lost his grandfather and father within a few weeks of each other; and when he had discovered the heartache of an unfulfilled passion.

He had remembered that feeling when he had discovered his son with a young housemaid some dozen or so years ago. He shook his head, recalling Edward's pleading that he wasn't taking advantage of a vulnerable servant, and that she loved him. Edward swore that he loved her and wanted to marry her. James had believed his beloved son, but knew he could not let it happen. Redfern Abbey carried a huge responsibility for its tenants and servants and Edward must marry a girl to support him as Countess of Redfern. Edward was a good son and he had listened to his father. Yet he still had not found a partner to share in that work. He hoped his trip to Europe would help in that task.

James's weariness was not relieved and he was not

stupid. His physician had told him what he already knew; his heart was weakening and it was to be expected as he grew older. He experienced a sense of urgency about the future of Redfern, which made him feel worse, and his chest started to hurt. Edward understood his duty and would, he was sure, find a good wife and have children. He, like his nephew Melton, understood the importance of producing a son and heir.

James hoped he was not developing a cough. Amelia had told him of the difficulty this caused with his miners. He staggered to his feet to return to the warmth of the Abbey. As he approached the sweeping drive to the front door he saw a horse and cart on the track towards the rear and raised his arm to hail it. The driver changed course and headed across the grassland.

'My Lord?'

Thank goodness the fellow recognised him, for James had no idea of who he was. 'Help me aboard, my good man. I am not in the best of health.'

The driver probably saved his life because he took him to the front door and summoned his butler who sent immediately for his physician. Later, when James took one look at his drawn, ashen features in the mirror, he knew that this was serious.

'James, James, my darling,' Amelia croaked.

'Don't upset yourself, dearest. I am in good hands. Dr Fleming is the best and I shall take his advice this time.'

'You will?' Amelia breathed a huge sigh of relief. 'You will step down from running Redfern?'

'I shall.'

'You have promised me that before. Will you keep your word this time?'

'I shall allow my stewards to do their job without my interference.'

Amelia managed a smile. 'I am sure they will welcome the opportunity.'

'I have been most favourably impressed by the men that Edward employed to manage the coalfield without him.'

'Will you change your mind about sending for him to come home?'

'No. I am firm on this, Amelia. I am not dying. Not yet, anyway. Dr Fleming says that if I take his advice I have a few more years left in me.'

Only a few! His words sent a cold shiver through Amelia and she worked hard not to show her distress. 'Are you being fair to Edward? He would wish to know.'

'Indulge me in this, my love. Next time I write to him, I shall tell him I am following his example and handing on some of my responsibilities, and how much you, my dearest, welcome the changes.'

'You should tell him you are ill.'

'I should not!' James gave her a disapproving glance. 'Neither should you upset me by disagreeing with my wishes.' Amelia frowned and he went on, 'Edward will come home when he is ready. He needs this expedition to help him see his future more clearly. Perhaps when he returns he will be ready to marry and have children, my dear.'

'He has not taken against marriage. I believe he wishes

it for himself as well as to please us but I have run out of eligible ladies to invite for him.'

'He wants the same as I did at his age. He will not marry without love and—' James raised his eyes to the ceiling in query.

'Perhaps he will find that in Anne?'

'I hope so. I do understand how he feels. He lost his heart as a young man and has not recovered it yet.'

'What *do* you mean?'

James took a deep breath and gazed out of the window. 'It is my fault. I acted for the best but I am the person to blame.'

'What *are* you talking about?'

'Ellen. I believe he truly loved her.'

'Ellen? Who is Ellen?'

'You must remember her. She was one of our best housemaids.'

Amelia eyes rounded. 'Do you mean Ellen who married your groom? But he was just eightteen, darling! That was nought but a youthful fling with a pretty servant girl!'

'It was more. He wished to marry her.'

'Edward? Wished to marry a housemaid? You did not tell me that.'

'Well he did not marry her, did he?'

'Then you must be wrong about him and he saw the error of his ways.'

'He obeyed his father against his own wishes and his own heart.'

'And so he should! He was young and it happened so

134

long ago I am sure he is over it by now. Didn't Ellen marry shortly afterwards and move away?'

'Then you do remember?'

The memory brought a tear to Amelia's eye. 'I remember being very disappointed in my son. I had expected him to behave differently from my rascal of a nephew. Edward would never talk to me about his fling, you know.'

'It was more than a fling and I asked him not to as I did not wish to distress you. I dealt with him.'

'I am grateful that he learned his lesson. I forgave him long ago. It is over and done with, past history to be forgotten. Will you come downstairs for tea today?'

'I shall if Cook has made pikelets,' he replied.

Amelia kissed her husband on his forehead and went off to find her housekeeper. Ellen Kimber was a widow now, and, she conceded, an attractive one who was proving to be a godsend to the vicar's wife in her welfare work. Surely James did not think that Edward was still holding a candle to her memory? Yet she wondered if Ellen Kimber was the reason that James had encouraged Edward to travel in Europe. One thing was crystal clear to Amelia. She was not going to rake over the past with her husband in his delicate condition. Her prime duty was to protect him from the least amount of anxiety.

She began by sitting down and writing to her niece Clara to put off her planned visit to Redfern Abbey. Clara was such a demanding guest, and she was coming without her children which upset Amelia. Even so, she would have welcomed her under normal circumstances. But

James was her priority now. It was still a hard decision for Amelia to make as the poor girl was pregnant again, so soon after her second child, and Melton was not the most considerate of husbands. But her darling James came first and she picked up her pen.

Chapter 10

Autumn, 1905

'I've put her in with you for now. I know you don't like it, Regan, but you will just have to put up with it. Kimber will be back in her own bed just as soon as the nursery is finished.'

'Thank you, Mrs Phipps,' Phyllis said. Her own nurse-maid's bedroom was being used as a day and night nursery during redecoration and she took the children outside as much as possible because the smell of fresh paint made them feel ill.

Phyllis sat on the vacant bed and looked around Violet's room. It was the same as every other servant's bedroom in the attic, painted cream, clean and very plain. Violet had put small pictures and other souvenirs on the wall around her bed and there were ribbons and dried flowers tied to her black metal bedstead. Phyllis opened the tiny attic window that was tucked behind a stone balustrade on the roof of Melton Hall and heard a prolonged and anguished cry. Alarmed at first, she realised that Her Ladyship was actually in labour for baby number four. Delightful as Miss Agnes, Miss Beatrice and Miss Charlotte were, everyone was praying, quite literally in church every Sunday, for a boy.

Mrs Phipps hurried away and Violet flounced across the room to flop on her bed. 'Don't think you can get too comfortable here. I don't share as a rule.' She gave a huge sigh. 'God in Heaven, can that woman squeal. You'd think she'd be used to childbirth by now.'

'I don't think you should refer to Her Ladyship as *that woman*. It's disrespectful.' Phyllis responded.

'Her Ladyship?' Violet pulled a grotesque face. 'I've been here for all the births and every one has caused chaos. That woman is a nightmare, I can tell you.'

'She doesn't seem to be a very happy person.'

'I can't see why, can you? She's got a husband with a title and she lives here in all this luxury.'

'Being rich is not everything,' Phyllis commented. Lady Melton's gloominess had become worse over the years. 'Anyway, everyone knows His Lordship hasn't got two farthings of his own to rub together.'

'Now who's being disrespectful? He's going to be rich one day. He's going to build a motor car like Mr Rolls and Mr Royce.'

Phyllis was genuinely surprised both at this information and also how Violet knew. 'Who told you that?'

The head housemaid looked embarrassed for a second and shrugged. 'Gossip in the servants' hall.'

'I've never heard it.'

Violet recovered quickly and answered, 'If you weren't too lah-de-dah to come downstairs more often, you'd know too.'

'The children take up all my time.' It was true. Nanny Byrne was still very much in charge, but she relied heavily on Phyllis to keep the nursery running smoothly. She began to unpack her clothes and said, 'I don't think we should be talking about His Lordship's affairs.'

Unusually, Violet agreed and muttered. 'You'd better not repeat anything you hear from me or I'll make sure His Lordship gets rid of you. I mean it.'

Phyllis believed her. No one actually spoke of it but everyone knew that Violet was a favourite of His Lordship and she exploited it shamelessly so that she was able to get away with not pulling her weight. Nanny Byrne was frequently called upon to do extra duties for Her Ladyship that should have been Violet's, as if she hadn't enough to do already. Nanny Byrne obeyed His Lordship without question but Phyllis felt it wasn't fair.

However, Nanny Byrne trusted Phyllis completely with all three infants, which gave her a sense of achievement. Mother was exceptionally proud of her and Phyllis never minded the extra work. Aaron kept his distance from her. She guessed it wasn't difficult for him because he spent much of his time with His Lordship's motor cars. He was polite and civil when their paths crossed. But she was disappointed that he wouldn't be friendly towards her as he was the only other servant she really liked.

She rarely had sight of Lady Melton either as she was

often 'too indisposed' to see her children. Her Ladyship was prone to bouts of depressing gloom. These were the times when Nanny Byrne was called upon to encourage her to 'pull herself together'. This meant that Phyllis had no time at all to join the other servants in the basement for recreation. However, Phyllis had her allies in the servants' hall and, with Mr Haddon's and Mrs Phipps' blessing, made her own arrangements with the bootboy and scullery maid, who were happy to help.

'Will Her Ladyship be joining the guests for dinner tonight?' Phyllis asked Violet.

'I shouldn't think so.'

'Don't you know? I thought you were supposed to be her personal maid.'

'I can't stick her. I see to her rooms but she doesn't like me either so she sends me away.'

'Couldn't you make more of an effort with her, like Nanny Byrne does?'

But Phyllis knew that Violet did not have the temperament for that. 'I can't be doing with her,' Violet said. 'She's too miserable all the time. It gets me down. I don't know how His Lordship puts up with her. Nanny Byrne knows what she's doing by keeping her well out of the nursery. There's no wonder His Lordship stays away all the time.' She became peevish. 'I wish he'd spend more time at home.'

'He's here now, and with a party of guests,' Phyllis pointed out. His Lordship was in residence every autumn for the shooting.

'That's it, you see. His Lordship is so different from

her. He's fun and he's always having house parties and banquets when he's home. He's very good friends with the Marquess of Branbury, you know, and his wife has royal connections.'

'Yes I did know that,' Phyllis said, but Violet didn't hear her.

'When I first arrived here, before your time, he entertained the King once, for luncheon. He was Prince of Wales then and in Yorkshire for the shooting.' Violet chuckled. 'It was a huge party, the Earl and Countess of Redfern came and all the local gentry were here. I was helping the footmen wait at table.'

'What, you served at table in the dining room?'

'I shouldn't have done, I was told just to keep the sideboard tidy and put dirty dishes in the dumb waiter. The footman had been round with sauce for the fish and placed the salver on the sideboard when His Majesty asked for more. Mr Haddon was serving the wine and he signalled to the footman but he didn't see him. I did, so I picked up the salver and took it over to His Majesty. I tell you, old Haddon was furious but he couldn't make a fuss in front of the King and the King didn't mind at all.' Violet's eyes were shining and her voice was rising with the excitement of telling her story. 'You'll never guess what he did!' She didn't give Phyllis time to reply. 'He squeezed my behind! He got hold of a real handful he did and then he winked at me, the dirty old bugger.'

Violet seemed very proud of her story but Phyllis was surprised by her language. 'What on earth did you do?'

'I winked back at him of course.' Violet guffawed. 'I

thought old Haddon would have a seizure! And I did worry that he might get rid of me after that, but His Lordship had seen it happen and he intervened.'

Intrigued by this tale, Phyllis forgot she was in a hurry. 'What did His Lordship do?'

'He told Haddon I wasn't to blame because the Prince of Wales would be King one day and he could do whatever he wished when he visited Melton Hall.' Violet laughed again. 'And His Lordship got an invitation to the Coronation when he was!'

'Ye-es, I remember that.' 1902 had not been a happy year for Phyllis and she had not taken much notice of it. The King had been ill and the original ceremony had to be postponed until he was better. The Earl and Countess of Redfern had been at the Coronation, too. The South Riding newspaper had a front page article with a photograph of them in their ermine trimmed robes.

'Lady Melton didn't go because she was—' Violet puffed out her cheeks and made a rounded shape over her stomach with her hands. 'I hope to God it's a boy this time.'

'We are all hoping for that,' Phyllis responded.

Phyllis found Nanny Byrne's strict reliance on routine comforting, because it reminded her of Lady Maude's. Indeed, if Phyllis closed her eyes when she was speaking to her, she could easily have been one of her teachers. But even Nanny Byrne lost her composure when Lady Melton gave birth to another girl. A fourth daughter for Viscountess Melton was a disappointment all round and

Nanny Byrne became quite agitated at Her Ladyship's weeping and wailing and inability to welcome her child.

His Lordship had no patience with his wife either and the doctor visited every day. Her Ladyship's father tried to cheer her with promises of an ocean cruise when she was better, and an orangery for the garden. Phyllis felt sorry for Her Ladyship as none of these people seemed to know what to do to cheer her.

A few nights later, Violet was unusually quiet except to demand when her nursemaid's room would be ready as she wanted her bedroom back to herself. The painters and decorators had left the nursery and the floors had been sanded and waxed. As it happened Phyllis was waiting only for new cupboards and chests to be delivered from the estate carpenter and volunteered to move back, taking just her overnight things until the furniture had arrived.

'The bed is there,' Phyllis explained to Violet, 'I'll ask Mrs Phipps for some bedding.' She was as anxious as Violet to move, as she didn't want Nanny Byrne to be on her own at night with four infants. But just when she was falling asleep that night she realised that her clean cap and apron were still in the drawers in Violet's room. Violet would be furious if Phyllis woke her before six the next morning and Phyllis needed to be dressed before then to see to the toddlers.

It was after midnight but reluctantly she pulled on her dressing robe and slippers and climbed up one floor of the back stairs to the attics. Moonbeams through the skylights cast the corridor in a blue gloom as she crept as quietly as possible to Violet's room. She didn't want to wake her so she turned the knob silently and opened the door.

'What the blazes!' A man's voice split the air. He was sitting on the edge of the bed, a dark shadow in a room lit only by the moon. He was wearing a white shirt and trousers with the braces down and pushing his bare feet into his shoes that lay in a patch of moonlight. They were rather fine leather carpet slippers and it was these that made Phyllis's eyes open roundly. Surely he was not one of His Lordship's guests!

'You have not seen me!' he hissed. He did not speak with the flat Yorkshire vowels of the servants and it wasn't His Lordship's steward, who was known to have an eye for the ladies, because he was a Scotchman and she had heard him talking to Mr Haddon. Phyllis noted his shirt reflected the soft sheen of silk. But it was his commanding presence that effectively stopped her from entering the room.

Astounded that a man would be in a maid's room at any time, let alone at this late hour, she thought at first that something must be wrong. Then as her eyes became used to the dark, she took in the tumbled bedclothes and a voice from behind the man groaned. 'Oh God, it's the nursemaid. What are you doing here, Kimber? You told me you'd gone back to the nursery!'

Violet was under the bedclothes but her shoulders were bare. Corsets, dress and chemise were strewn across the floor where she – Phyllis realised sickeningly – had taken them off in a hurry.

'I – I need a clean apron,' she explained. 'F-from the drawer.'

'She's been sharing with me while the new nursery is finished,' Violet added in a small voice.

But the man did not utter another word. He stood up and Phyllis was struck dumb as she recognised him. He advanced towards her hissing, 'Not a word to anyone, do you hear?' Then he pushed past her and left.

Violet sat up on the bed exposing her naked breasts and rubbed her hands through her hair. 'You picked your time, Kimber.'

Phyllis sank onto the empty bed, hardly believing her own eyes. 'His Lordship? With you?'

'Why not? I love him.'

'Don't be silly, Violet. He doesn't love you.'

'Of course he does! Why would he be here with me if he didn't?'

Phyllis half laughed. She wasn't naive and neither was Violet, who added, 'He does love me. He said so.'

Phyllis blew out her cheeks. There was no sense in arguing. 'But he can't marry you, Violet. He has a wife.'

'She is such a misery-guts and when he needs me, he needs me.' Saying this seemed to give Violet her confidence back. She raised her voice and went on, 'So you remember this is *my* room in future.' She thought for a second. 'That's if he lets you stay. You'll be in trouble for this, for sure.'

'Me? I haven't done anything wrong!'

'Just keep your trap shut like he said. I don't want old Phipps finding out.'

'Well you'll be dismissed if she does.'

'No I won't. His Lordship won't let me go. He promised me that.'

'Did he? How do you know he will honour his promise? Don't be stupid, Violet. What if you fall for a baby?'

'God, you are old fashioned! I know what to do to avoid *that*.'

Phyllis had heard plenty of dormitory gossip at Lady Maude's about what a girl could do to stop babies coming, including lurid tales of the consequences when it failed. Those things were for street women and ladies of the night, a lifestyle she would die before she would embrace. But she did dream that, one day, she would have her own follower and had decided the only way was to say no until she had a wedding ring on her finger, no matter how persuasive her sweetheart might be.

Phyllis shook her head in despair. It was not only the foolish risks Violet was taking that upset her. She said, 'But how can you betray Her Ladyship? She has just given birth to His Lordship's fourth child.'

Violet retaliated sharply. 'Aye, and it's another girl. He'll only do his duty by her until he has a son.'

'And have his fun with you in the meantime?'

Violet seemed to have fully recovered by now and laughed, 'That's about the size of it. Now get your bloody apron and go.'

Before she went out of the door, Phyllis turned, 'Have you thought that he might be having his fun with others, too?'

'He doesn't. He told me so. I'm the only one for him.'

'You're the only one for him *here*, Violet.'

She was surely right about that, Phyllis thought as she

went down to the nursery. Violet was by far the loveliest of the female servants and it was His Lordship's attentions that gave her the confidence to behave as she did. Phyllis wondered whether to say anything to Nanny Byrne and decided against it. Whether Nanny believed her or not she would be told it was none of her concern and be branded a gossip. 'Least said, soonest mended' was her mother's maxim, too.

Anyway, who else would know that His Lordship visited the attics late at night? Not his wife, for their bedrooms were at opposite ends of the landing and His Lordship's valet slept in the basement. Surely other maids would hear the door hinge creaking, not to mention the bedstead. But, she realised, they wouldn't dare breathe a word. It was none of their business if the head chambermaid had a follower. It was none of Phyllis's either. Violet was a favourite at Melton Hall and Phyllis would be the one to go if she caused a fuss.

Chapter 11

A couple of days later the bootboy came up to the nursery while Phyllis was making up the fire to say that Mr Haddon wished to see her and he was sending up a housemaid to sit with the children. The baby was settled and the toddlers were in their pen playing with toys. She had no idea where Nanny Byrne was as, normally, she would take Miss Agnes and Miss Beatrice for nursery lessons at this time.

'What's this about?' Phyllis asked the housemaid as she took off her sleeve protectors and jute apron, tidied away the wisps of hair escaping from her cap and cleaned her hands.

'I don't know,' the girl answered, 'but Nanny Byrne has agreed.'

'You're honoured,' Phyllis commented as she put on a

clean white apron, buffed her shoes and checked that her nails were clean before walking slowly down to the butler's room.

An interview with the butler meant trouble of some sort and she wondered if it was about Violet. Her mouth set in a firm line as she muttered under her breath, 'He can't dismiss me because I haven't done anything wrong.' But she fretted that her untimely intrusion might cost her this position.

She walked down the passage that separated the house-keeper's rooms from the male accommodation and tapped on the door to the butler's headquarters. It was a large square room with several doors leading off. One was open and led to another passage. He was sitting at his desk in the corner checking papers.

'Come right in, Phyllis. His Lordship wants to see you himself. Now tell me what this is about.'

'I don't know, Mr Haddon.'

'Neither does Nanny Byrne. So it must be something you have done without her knowledge.'

Phyllis thought of Violet with Lord Melton and cursed her blushes.

'Why have you gone red? Tell me, girl! I've seen the way you look at Wilson. Did His Lordship catch you with him in the motor car?'

'No!'

'It must be serious if His Lordship chooses to dismiss you himself.'

Oh no, it was her worst fear. 'Is that why he wants to see me?'

'Why else? You were recommended by his aunt. This is serious, Kimber. Nanny Byrne is most disappointed.'

'I haven't done anything wrong, Mr Haddon,' Phyllis said, miserably.

The butler stood up to check her appearance, straightened out the sleeve caps on her apron and picked up her hands. 'They are very red.'

'I had to scrub them clean, Mr Haddon.'

'Keep them behind you and follow me.' He was already marching through the door and along the passage to the back stairs.

In the grand marble-floored reception hall, Mr Haddon rapped on one of the wide mahogany doors opposite the drawing room. He opened it and stepped inside. 'Kimber, the nursemaid, My Lord.' He beckoned her forward and pushed her into the room in front of him.

It was a library, a bright, light room on the south east corner of the Hall, with shelves of books floor to ceiling on two walls and large sash windows on the other two. Leather armchairs were strewn around the room beside tables of inlaid walnut and rosewood. The dual aspect of the parkland that surrounded Melton Hall was breathtaking and for a moment Phyllis allowed her gaze to wander from the plush furnishings to the stunning views. Then she remembered her teaching and looked down at her feet. But not before she had noted where His Lordship was sitting and Nanny Byrne standing ramrod straight just behind him as though she were his guardian angel.

Viscount Melton was lounging in an armchair beside the fire. 'Over here where I can see you,' he said.

She went to stand in front of him. He was a handsome man, she thought, and she could see why he was popular with ladies. He had regular features and dark hair combed back from his brow. He wore plus twos and a hunting jacket but he hadn't let his whiskers grow as was the fashion. They would have covered his well-shaped mouth and fine jawline, Phyllis decided. His eyes were dark and piercing as they glared at her. Yet his next words were addressed to Nanny Byrne. Without taking his eyes off Phyllis, he waved an arm behind his head and said, 'Wait outside with Haddon.'

Nanny Byrne was startled and her mouth turned down at the corners, but she left immediately and Phyllis faced His Lordship on her own.

'Do you value your post here, Kimber?' he demanded.

So this was about dismissing her. She resisted the urge to purse her lips but she looked at him directly and answered, 'Yes, My Lord.' His eyes stared into hers. She should say something else, she thought and added. 'I am honoured to be looking after your children.'

'Quite so. You have a privileged position at Melton Hall. You are not required to mix with the lower servants or answer to Phipps or Haddon. You take orders only from Nanny Byrne.'

'Yes, My Lord,' she responded.

'Nanny has been at Melton Hall since before I was born. She is my most loyal servant and she has my complete confidence and trust.'

Phyllis remained silent. She wondered if Nanny Byrne would have such confidence if she knew about his

151

nighttime dalliances and guessed that, even if she did she would never indulge in any below-stairs gossip, inside or outside the Hall. Nor would she have an opinion about it. Servants did not have views of their own and their masters may do as they please. And Lord Melton most certainly did as he pleased.

She felt like one of the pinned butterflies she had once seen displayed in a museum. She considered saying that she had been brought up to be honest and truthful at all times but in the circumstances decided that it would not be the tactful thing to say. The aristocracy do things differently and her mother had taught her that discretion was the better part of valour, always. He lounged languidly in his chair and went on, 'I expect the same devotion to duty from her nursemaid.'

'Of course, My Lord.' She sounded more composed than she felt. It wasn't fair! He was going to dismiss her simply for being in the wrong place at the wrong time! What on earth would she say to Mother? She felt her heart start to thump and inhaled deeply to remain calm, adding, 'I have not breathed a word to anyone, My Lord. Truly I have not, nor shall I!'

'I have no idea of what you speak,' he replied. His bland facial expression did not alter. 'Of what do you speak?'

Oh, so that's how it is to be, she realised. The unfortunate meeting had not happened. He needed her reassurance that it had not and replied, 'I speak of nothing, My Lord.'

He measured out a smile. 'Quite so. There is nothing to speak of, is there. *Is there?*'

What was that phrase she had read in a story? *The smile on the face of the tiger.* She understood perfectly what it meant now and answered, 'No My Lord, nothing at all.' It was nothing to her. She was a servant and she did not have an opinion.

Unnerved by this she realised that she could do nothing to make a difference to his decision to dismiss her. He had made up his mind and was assuring himself of her future silence. Her mind was racing. Yes, of course, if she stayed silent he would instruct Nanny Byrne to give her a reference. She needed that, for how could she explain her dismissal otherwise? She'd never get another post without a reference.

His dominating presence was beginning to overwhelm her and she wanted the interview to be over so she could write to Mother and pack her trunk before nightfall. Eventually he raised his arm lazily, flicked his hand in the direction of the door and said, 'That will be all. You may leave.'

Was this it, she thought? She was banished from her post by the wave of an arm? He was the one who had done wrong! She wasn't even sure that he was dismissing her. Well, if he was she would not leave without making him say it! She was not a kitchen maid, she was his children's nursemaid and that surely counted for something. She straightened her back and raised her voice, 'I have done *nothing* wrong, my lord. Am I to be dismissed for *doing nothing*?'

His face registered surprise and he waited a few seconds before replying, 'Your work here has been exemplary. You

153

have not given me cause for such drastic action – yet.' It was the barely perceptible pause before he added the word 'yet' that said everything to Phyllis. He went on, 'Do not give me cause.'

He was not, after all, dismissing her from Melton Hall today. He was telling her to keep her mouth shut or he would. She answered clearly, 'Very good, My Lord.' He picked up a book from his side table and said, 'Send in Nanny Byrne.'

Phyllis bobbed a curtsey and hurried to the door, unbelievably grateful to have escaped dismissal and angry that she had this burden of knowledge to carry silently. Outside the library Nanny Byrne was tapping her foot on the mosaic marble as she waited. 'His Lordship wishes to see you now,' she said.

'What have you done, Kimber? I see no reason why His Lordship has to speak to you. I assured him your work was satisfactory. Mr Haddon is puzzled too. You came from Lady Maude's and your father was in service with Earl Redfern. Well?'

'Nothing,' Phyllis replied. 'It was about nothing at all. He said I must follow your example, Nanny Byrne.'

'He did not dismiss you?'

'No.' Phyllis was still struggling with her mixed feelings of relief at keeping her post and self-loathing for being party to this deception. She waited with Mr Haddon, whose impassive expression did not help her emotions. Nanny Byrne rejoined them almost immediately.

'Did His Lordship tell you what she did?' Mr Haddon demanded.

'He did not and it is not up to me to question His Lordship,' Nanny Byrne replied.

'Perhaps Her Ladyship asked him to intervene,' Mr Haddon suggested.

'Without speaking to me first? Tch!'

Their conversation turned to the way things were when they were young servants as though Phyllis were not present and she followed them to the servants' door at the back of the reception hall. Violet emerged from the shadow of a large aspidistra. She held a feather duster in her hand and began dusting the china and furniture that adorned the spacious entrance. Phyllis was sure she had been listening.

Mr Haddon queried Violet's presence at that time of day and she told him that His Lordship wanted his books dusting as the chimney had smoked that morning. As Phyllis pushed through the servants' door, she glanced over her shoulder and caught a glimpse of Violet's rounded rear disappearing into the library. She blew out her cheeks and shook her head. She couldn't be the only servant at Melton Hall who knew about their affair. But if they suspected, they knew better than to say anything or they would be asked to leave. Well, if there was going to be a scandal, Phyllis determined it would be none of her doing.

'Kimber, do keep up,' Nanny Byrne called from the back stairs.

'Yes, Nanny Byrne.' Phyllis hurried up to the nursery.

Chapter 12

Miss Diana's christening was a low-key affair compared with the first one Phyllis had attended at Melton Hall. A small family group surrounded Melton chapel font after a normal Sunday service. Nanny Byrne stayed, but Phyllis took the other children back to the nursery so as not to disturb their routine. As it was Sunday, Mr Haddon did not allow singing and dancing in the servants' hall, but His Lordship provided a barrel of ale by way of celebration.

'You'll have to have another nursemaid now,' one of the housemaids suggested when Phyllis joined the other servants that evening to drink the new baby's health.

The young maid had been a great help to Phyllis since Miss Charlotte was born and Phyllis had recommended her. But Nanny Byrne had disappointed them both.

'I am sorry,' Phyllis replied, 'but His Lordship has insisted on another nursemaid from Lady Maude's.'

'I've been trained,' the maid protested.

'Not at Lady Maude's, though.' Violet barged into their conversation with her sarcastic comment.

'Neither have you!' the maid retaliated.

Violet simply smiled and said, 'Push off.'

'There's no need to be rude,' Phyllis said. 'She is only trying to better herself. It's harder for those who don't do it your way.'

'Just because you're Nanny Byrne's favourite doesn't make you special either.' Violet lowered her voice. 'She does what His Lordship tells her.' In spite of her hushed tone Violet's voice was menacing. 'And he does anything I ask, so you'd better watch your step.' Violet drew her forefinger across her throat and made a rasping noise in her throat.

It was true. Violet had given up all her housemaid duties to be lady's maid to Lady Melton. Violet had suggested a daily afternoon drive in the Daimler for Her Ladyship, which His Lordship thought was an excellent idea. So every day Violet put on her hat and coat and sat next to Aaron in the front seat of the Daimler while he drove Her Ladyship around the beautiful Yorkshire countryside. However, when she returned she said she was too tired to see her children and retired to her bed, taking dinner in her room even when they had guests.

It was the only time Phyllis saw Aaron these days as his mornings were spent at Melton Halt with His Lordship in his motor car workshop. He passed most of his evenings in His Lordship's garages at the Hall, apparently preferring motor cars to the company of others. However, tonight was an exception. Phyllis noticed him arrive, as handsome as ever, and her heart lurched in spite of herself. He came over to them with a glass in each hand, handing one to Violet. 'Oh, you haven't got a drink yet, Phyllis,' he said. 'Here have mine, I'll get another.' He handed her the other glass and retraced his steps. Phyllis's eyes followed him involuntarily and Violet noticed.

'Oh you like him, don't you?' Violet exclaimed. 'Dear me, what will Nanny Byrne say when His Lordship tells her?'

'There is nothing between us. We are not even friends.'

'Well whatever you are, if you dare breathe a word to him of what you know, I'll have the both of you out of here as fast as lightning. Got that?'

'It is no concern of mine what you and His Lordship get up to, Violet, so why should I wish to talk to Aaron – or anyone – about it? Anyway, I gave my word to His Lordship.'

'He said you were the loyal sort.'

Violet moved away when Aaron came back with his drink. 'I haven't had a chance to speak to you since – since when?'

'Lady Charlotte's christening.'

'Is it that long ago? How old are you now?'

'I shall be seventeen in September.'

His eyes crinkled at the corners as he smiled. 'And growing prettier by the day.'

She thought he was making fun of her, felt her face

flush and looked down. Thankfully, he didn't expect her to flirt because he went on, 'What did Violet want?'

'Nothing.'

'Well don't let her push you around. I know she's a favourite with the mistress . . .'

'The mistress?'

'Yes, I thought you would have known. That's why she landed the lady's maid position. Lady Melton likes her around.'

'Really? Did Her Ladyship say that?'

'She hardly speaks to me apart from saying when she wants me to stop and start the motor car.'

'Well, who did tell you then?'

'Mr Haddon, who else? Violet has no idea how to behave when she's out and I mentioned it to him.'

Phyllis thought it best to change the direction of their conversation. 'I didn't see Lord and Lady Redfern today, or the Branburys. Did you recognise Miss Diana's godparents?'

'Didn't Nanny Byrne tell you? They were the Ashbys, Lady Melton's folks.'

'They don't visit her very often.'

'They're all too busy making money.'

Phyllis guessed this was true. In spite of Lady Melton being a difficult lady, no expense was spared in trying to cheer her and it must come from her family as Lord Melton didn't have any money. Lady Melton's good humour never lasted, though. In fact, sometimes Phyllis thought she became more miserable with each child she had.

They were interrupted by Violet looming between

them unexpectedly. 'What are you two doing with your heads together?'

Aaron looked surprised but Phyllis glared at her and said, 'We're just talking.'

'Well don't.' Violet took Aaron's elbow. He shook her off so she hissed, 'Her Ladyship's business,' and pulled him away into the corner.

Phyllis turned away and went over to watch the card game in the opposite corner. When she glanced across the room again, Violet had disappeared and Aaron was standing alone. He looked angry.

Phyllis wandered over as casually as she could and enquired, 'Is something wrong?'

'No.'

'You're cross about something.'

Aaron glanced at the clock on the wall. 'I have to leave to check the generator for tonight.'

'Wait! Don't go yet. Did Violet say something about me?'

He looked uncomfortable and didn't reply.

'She did, didn't she? What did she say? You must tell me. I have a right to defend myself.'

'Why do you think you have to?'

Phyllis felt desperate. Violet had a poisonous tongue and she wanted Aaron to have a good opinion of her. 'Because Violet is – is . . .' She struggled to find the right word. 'You can't trust her.' She realised from his expression that she had said the wrong thing.

His mouth turned down at the corners and his eyes clouded. 'Her Ladyship does.'

'No she doesn't!' Phyllis clamped her mouth shut.

Aaron stared at her for a few seconds then said, 'Do you know what I think? I think you're jealous of Violet.' He seemed genuinely confused and muttered, 'Why? I expected better of you, Phyllis.' Then he took himself off to attend to his duties.

The head footman appeared by her side. 'What's up with Aaron?' he said. 'It takes a lot to put him in a bad humour.' The footman turned his curious stare on Phyllis.

'How should I know?' she replied irritably. 'I'm only the nursemaid.' She left the room, taking the stairs to the nursery two at a time.

A couple of months later, in the height of summer, Mr Haddon announced at breakfast Violet would be leaving them to take up a housekeeper's position elsewhere. Phyllis wasn't present but Cook mentioned it to her when she collected the nursery tray later that day.

'Mr Haddon said to tell you, but I expect Nanny will already have done so. I can't think how she does it, that Violet. Came here as an under-housemaid and was a head housemaid before you could say Jack Robinson. Then she's a lady's maid and now this. I mean, Violet as a housekeeper? It doesn't make sense.'

'Do you know where she is going?' Phyllis asked the cook.

'Mr Haddon said Ireland. His Lordship's uncle has estates over there. I can't see it working myself. Not with Violet being so common. I've done scrambled eggs for the nursery so you'd better get going. Nanny Byrne doesn't like them dried up.'

Phyllis could not fathom why Violet would want to leave her comfortable position and the patronage of Lord Melton, unless – unless someone important had discovered their liaison!

Later that week she took a pot of tea into Nanny Byrne's sitting room and found her quite anxious. 'Her Ladyship is worse then ever with her depression,' Nanny Byrne said. 'The doctor says His Lordship shouldn't do anything to make her worse.' The old lady shook her head. 'Her Ladyship won't have Violet in the room with her now so His Lordship has asked me to sit with her *again*.'

'At least you can talk to her about her children.'

Nanny looked horrified. 'I should not discuss His Lordship's daughters with *her*. She has too many dreadful middle-class ideas.' Nanny's face became agitated and she muttered, 'She has no breeding at all. A baronet's daughter would have been bad enough but this – this – shipbuilder's offspring will never deserve the title of Lady.'

Phyllis assumed she was thinking aloud and did not reply. Then, out of the blue, Nanny raised her voice and added, 'I shan't do it.' Phyllis's mouth dropped open and her eyes rounded. Lady Melton must be very trying for Nanny Byrne to disobey His Lordship.

'You can attend Her Ladyship instead. You know what to do, don't you?'

Phyllis shut her mouth and swallowed. It was a long time since her training days but she still had her notebooks.

Nanny Byrne waited for her response. 'What exactly is it that you want me to do, Nanny Byrne?' she asked.

'She's dressing to go down to dinner tonight. You're a Lady Maude girl so His Lordship will not object.'

'Oh, I am sure that he will!'

'Don't be ridiculous! He trusts you with his children, doesn't he?'

But he won't want me to be working so close to his wife, Phyllis thought. I know too much. Nanny Byrne, though, had been thinking about this option and had made up her mind. 'Put on a clean apron ready to go down to Lady Melton as soon as you hear the dressing gong.'

In any other circumstances, Phyllis would have welcomed an opportunity to be a lady's maid, even if it was only for one night. 'Surely you must ask His Lordship first!' she protested.

'I beg your pardon?' Nanny's facial expression was severe. She was not used to anyone questioning her orders.

'I am so sorry, Nanny Byrne. I wasn't disagreeing with you. I – I have no experience as a lady's maid.'

'Her Ladyship won't notice. Violet had no idea at all and at least you know how to behave. You are perfectly adequate for such a role. You are bound to be better than Violet and that will cheer Her Ladyship.'

Reluctantly, Phyllis did as she was told, changing into a clean dress, cap and apron before hurrying downstairs. She met Violet unexpectedly on the servants' landing presumably on her way to the attics. She had stopped by the open window and was leaning on the sill, inhaling fresh air.

'Are you ill?' she asked.

Violet turned around and leaned against the white-washed wall. 'As if you cared.'

'Of course I do if you are not well. Shall I call Mrs Phipps?'

'Don't be daft. You might be as stuffy as old Haddon, but you're not stupid.' She closed her eyes and covered her forehead with her hands. She was pale and smelled vaguely of something sour.

'Have you been sick?'

Violet nodded. 'It's the same every morning. I'm just going for a lie down.'

Phyllis had seen the signs in others often enough and they were unmistakeable in Violet. So that was why she was going away! It had nothing to do with Her Ladyship's wishes at all. The realisation dawned on Phyllis's features.

Even when out of sorts, Violet was not as shrinking as the flower she was named after and challenged, 'Aren't you going to say I told you so?'

'Oh Violet, I am so sorry.'

'Well, I'm not,' she answered defiantly.

'Is this why you are going to Ireland?'

'It won't be for ever. His Lordship will look after me. He always said he would. He's pleased. If it's a boy it'll prove it's not his fault that she will always have girls. We all know it's her, anyway.'

'But you can't come back to Melton Hall with a baby.' *Unless you give up your child for adoption*, Phyllis thought. She saw Violet's lip tremble for the first time ever. She had enjoyed her privileged position for several years and now she would have to move to an unfamiliar situation to live with strangers. But Violet raised her head proudly. 'I'm going to live at the seaside, so there.' She pushed herself away from the wall, adding, 'And whoever has to look after *her* is welcome. Good luck to them, I say. She has a screw loose if you ask me. I don't know why he hasn't put her in the loony bin.'

Phyllis took a deep breath and blew out her cheeks as she stood outside Her Ladyship's bedroom. She tapped on the door and waited for a reply.

'Who is it?' Lady Melton's voice was weak.

'Kimber, My Lady.' Phyllis listened for a response and after a short silence heard, 'Come in.'

She entered the room, curtseyed on the threshold and opened her mouth to explain, but Lady Melton rushed across the room in a flurry of floating white georgette and swansdown. 'What do you want? Oh it's you. Shouldn't you be in the nursery?'

Phyllis had not seen this room recently and now it took her breath away. The curtains and bed drapes were a gossamer white and there was much more gilding than she remembered. Phyllis was so entranced by its sheer beauty and stark contrast to the dark wood panelling that dominated the rest of Melton Hall that no words came out of her mouth.

Lady Melton stood in front of her examining every detail of her appearance and demanded, 'Well, what is it?'

'I've come to help you dress, My Lady.'

Lady Melton's feet were bare and she was a small lady.

She had dark hair and eyes but her skin was sallow. She furrowed her forehead and glowered at Phyllis.

'Did *he* send you? You're another of his trollops, I suppose.' She continued to stare at Phyllis and added, 'You're not as pretty as the other one.'

Hurt by her insinuations, Phyllis wanted to walk away. But as a servant, she did not have that option and said, 'Nanny Byrne sent me, My Lady.'

'Oh her. His Lordship's guard-dog, the one who won't let me see my babies when I wish. *My* babies.' Her face crumpled. 'They are *my* babies; *mine*.'

Phyllis stood in front of her in silence wondering what to do next. It was true what the other servants were saying. There was a marked jitteriness about the Viscountess. She was tense and shrill. Her eyes were puffy and her skin so dull that she looked quite unwell. Perhaps she was genuinely ill, or perhaps she simply needed the lively companionship of her visitors to cheer her? Phyllis said, 'Have you decided on your gown for tonight, My Lady?'

'Where is she?' Lady Melton demanded in response.

Puzzled at first, Phyllis asked, 'Where is who, My Lady?'

'Where is the – the trollop with the swelling stomach?' Lady Melton enunciated carefully.

She had to be referring to Violet, which meant she knew about her husband's affair and the pregnancy. There was no point in feigning innocence about her and Phyllis answered as honestly as she could, 'I believe Violet is helping Your Ladyship's seamstress. Which costume shall I get out, My Lady?'

'I don't want to go down tonight. I'm too tired.' Lady

Melton scrutinised Phyllis's appearance and grimaced. 'You're a bit skinny for him anyway. You can stay.' She waved an arm in the direction of a small door. 'My dressing room is through there. You'll have to choose for me. Close the curtains as well.'

Phyllis had not seen anything else in Melton Hall that was quite as luxurious as Lady Melton's suite. Not only did it have an electric chandelier but Her Ladyship had her own lavatory and bath with a hot water geyser for the tub. Violet's life as her maid was certainly an easy one with no water to carry or slops to empty. Phyllis walked over to the window and took a lingering look at the view with its attractive calming lake and fine parkland beyond. She sighed with appreciation and pulled the heavy silk curtains.

She made up the fire and it was drawing well when Phyllis helped Her Ladyship into the silk dress she had chosen. It had a matching evening wrap and shoes. Phyllis dressed her long dark hair and chose a feathered ornament that she enjoyed fixing in place. When Her Ladyship was ready she stood for a long time in front of the cheval glass in her dressing room.

Phyllis turned her attention to cleaning and tidying the bathroom and dressing room. As soon as Her Ladyship went down to dinner she did the same in the bedroom, arranging the furniture and cushions to best effect, and then checking Her Ladyship's wardrobe for loose buttons and threads. Her earlier ambition had not gone away. She still really wanted to be a lady's maid. She could make Her Ladyship beautiful for her husband and then he wouldn't seek his pleasure elsewhere. If Her Ladyship knew about Violet there was no longer any secret for Phyllis to keep from her. And it was high time Her Ladyship was looked after by someone who cared.

Chapter 13

'What is it, Fraser?' Lady Redfern's butler hurried across the drive to meet her from the motor car. Her chauffeur was perfectly capable of escorting her to the front door and as Fraser approached her she knew immediately that something was wrong. His face was grey and he was agitated.

'My Lady, His Lordship wishes to see you urgently.'

What was so urgent that it could not wait another hour until luncheon? 'Very well, Fraser. Is His Lordship in the library?'

'He is in his bedroom, My Lady, with Dr Jenkins.'

'Dr Jenkins?' Amelia's heart missed a beat. 'His Lordship is quite well?'

'He is not, My Lady.'

With her heart now thumping, Amelia took the

staircase as fast as her seventy-five years would allow and ran across the carpeted landing into her husband's room, unpinning her hat as she went. Dr Jenkins rose to his feet as soon as she entered and came towards her.

'Please remain calm, My Lady. His Lordship must rest quietly.'

Amelia tried not to show her anxiety. 'Of course, Dr Jenkins, but tell me what has happened? He was perfectly well at breakfast and we were to have luncheon together.' She stopped as soon as she realised that she was gabbling and placed her hand across her brow. 'Oh dear Lord, no. Tell me the truth, Doctor.'

'Not here, Your Ladyship. He has a little time left but I have done all I can for him now. I shall wait for you in the library.'

Dear Doctor Jenkins. He gave her a sympathetic smile which said everything. She unbuttoned her coat slowly and inhaled deeply in an effort to quell the thumping in her chest. James was not sleeping and he raised an arm to acknowledge her as she approached his bedside.

Amelia had tried not to imagine a repetition of James's heart attack. He had been so careful to follow Dr Jenkins' advice that she thought – she thought he would go on for ever. But at seventy-two and with a weak heart she knew this was not so. Nobody was immortal no matter how much one might wish it, and her own heart cried. James couldn't leave her, he couldn't! What would she do without him? How could she go on?

'Amelia.' His voice was weak and as he spoke she watched his eyes close and his chest rise with the effort.

She took his cold thin hand in hers. 'James, my darling, darling James, do not try to talk. Dr Jenkins says you must rest.'

'But I must,' he wheezed. 'I must tell you – before I die, you should know—' He gave up, exhausted.

'Sleep will help, my love. Then you will feel stronger and we may talk.'

He opened his eyes and moved his chin up and down slightly, then closed his eyes again. She watched his breathing for a few minutes to reassure herself it was steady and crept quietly from the room. Edward was striding up the stairs.

'Don't disturb your father now, darling. He is sleeping. Dr Jenkins will speak to us in the library.'

James stooped to kiss her. 'May I look in briefly, Mama? I – I want to see him.'

'I'll wait here,' she responded.

Edward came out of his father's bedroom frowning, took her arm gently and they went down to the library together. Dr Jenkins stood up as they entered and they sat side by side on the chesterfield by the fire. Amelia gestured for the doctor to sit down and Edward took a firm hold of her hand.

'This is not unexpected, My Lady.'

'No,' she agreed. 'I am aware that his heart is weak, but how frail is he, Dr Jenkins?'

'Very, My Lady, I am sorry to say. His heart is failing now. It is only a question of time.'

Edward's grip on her fingers tightened and Amelia could not stop her mouth quivering and tears spring in her eyes. 'How much time does he have, Dr Jenkins?'

'It is hard to say exactly, but I would say weeks rather than months and it may be only a matter of days. It is my opinion that he will not survive another seizure.'

Amelia's whole body was rigid as she fought to maintain her composure. She swallowed hard and searched in a pocket for a handkerchief. Edward, darling Edward, took over for her.

'Tell us what we must do to ease his discomfort, sir,' he asked.

'He must remain in bed and I shall send a nurse for his medical needs. His Lordship knows how serious his condition is, and – and he is as well prepared as any I have known. If one of you is with him during his waking hours it will ease his suffering. If he is spared another seizure he will, eventually, lapse into an unconscious state. I do not know how long that will take but His Lordship has a strong will and does not give in easily.'

'He will lose all consciousness?' Edward queried quietly.

'When he does, the end will be close.'

Amelia gave her son's hand a squeeze and found her voice again. 'Thank you for being so frank with us, Dr Jenkins.'

'I shall stay with His Lordship until his nurse arrives and then call to see him twice a day. I shall make him as comfortable as possible. I only wish I could do more for him, My Lady.'

'Thank you. He could wish for no better. I am truly grateful for your ministrations.' Amelia stood up and the doctor left to return to his patient.

'I shall sit with him when he wakes, Mama,' Edward said.

'Your father was quite agitated earlier. He wished to speak to me. Call me as soon as he wakes. Whatever it is we must indulge his wishes.'

'Oh, Mama,' Edward groaned, 'I can't bear this.'

'Darling, you have to. Your father expects it of both of us and we shall not let him down.'

'I'll take it.' Amelia took the tray of beef tea and toast from her husband's valet and stood aside as he opened the door to James's bedroom. She took a deep breath and pasted a cheerful smile on her face. *Dear Lord*, she prayed silently, *help me to get through this most painful of times*. Her life as mistress of Redfern Abbey had been punctuated by helping estate and miners' families through similar distressing situations. She had felt helpless then and she felt helpless now. How does one come to terms with the death of a loved one? How does one keep going knowing that the person most dear to them is dying? She had gone through the gamut of hope; that his physician was wrong, that James was strong enough to recover; *and, forgive me Lord*, she prayed, *if this is the end, do not let him linger and slowly waste away*, for she knew that he would not want that for himself.

She had comforted wives, husbands and parents whose suffering was as prolonged as their ailing loved ones and considered then that those who had a quick end to their lives were, perversely, the lucky ones. Yet, she could not truly wish that on James for she did not want him to leave her, not ever.

'He is awake, Mama.' Edward rose to his feet, vacating the bedside chair and took the tray, placing it on a nearby table.

Amelia bent to kiss her husband's pale cheek. She noticed his eyes brighten and he returned her smile. 'A nurse is here already,' she said. 'Dr Jenkins is with her now.'

James made an effort to sit up and Amelia rearranged his pillows. 'I have some of Cook's best consommé and Melba toast.' She placed the bed-tray across his lap and unfolded the linen napkin, handing him the soup spoon.

'I must speak with you now, before it is too late.'

Amelia frowned before she could stop herself. 'Take your soup first, darling.'

'Edward, would you leave us and see we are not disturbed,' James responded, and waited until the door had closed behind his son. 'I have something to tell you that I have kept to myself for too long, and soon it will be too late.'

Amelia's heart twisted in her breast as she tried desperately to relax her frown. 'You must not distress yourself with matters that can wait. You are still very weak, my love.'

'I shall not regain my strength and I may go at any time, dearest. You must prepare yourself for you have to keep Redfern going without me and I know that with Edward's help you can. He sank back into the pillow and closed his eyes for a moment before continuing, 'I have struggled with this knowledge but it is only right that I share it with you before I depart this earth. He is your son, too.'

'This concerns Edward?'

'Try and find him a wife, dearest. A man needs a wife, especially when he has an estate the size of Redfern to run.'

'I shall do my best, as I have done for these past few years.'

James lowered his already weakened voice and Amelia had to lean forward to hear him clearly. 'I have kept this secret for too long. It has been my mistake.'

'You must not talk of it if it distresses you so.'

'I must, for no one else will say and you have to know. I shall leave it to your unfailing wisdom to share it with Edward. He has a child, my dear. We have a granddaughter.'

Amelia's well-bred tolerance of shock, borne of a childhood at Melton Hall, prevented a cry of disbelief escaping from her throat. But her astonishment must have shown in her eyes for James went on, 'Do not doubt me on this, beloved. I had only your sensibilities in mind when I decided you would not be a party to my deception.'

'But Edward is?'

James shook his head. His face was drawn and haggard but he went on, 'It happened over twenty years ago, my love. He was young and the girl was a servant. He could not have married her and he would have been the source of a scandal. I have spent years rebuilding the good name of Redfern but I shall not die leaving you with a lie.'

Amelia saw how tired James was after only a short conversation. His nourishment was forgotten and she feared for his condition. 'Tell me later, when you feel stronger.'

'Dearest, this is the end for me. I shall never feel stronger than I do now. I insist that you hear me out.'

She acquiesced. 'Of course I shall, my dear.' She moved away the bed-tray, drew her chair nearer and took his hand. 'Tell me, James.'

'She is a fine girl. When you are aware of her parentage you can see the resemblance.'

'You have met her? Does she know what you are to her?'

James moved his head from side to side. Amelia's mind was racing. James had spoken of Edward's youthful passion before. He wished to unburden himself. He had held this secret for too long already. 'Jack Kimber's daughter,' she stated. 'The girl you asked me to find a position for when he was killed.'

James squeezed her hand gently. 'Edward loved her mother then and I believe he still does.' He closed his eyes. 'Ellen Kimber could have created a scandal but she has been loyal to this day and never breathed a word about her daughter's real father. Promise you will do right by her when I am gone. Promise me, Amelia.'

'Why didn't you tell me?'

'I wished to spare you the heartache and worry that Edward may have grown up like your father and brother.'

'He hasn't. He is more like your sister, God rest her soul. Our son is honest about his affections. Do you truly believe that he loved Ellen?'

'I do and I hoped that I could carry the burden of

my knowledge alone. But I am dying so you must promise me you will not forget the sacrifice that Ellen has made for the sake of the Redfern name. Promise me, Amelia. I ask nothing more of you.'

'Oh my darling, of course I promise you. But you are not leaving me yet. Dr Jenkins—'

James raised his hand to silence her and went on, 'And Ellen's daughter, she is Edward's daughter, she is our blood, she is a Redfern. Promise me you will not forget that.'

'I promise you, of course I promise you,' she repeated. 'Had Edward no idea that Ellen was with child?'

'None at all. I dealt with everything and encouraged him to forget Ellen. He was – is – a good son but I did not comprehend the depth of his youthful passion. I believe he has tried hard to love again but has not been successful.'

Amelia gazed across the room. Her own father and brother were never steadfast in their devotions and she had grown up believing that her marriage would be the same as her mother's until she met James and knew the meaning of a deep and lasting love. Loyalty at any cost was her mother's overriding quality. Her mother had been happy enough despite her profligate and philandering husband who took his lead from the King's behaviour just as her mother had from the Queen. But Amelia's beloved James had opened *her* heart to a different kind of marriage where trust, understanding and forgiveness prevailed.

Yet now she was faced with a situation involving her own son she realised that nothing was as straightforward as it seemed. What should she do with this knowledge?

She dare not dwell on the problem now. James was her concern and she tried not to show her worry at his pale and haggard features.

'Thank you,' he breathed. 'I know you will do what is right.'

He sank back into his pillows and she thought his face relaxed its frown a little. She had made her promise. But what was the right thing to do in this situation? This was the twentieth century and the old ways were giving way to new ideas about women and their place in society. But how many were ready for them?

James's steady regular breathing told her he was asleep and she took the tray to the door to hand it to his valet. 'Thank you. His Lordship is too tired for this at present. Ask Cook to prepare it again in an hour, with some scrambled egg. Bring the newspaper too. I'll read to him.'

James, Earl Redfern died peacefully at Redfern Abbey in the South Riding of the county of Yorkshire with his family at his bedside. Amelia's eyes remained dry as Dr Jenkins expressed his condolences. James had been barely conscious for several days as his failing heart grew weaker and weaker until it expired. For Amelia it was a welcome release. She knew how unhappy James had been as a normally energetic man restricted to his bed. She knew he wanted to go. He was ready but she was not. No matter that she was aware he was dying, she was no less distraught when he took his last rattling breath.

She glanced at Edward who seemed as pale and haggard as his father had been. He was young and strong and would survive. Her nephew Melton was there too, but not his wife who, sadly, was coping less and less with her life at Melton Hall. James's half-brother, Albert, had been down from High Fell in the Yorkshire Dales for three weeks now. A gentleman farmer, he had been born late in life to their mother and her second husband Abel. Albert lived with his half-sister Daisy and her husband and ran the farm allowing Daisy and Boyd an extended trip to see their children and grandchildren in America.

Her husband's steward, also present, came forward too to offer his condolences. Amelia thanked him graciously and nodded briefly. He bowed and left. There was much to arrange as an Earl's funeral cannot be a private affair.

Edward, the new Lord Redfern, watched the last of the mourners leave in their carriages and motor cars. A funeral, he realised, was the first formal duty for an heir and it had drained him of all energy. This was what his life would be like without his father. The running of Redfern estates and industries was his alone and while once he itched to shoulder the yoke, now he quaked at the responsibility. So many people depended on Redfern for their livelihoods. His father had never let them down and neither would he.

He turned to his mother, his father's constant and devoted companion. His father had told him many times of how much he owed to his mother to ensure Redfern's success and, now Edward was alone in this task, the full realisation of the value of a supportive wife began to dawn. Amelia had exhausted herself these last few weeks caring for her dying husband and advising Edward on estate decisions but Edward could no longer ask for her support. She must rest and recuperate, perhaps travel as he had done a few years ago. As soon as his house guests had departed he would speak with her about an extended trip to Europe.

'Well, Edward, how does it feel to be an earl?' Lord Melton appeared at his elbow. 'I remember how strange it was when Father died and I inherited. But one quickly becomes accustomed to being a lord.' Melton's inborn confidence showed as he leaned forward and added. 'You'll always have me to advise you, cousin.'

Edward did not alter his expression. Melton Park was less than a tenth the size of Redfern and Mel's lands and fortune had been dissipated by his father. Mel was the very last person he would turn to for advice. It was Melton's father-in-law who had been the salvation of his cousin's estate.

'How is your wife, Mel?' he asked.

Melton was unaware of the slight. 'Clara? Oh she's having one of her depressions again. She is so difficult I wonder how the servants cope with her. But a viscount has to have an heir. So does an earl. You ought to take a wife, cousin. I hear that Anne Branbury has finished with all that university nonsense. I can't understand why her father paid for it in the first place.'

'He took a lot of persuading,' Edward commented.

Anne did not give up her ambition to go to university and he admired her for the stubborn stand she took against her father. He had fallen in love with her in Italy but a proposal from him then would have made life difficult for her at home. She would have been pressured to accept him and her parents would have insisted she gave up university for marriage and he couldn't do that to her. They had continued to see each other when possible and her behaviour allowed him to believe she loved him too. But she had not committed herself. He thought, wryly, that he was in the same position with Anne, that Lucy had been with him before she left.

'She isn't engaged or anything, you know. Shall I speak to her father for you?' Melton suggested.

'Thank you, Mel. I am sure I can win her affections without anyone else's help, least of all yours.'

Edward knew he had at last found a girl that he wanted to marry. Anne was all he could wish for and more. Although she was younger than he, she was wise and well-read, and had a mature head on her shoulders. She defended the suffragettes, arguing that the pre-1905 suffragists hadn't got anywhere so they were forced to take a more violent approach. Edward found the subject interesting and encouraged her discussions, much to the annoyance of Lady Branbury.

He continued, 'She is not going to London for the season this year but she has promised to join me for the shooting in the autumn.' Edward thought for a moment. 'I shan't be in London this year either. There is too much to do at Redfern.'

Melton shrugged and muttered, 'You don't have to behave as your father did.'

Neither do you, Edward thought but did not say it. He

turned to his right where Fraser was waiting patiently for his attention.

'Will Lord Melton be requiring his motor car this evening, My Lord?'

Melton had driven over from East Yorkshire himself. He enjoyed driving his Silver Ghost and it was a beautiful motor car. Edward raised his eyebrows at Mel, who answered, 'Have your chauffeur see to it, Edward. I'm leaving first thing tomorrow.'

'Clara will be pleased to see you back so soon.'

'I'm not going to the Hall. I'm motoring direct to Hull to persuade Ashby to invest in my motor car workshop.'

'I thought he had already given you funding for that.'

'He has so keep your voice down. It's costing more than I anticipated. But my Melton Motor rivals the Silver Ghost and it's going to make an absolute fortune for Melton Hall. Motor cars are the future, Edward. You make steel, you should build motors cars with it now.'

'I'll leave that to you. Will you excuse me? Mother would like a word with me.' He went over to Amelia who had been watching her son and nephew with interest. He bent to kiss her cheek and whispered, 'How are you?'

'Well it has been the most difficult day of my life but I am bearing up.'

'It will soon be over and in a couple of days the last of the guests will have departed. You look so tired, Mother. You should take a holiday abroad, in the sun.'

'I believe I may heed your advice this time, my dear, although I do not want to leave you to manage Redfern alone.'

'But that is exactly what I shall do, Mother. I shall manage Redfern alone with the help of all my staff. I am over thirty years of age.'

'Do not remind me, my dear! It makes me feel so old.'

Edward noticed a vestige of a smile in his mother's face for the first time in months. 'And still so beautiful,' he said. He took her elbow and steered her toward the French windows. 'Let us walk on the terrace and watch the sun go down.' He noticed her eyes become shiny with springing tears. He had not seen her cry once during the weeks of caring for his father and now was the time. He quickened his step slightly and led her out into the cool air and whispered, 'You can let go now, Mama. No one is here to see you and if they approach I shall send them away. Anne says that it helps to weep.' He took out a snowy white handkerchief with an ornate 'R' embroidered in the corner and handed it to her.

Amelia received it gratefully as her tears began to flow. 'Anne is a wise girl,' she sniffled.

'Yes, she is,' he replied, as his own tears threatened. 'Very wise.'

Chapter 14

November, 1908

Lady Melton's mood was low again and Phyllis was at her wits' end to cheer her. Her afternoon drives in the Daimler had been stopped long before Violet left, after Aaron reported empty brandy bottles in the motor car. His Lordship had sold his Daimler and moved Aaron to the motor car workshop at Melton Halt. He was given lodgings with another engineer so Phyllis rarely set eyes on him. But she felt he had misjudged her. There was unfinished business between them and it troubled her.

She had dressed Her Ladyship in a new Paris-inspired outfit made by a London couturier and taken special care with dressing Her Ladyship's hair. This usually helped. She was tidying Her Ladyship's bathroom when she heard the bedroom door open and His Lordship say, 'The dinner gong went ten minutes ago – oh, that's an improvement. The hair suits you.'

'You see, my dear husband,' Her Ladyship replied, 'A proper lady's maid does a proper job.'

'Indeed she does. I haven't seen you looking so – so desirable for months.'

'I'm pleased you think so. I still have my waistline after four children.'

'Four girls, Clara. *Four girls*. It's time to resume trying for a boy and if your idea is to tempt me you have succeeded.'

'But I haven't recovered from my last miscarriage. The doctor said—'

'He told me you were fine so stop putting it off.'

Phyllis wished she couldn't hear but the sound of the bedroom door closing and his footfall across the room was distinct. It was followed by a strangled groan from Lady Melton. 'Not yet, Melton, I need more time.'

'You can't put it off for ever. You knew what you were in for when you married me. Now shut up and get yourself on the bed before I lose interest.'

'Can you not wait a few more hours? I am dressed for dinner.'

'I shall not want you later, when you have drunk a bottle of claret. You are already trying my patience.'

Phyllis heard the bedstead creak followed by the sounds of a struggle and then the tearing of silk. Lady Melton cried out, 'No, Melton, I don't want you!'

Mortified, Phyllis grasped the door handle intending to dash in to Her Ladyship's aid. But they were husband

and wife and it was not her place to interfere. She just wished she didn't have to know about this side of their marriage. She was forced to listen to Her Ladyship's strangled protests and cries of anguish and His Lordship's curt dismissal of her complaints.

It was his right, Phyllis supposed, but she was frowning and shaking her head with her hands to her ears, unable to drown out Her Ladyship's resistance, or His Lordship's forceful demands. It was over quickly, she thought. At least, Phyllis became aware that Lady Melton had gone quiet.

She heard heavy footsteps across the floor. The bathroom door banged open and His Lordship filled the opening. 'You!' he yelled. 'Get out of here!' She hurried past him, noticing a long scratch down his cheek. Lady Melton was flat on her back on the tumbled counterpane. Her lovely silk dress was scrunched up around her waist, showing her stocking tops and garters, and her silk French knickers were torn and caught around one ankle. Her beautifully arranged hair was awry and the exquisite ostrich feather headdress crushed. She had her eyes closed. Her face was ravaged by tears but she was silent. Only the movement of her shoulders and the grimace on her features told Phyllis that she was sobbing.

His Lordship came out of the bathroom with a face-cloth pressed against the scratch on his cheek. He ignored Phyllis and said to Her Ladyship's closed eyes. 'It had better be a son this time. This is as distasteful for me as it is for you. Now tidy yourself, our guests are waiting.'

He left as abruptly as he had arrived. Phyllis selected

another evening outfit from the dressing room. 'It won't take me long to re-do your hair, My Lady. I'll bring you a cold compress for your face.' She went into the bathroom and when she returned with facecloths and eau de cologne, Lady Melton was already in her fresh costume. She was sitting at the dressing table, muttering, 'I can't go down there. I can't. Ring for the butler. I need a drink.'

'You'll feel better when I've done your face and hair, My Lady.' She stood behind her and handed her the compress. 'Hold this over your face for a few minutes.'

Lady Melton obeyed and Phyllis tackled her straggly hair. Within ten silent minutes Her Ladyship was presentable again. However, a sad face looked at Phyllis through the mirror.

'You look lovely, My Lady,' Phyllis smiled at the reflection. There was a tap on the door and Mr Haddon called urgently, 'Lady Melton, Cook says the guinea fowl will spoil if she doesn't serve the soup within the next fifteen minutes.'

Lady Melton stood up and walked unsteadily across the room. Her hand shook as she opened the door. 'Haddon, would you assist me down the stairs?' Before she left she said, 'Kimber, you will be here when I return, won't you?'

'Yes, My Lady.'

Phyllis made a half-hearted attempt to tidy the bedroom. After a while she sank into a chair and gave a shuddering inhaled sob. It was all very well to be told not to have an opinion on Lord Melton's behaviour, but she did. He was a selfish man. Poor Lady Melton, no wonder she was at the end of her tether. This was a side of marriage she had never been made aware of in dormitory gossip. There was not even a show of any love on His Lordship's part. His wife had a duty to give him an heir and that was all he cared about. He had turned to Violet for anything more, except that Violet was no longer around.

There had never been a housekeeper's post. Violet had been sent away to a convent in Ireland to bear his bastard child. The whole business sickened Phyllis to her stomach. She finished her work and went up to the nursery for a few minutes of sanity with her former colleagues. It was a sanctuary for her as well as the children in this unhappy house. Nanny Byrne was asleep in her fireside rocking chair as Phyllis expected, and the infants were sleeping soundly. She had two nursemaids now but they must have been downstairs. Phyllis slept in the attic now in her own bedroom and she missed the company of the nursery. She went back to Lady Melton's bedroom and prepared a lavender scented bath which would help her to sleep, if she could be persuaded to take it.

Phyllis was sewing on the dressing room day bed when she heard someone enter the bedroom.

'No, she isn't in here,' His Lordship called. 'She must still be walking in the grounds.' The door closed and Phyllis put away her sewing and rose to her feet. Her Ladyship would be chilled when she returned. She went into the bedroom intending to check the temperature of her bath.

'My Lord! You startled me.'

His Lordship stood in front of her in full evening dress. 'Didn't you hear me come in?' he barked.

'I – I didn't realise you were still here.'

'Have you seen my wife within the last hour?'

'No, My Lord.'

He moved to the window and muttered, 'Stupid woman. She took offence at something I said and walked out onto the terrace. Now she's outside without a wrap and cannot be found. She'll catch her death.' He was staring out into the night and repeated. 'No one in their right mind would do that, would they?'

He didn't expect an answer, of course, but Phyllis thought that if she had a husband who behaved like Lord Melton, then perhaps she might. Neither would she come back. As Phyllis realised that, a vestige of fear for Lady Melton's safety began to flutter in her breast. Should she say how unhappy Her Ladyship had been before dinner? She couldn't. It was not her place to comment and anyway His Lordship would say he didn't know what she was talking about, as though she hadn't been present earlier. She was well aware that he was expert in ignoring incidents as though they had never happened.

'Well, would you?'

He did expect an answer!

'I couldn't say, My Lord.'

'The servants are out there looking for her. Where do you suppose she is?'

'She enjoys walking by the lake during the day, My Lord.'

189

'She likes you, y'know. And you've stayed loyal to me,' he said. 'You've grown pretty, too. Very pretty.'

Phyllis was beginning to feel uncomfortable in his presence. He had never spoken to her in such an informal way before. She had detected an aroma of wine and cigars about him and moved towards the bathroom.

'Stay where you are.'

Phyllis held herself rigid, hardly daring to breathe.

Lord Melton continued to gaze out into the night. 'Is that her? Someone is moving out there, near the reeds.'

Phyllis went over to the window to look but it was too dark to make out any figures.

'My wife received several compliments on her hair this evening. What's yours like under here?' He took hold of her lace cap, which didn't cover much of her hair anyway, and pulled it off, taking some of her hairpins with it.

'Oh!' Her hands shot to each side of her head to hold up her heavy coil of hair. She could feel it slipping down as hairpins dropped to the floor.

He pulled her hands away so that a curtain of hair slipped and slid down her back. He seemed to approve of what he saw and murmured, 'Better. Much better.'

Phyllis felt a blush rise. Lord Melton touched a finger on her rosy cheek and smiled at her discomfort. 'Our thoughts are as one. Which room are you in up there?'

'No, My Lord! My thoughts do not coincide with yours. I am not Violet, My Lord.'

'Indeed you are not. You have much more to offer.'

'I have not!'

'You were born into service. You understand your position.'

She chose her words carefully so that he would not misunderstand. 'I will not sleep in Violet's bed, My Lord.'

He seemed genuinely surprised. 'You cannot defy me. You do not have a choice. I am the master here and I have decided that you will.'

Violet had been pleased to be chosen by His Lordship and even more so when she was carrying His Lordship's child. But Phyllis wondered what had happened to her since.

She replied, 'You can't make me.'

'Yes I can.' He lifted both her wrists and held them tightly. Do you want me show you now?'

He was a horrid man. She had witnessed the force with which he had taken his wife and applied all her strength to pull her wrists out of his grip. 'Please let me go, My Lord.'

But he just laughed and held on to her more tightly. 'They all give in to me eventually.'

He moved towards the dressing room, dragging her behind him and threw her onto the couch. He was an abominable man. He had not listened to his wife when she had protested against his strength so he certainly was not going to listen to a servant. She was on her back and her dress had ridden up to show her knees. She tugged at the hem and scrambled to sit up as he towered over her. She knew where to kick him to stop him, but she had to be on her feet and he was already pulling at her legs and pushing her on her back.

'I'll scream!' she protested. 'Someone will hear me.'

He leaned over and placed his hand over her mouth. 'Be quiet!' Then he was still. There were voices. There was some kind of upheaval going on. It was faint, on the stairs or landing. 'Stay here,' he hissed, and went back in to the bedroom closing the dressing room door on her. A few minutes later, the door opened a fraction and he threw in her cap. 'Put that on and come out here.'

The disturbance came into the bedroom and Phyllis pressed her ear to the door as she pinned up her hair and cap. She heard male and female voices. 'Quickly, put her on the bed. Where is her maid? Phipps, draw hot water from the geyser.'

Haddon and Phipps were there, and Nanny Byrne. Phyllis finished tidying herself in the cheval mirror and went into the bedroom. Her mind was made up. She enjoyed being Her Ladyship's personal maid but she would not stay under Lord Melton's roof if he wanted her to be his next Violet. She would have to find another post. There was no alternative. But Phyllis was determined not to obey Lord Melton's wishes in this respect. She planned to write her letter of resignation tonight. Feeling better with herself for having reached this decision, she inhaled deeply, straightened her back and shoulders and opened the dressing room door.

'There you are, Kimber. Her Ladyship needs a hot bath. She has fallen in the lake.'

Phyllis glanced at Lady Melton's pale and bedraggled form making dark damp patches on the silk counterpane and scooted across to the bathroom to top up the bath water. She lit the gas geyser and steaming water flowed slowly into the bath, then she took away her lavender and camomile and searched for mustard salts. Her Ladyship fell in the lake? She was familiar with all the footpaths around the lake. But what was she doing out there without a wrap at this time of night in November? Phyllis experienced a pang of guilt for not being with her.

Her Ladyship was chilled to the bone and Mr Haddon brought brandy to warm her. She was languid and incoherent and Phyllis was nervous of bathing her. Nanny Byrne stayed to help and when the doctor arrived to see her, Her Ladyship was clean and scented and looking better. She sat up in bed, supported by pillows. His Lordship had returned to his guests leaving Phyllis with her, his earlier behaviour apparently forgotten.

'Shall I come back later, My Lady?' she suggested.

'No, you can pour me another brandy.'

Phyllis glanced at the doctor but he was busy taking Her Ladyship's temperature and pulse and listening to her breathing. Haddon had left his silver tray with the bottle and brandy glass on a side table. She poured a small amount. It was probably too much claret and brandy at dinner that had caused Her Ladyship to miss her footing by the lake.

'I can't sleep, Doctor,' Lady Melton complained. 'I'm so tired all the time.'

It's true, Phyllis thought. It was so difficult to get Her Ladyship to do anything for most of the day.

'Leave me some more of your sleeping pills,' Her Ladyship went on. 'They are the only things that work.'

He opened his leather case, took out a bottle containing the pills and placed them beside her bed. 'Take one with water if you are still awake at midnight. However, I advise you not to drink brandy because it's not good for you.'

Her Ladyship stared into space with an empty look in her eyes. Phyllis didn't expect her to take her doctor's advice about the brandy. It was her favourite nightcap and she took it with her coffee and tea during the day as well. The doctor finished his examination and closed up his case. 'You are physically sound, Lady Melton,' he said. 'Have you thought of doing charitable works to occupy your time?'

Lady Melton closed her eyes and sighed.

'I'll call to see you in the morning. Goodnight, My Lady.' He left, closing the door behind him.

'Bring the brandy over here, Kimber.'

'But the doctor said—'

'Have I got to fetch it myself?'

'No, My Lady.' Phyllis carried the tray to Her Ladyship's beside table.

'Thank you, Kimber. I don't know what I should do without you.' Her Ladyship gulped the brandy and said, 'Another.'

Phyllis hesitated until Her Ladyship jerked the glass at her and said, 'One more and then you can go.'

'I have to clean the bathroom first, My Lady.'

'Yes, yes. Do what you have to.'

Phyllis finished tidying and cleaning Her Ladyship's suite. Her Ladyship had helped herself to more brandy and Phyllis said, 'Shall I take the tray with me?'

'No. Pour me another before you go.'

Her Ladyship watched the amber liquid and muttered, 'I should have put rocks in my pocket.'

'My Lady!'

Her Ladyship waved her glass around. 'It's too late now.' She stared at Phyllis and said, 'Off you go, Kimber.'

Phyllis didn't know what to do. She didn't want to leave Her Ladyship alone. Nanny Byrne might sit with her but she would have retired to her own bed by now and she had other responsibilities. His Lordship was probably still in the billiard room with his guests. She went down the main staircase slowly, formulating her words.

The billiard room was full of cigar smoke from several gentlemen who had taken off their dinner jackets and rolled up their shirt sleeves and were conversing loudly. She stood in the doorway and said, 'May I have a word with you, My Lord, about Her Ladyship?'

He waved her away. 'Don't bother me now. Haddon is downstairs.' He picked up his billiard cue and resumed his conversation.

Mr Haddon was more practical. 'I'll see that she is asleep, Kimber.' He picked up his keys. 'We don't want her wandering outside like that again.'

'Thank you, Mr Haddon.' Exhausted, Phyllis climbed slowly to her attic bedroom.

Phyllis was awake before the scullery maid called her the following morning and was anxious to see how Her Ladyship was. As soon as her morning tea-tray was ready, Phyllis took it upstairs. She was surprised to see

Mr Haddon's key in the door and had to turn it to open the door. She guessed he was as worried as she was about Her Ladyship.

She knocked and entered. 'Are you awake, My Lady? It's a beautiful morning. I'll put out your new tweed costume, shall I?' There was no sound from the bed but that wasn't unusual. Her Ladyship was always slow to wake. Phyllis put down her tea-tray and went to pull back the curtains.

Sunlight sparkled on the lake. Surely such a sight would cheer Her Ladyship? 'It's a perfect morning for a walk,' she said. She raised her voice. 'Your Ladyship.' Phyllis walked over to the bed and gave her shoulder a gentle shake. Then she noticed the staining on the pillow and the smell of vomit. She pulled at her shoulder and Her Ladyship rolled limply onto her back, her mouth slack and stained with vomit and her eyes – dear God – her eyes were open and staring. Phyllis shook both her shoulders vigorously and cried, 'Wake up, My Lady, you must wake up!'

She knew it was futile. She remembered her father and recognised death. Her Ladyship's skin was as cold as marble. Phyllis took in the empty brandy bottle and then, oh heavens, surely not, the bottle of pills tipped over and on its side. She picked it up and shook it. It was as empty as the brandy bottle.

Phyllis's knees buckled and she collapsed on a nearby chair, shock and horror distorting her features. Please God, no. Let it not be so. But it was so. She sat motionless, not able to believe the evidence of her own eyes.

She did not know how long she stayed there. A tap on the door brought her to her senses and Mr Haddon came in with the key in his hand. His eyes swept over the scene. 'Kimber, what do you think you are doing? Good God, no!'

Why hadn't she stayed with Her Ladyship? She was the only one in this household who had any sympathy for her and she had let her down when she was most needed. 'It's my fault,' Phyllis mumbled. 'I gave her the brandy and then I left the pills on the table and I went to tell His Lordship but he wasn't interested.' Her words were garbled and she couldn't move her limbs properly.

'Fetch His Lordship this minute!' Mr Haddon snapped and then peered at Phyllis more closely. 'On second thoughts, don't.' He walked over to push the bell. 'You're in no state to do anything. Go up to your bedroom until I come for you. Don't speak to anyone about this. Not a soul.'

Phyllis nodded and obeyed. Why hadn't she been more aware of how wretched Her Ladyship felt? Why didn't she *think* about the pills? She could have saved her. Instead she had failed her. Her Ladyship had died because her lady's maid had failed her. It was her fault. Lady Melton had not swallowed them by accident, just as she had not fallen into the lake by accident. How was Phyllis going to live with herself after this?

Chapter 15

January, 1909 South Riding

'It's been lovely having you at home again for Christmas. You will be going back to Melton Hall, won't you?' Ellen Kimber did not expect an answer. 'Lady Melton's death was a shock but surely those poor little children may need you in the nursery.'

'They have other nursemaids now and I don't want to be in service all my life.'

'It was good enough for me and your father.'

'But that was in Victoria's day. The Queen has been dead and gone for eight years.'

'Aye and more's the pity. The way the King behaves sometimes, he isn't fit to be her son.'

'Mother!'

'Well, philandering with floozies when he has a lovely wife and family.'

'Lord Melton was the same,' Phyllis murmured.

'What did you say?'

Phyllis raised her voice. 'Viscount Melton, your precious Earl Redfern's cousin, is a philanderer.'

'Phyllis! Where is your respect?'

'Where was *his*?'

Her mother's face paled. 'Is that why they've let you come home? Oh dear heaven, please do not say you are in the family way.'

Phyllis didn't lower her tone. 'I am not. But Lady Melton's former maid was.' No one knew what had really happened to Violet and her baby but Phyllis could guess it hadn't been as she'd described.

'Oh, poor child! He didn't – he didn't – oh, not with you?'

'No he didn't. But that was only because I didn't stay long enough.'

'Lord Melton can't be as bad as you say, he's Lady Redfern's nephew.'

'Yes he can.'

Lord Melton had not spoken to her since just before the death of his wife. Mr Haddon had let Phyllis go at her request without working notice, and with testimonials. It was then she realised he knew more than he let on, and probably always had. But it had been difficult to explain to her mother without giving her the unsavoury details. However, Phyllis felt stronger after a few weeks in the sanity of Chase Cottage and she had to be honest with her mother.

She said, 'Try and understand, Mother, I was fourteen

when I went there to look after babies and I never wanted to be a nursemaid in the first place. I wanted to be a lady's maid only because I wanted to travel.'

Her mother sighed. 'You were far too young for that when you left Lady Maude's.'

'I'm older now and more experienced. I've learned how to care for couturier clothes and I'm really good at dressing hair. I enjoyed it much more than being in the nursery.'

'But how can you be a lady's maid when there is no Lady Melton?'

'I'm not going back to Melton Hall, not ever.'

Her mother fingered her wedding ring nervously. 'If your father were alive he'd be very angry to hear you say that. Lady Redfern herself recommended you.'

'I can't go back there. I can't.'

'But Melton Hall is a *titled* household.'

'I don't want to be in service all my life. I want to see more of England, perhaps the world.' Now was the time to tell her, Phyllis thought and added, 'You might as well know. I've decided to go to London. I have applied for a position at a *salon* near to Bond Street.'

'What kind of *salon*?' Her mother's eyes widened with alarm.

'It's very highly regarded and discreet, where ladies attend to have their hair dressed.'

'*Ladies* have their own personal maids to dress their hair.'

'It's what I want to do. I shall be twenty-one in the autumn and the owner is a French gentleman.'

'French! Oh my dear, no. You cannot go and work for a *Frenchman*. It all sounds most unseemly to me.'

In spite of her rebellion, Phyllis really did want her mother's approval and began to plead. 'I can learn so much from him, Mother. If he will take me on it will be a wonderful opportunity.'

'But what do you know about him? London is so vast. Where will you live?'

'I have secured a room in a hostel for young ladies. It's run by a church mission and there's an omnibus to take me to Bond Street every day.'

'And who is going to pay for all this?'

'I have savings. I didn't have to send money home to you like other maids and – and I have a year's wages from His Lordship.'

'Lord Melton has given you a whole year's wages?'

Phyllis looked down at her hands. 'I – I know what happened because I found Her Ladyship when she – when she died. His Lordship asked me never to speak of it as a – as a mark of respect for his children.'

'You would not gossip anyway.'

Phyllis was wondering just how much to tell her mother, when Ellen went on, 'The newspaper report said Lady Melton had caught a fever that weakened her heart.'

'Then that is what happened,' Phyllis responded, still scrutinising her hands.

Her mother stared at her. 'Well clearly it was not, but I shall not ask you to break your word to Lord Melton. However, I am not at all happy with this *salon* notion of yours. I cannot understand why you would ever want to leave Yorkshire.'

Phyllis suppressed a sigh. She resigned herself to the time it would take her to convince her mother she was serious about her plans. 'I'm not going immediately,' she said. 'Perhaps I could help you with your welfare work for a few weeks?'

Ellen brightened. 'That is a splendid idea, my dear! I am sure the vicar's wife can find you plenty to do.'

Phyllis's nursemaid skills were put to very good use with a young mother of newborn twins who already had three children under six. Her husband left early for the glass factory in town and worked long hours to feed his growing family. Her own mother had passed on and she had no sisters in the village to call on. The poor woman was worn out and Phyllis was glad to lend a hand. In spite of her decision to leave Melton Hall she did miss the children and welcomed others to fill the void.

Yet this could have been me, Phyllis thought as she rolled up her sleeves in the tiny cottage scullery. If she had not been so lucky with her education and father's connections at the Abbey, she might have been in the same position as this woman. An hour later she was pegging out the washing in the garden when she saw the vicar's wife standing at the kitchen door. Phyllis picked up her empty basket and called out a greeting.

'Miss Kimber, may I speak with you?' She stepped outside onto the path. 'After our committee meeting yesterday, your mother mentioned your plans to go to

London. She is most concerned about you and Lady Redfern overheard our conversation. She has expressed a wish to meet you.'

'Me?' Phyllis was alarmed that gossip from Melton Hall might have reached Lady Redfern's ears.

'Do not look so scared. Lady Redfern is kindness itself and she wishes to help. She has arranged to take tea with me at the Rectory tomorrow and would be obliged if you and your mother will join her.'

'Of course,' Phyllis agreed, but the prospect of an interview with Lord Melton's aunt distracted her for the rest of the day.

The following afternoon, she took off her working pinafore, tidied her hair and buffed her shoes, then met her mother at the Rectory gate. A young maid showed them through to the drawing room and they sat silently with the vicar's wife waiting for Lady Redfern. She was shown in by the maid who went off immediately to bring tea. Phyllis bobbed a curtsey when she was introduced and thought that Lady Redfern stared at her a little too long for politeness.

'Please sit down ladies. I have had excellent reports of Miss Kimber's help in the village since she left Melton Hall.' Lady Redfern turned towards her. 'Lady Melton's passing was a great shock to all of us. Her poor children are now motherless.'

Phyllis chewed her bottom lip and felt uncomfortable. Was this about persuading her to return to Melton Hall? She sympathised with the plight of the children. It was not as though Lady Melton had been involved with the care of her children and they had the continuity of Nanny Byrne and her nursemaids. 'I hope that your nephew's children are well, My Lady,' she replied.

'I understand that you cannot be persuaded to return to Melton Hall. As with all young women these days, you are influenced by the times and want different lives from your mothers.' Lady Redfern frowned as though troubled by her thoughts.

Phyllis glanced at her mother who was sitting ramrod straight and staring silently at the wall. She felt she had to say something. 'There are so many opportunities in London, My Lady,' she stated.

'London is not the same as Yorkshire,' Her Ladyship responded. 'It is exciting, I grant you, but it is also dangerous, especially for a – a pretty young woman.'

Phyllis stiffened her resolve. Has she heard rumours about her nephew's behaviour? She prepared for a battle. 'I have friends from Lady Maude's who have positions there and – and I am twenty years of age, My Lady.'

Lady Redfern closed her eyes for a second and Phyllis noticed her chest rise and fall as she inhaled. Perhaps Her Ladyship was not well? She must be over seventy by now and seemed to be finding this interview difficult. However, she went on, 'Quite so, Miss Kimber. Your mother may not wish you to leave, but I am inclined to agree with you.'

'You do? Thank you, My Lady.' With Lady Redfern on her side Mother would not stop her now!

Her Ladyship's features relaxed. 'London will give you choices that the South Riding cannot. That is what young women want these days. As you know, His Lordship keeps a permanent staff at Redfern House in Belgravia.'

Phyllis interrupted her before she could continue. 'Forgive me, My Lady, but I do not wish to go back into service.'

'Phyllis!' Ellen Kimber exclaimed. 'Hold your tongue.'

Lady Redfern glanced at Ellen, swallowed once and went on, 'I am aware of that, Miss Kimber, and I have no intention of suggesting such a move. Indeed I wish to say expressly that I am against your being employed at Redfern House.'

'Oh.' Phyllis felt mildly affronted. Was she good enough for Melton Hall but not for the hallowed halls of Redfern? What exactly did Her Ladyship have in mind for her?

'However,' Lady Redfern went on, 'I have a house-keeper at Redfern House who has lived in London since – well, since you were born. She trained at Lady Maude's and excelled as a housemaid in the Abbey. She will be able to help should your plans not work out as you wish, or – or you find yourself in difficulties. Her support will give your mother peace of mind.'

'Not Mrs Simmonds!'

Three pairs of surprised eyes turned to Ellen Kimber's horrified face. She looked from one to another and muttered, 'I – I mean, she will be far too busy to worry about my daughter. I have no wish to impose on her.'

The awkward silence that followed was broken, thank-fully, by the arrival of tea and Ellen was able to compose herself amidst the passing of cups and saucers, plates and napkins, and dainty sandwiches. But her outburst was ignored rather than forgotten, Phyllis thought, for Lady Redfern's brow was troubled. However, after she had complimented the vicar's wife on her delicious refreshments, the Countess continued, 'As I was saying, Miss Kimber, for your mother's peace of mind, you will agree to visit Mrs Simmonds every Sunday for tea so that she may see how you are faring. In return, I shall write to Mrs Simmonds telling her that you will be visiting her and that she will be corresponding with Mrs Kimber accordingly.'

'But I shall write to Mother myself,' Phyllis protested.

'Mrs Simmonds will be your mother's eyes and ears.'

Ellen Kimber's voice was barely audible. 'You wish Mrs Simmonds to write to me?'

Lady Redfern raised her eyebrows. 'Do you not agree that this is a sensible safeguard for your daughter?'

'Y-yes, of course, if Mrs Simmonds agrees.'

Phyllis knew that Mrs Simmonds had no choice but to obey Lady Redfern and her mother wouldn't dream of going against Her Ladyship's wishes. For herself, it was a small price to pay for her mother to give her blessing to her plans. The interview came to an end and Lady Redfern stood up to leave. Her motor car was waiting at the Rectory gate and as it rumbled away the vicar's wife smiled benignly, 'Lady Redfern is wonderful, isn't she? Our sexton will take you home in my husband's trap.'

Phyllis waited until they had reached Chase Cottage and opened the damper to draw the fire before she asked her mother about Mrs Simmonds. 'I can see you're not happy with this arrangement,' she said. 'Who is Mrs Simmonds?'

'She is housekeeper for Lord Redfern at his London home in Belgravia.'

'I gathered that. Do you know her?'

'We were young housemaids together in Redfern Abbey.'

'You have never mentioned her before.'

'We – we were best friends once, but she went to London and we – we did not keep in touch.'

'Did you fall out?'

'You ask too many questions, Phyllis.' Her mother's firm tone told Phyllis that it was not a subject she was prepared to discuss, at least not this minute and she wondered what had gone on between Mrs Simmonds and her mother. But Phyllis acknowledged that this link with home would help her mother rest easy while she became settled in a position.

Later, when Mother had calmed down, Phyllis brought up the subject again. 'Will Mrs Simmonds remember you?' she pressed.

Her mother nodded and said, 'Oh yes. She will remember me.'

'But you are not happy with Lady Redfern's arrangement?'

'I suppose I am grateful for it does ease my mind to know you have someone to turn to. Mrs Simmonds was – is – fair and honest in all her dealings, so do not think you can pull the wool over her eyes. It will be very strange to correspond with her after all these years but you must promise me that you will do as Lady Redfern has asked and visit her every Sunday for tea, just as though she were your mother.'

The words were out of Phyllis's mouth before she thought. 'Mrs Simmonds isn't my mother, is she?'

The shock and pain that suffused her mother's face almost broke Phyllis's heart. What a foolish, stupid thing to say. She regretted it immediately and rushed forward. 'Oh I'm sorry, Mother, I didn't mean that. Of course you are my mother. Gosh I look like you, don't I?' She tried to laugh it off but the hurt was done.

'Why would you even think that?'

'Oh I don't know. But you have to admit that there was never much tenderness and love in this house when I was little. Sometimes I didn't feel that I belonged here at all. Father was so distant. I don't think he loved either of us as a father should.'

'He looked after us well enough.'

'It's not the same!'

'Don't raise your voice to me.'

'But why do you always stick up for him? He was self-righteous and cold-hearted!'

'He was a good husband and father.' She took a deep breath. 'He wanted to marry Mrs Simmonds!'

'He was in love with her?'

Her mother nodded.

'Yet he married you instead?'

'He protected me from scandal and gave you respectability.'

'Oh.' Everything fell into place now. Mother had been expecting her out of wedlock and father had shouldered his responsibilities, against the wishes of his own heart. She didn't dwell on his feelings or lack of them when he had seduced her mother but said, 'And so he should have done, Mother. He did the right thing.'

'Yes, dear,' her mother agreed. 'But I don't expect Mrs Simmonds saw it that way. She loved him too.'

Phyllis hugged her mother and whispered, 'I won't breathe a word of it to anyone, and I promise you that I will keep out of trouble. I have done so far, haven't I?'

Ellen Kimber leaned forward and kissed her on the cheek. 'You're a good lass, my love and I am very proud of you. I know you won't let me down.'

'Then I have your blessing to go to London?'

'You do.'

'Thank you, thank you, thank you. I have so much to do. Lady Melton, God rest her soul, was always generous with her cast-offs and I have alterations to do.' Phyllis went upstairs with a spring in her step.

'Tea's ready,' her mother called from the bottom of the stairs. Phyllis stood up, brushed away the cotton threads and went down to the kitchen were her mother stood at the kitchen range mashing tea. 'Sit down dear. I hope you are hungry.'

Phyllis sat down to a spread of cold ham, mustard pickle and bread and butter, with a fruit cake and slab of cheese on the dresser to follow. 'How do you manage this, Mother, without me sending home wages?'

'Lord Redfern does not ask for rent and normally I have a young lodger or two.'

Phyllis's eyebrows shot up in surprise. 'Mother!'

Her mother placed the teapot in the centre of the table and put the cosy on while it mashed. 'Oh, it's not what you think. I look after children here for the vicar's wife when their mothers are ill or not coping. It's temporary until they get back on their feet. Chase Cottage is so quiet without you and your father and it seems such a waste to have two bedrooms empty.'

Phyllis absorbed this information. 'Did you want more children after me, Mother?'

'What kind of a question is that for a daughter to ask her mother? We accept God's will in these matters.'

Phyllis didn't believe that any more and went on, 'I don't think Father did but would you have liked to have more?'

Her mother concentrated on her plate for a few seconds then raised her head. 'I wanted you more than anything in the world. That is all you need to know.' After a moment's pause, she went on, 'You really must not talk of such things at the tea table. People will get the wrong idea about you. Such a topic will certainly upset Mrs Simmonds.'

'Why?'

'Mrs Simmonds has been housekeeper at Redfern House since she left the Abbey. She has never had children and I know she would have wanted them.'

'Was her husband like Father, then?'

'That is enough, Phyllis. This is no conversation for a

young lady. I am beginning to think that Melton Hall has not been such a good influence on you after all.'

Gosh, her mother was cross. 'I'm sorry. I'm just curious, that's all.'

'Mrs Simmonds did not marry. Housekeepers are always addressed as *Mrs*.'

Phyllis wanted to ask much more about her and Father but did not wish to anger her mother further. Perhaps Mrs Simmonds would be more forthcoming about the past? She looked forward to meeting her and asked a more acceptable question.

'Is Lord Redfern's London house as big as the Abbey?'

'Dear me, no, Redfern House has only a dozen servants. Your father used to take hampers full of provisions from the Abbey kitchens to the railway station when His Lordship was in London.'

'Does Lord Redfern visit London often?'

'I have no idea. His father preferred his shooting lodge up on the moors towards the end.'

'Perhaps I shall see his son Edward at Redfern House?'

'Edward?'

'Lord Redfern,' Phyllis explained.

'I know who you mean. You will use not use his Christian name in conversation. You will use His Lordship's title when you speak of him. Dear me, what would Mrs Simmonds think of such informality?' Mother stood up, clearly agitated, and began to stack dirty plates. 'I – I've just remembered the hens. Go and shut them in for the night.'

'It's still daylight, Mother.'

'Do as I say,' she responded firmly. Phyllis realised that the matter was closed, and obeyed. She was excited about London anyway and looked forward to her new life as an independent woman.

Chapter 16

The hostel was dull and soulless with brown wood-panelled walls and brown oilcloth on the floor. Her room had a closet for clothes and was sparsely furnished with a bed, table and chair for writing and armchair for reading. She always had to queue for the bathroom at the end of her corridor. But she looked forward to it as it was the only opportunity to speak to the other girls that lived there apart from regimented mealtimes in the basement refectory. The food was awful and there wasn't much of it so she was always hungry.

Her fellow residents, all seemingly from respectable families, were shop girls and clerks or they worked in various capacities for church charities in the poorer parts of London. They all went out for the omnibus in the morning and came back tired but cheerful in the evening.

One or two took the same route as Phyllis on her first intrepid journey to Bond Street.

She made the trip three times without ever setting eyes on Monsieur Anton. At each visit she saw a different, harassed young male assistant who promised to show her papers to him before she came back the next day. She never progressed beyond the entrance lobby of this small house with its brass embellished front door. On the fourth day she gave up and asked for her papers back.

She had spent three days walking London streets with very little spare money, pressing her nose against shop windows and sheltering in an arcade when it rained. If she couldn't get into Monsieur Anton's to learn she would just have to find something – somewhere – else. But the shops only took girls with experience and she had none. 'How can I get the experience if you won't take me on?' she protested to be met with a very polite, 'Thank you, Miss.'

Motor cars competed with horses and carts attempting to deliver their goods. She bought a bread bun from a street kiosk and was eating it in a dusty doorway when a policeman stopped to ask her questions. When she realised he thought she was a woman of the streets she was horrified and spluttered, 'I am looking for – for Bramley Square.'

He gave her directions and watched as she moved off in that direction. It wasn't Sunday but she didn't have much choice. She wasn't allowed back in the hostel until supper time.

The houses were very, *very* grand and stood majestically around a tiny park surrounded by iron railings. She walked twice round the square admiring the buildings and the gardens and then stopped at the house railings of Earl Redfern's London home. Between the pavement and the house was the entrance to the basement where the domestic offices were. She looked at the stone flight of steps, the large sash window below ground level and the polished brass knocker on the painted door. There was no sign of light or movement but she opened the squeaky gate and went down the steps.

'Yes?' A harassed young maid in a brown dress and sacking apron stood at the open door.

'May I speak to Mrs Simmonds?'

'Mrs Simmonds? Is she expecting you?'

'Yes, I mean, no, not until Sunday.'

'Well it's only Thursday. What name is it?'

Phyllis told her, adding, 'Lady Redfern wrote to her about me.'

'Wait there.' The door clicked shut in her face.

She peered in the dusty window anxiously and waited. When the door opened again, the maid looked less fraught. 'Mrs Simmonds is very busy but she said to come in.'

Phyllis followed her through a large square kitchen with a stone staircase in one corner to another square room with a fireplace. The furniture arranged around the fire was comfortable and a long table surrounded by dining chairs filled the side of the room. It had a low ceiling and was gloomy without any lamps.

'Mrs Simmonds said to sit you down in here and make you a cup of tea. Are you her niece or something?'

Phyllis shook her head and went to sit at the table. It

was covered with a dark red velour cloth that felt soft to her fingers as she stroked it. When the young maid brought her tea it was on a tray with a slice of fruit cake. 'Down from Yorkshire, are you?' she asked.

'My father was a groom on Earl Redfern's estate.'

'She might be a while yet. We've had decorators in for weeks. Can't you smell the paint?'

'I'll wait.' Phyllis answered.

'Well, I've plenty to do. Cook'll be down from her nap to start our tea soon.'

Phyllis thought about what she would say to Mrs Simmonds without her spreading alarm in her weekly reports to Mother. She wouldn't be able to stay in the hostel without a job to go to every day.

'So you are Phyllis?' The housekeeper was standing in the open door and scrutinising her as she sat at the table.

She stood up immediately. 'Mrs Simmonds? Lady Redfern wrote to you.'

'She did. I must say, you have grown quite like your mother.' Phyllis was flattered because it was generally known that her mother had been very pretty as a young woman. But this woman, too, was quite beautiful with a smooth, if lined, skin and thick greying hair, carefully coiled and pinned under her black lace cap. Her long black gown was fashionably cut in pleated silk edged with satin. Phyllis was glad she had taken trouble with her own appearance that morning.

'Did you know her well?'

'She was an upstairs maid when I was an under house-keeper at the Hall.' The maid who had let Phyllis in appeared and handed her housekeeper a cup of tea then disappeared. Mrs Simmonds joined Phyllis at the table. 'Lady Redfern wrote to say you would be calling on Sunday.'

'Things haven't worked out as planned.' Phyllis told her about Monsieur Anton.

'I expect he's far too busy to have a girl under his feet all day. I've heard he has his own training school now.'

'Oh.' Phyllis cheered. 'Why didn't his assistant say?'

'He has a year's waiting list for pupils.'

'A whole year? Well I shall I have to do something else until then.'

'You're quite determined, aren't you?'

'I know I can do it, Mrs Simmonds. I can make a plain girl look pretty and turn a beautiful one into a goddess.'

'Really?' Mrs Simmonds appeared sceptical.

'I can show you. Give me an hour with the maid who let me in.'

'There's no need, and I don't want you turning her head and giving her ideas. But I will help you if I am able. Come for the servants' tea on Sunday as arranged by Lady Redfern.'

'Oh thank you Mrs Simmonds, thank you.'

'Now run along and catch your omnibus.' She walked to the door. 'Hetty! Where are you?'

The maid appeared carrying a small basket that she handed to the housekeeper.

'These are for you,' Mrs Simmonds explained, 'a taste of home. Bring the basket back with you on Sunday.'

'Thank you.' There was a white cloth over its contents

and Phyllis peeked inside as she queued for her omnibus. Yorkshire tea bread and Wensleydale cheese! *What a nice lady*, she thought. She didn't appear to bear her mother a grudge for taking away the man she loved. It was her mother who was being over-sensitive, she thought.

There were ten men and women for servants' tea on Sunday. The housekeeper and three housemaids including Hetty, the cook and her kitchen maid, the butler and two footmen, and the chauffeur to make sure the Rolls was always ready to meet His Lordship off the railway train from Sheffield. They eyed Phyllis with some suspicion until Mrs Simmonds told them about her father's connection with the Abbey. She made him sound very important, which was kind of her.

'Are you coming to work here?' Hetty asked.

'No, she isn't,' Mr Simmonds answered. 'She'll be here to see us every Sunday and tell us how she's getting on.' The housekeeper turned to Phyllis. 'Come into my office for a minute.'

When they were seated, the older lady said, 'I've spoken with my good friend Miss Morris at the Admiral Hotel. They have the highest standards of hospitality and the concierge is always asking her for help with providing for lady guests who arrive on the boat train from Southampton. I've arranged for you to see her first thing tomorrow. She'll explain everything.'

'I shall be forever in your debt, ma'am,' Phyllis responded.

The older woman sighed and said, 'Like mother, like daughter.'

Mrs Simmonds had been very kind to her and Phyllis wanted to clear the air between them. She said, 'I am sorry, Mrs Simmonds. I know you lost your sweetheart because of me. Is it any consolation to know that I believe it was a sacrifice for my father, too?'

'What has your mother been telling you?'

'Very little. Jack Kimber stood by her and she was loyal to him but he did not love her. Now I understand why. He loved you.'

Mrs Simmonds frowned. 'Not quite enough, it seemed.'

Neither spoke the words but Phyllis realised that her father must have betrayed Mrs Simmonds with her mother and it had hurt her deeply. The housekeeper went on, 'I wouldn't have taken this post if Jack had offered marriage but I have had a good life here.' She smiled. 'They say that every cloud has a silver lining.'

Mother used to say that about her, Phyllis thought. She was the silver lining of her marriage cloud. They joined the others for tea. Phyllis enjoyed the lively conversation of the other servants and looked forward to visiting again the next Sunday.

Miss Morris had a similar demeanour to Mrs Simmonds except that she was a Londoner and worked in an office behind the reception desk at Admiral's. She wore a plain grey costume over a high-necked blouse fixed with a large jet brooch and plain black shoes that you could see your face in. She was not as beautiful as Mrs Simmonds but her appearance was immaculate and she had not one hair out of place. Phyllis had taken special care with her own dress that morning but she felt untidy by comparison. Nonetheless, Miss Morris seemed to approve of her appearance when she sat behind a desk covered with papers. But her face was stern as she read her testimonials and she stood up.

'I am prepared to give you a one month trial as my assistant, if you survive the first week without complaint. The housekeeper will fit you with a purple Admiral's jacket for when you are on duty. You'll need three black skirts and plain blouses of your own. I'll start you off on errands to get the measure of you. You'll be mainly purchasing buttons, ribbons and hosiery from Bond Street. The doorman with call you a hansom cab who will wait outside the store and bring you back.'

'What shall I do about money?'

'You won't need money. Wear your purple Admiral's jacket and charge purchases to the hotel account. You'll be given dockets to bring to me. Lose them at your peril, young lady. I see that you have worked as a nursemaid and lady's maid in a titled household?'

'Yes, madam. I was there for over six years.'

'Excellent, excellent, I require the highest standards from you. The *Lytham Star* docks in Southampton later this month. When the boat train gets into Victoria station we shall be full. Then I shall really find out what you are made of. Do you have any questions?'

'My mother expects me to call on Mrs Simmonds every Sunday, ma'am, just so that she knows I'm safe.'

'Yes, it's in her letter. You will have Sunday free while you're on trial. On other days be here at seven-thirty.'

'Oh, hostel breakfast isn't served—'

'This is a hotel Miss Kimber, you won't starve. Catch the early omnibus.'

'Yes, madam.' Phyllis bent her knee and dipped.

'Yes, *Miss Morris*, and you don't curtsey to me. Save that for our titled guests.' Miss Morris glanced at a fob watch that she retrieved from a pocket where it was secured by a gold chain. 'My housekeeper is due for her morning briefing. Go and sit by the door. She will take you with her when I have finished.'

Phyllis's day was as confusing as when she started in service at fourteen. But Admiral's ran in much the same way as a large private household in the throes of the shooting season with guests coming and going, needing lodgings and sustenance on a grand scale. Her hours were just as long and exhausting and frequently she didn't get home for hostel supper. Not that she minded for she was well fed in a small basement dining room where Miss Morris ate with other senior staff.

She was fascinated by her tasks, enjoying the opportunity to visit London stores and occasionally seek out unusual foods for foreign guests. On such sorties, which were sometimes to parts of the city she preferred to avoid, a hefty doorman accompanied her for safety. Her major difficulty was keeping up the immaculate appearance Miss Morris demanded of her whilst living in the hostel and travelling on the omnibus. She loved the work and as her month's trial drew to a close, she became especially anxious to impress. But she'd need at least another year's excellent service before Miss Morris would offer her a permanent post at the Admiral.

PART TWO

MARTHA

Chapter 17

May, 1910 Pennsylvania

'Who do these dames think they are? They gotta invite you to their parties!'

'We are not one of their old Pennsylvania families,' Martha explained. She sighed inwardly. In fact her father was, but not one of the county set. 'They look down on us. Anyway, I don't care for their showy extravagant ways.'

'You oughtta care! Goddamn, Martha, my dough is as good as theirs. I can buy half of them out ten times over!'

She didn't doubt it. Since the turn of the century her father's steel business had prospered. Their ranch commanded one of the best positions in the county – a situation that irked their socially influential neighbours – and racehorse stables don't come cheap.

'It's not to do with your money,' she began. 'It's more—' She stopped, aware that her father was sensitive about any mention of breeding unless it concerned his horses. Thankfully, George Strayhorne wasn't listening to her.

'You gotta show 'em,' he went on. 'You gotta look like one of them fancy ladies instead of one of my jockeys!'

Martha cared about her appearance, but right now she cared more about her new horse and she was dressed to exercise him. 'I always ride in the mornings, Daddy.'

'You'd be as pretty as your mother was if you wore dresses the way she did,' her father glanced at her mother's portrait on the wood panelled wall of his grand staircase. He made twirling movements with his hand causing his cigar smoke to leave blue circles in the air, 'with feathers in your hair and jewels.'

Martha reflected for a moment on this beautiful woman who had died before her time and whose image was a constant reminder to both of them of their loss. She had not been blessed with her mother's fair European colouring but she was not unattractive. She had inherited high cheekbones, dark eyes and black hair from her father's Iroquois heritage. Sadly, Martha realised this was something of a disappointment to him as he had worked hard all his life to hide his native ancestry.

'Get one of those beauty parlour dames out here. I have some big shots down from New York next week.'

This could only mean business lunches and dinners where she was required to be her father's hostess. But it had its consolations for Martha. 'They are coming here? Will Michael be with them?'

Michael O'Mallon ran Strayhorne Steel for her father and Martha had been in love with him since she was sixteen. He had taken over the day-to-day management since her father had moved out of town to this country spread eight years ago. Daddy said the move was for the cleaner air but in reality it was an effort to raise his social standing in the county.

'Sure he will. You and Michael can show them my horses.'

Cheered by this prospect Martha made for the back of the spacious hallway and said, 'I'll tell Joe in the stables right away.'

'Wait. I mean what I say about the way you look. Don't let me down.'

'No, Daddy.' She hoped he didn't hear the resignation in her voice. *I'll telephone Aunt Shawna in Pittsburgh*, she thought and retraced her steps to open the heavy wooden front door for him. 'Riley has the automobile ready.'

Her father put a fashionable hat on his white hair, checked its angle in one of the gilt framed wall mirrors and picked up his cane. 'I'm bringing Michael for dinner tonight. We need to talk tactics. Have a guest room ready for him.'

Better and better, Martha thought. Michael had first shown an interest in her at her lavish twenty-first birthday party and a couple of months ago had told her that he loved her. He was simply waiting for the right time to approach her father about marriage. Daddy was sure to approve; as the steelworks would be hers one day it seemed right to her that she should marry the man who, eventually, would take over from her father.

After her morning ride, she went into her father's study

and telephoned Michael at his office. She held the mouth-piece close to her lips. 'Good morning, Mr O'Mallon. Has my father arrived yet?' Martha was always formal when she knew his personal assistant might be listening.

'He has, Miss Strayhorne. I have a meeting scheduled with him in half an hour.'

'You're coming over to the ranch tonight.'

'Tonight? But I'm going to the – ah, I guess my diary has been changed.'

He didn't sound very pleased. Though, like she, he was used to obeying her father without question.

'Ask him at dinner tonight,' she went on. She thought the line had gone dead. She was certain that he knew what she was talking about. 'Mr O'Mallon?'

'I'm here.'

'Ask him,' she repeated.

After another pause he answered. 'Okay, Miss Strayhorne. Is that all?'

'Yes. Goodbye, Mr O'Mallon.'

Martha put the earphone on its hook, replaced the telephone on her father's desk and stared at it. Michael had sounded uncertain. But she supposed he was as nervous as she about anyone in the office finding out about them before he had talked to her father. Her uneasiness soon receded, to be replaced by an excitement about her future. She guessed she'd have to return to live in the smoke and grime of Pittsburgh after their marriage. It was a small price to pay to be with the man she loved. And she would be able to see more of Aunt Shawna. Her father's aunt did not visit the ranch. Shawna

Strayhorne was proud of her native heritage and did not hide it. For that reason, and that alone, George Strayhorne did not invite her to his home.

Martha arranged the yellow roses, which Michael had brought for her, in a large vase on one of the antique French hall tables. She had placed them in front of a mirror for maximum effect and glanced at her image with a satisfied smirk. She didn't recognise herself.

Aunt Shawna had chosen well for her and the Pittsburgh stores had delivered the packages this afternoon. The red silk dinner dress had a long lean outline that suited her colouring and shape. In among her coils of hair, an ostrich feather headdress matched perfectly and she wore her mother's pearls at her ears and throat. Daddy could not fail to be impressed! She padded across the hall in soft kid pumps and put her head round the kitchen door.

'Everything ready, Mrs Hudson?'

'It sure is, Miss Martha.'

The Hudsons were relatively recent immigrants and had worked in the households of European aristocracy, which is why George Strayhorne employed them. Martha retreated to the drawing room, furnished with more French antique furniture and drapes. Hudson was busy with his drinks trolley and Michael was staring out of the window at the acres of Pennsylvania land that made up the Strayhorne Ranch. Her heart quickened at the sight of his tall broad frame and curling fair hair. Of Scotch and Irish descent, he had the brawn of a navvy and the brain of a lawyer and she adored him.

She crossed the room quickly to stand beside him. 'Is that one of Hudson's cocktails?'

He didn't take his eyes off the view. 'No it's straight bourbon. I hope you're right about this.'

'We can't put it off any longer. I want Daddy to know about us.'

Michael turned to face her and she noted his double take on her appearance with some satisfaction. He seemed lost for words at first. 'You look stunning, Martha.'

'Thank you.'

He bent to kiss her cheek and whispered, 'Is this a new you?'

'Maybe,' she answered and spread out the fingers of her left hand. 'It's just the ring that's missing.'

'I'm not sure now is a good time to ask him.' Michael seemed very wary.

'There's never going to be a good time for Daddy.'

Hudson loomed up beside her with a cocktail glass and napkin in his hand. 'Try this one, Miss Martha.'

She sipped it and nodded enthusiastically as the drawing room door opened and George Strayhorne came into the room. She turned to face him and he stopped in his tracks. 'Good God, Martha! Is that you?'

'It most certainly is, Daddy. What do you think? Will I do for your New York big shots?'

'You're going to New York?' Michael queried.

'They are coming here,' Martha explained.

'Next week,' George replied. 'That's what I want to talk to you about tonight. We'll eat first.' He ignored Hudson's proffered cocktail and poured himself a large bourbon from the trolley. 'We're ready, Hudson.' He went out, followed by Martha and Michael side by side.

They talked of horses and racing during the meal until Hudson cleared away the dessert plates and brought in cigars. She hoped Michael wasn't going to wait until she'd left them to their brandy and business before speaking. She caught his eye and mouthed, *Now*.

'A love of horses is not the only thing I share with you, sir,' Michael began.

Her father opened his humidifier and offered Michael a cigar. 'A love of tobacco from Havana?' he commented.

'It's my love for your daughter, sir.'

George's grip on the box faltered and it dropped to the table. 'Your what?'

'I love him too, Daddy,' Martha added.

Her father looked from Michael to her and back to Michael. 'How long has this been going on?'

'I want to marry your daughter, sir, and I'd like your blessing.'

'*How long has this been going on?*' George repeated.

Martha answered him. 'Don't shout, Daddy. I've been in love with Michael for years and since – since my twenty-first last year, he's felt the same way.'

'He can speak for himself. And he can tell me why he betrayed my trust!' George turned his angry reddened face on his works manager. 'I told you to look out for her, not to – by God, O'Mallon – not to seduce her!'

'He hasn't!' Martha protested. 'We haven't! And even if we had, I am twenty-two and don't need your permission!'

'You do if you know what's good for you! Who keeps a roof over your head and pays for your horses? And you, O'Mallon, you ought to know better. She not yours and she never will be.'

'You can't say that, Daddy!'

To his credit Michael raised his voice and said, 'Sir, we do love each other.'

'Be quiet, both of you. She's not marrying you and that's my final word on the matter. Now leave us, Martha. We have business to discuss before next week.'

Tight-lipped, Martha rose to her feet. 'Hudson, serve coffee in here tonight.'

'Yes, Miss Martha.'

'I'll be in my room.'

Michael's face was stony as she withdrew. She smiled at him with pleading eyes but he did not respond. Irritated, she transferred her anger to him. He hadn't put up much of a fight for her so far. She stomped up the stairs to her bedroom and slammed the door. The sight of her new image in her wardrobe mirror inflamed her anger more. She tore off her feathered headdress and ripped out the hairpins allowing her glossy black hair to fall in waves over her shoulders. But she stopped short of trampling her red silk dress into the carpet. Michael had admired her in this dress; she had seen desire in his eyes and it wasn't his fault that her father was so stubborn about them.

Her father's words echoed around her head, eating away at her normally calm manner. *She's not yours and she never will be.* This implied what Martha knew already;

that her father thought she belonged to him in the same way that her mother had. Her mother had been a compliant and dutiful wife and he expected the same of his daughter. She loved her father, he had looked after her generously and she wished to please him. He was not, in any case, a man to cross. He got what he wanted by fair means or foul. Her mother had learned that the hard way and so had Martha. But George Strayhorne was not dealing with her mother now and this was the twentieth century.

She's not yours and she never will be.

'Not true,' Martha said out loud. She *was* Michael's and she always would be his. But how could she make it a reality?

Her father and Michael talked late into the night. Martha tried to read, but her mind was on more personal things. She understood Michael's reticence. Daddy would not disown her from being his daughter, but he could ruin Michael's living, dismiss him from his job and make sure he never worked in Pittsburgh again. It was up to her to make Daddy change his mind. She waited until the house went quiet and crept along the landing to Michael's room. His electric light was still burning.

'Martha! What are you doing in here?' He was already in a dressing robe and slippers.

'We have to talk.'

'Well keep your voice down.'

'Did Daddy say anything more about us?'

'Not a single word. You know what he's like. The matter is closed.'

233

'Not for me it isn't.' She ran her fingers through her hair and let it fall onto the red silk of her dress. 'Make me yours, Michael. Show him he's wrong.'

'Whatta you saying, Martha?'

She didn't answer him. She sidled towards the bed and lifted her arms to undo the buttons at the back of her neck. There were only two left fastened and, as she released them, the silk slipped forward over the light chemise that she wore underneath. She held it in place with one arm across her breasts.

'Jesus, Mary and Joseph, you can't mean it!'

'You do love me, don't you?'

'But your father—'

'And you do want me?'

Three times since her twenty-first birthday party they had been alone long enough in the stables for their kisses to become passionate. She had been aware that his desire was as great as hers and he had said that he loved her. He slumped on the bed and covered his face with his hands. His robe fell open to reveal his strong legs covered with light hair. Martha's heart thumped and her juices flowed in anticipation. She had made up her mind hours ago and was not about to change it now.

'Make me yours, Michael, and Daddy will relent.'

'He won't. He's a ruthless man, you don't know him.'

'Of course I do. He's my father.'

Michael shook his head. 'It's much more complicated than you realise, Martha. He has plans for the steelworks and . . . for you.'

'So have I,' she whispered. She allowed the silk to slide

to the floor, revealing a short lace-edged chemise over French-style panties and long brown legs. Carefully she stepped out of the pool of fluid red leaving her white swansdown slippers in the middle. She watched his eyes darken as her nipples became obvious. When he had fondled her breasts in the stables he had told her he wanted to kiss them. Slowly she pushed aside her chemise straps and the flimsy garment fell to the waist of her lace-edged panties. 'I want to be yours,' she added and climbed onto the bed, lying on her back beside him.

He groaned. 'I can't do this, not now. Things have changed, Martha.'

She wriggled out of her underwear, sliding them to the floor and said, 'Look at me, Michael.'

He twisted his body, growled softly in his throat and bent to kiss her.

Chapter 18

Martha reined in her thoroughbred and stretched in the saddle, turning to look back at the ranch house. She had slept heavily for three or four hours and woke to the first streaks of dawn, slipping out of bed without disturbing Michael.

She had frowned at his tousled hair. Was he right to be so concerned about Daddy's reaction to him? He wasn't from an old county family but he was well-connected with the men who ran Pittsburgh and Daddy had employed him for that reason as much as for his ability. She had been so sure that Daddy would approve. Instead, she had found herself flitting like a spectre across the thickly carpeted landing to her own bedroom afraid she might be spotted.

'Are you as hungry as I am?' The horse's ears twitched. 'Come on, then. The stables will be awake now.'

She spurred him to a gallop, slowing only when they approached the ranch house. Daddy's automobile rumbled round the side of the house and she saw Michael appear outside the front door with him. They were up and dressed for the office already! She urged her mount to a trot.

'Riley,' she called, reining in her horse to fall into step beside the automobile. 'Is Daddy leaving for Pittsburgh now?'

'He sure is, Miss Martha.'

'Why are you out so early?' George Strayhorne demanded as Martha approached him. 'Mrs Hudson wants to talk to you about next week.'

'Good morning, Daddy,' she smiled. 'I'll see her right after breakfast. Good morning Michael.'

She could see that Michael was uneasy. 'Good morning. Miss Strayhorne,' he answered formally and followed her father to the automobile.

Martha backed away her horse as they climbed into the passenger seat behind Riley.

'You will telephone me, won't you, Michael,' she pressed.

'No, he won't,' her father replied.

'I'm gonna be busy,' Michael added.

'But you'll be here next week with our New York visitors,' she said.

Michael pursed his lips and looked at his employer. Why didn't he smile at her?

George stated, 'I can't manage without him. You make sure that everything this end goes well.'

'Of course, Daddy.'

'Get going then.'

'What are you planning, Daddy?'

'You'll be told when you need to know. That horse needs a rub down.'

'Yes, Daddy.' Disappointed, she clicked her tongue and tugged gently on the reins.

After a morning in the stables Martha took a bath, fixed her hair herself and put on a chiffon blouse with fashionably full sleeves. She wandered into the kitchen. 'Any telephone calls?'

'No, Miss Martha.'

Was this what it would be like married to Michael? He would obey her daddy first and she would come second. She went to the telephone in the hall and dialled his office.

'Mr O'Mallon is in meetings all day, Miss Martha.'

If she were honest, *Miss Martha* didn't expect anything different. She grunted impatiently and returned to the kitchen.

'Is lunch ready yet, Mrs Hudson? I'll eat in here today so we can talk about next week.'

'Very good, Miss Martha. Mr Strayhorne has told me what to expect.'

'I wish he'd tell me.'

'It's only a small house party.'

'No reception or dinner for the county set?'

'No Miss Martha.'

'It is strictly business, then.' Martha thought her father would have jumped at a chance to show off his New York big shots to some of the Pennsylvania privileged. 'What has he said to you?'

Mrs Hudson raised her shoulders and eyebrows at the same time. 'He wants the best of everything. I'm writing the orders this afternoon. Do you want to check over my menus?'

'I'll leave it all to you. You don't mind, do you?' Martha was confident that this was the right answer.

'I prefer it that way. Mr Hudson's niece and nephew are coming out to help. Will you do a final check on the guest rooms?'

'Sure thing.'

Mr Hudson joined them and they discussed preparations for next week. During the conversation, she realised how well the Hudsons ran Daddy's house without her. Every now and then they asked her what her views were but they were just being polite and she left them to it. Her responsibility was to look attractive and behave graciously for her father's guests. It was what her expensive ladies' academy had taught her to do. Well, she decided, she would, if only to get Daddy on her side about Michael. She was not about to give up on what she wanted.

'There'll be three of them and one is bringing his wife. You take care of her while we talk business and make sure everything is perfect.' George helped himself to a second helping of Mrs Hudson's fried potatoes. 'She's old money, one of the Boston families, and expressed interest in my racehorses.'

Martha experienced a glimmer of hope about enjoying the forthcoming visit. 'Does she ride, Daddy?'

'Can't tell you that but be prepared and for pity's sake

don't wear those goddamned breeches. Ride like a lady for once in your life.'

Martha guessed she'd have to for Daddy's sake. But it was a long time since she'd ridden side-saddle. Maybe that's why the local ladies avoided her?

'Of course, Daddy,' she smiled and passed him the salt and pepper. 'Why is this visit so important?'

'Transam Steel, that's why. Don't you breathe a word to anyone, not even Riley or the Hudsons.'

Martha was astounded. 'They're coming here to talk about Strayhorne Steel? You've always rejected any approaches from them before.'

'Times have changed. I have to think of you when I'm gone.'

'Not yet, you don't!'

'What would a dame do with a steelworks?'

'She could do a lot worse than marry the man who runs it.'

George pointed his finger at her. 'I've told you, that's out of the question. You deserve better.'

'You were good enough for mother,' she retaliated.

'Your grandfather never had the dough I have now.'

'Then why sell out? I don't understand.'

'You don't have to, you're a dame.'

She knew more than he realised and said, 'You'll keep some stock though, won't you?'

'What do you know about stock?'

'I read newspapers. There's not much else to do here apart from the horses.'

'I'll have Transam Steel shares and I'll have my leisure.'

Martha understood his thinking now and felt more sympathetic. 'You'll have more time for your horses.' With Daddy at home and no steelworks to bother him, they might have an evens chance of improving their relationship. Michael would be close by and – a sudden fear gripped her. 'What will happen to Michael?' she asked.

'He stays. He's part of the deal.'

For Martha, this was a good reason for her to make sure the visit went well. Once he was no longer employed by her father, Michael would be free to do as he pleased as far as she was concerned. She saved any further questions for after the visit. But preparations became more meaningful to her and she began to enjoy them. Deliveries from the best suppliers and stores in Pittsburgh arrived by automobile transport every day and Martha spent her afternoons trying on outfits and shoes from the selection she received.

The New York visitors stayed several days looking over Strayhorne Steel before checking out of their hotel to spend some leisure time at the Strayhorne spread. Martha watched the approaching procession of automobiles from her bedroom window with a growing feeling of excitement. Michael was with Daddy in the lead vehicle.

She checked her appearance then hurried down the wide staircase to join the staff lining up outside the front door to greet the party. Hudson marshalled them to order, checking their haircuts, new uniforms and boots. Martha hadn't seen all their ranch employees together like this before, all cleaned up and standing to attention. Hudson said it was how the aristocracy did it in his native England but Martha wondered who was keeping an eye on the horses.

The line of automobiles stopped on the gravel outside the front door and Martha hurried forward to greet them, delighting in the smile that Michael gave her. His business discussions must have gone well. Perhaps he had reached the same conclusion as she had about being free of her father's control?

After introductions they moved indoors through the line-up. Martha went in last, pausing to watch the chauffeurs unload valise after valise. Hudson held open the front door for her.

'Would you show Mr and Mrs von Stein upstairs, Miss Martha? Cocktails are in the drawing room.'

Mr von Stein placed a hand on his wife's arm and said, 'I'll be with Mr Strayhorne, dear.'

Mrs von Stein smiled at Martha. 'You have a charming home, Miss Strayhorne.'

Martha was showing her the bedroom layout and facilities when her chauffeur and a young woman came in with her luggage. She hadn't noticed the young woman earlier. Neither she nor Mrs Hudson had expected a second lady. 'Is this your daughter, Mrs von Stein?' Martha asked.

Too late! The woman's plain coat and hat should have told her.

'My maid,' the older woman replied. 'I'll leave her to unpack and find your housekeeper.'

Martha felt flustered for a second. She should have remembered that from her old academy. A lady does not travel without her maid.

'Mrs Hudson is in the kitchen at the back of the—'

Mrs von Stein took hold of Martha's hand. 'Come along, Miss Strayhorne. Smith can take care of herself and I need a drink.'

So do I, Martha thought and allowed her visitor to lead the way downstairs.

'Now don't tell me,' Mrs von Stein stood in the middle of the spacious hall, 'the drawing room is, let me see, that one.' She pointed triumphantly at the correct door.

Martha grinned. 'How did you know?'

'It will have the best view.'

'Yes it does.'

Martha warmed to Mrs von Stein who didn't judge her deficiencies as a hostess. She was immensely rich and Martha thought she would have liked to show her off to the local families of note. She opened the door feeling more confident. The men were already in the drawing room.

Mrs von Stein murmured in her ear, 'Ask my husband and his colleagues about horse racing,' and moved to stand between Daddy and Michael. Martha heard her say, 'Tell me about your beautiful county. What can I see from the windows?'

Martha marvelled at how smoothly the evening passed and how much of it was due to Mrs von Stein's skill and grace, which came to her rescue several times. She did, however, feel quite exhausted by the end and was relieved when Daddy took the men off to his smoking room and her only female guest retired to her bedroom. She had not had a chance to talk to Michael but he was staying for the remainder of the visit.

After breakfast the next day, the men shut themselves in George Strayhorne's office for further discussions, and to Martha's delight, Mrs von Stein responded positively to her suggestion of a ride. They went upstairs to change.

Martha's new riding habit was black and her hat had a fetching spotted veil. The older woman wore soft lilac which suited her colouring. Her leather riding boots were in a toning shade that Martha had never seen in Pittsburgh and she gazed at them in envy.

Mrs von Stein noticed and stretched out a foot. 'Do you like them? When you visit me in New York, I shall show you the very best stores. I have promised your father I shall take you under my wing.'

This was news to Martha and she expressed surprise. 'Daddy has not told me about any visit to New York.'

'Gentlemen can be so thoughtless about these details. Were your mother alive, I am sure she would be discussing it with you this very minute. You must miss her dreadfully.'

'Yes I do.'

'How long have you been without her?'

'Fifteen years.'

Half a lifetime.

'I am surprised your father has not re-married.'

Martha hadn't given this any consideration before as Daddy's life was at his steelworks until recent years. Perhaps that is why he wanted more leisure, to find a wife? She assumed he was going with her to New York too.

'Come. Show me these fine horses I have been hearing about.'

They walked over to the stables where Joe had saddled two horses of similar age and stamina. He helped them mount and said, 'Both fillies are in need of a good gallop, Miss Martha. You can easily take them as far as the river bend.'

'If we go that distance we'll be out all morning at least,' Martha explained.

'Excellent,' Mrs von Stein commented. 'We shall make a day of it. The gentlemen do not need us. They will be locked in their meeting until dinner.'

'Sounds good to me,' Martha responded and turned to Joe. 'Have Mrs Hudson send over a picnic lunch for us.'

'Sure thing, Miss Martha.' Joe gave them an informal salute and waved them away.

'May I call you something less formal than Miss Strayhorne?' the older woman asked as they walked their horses towards the gate.

'I'm Martha.'

'That's settled then. I'm Ingrid.' She pulled her veil down over her face and Martha did the same.

Ingrid was an experienced horsewoman and more at home on a side saddle than Martha. Martha concluded that she must have her own horses somewhere other than New York. She recalled Daddy describing the von Steins as 'old Boston' and guessed they had a spread out there.

'As soon as we're through the gates,' Martha called, 'follow the dirt track. If you get ahead of me go left at the fork and keep on until you reach the river.'

It was an exhilarating ride and they were both hot and tired when they reached the water. Martha slid carefully from her saddle and offered the older woman a hand. 'There's a rock pool for the horses and a spring above it. I have a canteen on my saddle.'

This was one of Martha's favourite spots and she had hoped, one day, to get Michael to ride out here with her. But she had hoped Daddy would approve of their relationship too.

'You look sad,' Ingrid commented as she took her horse to drink.

'I was thinking how my life might change now.'

'Your father certainly wants that for you.'

'He has spoken about me?'

'He's worried about leaving you alone in the world. It was my suggestion that you visit New York to spread your wings and—'

'And what?'

'Your father wants you to marry well.'

'He's not going to die, is he?'

'Not as far as I know. But you have no one else.'

'I have my Aunt Shawna.'

'You have? He hasn't spoken of her.'

'No, he wouldn't.'

Her aunt was as committed to remembering her native ancestry as Daddy was to forgetting it. Martha loved her well enough but she was inclined to browbeat her about Daddy's 'betrayal of blood' as she called it.

Ingrid must have picked up the irony in her voice. 'Be patient with him. As soon as the sale of Strayhorne

Steel is complete, he will speak to you of his plans.'

Martha could already guess at his plans. Daddy wanted to move her away from Pittsburgh and from Michael. But she had no quarrel with Ingrid whom she found friendly and easy to be with in spite of the difference in their ages.

'You're a nice lady, Ingrid, but I am sure your own family keep you occupied in New York.'

'Both my daughters have made good marriages and moved away.'

And Daddy wants the same for me, she thought. She leaned against a rock, turned her face to the sun and murmured, 'Why would I want to move from here?'

Ingrid did not argue with her. *How pleasant*, Martha thought, *to have a conversation with an adult who does not try to bully me.*

They allowed the horses to drink and rest before returning to the stables at a more relaxed pace. Ingrid insisted on rubbing down and stabling her own mount as Martha did. It was only after they had cleaned themselves up in the tack room that they could sample the basket of food sent over from the kitchen. It was mid-afternoon and they spread a horse blanket on a grassy slope.

'Oh! Your skirt and boots are ruined by dust!' Martha exclaimed.

'My maid will have everything pristine again for tomorrow. Who will do yours?'

'The Hudsons take care of anything I put out.'

'You ought to have a maid, my dear, if you are to

247

travel. Smith will look after you while you stay with me in New York, then you will know what to expect when you employ one for yourself.'

Ingrid seemed very sure that Martha would be visiting New York. But then she didn't know about Michael. Later, Martha bathed luxuriously and spent a long time on her appearance for the evening. But her thick dark hair did not behave itself. Or maybe she had lost a little of her patience in her excitement? She had heard the gentlemen talking when they came upstairs to dress. It had been a long day of legal and financial detail for them but they sounded jocular and pleased with each other. Tonight would be the celebration they had planned. Then she and Michael could talk about their future.

A heavy coil of hair slipped through her fingers again. 'Damnation,' she muttered. 'How do these society ladies manage?' She knew, of course. They had personal maids. That is how they did it. She inhaled deeply and counted to ten. She had to do this herself. She wanted Michael to be proud of her but he wouldn't be able to afford a houseful of servants.

Her new red silk lay waiting on the bed. Mrs Hudson had freshened and pressed it beautifully. Martha slipped into it and fastened on her feathered headdress. Daddy had told her to wear it but she had made her own decision beforehand. In reality it was Michael's reaction she craved. The dress was a vivid reminder of their night together and their love.

248

Chapter 19

She was not disappointed, not at first anyway. Michael was, as she anticipated, wonderfully startled by her appearance. His jaw dropped and she gave him her widest smile. But he did not return her warmth. Instead, he snapped his jaw shut and looked away, resuming his conversation with the lawyer. Martha's eyes clouded with irritation and she turned towards Ingrid who looked elegant in blue and gold. Ingrid's expression did not alter and, although Martha was convinced she had noticed Michael's snub, she did not react.

Mrs Hudson's handsome nephew circulated with a silver tray of champagne coups and tasty canapés. As soon as all were assembled with charged glasses George Strayhorne jerked his head at the young waiter, who immediately put down his tray and left the room. George cleared his throat and announced, 'A toast, ladies and gentlemen. We have reached agreement on all frontiers including a statement for the Pittsburgh press. Please raise your glasses to Transam Steel.'

Five voices murmured 'Transam Steel' after him and drank. Mr von Stein responded, 'It has been a pleasure negotiating with you, George.' He turned to Michael and added, 'Welcome aboard, Mr O'Mallon.'

'Thank you, sir.' Michael said. His face was impassive.

Martha stared at him. They had agreed to take him with the company as Daddy had said. He must be proud of his achievement. She was, and she couldn't love Michael any more than she did at that moment. Why wouldn't he look at her? Why didn't he appear more pleased with himself? This was a major success for him! His picture would be in the newspapers as the youngest general manager at Transam Steel. And he was free of any pressure from Daddy!

There was an awkward silence before conversations resumed. Martha picked up the abandoned tray and circulated with it until, shortly afterwards, Hudson came in with more champagne. He took the tray from her and whispered, 'Mrs Hudson has everything ready.'

Martha had arranged the seating according to Hudson's advice with Daddy at one end of their dining table and Ingrid on his right. She was at the other end with Mr von Stein on her right. She had put Michael on her left with the accountant between him and Ingrid and the lawyer opposite sitting next to Ingrid's husband. Seven was an awkward number around an oblong table and Martha had suggested inviting another lady to join them.

But Daddy would not risk the secrecy of the deal with anyone and in truth, Martha agreed.

However, she was not prepared for him to ask Michael to change places with the lawyer so he was not next to her. George said it was because Mr von Stein wanted to speak with Michael, but they had time tomorrow for that. Even Michael seemed a little put out. However, like she, he did not argue with Daddy in the presence of company. Nonetheless, dinner went well, lubricated by champagne, fresh lobster brought in by the railroad and beef fillets from a local Scotch herd that was coveted by the Scotch and Irish power brokers in Pittsburgh.

They talked of horses, the future of the automobile and golf, a sport gaining popularity especially in the New England states. Martha was impressed by Ingrid's grasp of all three topics as the conversation continued in the drawing room. But it was late, the food and wine had overheated her and she needed fresh air. After stifling a yawn she stood up and said, 'Would you excuse me? I'm going to take a stroll before bed.'

'That sounds a good idea to me,' Michael responded. 'May I join you?'

Ingrid went upstairs and the other gentlemen took their bourbon and cigars to the smoking room. At last, Martha thought, we can talk. She went out onto the terrace and down the steps to the lawn. The night air was cold with no sign of a moon.

'Daddy must have been planning this for weeks,' she began. 'Everyone seems pleased so I assume they have what they want.'

'Yes, they have, including me.' Her heart lifted. He was out of Daddy's control at last.

'Are you happy with the deal, Michael?'

He seemed to choose his words carefully. 'It's for the best.'

Martha frowned. He didn't sound very joyful. She placed the palms of her hands on the lapels of his tuxedo and said, 'Kiss me, then.'

'I'd rather not.'

'Michael?'

'Well, how do you feel about it, Martha?'

'I'm elated, of course. You won't have to do what Daddy says any more. We can marry without his blessing if we wish.'

'If you think that then you don't know your father as well as you should.'

'I know he always wants his own way.'

'Always gets his own way,' Michael corrected. 'This deal won't make any difference to me. He will hold on to his influence and he's ruthless. If he wants to break me, he can. I've seen him do it to others.'

'But he won't, not if you are his son-in-law.'

'Even more so if we go against his will. He'll run me out of town one way or another. I can survive that. I'll find work elsewhere, but what will happen to you?'

'Well, I'll come with you, of course.'

'And be cut off, disowned, by the only family you have, living on a manager's wage in grimy coal city at the back end of nowhere? Don't be naive, Martha.'

'He wouldn't do that!'

'Are you sure? I think he would.'

When she thought about it, she worried that Michael was right. Daddy was unbending in his views and expected others to do as he ordered. His treatment of his own sister was a testament to that. Martha didn't answer.

Michael went on, 'You think so too, don't you? I can't let him do that to you, Martha.'

She recognised a firmness in his tone and dropped her hands from his lapels. 'What are you saying, Michael?'

'We can't be together. I won't marry you against your father's wishes.'

Stunned, she replied, 'Then you can't love me as much as you say you do!'

'It is because I love you that I'll not do it! I'll not see you ruin your life for me.'

'No. You'll see me a dried up old spinster instead. Isn't that as much a ruin for a woman?'

'Don't be melodramatic. You're an heiress. You'll soon find someone else.'

Cut to the quick she choked on her words. 'How can you say that?'

'I'm not saying I don't believe you love me. But you'll meet other guys on your travels.'

'What travels?'

'Hah! Your father hasn't told you all of his plans yet? Make no mistake about this. He means to separate us, Martha.'

And, she thought, it hasn't taken much for Michael to roll over like a pet puppy dog! If he wasn't prepared to stand up to Daddy now, what hope was there for them?

At that moment she didn't feel like kissing him either and snapped, 'There's a frost in the air. I'm going in.'

When she had calmed down she reasoned that Daddy might want to travel around with his horses to race meetings across the States and that he would expect her to be with him. But they had good railroads and if it was easy to get there, it was easy to get back, too. Michael had given up on her too soon and he most certainly wasn't like that in his business dealings. She began to suspect him of not really wanting to marry her.

Or – or – no, she wouldn't, couldn't, countenance it at first. Michael was an ambitious man, like many young men seeking to make their fortune from steel. Had he been interested in her only because she was his boss's daughter?

The notion ate away at her and Martha tossed and turned that night not wanting to believe it about the man she loved. But even if she only suspected him, surely that meant she did not truly love him? Love meant trust and – she sickened at the thought – she had trusted Michael to fight for her but he had betrayed her instead.

She rose at first light. She pulled on her riding breeches and boots, and walked briskly to the stables to check over the horses selected for today's ride. If she hurried she'd be back and changed well before Daddy's guests stirred for breakfast.

Joe who ran her father's stables and Riley the chauffeur were from the same Pittsburgh family and Joe knew as much about local affairs as he did about horseflesh. Martha enjoyed her conversations with him as they tended the horses together. Joe was tuned in to local feeling and she enjoyed listening to his homespun philosophies.

'Which have you selected for this morning's ride?' she asked. 'Ingrid and I will take the ones we rode yesterday.'

'Your father will be wanting his hunter and Mr von Stein will be having the half-brother. I have two geldings for the others.'

'What about Michael?'

'Oh, our Michael will be taking his usual mount.' Michael was not related to Joe but their common Irish ancestry gave Joe permission to speak of him as family. 'Our Michael is easy to suit, though he won't be having the time for riding now.'

Martha was surprised. How could Joe know about her father's plans? She made light of it and asked, 'Why do you say that?'

'Sure and won't the politics be taking up all of his life.'

'Politics?'

'He's an O'Mallon. He'll be running the city for us one day and maybe even the State.'

Martha gave a short laugh. 'You've gotten it wrong this time, Joe. Daddy's guests are not politicians.'

Joe didn't comment further and carried on with his work, a sign that he knew he was right. Michael would have told her, wouldn't he? He would have told Father. Perhaps he had, so why not tell her too? She felt an instinctive urgency to find out how much of this was true and left the stables immediately.

The upstairs was quiet when she knocked on Michael's bedroom door. 'It's me. I'm coming in.'

She did not wait for his reply. He was in his dressing robe and sitting at the French writing desk with the balcony doors open. 'You're up early. What are you doing here?' He seemed irritated by her intrusion.

'I want to ask you something.'

He put down his pen and swivelled round in his chair. 'I won't change my mind. I'm sorry.'

'When did you decide to go into politics?'

'Who told you about that?'

'It doesn't matter. Is it true?'

He didn't deny it. This was no overnight decision, Martha realised with a growing anger. Michael had not and never had the slightest intention of leaving Pittsburgh for her or anyone else! 'Were you ever serious about marrying me?'

'Yes I was. Without your father, you'd be a perfect politician's wife.'

'Then why change your mind? Surely this makes a difference to Daddy's opinion of you.'

'You don't understand all the ramifications.'

She plonked herself firmly on his unmade bed. 'Then explain it to me.'

'You're a Strayhorne.'

'So? Daddy's wealth can support your campaigns.'

'This is not about money.'

'Everything is about money. Daddy taught me that from an early age.'

Michael was frowning and shaking his head as though he disagreed with her. Martha's patience ebbed and she demanded, 'Well what is it about, then? Tell me, Michael. You owe me that at least.'

'Oh, Martha, I didn't want to have to say this to you. But your father is not the man you think he is. Yes, he's built a fortune in his lifetime, but he hasn't done it without making enemies. And now he's gonna make more by selling out to Transam Steel. He thinks he can buy his way into respectability but he can't. Folk in these parts have long memories.'

Martha acknowledged that there was some truth in this. Aunt Shawna often hinted at Daddy's ruthless dealings in the past but never gave her details. The rift between Daddy and his sister was not one-sided.

'If I'm to win votes, I can't marry a Strayhorne.'

'You snake! How long have you known this?'

'Don't shout. Transam Steel will keep this town going for years to come. They will take down the Strayhorne name and your father will leave.'

'We are being run out of town?'

'I wouldn't put it quite like that.'

'No? Well you're a politician, I can see that now.'

'He's doing it for you, Martha.'

'Then it's a pity you didn't think to tell me of your plans!'

'I can't tell anyone until Strayhorne Steel no longer exists.'

'But you said you loved me!' Martha looked from him to the bed and back to his impassive face. 'And our night together? Was that all part of the deception?'

'I didn't want to – I didn't want to hurt you. I tried to stop myself.'

She was so angry with him she could have hit him.

'You knew that I loved you,' she cried, 'and you deceived me!'

'Keep your voice down.'

'Oh, we mustn't cause a scene while the New York big shots are here in case they renege on the deal!'

'The deal is done, Martha. I am part of it and so is my obligation to sever all connections with the name of Strayhorne. I'm sorry.'

He said it with such finality that she stood up. 'You are *sorry*?' I wish I'd never set eyes on you.'

He had the grace to look guilty and she hammered home her disgust. 'You were in the pocket of Transam Steel all the time, weren't you? You've been scheming against Daddy for your own political ends. Daddy and I were your pawns! My God, Michael, where is your integrity? Daddy made you what you are and you do this to him? He is ten times the man you will ever be.'

'He's an Iroquois and so are you,' Michael replied. 'Neither of you are part of my future.'

She hit him. She slapped his face so hard that her palm was stinging. Shock registered in his eyes but he took it calmly and said, 'I guess I deserve that.'

'Goodbye Michael,' she announced and walked out without a backward look. She felt so betrayed by him. His reluctance to speak to her father about their relationship, her father's angry refusal when he did, it all made sense now. Michael had been the turncoat here, using the sell-out of Strayhorne Steel to throw his hat into the political arena.

She groaned as she changed out of her riding clothes.

She had loved him; *had* loved him. How could she love a man who betrayed her so deliberately? She was worth more than that. If that was love then he could keep it. Love was part of her past now. Daddy was right. Money was all that mattered in the twentieth century. Martha closed the door behind her with a satisfying click. At that moment, New York seemed a much more attractive place to be.

'How do I look, Ingrid?'

'Oh Martha! Your father should be here to see you. I told Herbert not to whisk him away so early. Smith has done a magnificent job with your hair. A cream ostrich feather with pearls! Perfect.'

'I'm so excited!' She twirled around in her cream chiffon and satin dress with matching satin shoes. 'But will all the other girls be in white?'

'You don't have to worry. In that outfit, you'll knock 'em dead – the gentlemen, I mean.'

'Do you think so? I'm too old to pass as a debutante.'

'You're new in town and staying with me, that's what counts. I'm hosting this tea dance to introduce you to New York society. No one turns down an invite to the von Steins of Manhattan.'

Neither would Martha if she weren't already staying in their grand house. It was built in a classical style and glittered with gilt and crystal and electric light. But they had arrived at the end of the season and the weather was already getting too warm for the city.

'Will Daddy be back before we leave for the play?' Martha asked.

'He and Herbert will join us for supper afterwards. Come with me to greet my guests.'

Martha soon gave up trying to remember who everyone was. She had her dance partners' names written on her card. Many of the other girls were younger than she, but not the gentlemen, including several from the Athletic Club where Mr von Stein had taken Daddy. Mrs von Stein's guests from the club were out-of-towners who were staying at this exclusive haven for gentlemen. After one visit to the club's premises overlooking Central Park, Daddy had resolved to become a member and make it his New York home.

It was then that Martha realised just how serious her father was about finding her a husband. This visit to the von Steins, accounts for her in the best Fifth Avenue stores, and an interest in Ingrid's guest list were witness to this task. Now he had Ingrid on his side vetting her introductions, all he needed to do was approve of her choice.

Martha thought this was fun, but new to her and very confusing. Although she was enjoying New York, she missed her horses. And she was still angry that she had been taken in by a traitor! Michael had broken her heart but she had learned from the experience and prepared herself for any similar imposter who made it through Ingrid's barriers.

'Martha?'

'Oh, excuse me, Ingrid, what did you say? The band is so loud.'

Ingrid gave her a mildly disapproving look and whispered, 'Orchestra, my dear. Do concentrate, my dear,' then raised her voice. 'Miss Strayhorne, may I present Duke Fairleigh?'

A fair-haired young man with a fresh face and earnest expression kissed the back of her gloved hand in a most gallant manner. 'Delighted,' he murmured. 'I'm absolutely delighted, Miss Strayhorne. I do hope you have space on your dance card for me.'

She was so thrown off balance by the way he talked that she fumbled with her tasselled pencil. Where did he come from? Not Texas or California, she knew how they sounded. He was East coast, she decided. Boston. What was his name again? Duke something. He wants two dances. Two? She glanced at Ingrid who nodded approvingly. He seemed pleasant enough and she hoped he was a good dancer.

He was, and he led her firmly so that she felt confident. 'Is Mrs von Stein your aunt?' he asked.

'Her husband is a business associate of Daddy. They are both in—'

'Steel. Yes, I know.'

'Well, Daddy has retired now.'

'Yes I know that too,' he repeated.

'Have people been talking about him?'

'Only as it affects you,' he murmured.

'Oh no! What have they been saying?'

He smiled at her but didn't answer. She noticed his light blue eyes and they distracted her for a moment as he spun her round.

261

But if there was gossip about her or her father, she wanted to hear it. What was his name again? Duke something. 'Duke,' she began, 'May I call you Duke?'

He seemed to find this amusing so she carried on, 'Please answer me, what are people saying?'

'Only nice things, I promise you.'

The music finished and he took her hand to lead her back to Ingrid's table, thanking her and his hostess in a very gracious way.

'Charming manners,' Ingrid commented. 'Do you like him?'

'I hardly know him.'

'Oh well, you have another dance with him. He would be a good match for you. Your father would be pleased.'

Martha blinked. 'Why?'

'Why do you think, dear?'

Martha didn't know and was reluctant to admit it because she hadn't recognised his name when she tried to read it on her dance card. She could make out an F and an L but the rest was a squiggle. Was he very famous? Or perhaps he was very rich? When she saw him on the dance floor his partners were girls Martha knew to be heiresses, as she was. Perhaps Daddy wanted her settled quickly so that he could follow his racing pursuits? She wanted to please her daddy more than anything. He was all she had in the world. The next time she danced with Duke she was honest.

'What was your name again?' she asked. 'It was so noisy earlier, I didn't hear all of it.'

'Fairleigh. I'm Fairleigh.'

No, she hadn't heard of him. He smiled and went on, 'Duke is fine by me, especially when you say it.'

Unfortunately, she thought he was making fun of her Pittsburgh drawl and frowned. 'Where are you from?'

'England.'

'Oh, that's why I haven't heard of you. How long have you been over here?'

'I'm here for the season.'

Does that mean you'll go back in the fall?'

'Autumn. We call it autumn and yes, I don't want to miss the hunting at home. Have you ever visited England?'

''Fraid not. And this is my first trip to New York.'

'Do you like it here?'

'I miss my horses.' She hadn't realised how much until she said it. She missed the ranch and Joe and her early morning rides. She knew where she was on Daddy's ranch. City life was different and her mind wandered.

'. . . in Central Park.'

'Excuse me?' she apologised.

'I said you can ride there, if you've a mind to, in Central Park. I do.'

'It wouldn't be the same,' she reflected, dreaming of the river back home.

'Suit yourself.'

'Oh I – I mean, I mean, oh not you, I don't mean you.'

She gave up explaining as the music stopped and quickly realised his attentions had moved to Bette Winthrop, a seventeen-year-old New Englander. *So that's how New York society works*, she thought. Bette Winthrop is much more suitable for him, anyway. He was too small and thin for her. She liked a man who looked as though he could handle his end of a two-man saw if he had to.

She travelled to the play in Mr von Stein's chauffeured automobile chaperoned by Ingrid and escorted by a tall broad-shouldered young man from the Athletic Club. He was Mitchell Something-Something the Third but everyone called him Mitch. He was lively and attentive and knew lots of other people at the play. Martha liked him because he made her laugh and she looked forward to sitting next to him at supper, when they could have a proper conversation.

Ingrid had other ideas and deftly separated them in the hotel lobby.

'He was fun,' Martha complained.

'He's not for you,' Ingrid replied.

Martha was reminded of Daddy's words about Michael and wondered if she'd had a lucky escape. 'Why isn't he?' she asked.

'No money and nothing to make up for it.'

Martha disagreed. She had experienced a man's body with Michael and, at the time, it had been good so she had already fantasised about a wedding night with her escort, but she was wise enough to keep silent. Anyway, Ingrid meant his family name or land or a company like Daddy's. But, Martha decided, that needn't exclude other attributes she thought necessary for a good match. It was her life they were planning and she wanted it to be fun.

'Do not forget that you are an heiress and that makes you desirable,' Ingrid added.

Martha was beginning to get the drift of how she should behave and asked, 'Who should I speak to next?'

Martha was seated between Mr von Stein as host and another possible suitor who talked of nothing except of the number of square miles of Texas his pappy owned and how the railroad wasn't big enough to transport his cattle. He was handsome enough but he bored her and when she tried to talk about her horses he said that automobiles were the future. Martha guessed he was right because New York seemed full of them and this depressed her.

At the other end of the long table, Ingrid was in conversation with Daddy and they kept glancing in her direction. Later as they stood in the von Stein's spacious marble hall, handing coats and cloaks to the butler, she realised there was to be a post mortem on her progress.

'Bring Scotch for the gentlemen and brandy for me. Martha?'

'Bourbon, please.' She didn't care if it was a provincial taste. She liked bourbon and needed a proper drink. She followed Ingrid to her comfortable art nouveau drawing room and kicked off her shoes. 'That was some introduction, Ingrid. I can't begin to thank you. Did I do all right?'

'You could have done better. The Duke escorted Bette Winthrop and her mother to the play and they didn't join us for supper.'

'And you said he had charming manners,' Martha commented.

'Mrs Winthrop has snared him for her Bette. She'll

have him visit New England tomorrow and they'll be engaged before the fall.'

'He told me he's going back in the fall. Bette will have to go and live with him in England.'

'It might have been you, dear.'

Herbert von Stein drew on his cigar. 'Give the lady a chance, Ingrid. It's her first introduction.'

'What's so special about Duke Fairleigh, anyway?' Martha asked.

'The Duke *of* Fairleigh,' Ingrid corrected. 'He's kinda English royalty.'

'He ain't as rich though,' Herbert added.

Oh. Had she had danced with real English royalty without realising it? Martha took a swallow of her bourbon. No wonder Fairleigh had been amused by her. He must have thought she was stupid.

'I don't think he was interested in me, anyway,' she said.

'You are prettier than the Winthrop girl,'

'Not quite as rich, though, honey,' Herbert said.

Ingrid ignored his comment and went on, 'It looks like she will land the catch of the season now. Mrs Winthrop will be even more insufferable with a daughter married to an English Duke.'

'What will that make the daughter?' George Strayhorne asked.

'A duchess. The Duchess of Fairleigh if she marries him, which she will.'

Herbert made light of it. 'You've missed your chance there, George. You'd have no problem with getting into the Athletic Club if your daughter was Lady Fairleigh.'

'Is that so?' George commented.

'Herbert!' Ingrid said. 'This is not a joke.'

'Sure it's not, honey. It's darn well true.'

Martha maintained her silence. She had fallen at the first hurdle. What did it matter if her husband was thin and unattractive if she pleased her Daddy?'

'We'll find one for Martha,' Herbert said. 'What happened to that viscount, the one who wanted me to invest in his automobile works in England? Why don't I take George to dine with him at the Club?'

'He's not in New York right now. I sent an invite to his hotel and it was returned.'

'There'll be others.'

'Not this season, dearest one. We aren't getting as many over here as we used to.'

'Not enough destitute dukes to go round,' her husband responded.

'Herbert!'

'We all know why Fairleigh is here.'

'Yes and Bette Winthrop's unmarried cousins will be out visiting her in England next year if their mothers have any sense.'

Martha noticed her father had been frowning at this exchange until he brightened and said, 'Then I'll just have to get Martha over there before them. How do would you like to go to England?' Martha opened her mouth to protest but her father went on, 'I'd appreciate a chance to see their horseflesh.'

Herbert leaned forward. 'I'll give you some contacts for the races.'

Ingrid's eyes were wide. 'You just have to see London – and the Tower, where King Henry chopped off his wife's head.'

'Is that what they do in England?' Martha asked.

Ingrid ignored her question and said, 'Herbert and I went on honeymoon to Europe and have been over a few times since. The von Steins are from the Netherlands. Wasn't your mother European?'

'And two of her grandparents,' George added pointedly.

There was a short silence, giving Martha an opportunity to speak. After her initial resistance to travelling outside her home country, going to England sounded a more exciting diversion than a hot summer in New York. Didn't the English live in castles with walls covered in oil paintings, and go horseback riding in their deer parks?

She said, 'Yeah. My grandparents came over from Europe. I'd like to see where they were born.'

'Well, folks, that's decided. The *Lytham Star* leaves from Chelsea Pier, right here in Manhattan,' Herbert concluded. He leaned back in his chair, puffing on his cigar.

Chapter 20

'Mr Strayhorne, welcome aboard the *Lytham Star*.'

Through the open door, Martha recognised the clipped vowels of an Englishman speaking to Daddy in the neighbouring stateroom. She moved into the mahogany lined corridor and hovered outside to catch her father's eye. He didn't disappoint her.

'Ah, here is my daughter. Come in, honey, and meet the Captain of this fine ship.'

He was quite old, she thought, with a lined face and grey hair. But in his captain's uniform with gold braiding and brass buttons, he looked *very* handsome. He turned and bowed his head. 'I am delighted to meet you, Miss Strayhorne. I trust you will have a comfortable crossing. May I apologise again for not being able to place you in the suite your father requested. The Count and

Countess reserved it weeks ago. They are French. Do you speak French, Miss Strayhorne?'

Martha shook her head.

'Mr Strayhorne?'

'I can't even understand English the way you talk it, Cap'n.'

The Captain's eyes clouded as he frowned. 'As a rule, I should ask you to dine with me and the Count's family, but I fear the conversation will be in French.'

Martha watched her father's face set into a scowl and she moved to stand by his side. Herbert von Stein had assured them they would dine at the Captain's table. Ingrid had personally chosen Martha's wardrobe for the crossing and Smith had even come aboard with her to unpack her cabin trunk.

'So whatta you gonna do about it?' George replied.

'We have a viscount sailing with us, sir. In a normal state of affairs he and my First Officer would dine with me but as we have so many distinguished passengers on this trip, my First Officer will host another table for the Viscount.'

'Who is this viscount guy?'

Martha answered, 'He's an English aristocrat, Daddy. Ingrid gave me a book about it.'

'He's an English lord?' George demanded.

'He most certainly is, Mr Strayhorne. He is very interested in meeting you and would deem it a privilege if you would join him, sir.'

George's expression changed to one of satisfaction. 'I guess that settles it, then. Whaddaya say, Martha?'

Martha smiled and nodded. She wondered if this viscount knew the Duke of Fairleigh.

The Captain returned her smile and seemed relieved that they had agreed. 'Splendid! Would you do me the honour of taking cocktails in my private salon before dinner?'

George brightened. 'You gotta deal, Cap'n.'

The Captain left and George commented, 'They sure talk funny, these limeys.'

'Maybe when we've gotten used to it we'll speak the same.'

'Get this straight, Martha. Your ma's family left Europe for a better life. Your ma was an American and I am an American and I ain't changing that for nobody.'

Martha didn't argue and George went on, 'You concentrate on looking pretty, honey, and leave me to work on the invitations. I may have let that duke slip through my fingers but I'll make darn sure about this viscount. If he ain't married, you gotta head start on the Winthrops.'

Since staying with the von Steins in New York, Daddy had two ambitions. Martha would marry a title and he would get in the Athletic Club. The second of these would follow if Martha achieved the first and Martha was game. She didn't have to love the guy, did she? It was all about money. They wanted it and she had it. It seemed a perfect arrangement to her. She said, 'Let's go out on deck. Ingrid and Herbert are on the dockside to see us off.'

The decks were as crowded as the dockside and the noise was deafening. 'There they are, Daddy!' Martha waved enthusiastically as she spotted Ingrid and Herbert. They waved their handkerchiefs in response. Martha clutched at a handful of coloured streamers from a white suited crewman and released them over the side to tangle with a myriad others. A brass band played on the dock and automobile drivers sounded klaxons as the ship blasted its foghorn and the graceful white hull slipped away from the dockside. George picked up two glasses of champagne from a circulating waiter and handed one to her.

Martha's head spun and her stomach turned as the docks seemed to move before her eyes. Saliva collected in her mouth and she swallowed, gulping at her champagne. Her dizziness receded and she oriented herself to being afloat. She had gotten used to travelling on the railroad and in automobiles. The ocean was Martha Strayhorne's next frontier!

The water was flat calm as they sailed past the Statue of Liberty and for a second Martha had misgivings. Was this a crazy idea? She was going to a continent that her grandparents had risked this sea journey under canvas sail to escape. But that was in the last century before steam driven engines and these huge ocean liners. Why, they even had the telegraph now that ran through a cable underneath this vast ocean she was crossing. This was a new era for everyone and an exciting adventure for her.

When she thought of Michael, what was left of her heart hardened and she reckoned she had had a lucky escape. She and Daddy were together on this one. Daddy wouldn't let her down and she was darned sure she wouldn't disappoint him. Between them, they'd show

New York and Boston society what they were made of! She'd return as an English Lady and everyone would want to dine with Daddy then! After all, a lord didn't have to be rich, Daddy would see to all that side of things. She was young, attractive — Ingrid and Herbert had said so — and she was an heiress so how could she not succeed? If fat, plain Bette Winthrop could do it then so could she! Daddy would be so proud of her. And those Pennsylvania matrons could go whistle. She'd show 'em! She and her daddy were a team.

When she opened her stateroom door, her emptied cabin trunk and valises had disappeared and her only problem was deciding what to wear for the Captain's cocktail party where she would meet the Viscount. First impressions were important. The cream chiffon and satin with matching ostrich feathers in her hair, she thought. It was a classy outfit.

When she met him that evening she hesitated. He was older than she'd imagined and his hair was receding and going grey at the sides. But he was handsome, more handsome than Michael in spite of the lines around his eyes and mouth. This more than made up for his age. He was a real live viscount and that was enough for her. She kept him in her sights as they circulated then approached him to break into his conversation with the ship's First Officer. A waiter prevented her interruption and the Viscount picked up two champagne cocktails from the passing tray as she hovered behind him.

'Thank God I am not on the Captain's table for dinner,'

he said, handing one of the coups to his companion. 'That French Count and his family are insufferable.'

'They have the two largest suites on board, My Lord.'

'Who will be on my table then? I hope to God they aren't boring. Do they at least speak English?'

The First Officer tried to hide his dismay. 'I understand that you did agree to assist the Captain in his social duties in exchange for – er, financial benefit.'

'Keep that to yourself! That's between me and the line's director. He's a friend of my late wife's father so don't look so worried, fellow. I'll sing for my supper.'

Better and better, Martha thought. The Viscount is a widower in need of a certain financial help. She cleared her throat and the First Officer caught sight of her. He turned and offered her his untouched cocktail, saying, 'Ah, here is one of your dining companions, My Lord.'

Martha took the coup and raised it to the Viscount. 'I'm travelling with my father,' she said with her widest smile. 'He is George Strayhorne of Strayhorne Steel. You may have heard about his sell-out to Transam.'

The Viscount gave her a second glance. 'You're the Strayhorne girl?' She had been announced by the Master of Ceremonies when she had arrived at the party with Daddy but clearly the Viscount had not given them any attention at the time. So much for her cream chiffon, she thought. 'Please call me Martha, My Lord,' she said.

'Lord Melton,' he muttered, looking over her head. 'Where is your father?'

'He's by the palm trees talking to the Captain.'

Lord Melton placed his hand on her elbow, steered

her towards the bank of potted greenery and whispered in her ear. 'I want to talk to your father. Take the First Officer off with you to get a drink.'

He left her standing alone and walked over to the Captain. Martha tipped her cocktail down her throat and looked around for the First Officer. Fortunately he remembered his manners, which she thought were without fault and approached her with a smile.

'Your glass is empty, Miss Strayhorne,' he commented.

'So it is,' she said, handing it to him. He went off immediately to find her a refill.

This was no hardship, Martha thought as she followed him, noting that his height and shoulders reminded her of her escort to the play in New York. She asked him lots of questions about the *Lytham Star* and hooked her hand in his arm as they filed into the glittering first class dining salon for dinner. During their six courses, Lord Melton spoke a good deal to Daddy. In fact at one time their voices were so low and their heads so close together that Martha thought Daddy was already hatching a deal.

As the end of the meal she felt queasy and didn't know whether it was the ship's rolling or the French style cuisine on the *Lytham Star*. Daddy went off with Lord Melton in deep conversation and she hoped the First Officer would ask her if she wanted to stroll on the deck. However, one of her other dining companions insisted that he accompany his timid daughter to her cabin as she was in fear of becoming lost. So Martha was left on her own until Daddy joined her after saying goodnight to the Viscount.

'He is retiring early,' she remarked.

'He's off to the gaming tables. Do you want to go after him?'

'Do I have to, Daddy? I don't feel too good. I guess I'm not used to the ocean yet. What were you talking about through dinner?'

'He'd heard that I once made a bid to sell metals to Henry Ford for his automobile manufacturing.'

'I thought you lost that order to a rival.'

'I did, but I had the specifications.'

'Isn't that confidential information?'

'Sure it is, honey, in the United States. Viscount Melton is building an automobile in England. How about a bourbon to settle you for the night?'

Martha shook her head. 'No thanks, Daddy, and I'll breakfast in my stateroom tomorrow. Maybe I'll join you for lunch.'

'Do you want me to call the ship's doctor?'

'Wait until the morning. It may be the oysters that have disagreed with me.'

'You get some rest, honey. Leave the Viscount to me.'

Martha stayed in bed the following morning leaving her breakfast untouched. When George came to collect her for luncheon she felt better but was still in her dressing robe. She took one look at her pasty face in the mirror and said, 'I can't have the Viscount see me like this. Make my excuses, Daddy.'

'I'll send the ship's doctor to you.'

'It's only the ocean sickness. Remember when I first went on the railroad? It took me an age to get used to the motion.'

'And you hated your first ride in my automobile.'

She raised a weak smile. 'Gimme my horses any day.'

Alone in her stateroom, Martha pulled a face at her reflection. She needed Smith with her. She resolved to find her own Smith as soon as she reached England. Her nausea had been short lived but when the ship's doctor called he left her some pills in case it came back. He said they would make her sleepy and advised her to go out on deck in the fresh air instead. As soon as he had gone she called for the steward and arranged for a visit to the ship's beauty parlour and a maid to help her dress for dinner.

The maid was English and she had worked in a big country house in a place called Dorset. She chose a French designed maroon gown trimmed with cream lace, pinned her heavy black hair firmly in place and fixed a feather and ruby headdress that flattered her features. When Daddy came to collect her she was satisfied that she looked her best.

'You sure are a stunner, honey. I guess you're feeling better now.'

'I won't eat the oysters or the lobster tonight. How did you get on with Lord Melton?'

Her father's swarthy features assumed a poker-faced expression which told her that he was pleased with his progress so far and she knew better than to ask for more details. He held out his arm for her and said, 'You just be your charming self with him and remember Ingrid's advice.'

They were the first to arrive and chose the same places

at the dinner table as they had the night before. But when Lord Melton appeared he didn't sit next to Daddy; the steward drew out a chair for him next to Martha, where the First Officer had sat before. The First Officer took his seat next to the timid girl who was wearing exactly the same outfit as the previous evening. Martha was satisfied with the changes and when she glanced at Daddy he gave her an approving nod.

The general conversation was of the weather forecast to begin with as the Captain had warned of heavy rain and a possible storm. 'I hope it doesn't last,' Martha groaned.

Lord Melton laughed. 'There's no chance of that in the North Atlantic. I think of sailing on an ocean liner as riding my best hunter jumping my highest fence.'

'I'll try that,' Martha responded.

'Your father tells me you ride well.'

'At least as well as I can walk. Daddy breeds horses on his ranch.'

'So I hear. Do you ride to the hounds?'

'Can't say I do, but you bet your bottom dollar I can learn.' In fact, Martha was excited about the prospect of visiting an English country estate and riding horseback to chase a fox through the countryside. It'd certainly be a darn sight more interesting than taking tea with some frosty old matrons.

'My cousin is Master of the South Riding Hunt. He has one of the best chases in the county on his estate.'

'Is that what you call a hunt in England?'

'A chase?' He laughed again. 'A chase is a hunting

forest. All of 'em used to belong to the Crown. My cousin's ancestors had rights to Redfern Chase granted from the King three hundred years ago. Most disappeared in the last century, but Redfern kept part of theirs.'

'Is your cousin a duke?'

'An earl.'

'Right.' Ingrid must have told her that but she'd forgotten. 'An earl is like a duke, isn't he?'

He frowned and appeared to lose patience so Martha went on, 'I'm looking forward to riding horses again instead of these ocean waves.'

Apparently he didn't want to talk about horses either and he concentrated on his soup. They lapsed into silence until the lady on his left turned to him for the next course and Martha struck up a conversation with the gentleman on her right. He was an English banker and the father of the timid girl who was getting on very well with the First Officer. But he was more amenable to her questions than the Viscount, telling her all he knew about Yorkshire, where Lord Melton had his country seat. Country seat? That was his ranch she reckoned. Gee, it was a whole new language to her.

But some aspects were familiar. 'They have coal and steel in Yorkshire?' she commented. 'We have the same in Pennsylvania.'

'Redfern Abbey, in the South Riding, has coal but Melton Park where the Viscount lives is to the east and only has farms. Lord Melton uses some of his land for his motor car workshop.'

'Is that a factory, the same as Henry Ford's?'

'Good gracious no, Miss Strayhorne. Lord Melton builds each of his motor cars to order. The Melton Motor is set to rival the Silver Ghost.'

'There's an automobile called Silver Ghost?'

'It is so named because its engine is so quiet. I have one myself.'

'I see.' She pushed aside her untouched lobster and prepared her conversation about automobiles with Lord Melton for during the entrée. He was monosyllabic in his responses so she gave up and turned her attention to her fillet of beef, which was very good. She declined the remove course but enjoyed a delicious poire belle Hélène and watched the gentlemen relish cheese and celery to finish.

She had barely touched her wine and refused a bourbon, preferring some fresh air before retiring. She hoped, again, that Lord Melton would suggest a stroll on the covered deck. However, he excused himself after coffee and went off to the gaming tables so she took the cold sea air with Daddy.

'Well, honey, how did you fare with our Viscount?'

'We talked a little about horse riding but I think I bored him, even when I asked him about automobiles.'

'Leave him to me, honey. You can spend your days making friends with our other dining companions, especially that banker and his wife.'

This seemed a much better prospect for Martha, in spite of their mousey daughter. Nonetheless, she found it was hard to be sociable when she felt ill for most of the time. The mornings were the worst and she spent the middle of the day on the exposed deck, well wrapped against the biting winds but alone apart from a mug of hot soup.

With the help of the ship's beauty parlour and the maid from Dorset, she presented herself well at dinner and Viscount Melton continued to sit next to her. His conversation did not improve although he enquired about her well-being and echoed the advice of the ship's doctor. The banker's wife was fully occupied dissuading her daughter from her interest in the First Officer which anyone could see was a wasted effort.

They were in sight of land a whole day before the *Lytham Star* docked at Southampton. Martha's excitement at reaching England was quelled by her relief to be on dry land once again. She and Daddy took the boat train to London where they had reservations at the Admiral's Hotel near Bond Street and an invitation to dine with Lord Melton at the races.

Chapter 21

'Do you speak any French, Miss Kimber?' Miss Morris asked one morning.

'I know some of the language. I learned vocabulary at my training school. I used to practise with books in the nursery so that I could speak to the children in French.'

'You did?'

'Of course, the nanny in charge of the nursery encouraged it.'

'Perfect,' she answered, 'the *Lytham Star* has docked at Southampton. The Count of Monte Breton and his family are due in on the boat train. They have taken both royal suites and we shall need help with their children.'

'Surely the Count has his own governess for them?'

'They are wakeful at night and I need you on call. Tell your hostel you will be away for five nights.'

'Nights?'

'You'll have a room on the staff floor at the top of the hotel.'

That meant the attics. Phyllis was used to those. 'Very well, Miss Morris.'

The Count's family occupied a whole floor of Admiral's and every other room was taken so the hotel was working at full stretch and Miss Morris kept Phyllis very busy all day. The French children were lively and ill-disciplined and all the Admiral's staff breathed a sigh of relief when they were dressed to go out. However, they were usually over-excited by evening and therefore difficult to settle for the night. If they were tired and went to bed early they tended to wake in the night and if they were kept up on the evening, they were badly behaved and disrupted the whole of dinner. One governess was not enough for six children and anyway she was in a state of permanent exhaustion.

At the end of their first day in residence, Miss Morris burst into her office shutting the door firmly behind her. 'What can I do with those children, Miss Kimber?' She sounded quite desperate.

Phyllis thought of Nanny Byrne's methods and said, 'Must they eat with their parents in the restaurant? I should give them a children's tea in their suite, a calm evening of stories and reading and then early to bed.'

'Me too, but I guarantee the night porter will be called by guests on the floor beneath about disturbance to their sleep in the middle of the night. If we wake the governess she is cross and chastises them. She makes them worse, so what is the solution?'

'Warm milk with a little malt extract and stories. All children love stories.'

'Then you must be prepared to do that, Miss Kimber. The night porter will be instructed to call you.'

'But I haven't any storybooks in French!'

'Then you'd better go and find some.'

London is a wonderful city if you have means, Phyllis thought. She journeyed to Knightsbridge and found French translations of her favourite children's stories and retired to her attic bedroom, which she found disappointingly similar to her hostel room. For five weird nights when she was summoned, she rose and put her Admiral's skirt and jacket over her night clothes, and crept softly down to the royal suite in her carpet slippers. She allowed the siblings to squeeze into the largest bed where she read stories until her own eyelids drooped. The children were captivated by English tales they had not heard before and giggled at her pronunciation of their vowels.

The benefits were all Phyllis's. Her own sleep routine went haywire but she had experienced that before at Melton Hall and complaints from Admiral's other guests at night disappeared. The hotel gave a collective sigh when the Count and his family departed for Scotland.

Phyllis was in reception as they left. 'Well done, Miss Kimber,' Miss Morris said. 'You have secured yourself a permanent position on the staff of Admiral's.'

'Thank you, Miss Morris.'

She could barely contain her excitement. She had a position at the Admiral with a smart uniform and regular wage! She sat down at her desk with a smile on her face, staring at but not seeing the pile of papers she had to sort.

'Get on with your work, Miss Kimber.'

'Yes, Miss Morris.' She pulled herself together and gave her full attention to the backlog of dockets and invoices that Miss Morris had placed in her in-tray.

'Package for Miss Kimber.' The bell boy came in after a brief knock, left a small parcel on Miss Morris's desk and departed.

'Delivered here already?'

Phyllis got up from her own desk to collect it. 'It's from my mother. I wrote to tell her where I would be staying this week.' She returned to her work.

'You may open it if you wish.'

'May I? Oh, thank you. I know what it is.' She untied the knots and removed the brown wrapping paper carefully. She had asked Mother to send it because she was horrified by the cost of such things in the London shops. There was a note from her mother inside.

London sounds so exciting and I rest easy now that I know you are in the care of a friend of Mrs Simmonds. She is a good woman, but soon she will be very busy as Earl Redfern is travelling to his London home for a short visit before the grouse shooting gets underway. Do look after yourself and be sure to come home if you are at all unhappy. I have enclosed a jar of my nourishing cream. This is the lighter recipe that you prefer for your face. Remember to use it night and morning and to rub it in how I showed you.

All my love, as ever
Mother

Phyllis slid open the top of the small wooden box, then unclipped the metal spring holding down the glass lid of the small preserving jar. She inhaled the delicate aroma of rose petals, and slid her fingers over the top of the cream before transferring a little of it to her cheeks.

'Miss Kimber? Your accounts, if you please.'

'Beg pardon, Miss Morris.' She replaced the lid and put the jar in her desk drawer. 'I'll take it to my room when I go and pack my bag later.' Phyllis wasn't looking forward to going back to the cheerless hostel and its frugal supper that night.

'I can't have you moving out now.'

'Oh. I said I would be in for—'

'Send a message. Miss Strayhorne in the Victoria suite is travelling without a maid. These Americans like to do things their own way. Her father has approached an agency but experienced lady's maids are in short supply at this time of year. I need a member of the hotel staff just for her until he finds someone suitable.'

'Do you mean me?'

'Who else have I got with your experience? As soon as you have finished filing, present yourself at her suite and put yourself at her disposal. You will supervise her personal laundry, mending and purchasing, even help with dressing if she asks. Take one of the notebooks, write down everything you do for her and leave it on my desk at the end of the day.'

'Yes, Miss Morris.'

Miss Morris turned her attention to other matters.

The Strayhornes had arrived at the same time as the Count but Phyllis had seen very little of the American steel millionaire and his daughter. Once, when she had been returning from an errand she had seen them leaving in a chauffeur-driven motor car and later the doorman had told her who they were.

The Strayhornes were going out for the day and, Phyllis acknowledged, Miss Strayhorne was an attractive young woman, but she wasn't making the best of herself. Phyllis noticed she was wearing a wide brimmed hat that Miss Morris had given her the day before with instructions to repair damaged feathers. It had taken her all morning to find a milliner who was able to do the work immediately. Then he had sent her off to Bond Street to purchase the replacement trims. Miss Morris was pleased she had succeeded and it was a beautiful hat. But, Phyllis thought, Miss Strayhorne wore it at totally the wrong angle for her hair and features.

'He's after a husband for her,' the doorman said. 'It should be easy for him.'

Phyllis wasn't sure she agreed. Miss Strayhorne appeared to be languid and her skin was dull. 'Why's that?' she asked.

'She's an heiress.'

'That maybe so but she looks ill to me.'

'Apparently she had a bad crossing on the *Lytham Star* and spent most of the voyage in her cabin. Besides, not all ladies are blessed with your complexion, Miss.'

Phyllis gave him a surprised sideways glance and he grinned. 'Where are they going today?' she asked.

'A race meeting, I'm told. He wants a title for her and it is the sport for kings.'

'Oh.'

'The Americans like our titles.'

Phyllis recalled the behaviour of her former employer at Melton Hall and was unimpressed by this ambition. 'I hope he finds one for her,' she answered and thought no more about the Strayhornes until Miss Morris gave her this new task. Phyllis tidied her appearance and put on a fresh jacket from her cupboard in Miss Morris's office.

'Miss Strayhorne and her father usually have coffee together in their suite before they leave for the day,' Miss Morris said without looking up from her work.

'I'll take their tray and introduce myself.' She hurried through the back door and down the stone steps to the basement where cooks, waiters and maids were scurrying around like a swarm of underground ants.

'Coffee for the Victoria suite?' she called.

'In the still room,' someone replied.

'Thanks.' She went in search of it.

'I'll take the Strayhornes',' she suggested to the floor waiter who was putting the finishing touches to the linen and china on a large silver tray.

He turned and scowled at first, then relaxed. 'Oh, you're Miss Morris's assistant. Are you sure you can manage it?'

She tested the weight carefully and frowned.

'The coffee pot isn't on yet, or the cream jug. Go on up and I'll put the tray in the dumb waiter for you. Use the dinner trolley on the staff landing.'

Phyllis hurried towards the staff staircase and was

outside the Victoria suite within five minutes. She checked her appearance in one of the gilt framed mirrors hanging on the walls of the carpeted corridor and knocked on the door.

A male voice called, 'Who's there?'

'Your coffee, sir.'

The door was opened by Mr Strayhorne and Phyllis trundled her trolley into the suite drawing room. 'My name is Miss Kimber, sir, and I am at Miss Strayhorne's disposal for the remainder of her stay.'

'Oh yeah, Miss Morris told me she was sending a maid.' Miss Strayhorne stood in the door of her bedroom, dressed in a blue silk and organza gown with matching shoes. She still looked, as Phyllis's mother would say, 'peaky'. It must have been a really rough voyage. 'Whaddaya think, Daddy?' Miss Strayhorne asked.

Her father wore a newly pressed linen suit and Phyllis had noticed a cream felt gentleman's hat on the ormolu and gilt side table by the door. 'It's a mighty pretty colour,' he said. 'Where's the hat?' Miss Strayhorne went back into her bedroom.

'May I pour your coffee, sir?' Phyllis volunteered.

'I take mine black.' He added, 'What kinda maid are you?'

Phyllis decided he only needed to know how she could help his daughter and replied, 'A lady's maid, sir. I was employed by a titled family before I came to the Admiral.'

This answer seemed to please him and he took his cup and saucer to the window until Miss Strayhorne returned wearing her wide-brimmed hat trimmed lavishly with blue feathers and perched precariously on the back of her head.

'What is it with the hats and you, honey?'

'I don't know, Daddy. They look fine in the store, but I can't fix them the way they do.'

'Would you allow me, Miss Strayhorne?' Phyllis offered.

'Sure. Come on through.'

The bedroom, furnished lavishly in bird's eye maple furniture inlaid with jet and ormolu, was in chaos. Wardrobe doors and drawers stood open and clothes and hats were strewn across a crumpled silk counterpane.

'I can't decide. It's the hats that look wrong and I can't go to the races without a hat, can I?' Miss Strayhorne slumped on the corner of her bed. 'It was so much easier in New York with Ingrid to advise me.'

Although Miss Strayhorne had black hair, her skin was fair and positively pallid this morning. Phyllis placed a chair in front of the mirrored dressing table. 'Sit here, Miss Strayhorne. It isn't your hat, it's your hair. You have to get your hair right. It needs to be higher.'

'I've tried. It won't stay. I'll have to get that French hairdresser out again.'

'I can – er – fix your hair for you, Miss Strayhorne.'

'Oh can you? I'm too exhausted to bother and I don't want all those Lady Marys and Lady Mauds smirking at me from behind their parasols again.'

Phyllis unpinned Miss Strayhorne's hat and re-did her hair, placing the coils much higher on her head to provide a sound base for her hat. She concentrated on her task and secured the hat in front with a fashionable tilt forward to show off the feathers.

'Oh yes, I see how they do it now. Hey Daddy, come in here and look.'

Phyllis had already made a start on dealing with the room's chaotic state when Mr Strayhorne came through the open door with a cup of coffee for his daughter.

'Honey, you look as pretty as your ma. Will the hat stay there? We are lunching at the racecourse today.'

'With the banker from the *Lytham Star* again?'

'With another real live lord. He'll be watching the racing with us later.'

'I'd rather be riding than watching. I'm sure I'd feel better if I could have a good gallop somewhere.'

Phyllis thought this might bring some colour to her cheeks and said, 'Pardon my interruption, Miss Strayhorne, but you can ride in London if you wish.'

'Oh can I? Where?'

'On Rotten Row in Hyde Park, Miss Strayhorne.' Phyllis told her.

'Don't bother with that, Martha,' her father interrupted. 'If today goes to plan I'll get an invite to this lord's ranch and you'll have all the riding you can handle.'

'They don't call them ranches here do they, Smith? They call them country seats.'

'I'm Kimber, Miss Strayhorne. Yes, a lord will have a country seat. It is the mansion where he lives, and it will be surrounded by his estates.'

'How many estates will he have?'

'Estate is the word we use to describe his land. They

usually have hundreds of acres of parkland, hunting forests and farms, as well as villages where his estate workers live.'

'There you go, Martha. A lord will have his own parkland for you to ride in.'

'How do you know he's gonna ask us to stay, Daddy?'

'I said leave it to me, honey.' Mr Strayhorne handed his daughter her coffee.

'Is there one of those plain cookies out there? I think I could manage one now.'

Phyllis brought her the dainty china plate of biscuits.

Miss Strayhorne nibbled the edge of a small Bath Oliver. 'What was your name again? Kimble? Kimber? Can I call you Smith? I had a maid in New York called Smith.'

'Smith?'

'Yeah, you look like Smith in that outfit.'

'Well, if you wish to, Miss Strayhorne, of course you may.'

'Oh good.' She waved at the chaos in the room. 'Will you make some order of all this? Each store sends me so much after just one trip.'

'Certainly, Miss Strayhorne.' She extracted the matching parasol for her gown from the heaped paraphernalia on the bed, checked that it opened and closed smoothly and placed it by Miss Strayhorne's waiting gloves and wrap in the drawing room.

Mr Strayhorne picked up his hat and placed it firmly on his head. He spent a long time in front of the mirror tilting it this way and that until he was satisfied with the angle. 'I'll wait for you downstairs in the lobby, honey,' he called, and went out into the hotel corridor.

Phyllis returned to Miss Strayhorne's bedroom to find her peering in the dressing table mirror at the two spots of rouge she had placed on her cheekbones.

'I look like a stage actress. It's too much, isn't it?'

'It is, Miss Strayhorne, and it's the wrong colour for you.'

'The girl in the store said it was the one for dark haired ladies.'

'But your skin is fair.' Phyllis brought clean facecloths from the bathroom and selected one of the pots of cream that littered the glass-topped wooden surface. 'This will take it off. You are very pale, though. Are you quite well?'

'I was sick on the ocean crossing and I've looked like a ghost ever since. I'm afraid London doesn't suit me.'

'You need some country air. A day at the races will bring out your colour.'

'It won't.' She pushed aside several small bottles and pots. 'What shall I do? I'm here to find a husband and this lot gives me pimples. Take it to the trash.' She met Phyllis's eyes through the mirror. 'You have a nice complexion, what do you use? Get me some o' that while I'm out.'

'Oh, but I use—'

'I don't care,' Martha interrupted. 'I'll give it a try.' She stood up. 'I sure want Daddy to secure this invitation to the country, so I guess I have to play my part and smile.'

'You look very lovely, Miss Strayhorne,' Phyllis said and she meant it.

* * *

293

The hired chauffeur parked his automobile alongside another at the race course and helped Martha step down from the passenger seat. She removed the silk chiffon scarf that had held her hat in place during the journey and thought that next time she would bring Smith with her to make sure she looked her best on arrival. A gentleman in a black tailcoat approached her father, bowed in a deferential manner, introduced himself as His Lordship's butler and requested that they follow him. Martha took her father's arm and walked behind the butler to a luncheon marquee with an entrance guarded by two liveried footmen. Martha grinned at them as she swept into this open air dining room and noted that their faces remained impassive. Gee, would she ever get used to this formality?

A silver tray of champagne coups appeared before her. She took one and scooped it to her lips, picking a canapé from another passing waiter. She had watched others do this and copied them, but regretted her actions as she swallowed the caviar and it reached her queasy stomach. Saliva gathered in her mouth and she gulped at her champagne to quell her nausea.

'Oh look Daddy, there's Lord Melton from the *Lytham Star*.'

'I'll take you over to him.'

'You're wasting your time, Daddy. He isn't interested.'

'He is, honey. Trust me.' Her eyes widened and Daddy nodded. He was in a buoyant mood and Martha was pleased to see him so cheerful. She knew how much it meant to him for her to marry a title. He tugged on her arm, 'Come and say howdy to the Earl first. He's Lord Melton's cousin from York Shire.'

After she was presented to her host and his party, Martha tried to open a conversation with Lord Melton. He was polite and friendly, introduced her to his friends, a Marquess and his family, and then left her with the Marchioness and her daughter to join a group of gentlemen surrounding her father. The interior of the marquee was hot and humid, which added to Martha's discomfort. She guessed she'd never get used to this English climate.

'This way, Miss Strayhorne.' The butler loomed by her side and she followed him to one of the tables laid out with crested china and silver, relieved that she and Daddy were not lunching with Lord Melton. Instead they were seated at the Earl's table with his mother, the Dowager Countess. Daddy looked immensely pleased with himself and Martha noticed more than one set of raised eyebrows among the other ladies as the butler pulled out a gilded chair for her next to the Earl.

Earl Redfern seemed about the same age as his cousin but he had a more serious air about him. His mother was charming and Martha felt more comfortable in her presence. She guessed that being a viscount's wife was an important position and, heiress or not, she had to pass muster. But she was better prepared than she had been in New York.

A succession of footmen carrying silver tureens of asparagus soup appeared from behind a canvas screen, the butler poured wine into the empty glasses on the table and Martha relaxed. She picked up a silver soup spoon bearing an engraved crest and answered questions about her ocean trip. Daddy talked coal and steel to the Earl, who seemed genuinely interested in what he had to say.

When the Dover sole arrived the Earl turned to her. 'Lord Melton tells me that you live on a ranch at home and that you ride well, Miss Strayhorne.'

'He flatters me, sir, but I do enjoy horse-riding.'

'I have a stable of hunters in Yorkshire. Do you hunt?' he asked, picking up his fish knife and fork.

'Not yet,' she answered, 'I guess that's something I have to look forward to.'

'Fly fishing?'

She shook her head. 'But I can handle a gun, My Lord.'

'You can?'

'I sure can,' she added confidently.

'Excellent. You must come for the shooting. Melton always brings a party to my grouse moor for the start of the season.'

'Thank you, I'd enjoy that.' They lapsed into silence to eat the fish and Martha guessed that the purpose of their conversation had been accomplished.

The racing started after luncheon and, as she expected, Lord Melton did not seek her out. He was more interested in the betting odds on the racecourse. Martha wandered over to the paddock with her Daddy to watch the runners parade before placing her own bets. It was a warm sunny afternoon and the grass was firm underfoot.

'Whaddya think, honey?'

'My money's on the chestnut two-year-old, over there.'

'I'm not talking about the horses. You've made it honey. We go to this lodge place of the Earl's then on to Lord Melton's spread to see where he lives.'

'Is he really interested in marrying me?'

'He sure is. You've met his rich cousin and you'll have to see the daughters next. They have a nanny to take care of them. How does Lady Melton sound to you?'

'It sounds about right to me, Daddy.'

She smiled at him and he puffed proudly on his cigar. This meant so much to him that she could not refuse him. Not that she wanted to. It was the reason for this trip to Europe and Martha couldn't believe how lucky they had been to meet Lord Melton on the *Lytham Star*. He was a bit older than she'd imagined, but he was hand-some enough and she knew what he'd expect from her as his wife.

'If this trip to York Shire goes well, you'll be engaged before the fall.'

'Will I have to live over here all the time?'

'Don't you worry about a thing, honey. You can have anything you want.'

'What does he get out of the deal, Daddy?'

'He gets you, honey. He's a lucky man.'

Martha leaned over and kissed him. 'Thank you, Daddy.' The sun was hot on her back and making her feel ill. 'I think I'll go to the rest room. You won't stay late, will you?'

'I thought you liked the races?'

'I do, but the climate over here doesn't suit me. I feel tired all the time.'

'D'ya wanna go back to the Admiral right away?'

'We gotta shop for clothes for the shooting lodge.'

'Yeah, I guess we have a lot to do. This is your big chance, honey. Don't spoil it like you did in New York. It's a coupla hundred miles north so I'll hire an automobile and chauffeur, and I'll need a valet. Has that goddammed agency sent you a maid yet?'

'There was a French girl. She might do.'

'French?' Daddy shook his head. 'Have you forgotten that Count and his family?'

'Well, I'm gonna need to get one before we leave.'

'What about the maid who fixed your hat? She's made you look real pretty today.'

'Smith? She works for the Admiral.'

'So?'

'They won't want to let her go.'

'Everybody has their price. I'll make 'em an offer.'

Chapter 22

Miss Morris was not pleased with Miss Strayhorne's request.

'Her father approached the manager of the Admiral directly,' she said. 'I argued that I should not be able to replace you and he replied that Mr Strayhorne had offered him enough to pay for three of you if I would let you go immediately. I assured him you had expressed a wish not to go back into private service, but I am obliged to ask you.'

Phyllis thought of the opportunities she might have for travel with the Strayhornes, and then of Miss Strayhorne herself and how much she could improve on her appearance.

'Did he say how long she wants me to work for her?'

'Does that mean you are considering the position?

Dash it all, Miss Kimber, where is your loyalty to the Admiral?'

Phyllis stood in silence while Miss Morris glared at her and tried to make her feel guilty. Lord Melton had behaved in a similar way when she had refused his advances and she had kept her resolve then. This was a chance she had been waiting for! Working for Miss Strayhorne would be nothing like her task at Melton Hall.

She was thinking of the words to justify her decision when Miss Morris went on, 'What will you do if Miss Strayhorne returns to America without you? Do not imagine you will be welcome back here. The Admiral does not take kindly to employees who use our training to move on.'

'I am sorry you feel that way, Miss Morris. I am grateful for the opening you have given me, but this is an opportunity of a lifetime. I shall of course work the required notice.'

'Miss Strayhorne wants you immediately. How shall I replace you in such short time?'

'Have you considered one of the private agencies? If Mr Strayhorne is paying—'

Miss Morris let out an exasperated cry. 'I can see that you have made up you mind.' She waved her hand to dismiss Phyllis and continued, 'Go now. Mr Strayhorne wishes to discuss terms with you. He is departing for Yorkshire in a few days.'

Yorkshire! That was hardly the travel Phyllis had anticipated but she was none the less excited by the prospect of visiting Scotland, Europe and in spite of Miss Morris's comment, crossing the Atlantic. However, Miss Morris had not finished with her.

'I'll take your Admiral's jacket now, thank you. You may stay in your room for the next few days. Mr Strayhorne will take care of the account, but remember that you will no longer be a member of the Admiral's staff.' Miss Morris stood up, walked around her desk and held open her office door. 'Goodbye, Miss Kimber.'

Phyllis felt naked as she walked through the reception area in her high necked white blouse and ankle length black skirt. She imagined everyone was looking at her but in fact no one noticed as she made her way quickly to the carpeted front stairs and up to the Victoria suite.

She was unbelievably busy for the next few days accompanying Miss Strayhorne on shopping expeditions to Bond Street to buy her country clothes, and spending her evenings preparing and packing Miss Strayhorne's complete wardrobe for the trip. Mr Strayhorne was similarly occupied with his new valet until they had filled the Victoria suite drawing room with pieces of luggage. Phyllis labelled the portmanteaus Ferndale House, Ferndale Moor, Ferndale, North Yorkshire to go by train, leaving the smaller valises to travel with them strapped to the back of the motor car. She didn't know the Dales at all, but had a vague recollection of the name and racked her brain to remember. Had she heard of it at Melton Hall? She couldn't recollect a connection. More likely it had been mentioned at Lady Maude's where she learned about most of the country seats in England. She planned to ask her mother in her letter home, if she ever got the time to sit and write it! The next day, Mr Strayhorne's hired motor car and chauffeur arrived to begin their journey northwards.

Phyllis travelled in the front seat which was open to the weather and he gave her a pair of driving goggles to protect her eyes from the dirt. She tied a long scarf around her straw hat to stop it blowing away and glanced at the chauffeur. He was a young man who, dressed in his livery, reminded her painfully of Aaron. She wondered if Aaron had stayed at Melton Motor Works, and whether he had thought differently of her after Violet left. As the chauffeur negotiated the tangle of horses and motor cars through London, she fretted that Aaron thought ill of her. He would have heard of her position with Lady Melton and her tragic death. But it would be difficult to explain her sudden departure without breaking her promise of silence. She had no concern for Lord Melton's reputation but his children would not wish to have details of their mother's last night spread around.

'Have you been to Yorkshire before?' she called out to the chauffeur.

He frowned at her and squeezed his klaxon as he negotiated an intersection of roads and she realised that conversation was impossible. Her excitement of the journey was soon replaced by alarm as he dodged and weaved omnibuses and horse-drawn carts until they were clear of London streets and cruising through the countryside. It was a fine August day and the fields were turning golden with ripening wheat.

The motor car garage in London had planned their

itinerary with venues and approximate times for coffee, luncheon and tea before their overnight stop. The chauffeur had no time for pleasantries at the first stop as he checked over his vehicle and added fuel for the engine. And Miss Strayhorne insisted that Phyllis spend half an hour checking her travelling costume and re-doing her hair and hat before they set off again.

They stopped for luncheon in a small market town where the largest hotel had a grand restaurant frequented by local landowners. Mr Strayhorne was expected and met by the manager who conducted him and his daughter upstairs to a private suite. However, the chauffeur seemed to know the layout. He led Phyllis to the saloon bar where they were served hot game pudding and beer followed by cold stewed rhubarb and cream.

'You have been here before?' she enquired politely.

'I do this run on a reg'lar basis when the shooting starts, but mostly at the weekends. It's a new thing for Londoners, this weekend lark.'

'We shall be there longer than a weekend. I have sent on luggage for an extended stay.'

'Yeah. I'm collecting a Russian lot in York for the return trip.'

'London seems to be full of foreigners.'

'Weird, aren't they? You never know where you are with them. I'm surprised a nice girl like you has taken up with them, but I suppose some folk will do anything for money.'

Stung by this insult, she retaliated, 'Well, you must work for a lot of them in London.'

'The garage pays my wages. I go where they send me.'

'Where exactly is Ferndale?' she asked.

'North-west Yorkshire. Back of beyond if you ask me.'

Irritated by his attitude, Phyllis lapsed into silence and was pleased when he left her alone to join men of his own kind in the blue smoke of the back bar. She was surprised that someone so boorish did this kind of work and was shocked by his attitude. If a butler had heard such disrespect for his employer, the servant would have been severely reprimanded if not dismissed.

It was a caution for her. Formerly, as a nursemaid and lady's maid in a titled family she had automatically commanded respect from the servants of other households who visited and she was expecting the same now. Perhaps she ought to prepare herself for different treatment as lady's maid to a family from a country that lacked hundreds of years of aristocratic ancestry, no matter how wealthy they were.

The journey was interminably long and increasingly chilly. Even with the protection of a fold-up hood for the rear seats, Miss Strayhorne complained of draughts and the cold. The terrain became hilly and then mountainous as the light faded. They continued into the evening dusk stopping only for tea and cake at another inn until the motor swung in through a pair of open wrought iron gates hung on stone pillars topped with carved stone stags. Dry stone walling stretched for miles in each direction and a winding road followed moorland undulations to a distant and disappointingly small stone-built manor house. Phyllis was cold, hungry and stiff, and Miss

Strayhorne was fractious with boredom. Mr Strayhorne was unusually quiet and Phyllis guessed he wanted nothing more than a brandy, bath and bed. It was dark and Phyllis's heart sank. There was no sign of electric light burning in the windows and she was sure there'd be no hot water on tap. Shooting was a muddy business and she prayed that it would not rain.

Phyllis had some knowledge of Yorkshire's titled families from her childhood in the South Riding and had racked her brain to think who in North Yorkshire might own this lodge. After leaving Miss Strayhorne with her father into the capable hands of a butler at the front door, Phyllis motored with the chauffeur and luggage to the domestic offices at the rear. A busy housekeeper sent the chauffeur off to a stable block a hundred yards away where the visiting male servants were housed and looked after by their own cook housekeeper. The female servant slept in the attics as usual. Phyllis was shown around the kitchen, laundry and extremely small servants' hall by a housemaid in a dark green dress, who spoke with the familiar flat vowels of Yorkshire folk.

Phyllis glanced at the monogrammed china of the dining room waiting to be filled by the cook and let out a surprised gasp. 'That's Redfern china! But it can't be!'

'Why can't it?' the maid commented. 'This is Lord Redfern's shooting lodge. Didn't you know?'

'No.' Phyllis shook her head.

That was how she had heard of Ferndale. It must have been mentioned by father when he was alive. He couldn't have been here, though, as it was miles away from the South Riding. Phyllis considered telling the maid of her connection and decided against it. She was Strayhorne here and ought to get used to it. Visiting servants were always known by the name of their master or mistress when visiting grand houses. That way you knew who to call when they were needed.

The Earl had been instrumental in finding her the position at Melton Hall. She wondered what he would think of her present post. 'Is His Lordship in residence?' she asked.

'He's the host.'

Of course, she was aware that Earl Redfern had several thousand acres of moorland in the Dales, but she had not imagined in her wildest dreams that the Strayhornes knew him and wondered how they had secured this invitation. Then she recalled that the Earl, in common with many of his peers, harboured a liking for horse racing and guessed that this was the connection.

'Anything else?' the maid finished. 'Cook needs me.' She seemed anxious to get on with her work.

Phyllis unbuttoned her travelling coat. 'Where are the water jugs?'

'We keep them in the scullery next to the boiler. All the bedrooms have names and Miss Strayhorne is in Partridge.' The maid raised her eyes to a line of bells high on the kitchen wall. 'See up there. Partridge is fifth from the end. You have an hour before dinner is served and after that servants' supper is through here.' She waved her hand towards the small servants' hall. 'The men eat separately here so we've enough room.'

Phyllis glanced at the kitchen clock on the wall opposite the bells then hurried upstairs with hot water wondering how Miss Strayhorne was feeling after the journey. She had certainly looked miserable when they stopped for tea. Phyllis found her stretched out on the four poster bed still wearing her hat and coat and surrounded by portmanteaus and valises.

'Come along, Miss, dinner is in an hour.'

'I'm not hungry. I'm exhausted. How can sitting on my rear all day make me so tired?'

'I don't know, Miss Strayhorne. May I have your luggage keys?'

Miss Strayhorne lifted a languid arm. 'In my purse. You can look after them now.'

Phyllis hesitated, then opened the small handbag and found them easily among the handkerchief, lipstick, travelling powder compact and loose coins. As she laid out the dressing table and prepared an outfit for dinner she heard Miss Strayhorne sigh, 'I can't understand it. England makes me feel queer all the time. I haven't been the same since the ocean crossing.'

'You'll be fine, just as soon as you have some fresh Yorkshire air in your lungs.' But, as Phyllis said it she thought, she's too pale, there is something amiss with her and I think I know what it is.

'Get my riding things ready for tomorrow, Smith.'

'Of course, Miss Strayhorne.'

'The Earl promised me horse-riding.'

'Would that be Earl Redfern, Miss?'

'That's him. This is his lodge.'

'Did you meet him at the races?' Phyllis would never have dreamed of asking such a question at Melton Hall, but Miss Strayhorne didn't seem to mind at all.

'That's right,' she answered.

Phyllis finished her duties in Partridge and made her way down the back stairs to the servants' quarters for her own supper. The Lodge maids were a jolly crowd and there was a laxity about them that wouldn't be tolerated in a larger establishment. She found out quickly that none of the maids was visiting from Redfern Abbey because the Dowager Countess wasn't here with her son. Phyllis fitted in well, the food was good and plentiful and the butler was not mean with his ale. However, she was tired and no one had shown her the attics yet.

The maid she had met before answered her query. 'You're in with me, Strayhorne. I'm acting as lady's maid for those without their own so we'll keep the same hours.'

'My mistress wants to ride before breakfast tomorrow.'

'She'll be lucky. We don't keep horses here any more.'

'None at all? Miss Strayhorne will be disappointed. She's expecting horses.'

'Not here. The moors can be treacherous, what with the bogs and the weather. His Lordship has stables at Redfern Abbey but he uses motor cars for everything now. He's got shooting brakes to go out to his grouse moor.'

Phyllis wondered how Miss Strayhorne would react to this news and decided that bad news is best delivered straightaway. She stood up saying, 'I'll go and tell her now.'

'Sit down, Strayhorne. The ladies will retire at ten and

we take them hot chocolate so you can tell her then. Besides, I might need you to help me with the others. They're all foreign and you're the only lady's maid.'

'Who are the others?'

'We have four couples as well as your two and they're not the usual visitors. They're new money and not what I'm used to. The butler said they were money men. One of the ladies is from Germany. Her husband is, too. But the others are bankers and their wives who are living in London. I can tell you, I'll really have my work cut out.'

'Oh, I'll help you with them. I've worked at Admiral's in London and I'm used to different ways.' *The Strayhornes are new money too*, she realised and felt disloyal to them as soon as she'd thought it. But it was true and she wondered why Earl Redfern had invited them.

'No horses? But this guy is rich!' Martha slumped on the carved ottoman chest at the foot of the oak four poster bed in her nightclothes. This was the end. He'd told her he had hunters. 'I'm not spending the whole day with those frumpy women. One of them can't even speak English!'

'I believe you may accompany the gentlemen in the shooting brakes if you wish.'

'Smith, what would I do without you! I'll wear that tweed outfit. The store told me it was the colour of moorland heather.'

'I'll make sure it is pressed and ready for you, Miss Strayhorne.'

'Miss Strayhorne makes me sound like one of my old academy teachers. Can't you call me something else?'

'Have you any suggestions, Miss?'

'Martha, of course. It's my name.'

'I'm sure your father wouldn't allow that and Earl Redfern would be horrified if he heard your maid address you by your Christian name.'

'Why, what do their maids call the Earl's daughters?'

'He doesn't have any, but if he did they would be Lady Something.'

'Like Lady Martha, you mean. Father would be pleased with that.'

'I can't call you that because your father is not an earl or a duke.'

'Yeah, I get it. I only get to be a lady if my father has the title.'

'Or your husband, Miss.'

Martha gazed into the distance. 'Yeah, I know that too.' She caught a whiff of the cooling chocolate and her stomach turned. 'Can you take that away, Smith?'

'Don't you like it?'

'I used to. Since the ocean crossing, I've kinda gone off it. Get me a soda, like the ones I had at the Admiral.'

'I don't believe the butler keeps such things here, Miss Strayhorne. The gentlemen take plain soda water with their whiskey.'

'That'll do. And call me Miss Martha. That's allowed isn't it?'

Dinner had been interminable and not what Martha had expected. The bankers were boring and their wives

310

stuffy and strait-laced. Lord Melton's party was not due to arrive until tomorrow. That young earl was a nice guy and he explained that his horses were kept at his seat in the South Riding. He didn't invite her there, though, and she guessed she needed a ring on her finger first.

Thank goodness for Smith. Martha would have welcomed her as a friend. But she couldn't do that in England. It was crazy. Smith dressed and undressed her like a mother and attended to her bathing but she couldn't be her friend. Smith was the best. She seemed to sense her mood before she knew it herself and her rose petal skin cream was the best she had ever used. Her ma made it and sent it through the post. She wished she had a mother like that.

Smith brought her a supply of plain soda and checked that her bed was aired. When she woke the following morning, sure enough, her tweed shooting costume was pressed and ready. The prospect of a day out on the moors was enough for Martha to ignore her nausea when she rose early to breakfast with the gentlemen. The German frau was there before her, working her way through devilled kidneys, smoked bacon and fried eggs. Martha nibbled at some dry toast and shunned the coffee, opting for tea instead.

'Not eating much, honey,' Daddy observed.

'I'm still digesting dinner from last night. The open air will give me an appetite.'

'The Earl's gamekeeper is going to look after you and the German frau.'

'I don't need looking after, Daddy.'

'I know that but these folks don't.'

Chapter 23

The men were loud and jovial as they gathered in front of the house and climbed into automobiles laden with guns and people. They drove uphill for a few miles and then trekked by foot across the exposed moors to where the low rise peaks formed hidden dips and valleys. They split into pairs to take up their positions. An army of beaters was already in position and waiting for a signal from the gamekeeper.

Martha's German companion examined her allocated gun in great detail before commenting in her native language and striding off on her own. The gamekeeper watched her crossly and then shrugged. Martha checked over her own gun expertly and smiled at him. 'I reckon those two London gentlemen need you more than me. We don't want them shooting too early and taking all the easy birds.'

They would, though. Martha didn't mind too much. The air was crystal clear and as good as mountain air back home and she enjoyed the day, including the warming whiskey tot offered as servants unpacked the picnic food.

The dogs brought home their kill and the gamekeeper displayed them on a wooden rack.

'How was your gun, Daddy?' she asked as they trailed up to their bedrooms at the end of the day.

'Not bad. What about yours?'

'Well I hit a few birds so I guess it'll do for me.'

'Lord Melton is arriving with his party for dinner tomorrow.'

'He's gonna miss another day's shooting.'

'Honey, he'll announce your engagement at the banquet. The champagne is already on ice.'

'He will? You've done the deal, then?'

'I sure have.' Daddy leaned forward to kiss her again. 'Lady Melton.'

'Maybe His Lordship'll have more to say to me this time.'

'It's the way these English are with foreigners. They call it reserve. You kinda get used to it after a while. It don't mean nothing.'

'Well I'm gonna be too exhausted to fawn over him. I think I'll skip dinner tonight.'

'That's not like you, honey. Not coming down with something, are you?'

'I've been feeling odd since the ocean crossing.'

'Get some rest. I'll make your excuses.'

She gave Daddy a kiss and headed down the corridor to her bedroom. Smith had already built up the fire and set a tub in front of it. Another maid was helping her fill it with hot water from cans. She watched the steam rising as they poured it into her tub. Smith drew a screen around the hearth area and said, 'Your bath is ready for you, Miss.'

Martha stared at the ornate plaster ceiling. 'This earl is rich, isn't he, Smith?' she asked.

'He is, Miss Martha. Earl Redfern is one of the richest gentlemen in England.'

'Then why doesn't he have bathrooms in his houses?'

'Well he does have them in the larger bedrooms. But they aren't like the ones at the Admiral. We still have to carry water from the downstairs boilers. Which outfit shall I put out for tonight, Miss?'

'I ain't going down to dinner. I can't face any more roast venison or jugged hare.'

'I'll arrange for a tray, Miss. Would you eat a little cold pheasant, perhaps?'

Martha felt her nausea rise again and saliva ran into her mouth. 'Don't they eat chicken up here?'

'Cook has guinea fowl, Miss. It is very similar.'

'Sure. I won't eat much of it anyway. What's wrong with me?'

'Don't you know, Miss Martha?'

'I reckon I'm just plain homesick.'

Smith didn't reply.

'Do you reckon I'm homesick?'

'More like you're love sick, Miss.'

'Love sick?' Martha sat down on the ottoman with a

jolt and pressed the heels of her hands to her eyes as realisation dawned. It wasn't the travelling that had upset her system. It was Michael. She was going to have a baby, his baby.

'Jumping jack-asses, I can't be pregnant!'

'You are, Miss. I've seen it two or three times in others and I'd stake my life on it.'

'Daddy's gonna kill me when he finds out!' Panic overtook her as she saw her daddy's carefully laid plan crumbling away. No lord, destitute or not, would marry her with someone else's baby inside her. In fact, no one would marry her at all now. 'What'll I do?' She wailed. 'I've said I'll marry him.'

'Marry who, Miss?'

'Coming here is a kinda trial for me. I guess I'm gonna fall at the first fence.' Martha thought of how disappointed Daddy would be. 'I can't! I just can't.' She noticed her hands shaking and put them behind her back.

'You should try to stay calm, Miss. Shall I get you a drink?'

'You gotta help me, Smith. What'll I tell Daddy?'

'Has Earl Redfern actually offered you marriage?'

'Not him. Daddy wants me to marry his cousin. He's arriving tomorrow to announce our engagement.'

She heard Smith gasp and say, 'That wouldn't be Lord Melton, would it, Miss?'

'That's him. He was on the *Lytham Star* when we came over.'

Smith seemed as shaken as she was and mumbled, 'May I sit down for a moment?'

'Hey, don't look so shocked. I know he's a widower and broke. Daddy said he'd fix it. I'll be a proper Lady, with a title. It's – it's all he wants from this trip.' *It's all he wants from me*, she thought, and felt tears filling her eyes. She was going to cry! She couldn't stop herself. A baby will spoil everything!

'I can't let Daddy down,' she choked.

Smith brought her a glass of water and said, 'Try not to get upset, Miss.'

'I can't help it. This will ruin Daddy's plans.'

'Crying won't do any good now, Miss.'

'But I can't have this baby. I just can't.'

'You really don't have any choice, Miss. And you ought to tell your father.'

'You don't understand,' Martha cried. 'I can't tell him. It'll kill him. I have to marry this lord. I just have to.'

'I assume that if you didn't know about your baby, then His Lordship doesn't, Miss. He might be pleased.'

She swallowed her tears. 'You have to be kidding me?'

'I – I understand Lord M—' Smith stopped mid-sentence as though she'd changed her mind, then added, 'Your bath is cooling, Miss.'

'Forget the bath. What were you gonna say?'

'I believe Lord Melton is anxious for a son to inherit his title. He has four daughters, you see.'

Gee, Smith thought the baby was Lord Melton's. If she had a boy he could be the next Lord Melton. She liked the sound of that, and so would Daddy. But the baby wasn't Lord Melton's. If she could have interested him in her on the ship, she might've been able to pass off the baby as his, but it was too late now – unless – unless . . .

Her mind was in chaos. The only way was to deceive him – and Daddy too. Lord Melton was a pig anyway and she didn't care about him. But deceiving Daddy? Her shoulders sagged. Truth or lies, this would break his heart. She said, 'I gotta think. Get me a bourbon.'

'Very well, Miss.'

As Smith opened the door to go downstairs, Martha added, 'Don't breathe a word about this to anyone.'

'Of course I shan't, Miss Martha. I shouldn't dream of it.'

Phyllis was in two minds about Miss Martha and Lord Melton's imminent engagement. On the one hand she wanted to plead with Miss Martha not to have anything to do with Lord Melton. She wouldn't wish Lord Melton as a husband on anybody. But how could she explain why without breaking the promise she had made for the sake of his children? She didn't want to go back to Melton Hall either, except – except that Aaron would be there if he was still working at Melton Halt.

Her mind filled with a fantasy of meeting Aaron again and showing him the fashionable young woman she was now. She could defend her former behaviour so easily. He knew what kind of man Lord Melton was. She sighed. That hadn't made a difference to Aaron's opinion of her before because he had made no attempt to contact her. She wouldn't get the chance anyway because she knew too much. As soon as Lord Melton found out about her he would insist that she resign as Miss Martha's lady's maid.

On the other hand, if Miss Martha was pregnant by His Lordship and he was prepared to marry her, she would not suffer the same fate as poor Violet. And Miss Martha might have a boy, which would surely please everyone. They would have to marry quickly, and say the child was premature when he was born. Everyone would accept it and no one would believe them but that would not matter if it was a boy. Phyllis hid her inner turmoil well. Her duty at present was to support Miss Martha in whatever direction she chose.

Later that evening when she took up warm milk on a tray, she commented, 'I'm sure your father will understand your condition, Miss. It is so romantic to fall in love on board ship.'

Miss Martha almost bit off her head. 'That's just it. He didn't show any interest in me at all. I'm only marrying him for his title.'

'But he must have found you attractive, Miss. I mean, you are carrying his child.'

'No, I'm not. It's not his.'

'Oh.' Fearful of dropping the tray, Phyllis laid it carefully on a table. 'You are in love with another gentleman?'

'I was. Back home in Pittsburgh. He let me down, though, and Daddy too, so Daddy took me away to New York. But it was too late.' Miss Martha passed her hands over her stomach.

Phyllis tried not to show her surprise and dismay. 'Then it must have happened several weeks ago, Miss.'

'I was so angry with him. He put his career before me and I could not forgive him for that. It never occurred to me I would be pregnant. We only did it once.' Martha gazed across the darkened room. 'I thought it was the most wonderful night of my life. Daddy will be furious if he finds out. He's all I've got and I love him. It'll kill him and I can't do that to him. Help me, Smith. You always have an answer. What do other girls do in my situation?'

Phyllis was unable to respond. What could she say? She inhaled heavily. 'I don't have much experience myself in these matters, Miss. But I do know that if marriage isn't an option it – it's very hard on the girl. Although it is not so bad if you have means.'

Miss Martha laughed. 'I got enough dough. I only have to ask my daddy and . . .' She turned her head sharply to face Phyllis. 'Are you suggesting I have a doctor to take care of it?'

'Good heavens, no!'

'You hear so many stories about girls being butchered and even dying. Anyway, I couldn't do that to my baby.'

Phyllis was relieved to hear it. But she knew of only one other option in these circumstances. 'It must happen in America too, but over here a young girl can go abroad for a while to travel or learn a language and the baby when it's born is adopted so that she returns with her reputation intact.'

'You're saying I'd have to give him up.'

'The baby would be adopted by a very worthy couple who will bring up the child as their own.'

319

Phyllis saw the hurt look on her face and tried to moderate her pain. 'Would you want a reminder of the man who had turned his back on you?'

This only made things worse and tears welled in Martha's eyes. 'I thought I loved him at the time.'

The distress on her face rang alarm bells for Phyllis. She had seen similar anguish in the late Lady Melton. 'Don't you love Lord Melton at all?' she asked gently.

'No. But Ingrid said love doesn't matter when you make a good marriage. Love comes later.'

Not with Lord Melton, Phyllis thought, remembering the late Lady Melton. Lord Melton was an incurable philanderer. He had married Clara Ashby for her father's wealth and he was about to repeat the same behaviour with Martha. His Lordship escaped scandal by dismissing his problems as poor unfortunate Violet had found out to her cost. Only a few servants were aware of the truth and they knew their positions depended on keeping silent. It did not seem fair to Phyllis and she considered that if Lord Melton could hide an illegitimate child then so might his future wife. Phyllis pondered on the poetic justice of the situation and determined to help her mistress and friend. She did not know how but one thing was certain. If Miss Martha's reputation was to be saved, then this baby must be kept a secret.

She turned down the lamps. 'Drink your milk and sleep on it, Miss.'

'These girls you talk about, where do they go?'

'France or Ireland are the nearest. Ireland is best because they have convents that arrange everything for you.'

'Thanks, Smith. Goodnight.'

'Goodnight, Miss.'

The betrothal was announced as expected at dinner the following night and the party celebrated with a whole case of champagne.

'I've never seen Daddy so happy. That makes me happy, too.'

Phyllis unpinned Miss Martha's hair and began to brush it. 'I'm sure Lord Melton is very pleased as well,' she commented.

'He barely spoke to me. He kissed my hand and then talked to my father about motor cars. At dinner, I was placed between two boring young men who later took turns to dance with me. But he has made his promise. Look.' Miss Martha held out her left hand. Phyllis had already noticed the size of the diamond sparkling on her finger.

'Did he set a date for the wedding?'

'Daddy was on my side. I told him I wanted to be married in the summer and he asked Lord Melton. As long as our engagement was announced, they both agreed to my plan.'

'You have made a plan already?'

'Daddy is very generous with my allowance. I shall see a little of Europe first and winter in the sun for my health.'

'Will he let you travel alone?'

'We-e-ll, Lord Melton wanted me to take his aunt but she's an old lady and I was dead against her, of course. This is the twentieth century and I have you.'

Phyllis remembered that His Lordship didn't know who she was. He hadn't brought any female servants from Melton Hall and his valet was housed in the stables. She was Smith: *no one* knew who she was.

Miss Martha went on, 'I persuaded him that as long as you are with me and we stay in the best hotels I shall be quite safe. Our experiences at the Admiral convinced Daddy and he agreed with me. We – you and I – will travel first to Paris for my wedding gown and trousseau.'

'Trousseau? Surely that is out of the question? You cannot hide a growing baby from a couturier!'

Martha sank to a chair. 'I know. You'll have to help me here. I can't have anyone find out, I'd rather die.'

Phyllis felt in involuntary shiver down her spine. 'Please don't say things like that, not even in jest.'

'I'm not joking, Smith. I couldn't live with Daddy's disappointment. Since Mommy passed on, he has done everything for me, for my future.' In the mirror, Miss Martha's eyes were wide with fear. 'Tell me what I should do, Smith?'

'You really are going to marry Lord Melton knowing that he does not love you?'

'I don't love him either, so there is no loss. He wants my father's money and I want his title. We understand each other.'

'And you will have your baby in France?'

'You said Ireland was the best. You must help me, Smith. You will, won't you?'

Phyllis stared at her in the glass. 'You are sure about giving up your baby?'

'I haven't got a choice, have I? Find me somewhere.'

Phyllis saw that Miss Martha meant what she said. 'I have contacts in London from Lady Maude's. I'll write to them immediately. I believe we can get to Ireland from Brittany in France.'

'And afterwards, I shall return to France for my wedding gown.'

'I can get a mannequin made up to your original measurements to leave with the Paris couturier. I shall need good photographs of you as well. Any alterations can be done after the birth.'

'You're a marvel, Smith. I don't know what I'd do without you.'

Although Phyllis did not approve wholeheartedly of Miss Martha's plan, she went along with it as much of it was her own doing. She believed it was a mistake for Miss Martha not to tell Mr Strayhorne. As father and daughter, they were very close. Surely if he knew about the baby he would wish to keep his own grandchild? Yet Miss Martha was unwilling to give him that chance.

However, Phyllis considered that there was a certain poetic justice in the way Miss Martha intended to deceive Lord Melton. She was turning the tables on him! In fact, the more she considered their plan, the more she thought that Lord Melton deserved it. Phyllis was determined to make sure the plan worked.

Chapter 24

They had motored from Paris to Brittany. The sea journey to the south-west coast of Ireland had been short and uneventful, but they were unable to hire a motor car to take them to Doolin on the west coast of Ireland so the latter part of their journey was slow and uncomfortable in a horse-drawn carriage. Phyllis contemplated how quickly she had become used to the motor car since working for Miss Martha.

They travelled north, hugging the coastline and seascapes of salty breezes and wild untamed waves. They were set down some distance from inn or town before the road began to climb. A horse and open cart was waiting and Phyllis tucked in woollen blankets around Miss Martha as the driver loaded their luggage. It was cold and dark and windy. Phyllis listened to the sea crashing against rocks as they trundled on.

The horse and cart turned off the track into a clearing dominated by a small stone-built house. Phyllis noted with relief that there was a light in the window. A moon appeared as they passed a large wooden barn raised on stones. The driver stopped outside the unpainted wooden front door.

'Wake up. Miss Martha. We're here.'

The driver unloaded their valises, boxes and supplies. The front door opened and a woman carrying a lantern emerged on the steps. She said a few words in what Phyllis took to be Gaelic, disappeared and re-emerged wrapped in a thick coat and boots to leave with the driver.

'You will come back tomorrow?' Phyllis asked hopefully, and was met with a blank stare.

Miss Martha staggered up the wooden steps holding onto the handrail. By their reckoning she had two months to go, and then what? When the cart had rattled away with their housekeeper, Phyllis realised that they were totally alone in this windswept landscape.

'There's a fire in here,' Phyllis called from the sitting room at the front of the house. It had whitewashed plastered walls and a wooden floor covered with rag rugs. 'Think of it as your beach house.'

Martha stood in the small room. 'This is some place to spend my Christmas.' She lowered herself into an armchair by the crackling logs; her swollen stomach pushed though the front of her coat. 'Do you think anyone will find us?' she asked.

'I doubt it. I wrote to the convent as Miss Kimber, telling them I shall be travelling with my maid Smith. Your father thinks you are in the South of France and by the time he realises that you've changed your plans, it will be over and we shall be back in Brittany.'

'It will be over? Say what you mean, Smith. I shall have had my baby.' Tears shone in Martha's eyes. 'I don't think I can go on much longer.'

Phyllis sympathised but they had been through the alternatives time and time again. Martha was adamant that her father must not know about her child and that she would go through with her marriage to Lord Melton in the summer. 'You'll feel better after some tea.'

'You English and your blessed tea!' Martha closed her eyes and Phyllis went out quietly.

The kitchen was larger than the sitting room and similar to her mother's at home. Phyllis set to work noting with relief that the cooking range was hot and the larder as well stocked as promised. She wondered briefly how many other ladies of means had come here to have their unwanted babies, and decided not to dwell on it. A nearby convent would send a midwife when necessary and Miss Martha's child would be taken from her and placed with a wealthy childless couple to bring up as their own. But as Martha's time drew near even Phyllis dreaded the wrench of separation so she could not bear to imagine how Miss Martha must feel.

Phyllis had been calling her Miss Kimber for several weeks now so she was used to it. It was important for her to respond naturally to the nuns when they addressed her. She had become used to Smith quickly enough and Miss Martha was determined to go through with her plan. In spite of her earlier sickness, Miss Martha was a strong young woman with a sound constitution so, although the birth was long and painful, she survived it well and took to her baby girl immediately. The midwife nun did not take the child from her as Phyllis expected. It was February but the cottage was warm and although the housekeeper did not speak English she had turned out to be reliable.

'I'll feed her for a few days,' Miss Martha stated when the midwife left. 'The nuns won't argue. I'm paying well to call the shots here and the dough is all they care about. They know I can't keep her.'

But Phyllis thought it was a mistake to feed her and suggested using a patent baby formula. Even Nanny Byrne had approved of feeding bottles.

Phyllis loved the wildness and the beauty of this part of Ireland and when Miss Martha had felt well enough, they had enjoyed walking in the fresh air together. They were not far from the majestic Cliffs of Moher and even though Miss Martha had found the climb too difficult before the birth, she had marvelled at their rugged beauty. Phyllis considered this a good sign but Miss Martha was unusually quiet after the birth and seemed uninterested in them. Phyllis remembered the late Lady Melton's lethargy especially after her fourth child was born and became increasingly worried.

Despite Phyllis's constant reminder, Miss Martha would

not fix a day to hand over her child. Two weeks after the child was born, Miss Martha was calling her baby Shawna May and alarm bells began to ring in Phyllis's head. She immediately arranged for a convent sister to call and take away the infant. Miss Martha seemed to agree; at least she did not argue. On the appointed day Phyllis took in Miss Martha's early morning tea and found her bed and the baby's cot empty. Neither were they anywhere in the cottage or its surrounds.

Panic seized Phyllis's breast. She grabbed her hat and coat and dashed outside. There was a cold wind blowing in from the Atlantic and she could hear waves crashing on the rocks at the foot of the cliffs. She ran towards the cliff track and spotted Miss Martha climbing the path with the baby in her arms. She raced after her but Miss Martha was at the top before she reached her. Phyllis's breath was coming in rasps but she could hear the baby crying.

'Miss Martha!' she called. 'Where – where are you going?'

'Stay away from me, Smith!' Miss Martha shouted. 'I know you mean well but I can't do it! You don't know what it's like. I can't give up my child. She is my flesh and blood and I love her!'

'But – but you have to! You must think about your future.'

'Don't you understand? I have no future!'

'I'm sure your father won't see it that way.'

'I have only disappointment and disgrace to offer my father. I'd rather die.'

She stepped off the path and walked towards the cliff

edge. She was looking out to sea. Her hair was awry and the baby's wrappings were flicking about in the wind.

Phyllis stifled a scream. 'Miss Martha, don't! Come back with me and talk about it. You're making Shawna May cry. She is cold and hungry. Let me take her.'

'You're not having her. She's mine and she's coming with me.'

'No! I won't let you do this.'

'You cannot stop me, unless you wish to die yourself.'

Oh dear Lord, no. Anger took over from panic and Phyllis shouted again, 'I won't let you do this!'

Her outburst must have surprised Miss Martha because she turned. Phyllis ran towards her and took hold of her clothes, dragging her away from danger.

'You can keep her! I'll say she's mine!' she choked. She tugged at the distressed bundle in Miss Martha's arms and tried to wrench the baby free. But Miss Martha would not let her go. Phyllis saw the hopeless despair in Miss Martha's eyes and said, more quietly, 'We'll take her back to England and I'll say she is my child.'

Miss Martha stopped struggling and stared. Phyllis stopped her tugging as it dawned on her that she had a solution. She felt a shiver travel down her spine and realised that it was the answer.

Miss Martha whispered, 'Will you? Will you do that for me?'

The two women stared at each other and Phyllis replied softly, 'Of course, I will. I don't know why I didn't think of it before.'

Phyllis saw the light return to her eyes but her own knees were beginning to buckle. 'Let's go back to the cottage,' she said. 'I won't let the nuns take her, I promise. Shawna May is innocent. No one need ever know the truth.'

Martha's eyes were full of tears. She seemed to summon all her strength and lifted the child towards Phyllis's waiting arms. 'You are the only person I should ever trust with her. Take her, Smith. She owes her life to you.'

Phyllis cradled the tiny child in the crook of one arm and reached out for Miss Martha's hand with the other. Miss Martha gripped her fingers and did not let them go until they were in the warmth of the cottage. Then she said, 'You won't ever leave me, will you Smith?'

'No, Miss Martha.'

Phyllis meant it but as she spoke the words she realised that she had no idea of how. What had she offered in the heat of the moment when she feared for the life of both mother and child? But the image of the late Lady Melton's limp and lifeless body, slumped in her luxurious bed, was imprinted on her mind for ever. She dare not risk history repeating itself.

Yet how could she care for a child and remain as Miss Martha's maid? She did not know and she could not go back on her word. Miss Martha's mind was fragile and understandably so. Phyllis could not have given up her own child so why should she have expected it of Miss Martha? But she had not stopped to consider the practicalities of her idea. The convent will get its money and another baby found for the prospective parents. But when they returned to England, what then?

'How are we going to do this, Smith?' Miss Martha was feeding her baby by the fire in the sitting room.

'I don't know yet. But you will have to give up breast-feeding. As soon as you feel strong enough, we'll leave for Cork and begin our journey back to Paris.'

'Make the arrangements right away. Do you think it will work? I've not heard of a lady's maid with a child before.'

'Me neither.'

'I'll hire a nursemaid for her.'

'I haven't heard of a servant who could afford her own nursery maid.'

'I shall say that I did not want you to give up your duties so I have paid for her.'

'Or you could hire a new lady's maid and I'll look after Shawna May.'

'My idea is better. We'll find a girl in Cork who will come with us to England. She has to believe from the beginning that Shawna May is yours. When can we leave?'

'As soon as we have a nursemaid and I can book the passages.'

'I gotta get back to France as soon as possible before Daddy gets suspicious.'

'I'll go into Doolin tomorrow and telegraph the shipping office. Everything takes so long in Ireland so why don't you write again to your father on the Paris note-paper. I'll send the letter in a packet to the concierge to post on to England. That way your father will believe you are in Paris already.'

'I hope this will be the last time I have to deceive him. I gotta collect my wedding gown and trousseau in Paris.'

'That is another reason to wean Shawna May onto bottles. You must allow your breasts to go down before your final fitting.'

'Do I have to?' Miss Martha whined.

'Yes! You will have to get used to being away from her! You cannot have her with you all the time.'

Miss Martha gazed at her sleeping infant. 'Maybe I can buy a French Layette for her while we are in Paris.'

'I don't think that's wise. She is supposed to be the daughter of a lady's maid.'

'I can get her a gift, can't I?'

'Of course, Miss Martha, as long as it isn't too luxurious.'

The two women stared at each other in silence until Miss Martha said, 'It's not gonna work, is it?'

'I don't know.'

When Phyllis came back from Doolin she felt more confident about their return to England. She brought letters forwarded by the concierge in their Paris hotel and had an address for a convent nearer to Cork where she would find a respectable girl who had given up her own illegitimate child.

'We'll have to find a foster home for Shawna May and her nursemaid until after your marriage,' Phyllis explained.

'A foster home?'

'My mother does it through the church at home. She

looks after children when their own mothers are poorly or in difficulty.'

'Your mother lives in Yorkshire. I could go and see her.'

'Oh, I wasn't suggesting my mother.'

'I was. Shawna May is supposed to be yours. I can take my personal maid to see her child, can't I?'

'You'll arouse suspicion. Besides, after your marriage you'll be away for your honeymoon so you'll have to get used to not seeing her.'

Martha sighed and sank down to her chair. 'This isn't going to be easy.'

Phyllis didn't respond. She didn't exactly regret making the offer. At the time it had been the best solution to bring Martha back to safety. After a while she said, 'You know, your father loves you very much. If you told him the truth I don't think he would disown you.'

'No, it would be worse. It would kill him, and if it didn't, the disappointment and hurt would be etched on his face every day he looked at me. I couldn't live with that. I must marry Lord Melton. I have made my promise.'

'Well, if your mind is set on it . . .'

'It is. The concierge has sent on another of Daddy's letters. He went shooting with a royal duke! Then they had dinner and played cards into the night. Imagine! My father has dined with an English duke of royal blood. A duke is the highest title in the land after the King, isn't it? That will be something for him to talk about at the Athletic Club.'

'Will he return to New York?'

'We shall all go there after my marriage. I've asked Melton if we can take a late honeymoon on an ocean liner. There's a new one to be launched next year and Daddy wants to be on its maiden voyage.'

'But you will be away from Shawna May for weeks!'

'I'm not leaving her behind,' she stated.

'Oh.' This meant Phyllis and the nursemaid would be going to New York as well. She tried not to worry about the complications that might arise, least of all her dismissal when Lord Melton discovered who she was. Miss Martha was used to being able to do what she wanted.

'Did you telegraph the Admiral in London?'

'Yes. They will expect us on the boat train from Paris.' Phyllis wondered what she would say to Miss Morris about the baby and whether she would talk to her friend Mrs Simmonds at Lord Redfern's London home, who would surely communicate the news to her mother. She went on, 'I do think we should keep a low profile until we have settled Shawna May somewhere in the countryside. The fewer people who know about her the better.'

'I guess you're right. We'll take her to your mother's before we go to Melton Hall.'

Surprised that Miss Martha had made this decision, Phyllis responded, 'Oh but I haven't written to ask her yet! She doesn't know.'

'You'll have to tell her sooner or later. It has to be your mother. I wouldn't trust Shawna May with anyone else.'

Actually, neither would I, Phyllis thought and wondered if she dared tell her mother the truth. Of course she

334

daren't! Her mother worked with the vicar's wife who shared confidences with the dowager Lady Redfern who was Lord Melton's aunt. All the humiliation and shame of having an illegitimate child was hers to bear alone. What on earth would she say to Mother?

Chapter 25

Phyllis found a gentle and kind-hearted girl working in a convent laundry who had given birth to a child at sixteen and been disowned by her well-off father. Mary, now eighteen, seemed to be a natural with babies and was pleased for a chance to escape daily drudgery and travel to England.

Miss Martha compensated the convent for their loss and her physical and mental strength returned quickly so that Phyllis's concerns for her and Shawna May eased. The child was adorable and Phyllis was delighted to be her surrogate mother. She understood Nanny Byrne's possessiveness with Lord Melton's daughters and had to force herself to hand Shawna May to Mary and resume full lady's maid duties.

Miss Martha had her final fitting at the Paris couture

house and had designs made up and sent on to Melton Hall for her future step-daughters as her bridal attendants. The finished gowns would be despatched to Melton Hall where her marriage would take place in the private chapel.

The arrived at the Admiral, all four of them and their collection of luggage, in two motor cars, sent from the hotel to meet the boat train. Miss Martha stayed alone in the Victoria suite she had shared with her father. Phyllis and Shawna May with Mary occupied less luxurious adjoining rooms on an upper floor.

'This will not do, Smith,' Miss Martha complained as Phyllis unpacked her valises. 'I want Shawna May with me in my suite.'

'That is quite impossible, Miss. She is supposed to be my child. You have to become accustomed to being apart from her.'

Her face contorted and she sank down on the bed. 'Don't ever leave me, Smith. Promise me.'

'I shall do everything I can to stay with you. Surely this compromise is better than what might have been? Shall I telegraph your father to inform him that we have arrived safely?'

While she was at the reception desk, Miss Morris came out of her room. 'Miss Kimber? It is you? I could hardly credit it when I heard you were staying here with a *baby*! And you have a nursemaid to care for her. Well, you always were a modern woman. Miss Strayhorne must be very understanding.'

'She is, Miss Morris. Like you, she did not wish me

337

to leave her service. As you used to say, these Americans do things their way. Miss Martha adores my daughter.'

Miss Morris raised her eyebrows, and turned away. Phyllis felt a frisson of fear that Miss Morris might talk about her to her good friend Mrs Simmonds and reached out her hand to touch her former superior. 'Please don't tell anyone,' she whispered hurriedly.

'Need you ask, Miss Kimber? You are a guest at the Admiral and confidentiality is our maxim at all times.'

'Thank you. Those who need to know will hear it from me.'

'I do hope that includes the baby's father, my dear.'

The softness and empathy in her voice overwhelmed Phyllis and she felt tears well in her eyes. She was miserable that she had deceived a woman she admired. She had done so for a very good reason but it didn't make it any easier.

Miss Martha was cheerful. She had everything she wanted and was pleasing her father at the same time. Phyllis would have felt much better about her future happiness if she were not planning to marry Lord Melton.

'I have had a letter from father.'

Phyllis took pleasure in watching Miss Martha feed her baby using formula and a bottle. She took Shawna May into the Victoria suite every morning after breakfast for her 10 o'clock feed. Shawna May was bathed and changed and sweet smelling and adorable. Any man would surely welcome such a delightful grandchild. 'Will you not change your mind about telling your father the truth?' she suggested.

'Don't ask me again, Smith. My mind is made up. I know Shawna May will be in good hands and I shall find a way to be with her. Melton will soon tire of me when he has father's money to occupy him. Your English aristocracy have their own marriage rules and I shall abide by them and play their game.'

Phyllis agreed silently but did not speak. Perhaps Lord Melton had found his match in Miss Martha. She would betray him from the beginning; not with another man but with her child. Phyllis admired her for her stance, immoral as it seemed. She attempted to lighten the conversation. 'Is Mr Strayhorne well?'

'He is sending a motor car to bring me up to Yorkshire.'

'Does he say when?'

'Not exactly, but I wish to leave soon. Shawna May will ride with me.'

'Then Mary must travel in the motor, too! I shall go by train with the luggage.'

'You will do no such thing! A lady never travels without her maid. Send the luggage on separately. Father wants me home.'

'Where is home for your father now?'

'Lord Melton has offered him the Lodge at Melton Park. He has had an electric generator installed and a bathroom with hot water from fawcets. I shall motor to Melton chapel from there on my wedding day.'

'Have you decided when you will tell His Lordship who I am?' Phyllis asked.

'Don't worry about it. I shall say I took you on because of your excellent experience and I cannot let you go now.'

'I hope that works,' Phyllis answered. She concentrated on preparing for the journey and preparations for the wedding. She looked forward to seeing Lord Melton's daughters again and helping to dress them as bridal attendants and wondered if Nanny Byrne would wish to take charge of that.

Her familiarily with the Admiral and its working made her life much easier and although there were whisperings about Shawna May, no one who had known her before was tactless enough to ask direct questions. She believed Miss Morris was discreet and felt that her secret was safe from her mother, at least until she told her herself. Miss Martha laid a towel over her shoulder and rubbed Shawna May's back gently until she burped and smiled.

'I'll take her now, shall I?' Phyllis said.

Miss Martha wiped her baby's mouth with the towel. 'I suppose you must.'

'She needs fresh air. Mary will take him into Green Park in the perambulator.' Phyllis almost envied Mary. Taking the infants for their morning air had been her favourite time of day with Lord Melton's children.

'Miss Kimber! There is a message for you.'

Later that afternoon, Phyllis stopped in her tracks as she crossed reception on her way to Miss Martha's suite from her shopping in Bond Street.

'It's addressed to Miss Smith, lady's maid to Miss Strayhorne. That's you, isn't it?'

'It is. Thank you.' She took the small envelope, opened

it and unfolded the sheet of paper carrying Lord Melton's family crest.

She read it quickly and then sank down into one of the reception armchairs, dropping her package on a small table. The note was from Aaron. He was here with the motor car to take Miss Martha to Yorkshire. She read the note again and breathed deeply to quell her – her nervousness. Her heart was pounding. She had things to say to him. They had parted on bad terms and she wished to set the record straight. As soon as she had recovered she returned to the desk.

'When did Miss Strayhorne's motor car arrive?'

'Late last evening, Miss.'

'Is the chauffeur staying here?'

'He has a room on the servants' floor.' He slid a piece of hotel notepaper across the polished mahogany. 'Is there a reply, Miss?'

Phyllis picked up a pen and shook off the ink, thought for a moment and replaced it. 'I should prefer to speak to him,' she said.

'He's likely gone to his room by now, Miss. It was well into the early hours of the morning when he garaged the motor car.'

Phyllis raised her eyebrows in a questioning manner. 'Which room?'

Stiff lipped he replied, 'Top floor, room 535.'

'Thank you, sir.'

'Don't let the housekeeper catch you up there.'

'I am no longer employed by the Admiral,' she answered. She retrieved her package and walked slowly up the grand staircase to Miss Martha's suite, but she didn't go in. She went past the large panelled doors around the corner through a smaller door to the staff landing and began her climb of the narrow wooden stairs with a beating heart.

'Who is it?' She recognised Aaron's strong voice and hesitated. Within half a minute the door opened and he stood there in an under-vest and trousers with his braces down.

'Good God! Phyllis Kimber! You're the last person I expected to see.' He lifted his braces onto his shoulders and reached for a jersey, struggling to pull the neck over his head. 'What are you doing here?'

She stood on the threshold and watched him run his capable fingers through his tousled hair. All she could think of was that his first reaction had not been one of anger towards her. She gazed at his handsome face and thought he looked tired. She forgot her rehearsed words, aware that her heart was already melting.

'I − I work for Miss Martha − Miss Strayhorne, that is. Didn't you know?'

Bewildered, he shook his head. 'How could I? You left Melton Hall without a word to anyone and Mr Haddon wouldn't say anything.' He raised his shoulders in a shrug. 'Everyone thought the worst about you, of course.'

'The worst?'

His mouth twisted. 'You had replaced Violet.'

'No!' she protested. Surely *he* did not think she had replaced all aspects of Violet's service to His Lordship?

'Oh, none of the servants blamed you. They know what

His Lordship is like with a pretty face.' His expression turned serious. 'But I – I thought more of you, Phyllis.'

'I never gave in to him! That's why I left! He wanted me to take Violet's place and I refused! And after Lady Melton died – oh, it was so awful, I couldn't stay. I just wanted to be away from there.'

'Her death was a shock for all of us. Imagine your heart giving up at such a young age.'

'Is that what they said?'

'It was in the papers.'

Yes it was, Phyllis thought. There was no point in dragging up the truth now.

She said, 'I was right about Violet, though, wasn't I?'

'Well if you knew what they were up to why did you climb into her bed?'

This conversation was not going as well as Phyllis wished. She gave him a questioning glare. 'Do you really believe that I did?'

'I didn't know what to believe. I would have liked to speak to you before you left. I was building a prototype motor for His Lordship and couldn't get away from the workshop. I sent you a note from Melton Halt.'

'I didn't get it! Who did you give it to?'

'His Lordship was at the workshop every day. He said he'd give it to you.'

'Well he didn't!' Phyllis remembered how keen His Lordship was for her to leave. He wouldn't have wanted her to stay friends with any of his servants. She considered again that he wouldn't allow Miss Martha to keep her after the wedding.

'Well, I'm sorry, Phyllis.' Aaron sounded genuinely upset. 'When you didn't show I suppose I must have thought there was some truth in the rumours, and that made me angry. It's the way things are with Lord Melton.'

'But not with me, Aaron! I admit that I couldn't get away fast enough, but I did want to explain myself to you and you didn't give me the chance!' Phyllis sounded – and felt – belligerent.

'But I just said—' Aaron stopped and groaned. 'Come on, Phyllis. Why do we have to argue? I haven't seen you for over two years. Sit down and tell me where you've been since you left Melton Hall?'

She accepted his offer of a chair. Aaron sat on the bed. 'What happened to you?' he asked.

'I went home to my mother and then to London, where I found work here.'

'Here, as in here at the Admiral? So that's why you're knocking on my door.'

'I was given your note for Miss Smith. Miss Strayhorne always calls me Smith.'

'You mean that you really are Miss Strayhorne's maid?'

She nodded wordlessly then heaved a sigh. 'She's an American. They do things their way.'

'Does His Lordship know?'

'I don't think so. The engagement was announced at Lord Redfern's shooting lodge up in Ferndale. I was there but I saw neither hide nor hair of him or any of his servants.'

'Didn't anybody recognise you?'

'The aristocracy never notice servants' faces, especially

those employed by others. I did see Lord Melton's valet from an upstairs window, but he was doubling as his loader and out on the shoot all day. When he wasn't looking after Lord Melton, he spent his time with the other male servants. They ate and slept in a separate stable block.'

'Well, His Lordship did calm down a bit after his first wife died. He found himself a new interest.'

'Yes I know. It's Miss Martha.'

'I don't mean her. I mean the Melton Motor. He's gone into partnership with her father and Mr Strayhorne is financing the workshop. I work for him now and I like him. He's a self made man who has earned every bit of his wealth and he appreciates other men who do the same regardless of their background. A man can make his fortune in America.' For a few moments he gazed at the few stars he could see out of his skylight window. 'I'm pleased you've done well for yourself, Phyllis. In spite of what Mr Haddon said, I was worried about you.'

'Were you?'

He nodded silently.

'You needn't have been. I grew up.'

'Yes I can see that.' For a second she thought he was going to get up and come over to her chair. She was ready to stand up and embrace him, kiss him even. Then he looked away.

'I – I think I should go,' she said.

'I don't want you to.'

'Then I must. I shouldn't be here anyway.' Phyllis couldn't trust herself to stay, alone, in a bedroom, with a man she adored. She stood up.

'We'll leave in the morning if that's possible,' he said.

'We shall be ready. You know there are three of us – and a—' Oh Lord, what should she say? 'Well, you'll see tomorrow. Goodnight Aaron.'

He opened the door for her and gave her a brief kiss on her cheek as she walked past him. 'Goodnight, Phyllis.'

She placed the palm of her hand where his lips had touched her and held it there.

'What's troubling you, Smith?'

Phyllis was in the Victoria suite making sure that everything was packed and they were ready to leave the Admiral. Mary had been waiting with Shawna May for half an hour.

'Aaron is downstairs, Miss.'

'Aaron?'

'I mean Wilson. I know him from my days at Melton Hall.'

'Let's go then.' Miss Martha checked her image in the mirror. 'Something's on your mind, Smith.' She turned to face her. 'You never told me why you left.'

'Her Ladyship died, Miss.'

'You could have gone back to the nursery. Was it anything to do with this chauffeur guy?'

Phyllis had decided long ago to reveal the minimum about her former life at Melton Hall. Miss Martha did not need to know about her future husband's past and, according to Aaron, His Lordship had changed. So her reply was vague. 'I thought we might have been friends.'

'Anything more?'

'I was young, Miss. I might have had hopes.'

'There's nothing between you?'

'No, Miss.'

'Well, there'd better not be. You won't let me down over this, will you?'

'What on earth do you mean?'

'What will you tell him about the baby?'

What could she say to anyone without ruining either her own or Miss Martha's life?

Chapter 26

Aaron held open the car door for Miss Martha and bowed smartly as she climbed into the motor car.

'Are those valises well secured?'

'They are, Miss Martha, though I had not expected so many.'

'There are three of us, and of course, the infant.'

'The infant?'

'Ah here she is, with her nursemaid.'

Mary went out of the hotel entrance with a sleepy Shawna May in her arms and Phyllis followed carrying a small crib.

'Are you sure you have sufficient wrappings, Mary?' she said, avoiding Aaron's surprised gaze as Mary placed the cradle on the wide leather seat beside Miss Martha. 'It will be a long journey and motor cars are draughty.'

She peeped inside her cocoon of Bond Street baby cashmere. 'She will be safe on the seat beside you.'

Mary climbed out and fished in her coat pocket for her gloves. 'Will I ride up front with the driver?'

'Yes, Mary. Make sure you are well wrapped against the cold. Shawna May will stay with me and Miss Martha.'

'Yes, Miss.'

The motor car was spacious so that there was plenty of room for the baby's basket on the seat between them. Aaron continued to stand to attention and Phyllis lingered for a few moments with the opened motor car door between them. She wanted to explain, but she couldn't form the words and her mind was in turmoil. 'Does Lord Melton know about your baby?' he whispered fiercely.

Hastily she shook her head. But the confusion that she felt must have shown on her face. 'I – I . . .'

'Don't speak to me,' he added. 'Just get inside.' As she settled herself beside the small crib, Aaron shut the motor car door soundly and marched around to climb into his driver's seat.

The journey was long and tedious as Shawna May became fretful and they had to make unscheduled stops for Mary to attend to her infant needs. They took lunch unfashionably early at an inn in Leicestershire and stopped again in Nottinghamshire for tea and toasted muffins.

'I think you would be wise to stay here for the night. Shawna May is fractious and you must be tired, Miss.'

Miss Martha yawned. 'I am tired of sitting and hearing only the sound of the motor car. Enquire if they have a suite here. I shall go for a brisk walk to clear my head.'

Phyllis left the remainder of her tea to arrange their rooms and an escort from the hotel staff to walk with Miss Martha. There was only one suite with two bedrooms and a sitting room so one of the bedrooms became the nursery for Shawna May and Phyllis. Mary had a servant's room at the top of the building and Aaron a coachman's room in the adjacent mews. Phyllis gave Mary the night off and undertook care of Shawna May herself. Miss Martha chose room service for dinner and breakfast in her suite and retired to bed early.

After settling Shawna May, Phyllis was in need of some air herself. Her head was throbbing and she went down to the lobby and spoke to the night porter.

'Don't go outside on your own at this time of night. I'll get a footman to go with you, if you don't mind, Miss.' He disappeared into the back and several minutes later returned with Aaron. 'You're in luck, Miss. Your driver was still up.'

Aaron was standing at a door behind the reception. 'Come through the back, Phyllis. There's a quiet lane beyond the mews and the moon is rising.'

He spoke gently and politely and she forgot his questioning anger of earlier. But once they were clear of the buildings and the sundry hotel staff sitting around and smoking cigarettes, his mood changed.

'A baby! A baby, Phyllis! That was something you forgot to mention last night. I thought there was a chance for us. I thought you came clean about Melton and told me the truth.'

'I have! Well mostly.'

350

'You lied to me! All I wanted was for you to be honest!'

'Aaron, you don't know what I've been through!'

'Did he force himself on you?'

Phyllis considered saying yes but more lies would only compound her already tangled situation. 'No!' she answered.

'You were willing?'

Exasperated she cried, 'No, it wasn't like that either!'

'Then what was it like?' he shouted.

'I am so, so sorry.' She spoke more to herself than to him. Perhaps she should tell him the truth. She trusted him enough. But his job would be at stake if he became implicated in this deception. It had seemed the only solution in Ireland, but she had made a hasty decision and one that she had not thought through. She could not retract her promise to Miss Martha but losing Aaron's good opinion of her was too high a price to pay. She was more angry with herself than with him.

'What's done is done,' she muttered.

'I take it that Lord Melton doesn't know about this child.'

'It's – it's not his child.'

The shock on Aaron's face was almost too much for her to bear. 'I don't believe you. I can't believe you because if it isn't his there was someone else and that makes it worse.'

Phyllis must have shown guilt and shame.

'Dear God, there was someone else. I thought I knew you but I didn't, not at all. You were lucky not to be thrown out of your employment.'

'Miss Martha did not want me to leave her service—'

'—so she hired a nursemaid for you? She must be very understanding. Well I don't think her father will be quite so accommodating, and I'm sure Lord Melton won't even allow you over his threshold. What will you do?'

'I'll keep her a secret, of course.'

His incredulity increased. 'How can you keep a baby a secret?'

'I – I won't give up the child.' It was the truth, yet she knew she was deceiving him and it broke her heart.

'Are you insane?'

'No one in Yorkshire would have known about her if Mr Strayhorne had not sent you with the motor car. I planned to break our journey in the South Riding and leave her with my mother until – until something more permanent can be arranged. Miss Martha has agreed.'

'What happened to the baby's father?'

'Oh, he's – he's abroad. He doesn't know about his child.' That much was true, she thought.

'Phyllis, Phyllis,' he groaned. 'Why? Did you love him?'

She shook her head. 'Please don't judge me too harshly.'

'Why shouldn't I? You lied to me and you – you – last night you gave me hope. Your behaviour cannot have been much worse.'

Phyllis thought her heart would break. There was nothing she could say to make things right between them. In saving Miss Martha's life on that windswept cliff in Ireland, she had lost any chance of happiness for herself.

* * *

'Try not to cry, Miss Martha. You will upset Shawna May. Say goodbye to her now.'

They were in the foyer of a hotel in Doncaster where they planned to stay the night before driving to Melton Lodge tomorrow.

Miss Martha took a deep breath and hugged the bundle of wrappings cocooning her child. 'I'll come for you soon,' she whispered and kissed her gently on her forehead.

'Mary will take good care of her.' Phyllis handed her to Mary and said, 'Put her in the crib in the motor car. Aaron is waiting outside.'

'I shall be Viscountess Melton when I see her again,' Miss Martha commented.

'The time will fly by,' Phyllis responded as cheerfully as she could. 'There is a great deal of preparation for your wedding to keep you busy. You must be strong, Miss Martha. Your father will be so proud of you when you walk out of the chapel as Lady Melton.'

'I know,' Miss Martha agreed. 'I have so much to thank you for, Smith. You'll never leave me, will you?'

Phyllis shook her head and smiled. 'We are already in Yorkshire and my mother is expecting us. I shall not be away from you for long,' she promised.

'It will be like old times with just the two of us again.'

Phyllis went out of the hotel foyer to where Aaron was cranking the motor car engine. It roared into life and he stowed away the crank handle. Phyllis climbed in beside Mary and Shawna May.

Mary was excited. 'I've never been inside a motor car

before,' she said. 'Not properly, like this.' She sat back in the seat and smoothed the leather with her hands.

The journey was uneventful yet Phyllis felt a tension building inside her with every mile. She had not exactly lied to her mother but had not written the whole truth in her letter, and there had not been time for Ellen to reply. Eventually, the large and graceful motor car bumped quietly along the lane to Chase Cottage.

Ellen Kimber appeared at the gate in her apron and waited for them to get out. Her hand gripped the gate-post as though she needed it for support. She gave her daughter a brief hug and whispered, 'Phyllis! What have you done?'

Phyllis replied, 'Not here, mother. We'll talk indoors.' She took her mother's arm and propelled her to the front door. There was a good fire in the front room and a small table was laid out for tea and cake. 'This way, Mary,' she called over her shoulder.

Ellen hung back to look at the child, sleeping in Mary's arms. She pulled away the wrappings cocooning her tiny head and Phyllis noticed Ellen's face soften as she said, 'Bring her in by the fire. No, dear, take the other chair away from the draught.'

Phyllis felt tears prick the inside of her eyelids. She hated deceiving her mother in this way. But she had got herself into this mess so she had to deal with it. She thought back to that windswept morning on the cliffs in Ireland and knew she had done the right thing at the time. But was it the right thing now? The more she thought about it, the more she realised that her promise to Miss Martha had been a huge mistake. Mother disappeared to the back kitchen to fetch the tea.

Phyllis took off her fashionable London coat with its luxurious fur collar. It was out of place draped over her father's old rocking chair that used to be in the kitchen. She mentally shook herself and said, 'Shall I hold Shawna May while you take off your coat, Mary?'

Ellen returned with a laden tray that Phyllis took from her and placed on the table. Ellen went back for more and Phyllis heard voices in the hallway. Aaron was stacking bags and baby items at the bottom of the stairs. Ellen brought in a large tea pot shrouded in a knitted tea cosy and commented, 'You didn't give me much notice, dear. You are very lucky I have space and time at the moment.'

Phyllis answered, 'Mary is very good with the baby, Mother.'

Again Ellen's face softened. 'I am sure we shall get along very well, my dear.' Her tone hardened a little as she turned to Phyllis and added. 'I have made space for a baby's cot in your bedroom and Mary will sleep in the middle room.'

'Thank you, Mrs Kimber,' Mary said.

'Phyllis, why don't you help the chauffeur to take up the luggage? Mary and I can talk while the tea is mashing.'

'Very well, Mother.'

She is angry with me, Phyllis thought, *and with good reason*. She went out into the hall to meet another angry face.

'This is Lord Redfern's estate, isn't it?' Aaron commented. 'My father was head groom for His Lordship.'

'Where is he now?'

'He was killed in a riding accident.'

'I'm sorry. I didn't know. You never said.'

'You never asked.'

He seemed lost for words for a minute. 'Your mother is a very capable lady.'

Phyllis's emotions rose in her throat and she couldn't speak. She nodded, feeling overwhelmed by the situation. Must she lie to her own mother? Must she deceive Aaron? These were people she loved and she was betraying them with every breath she took.

'Where do you want the baby cot?' he asked.

'Follow me,' she replied, picking up one of Mary's bags and going upstairs.

The wooden cot, purchased specially by Miss Martha, had been dismantled for the journey and had to be put together. Aaron was prepared for this task. He placed a canvas tool bag on the bedroom floor. Phyllis stepped inside her old bedroom and looked round. Her bed had been pushed under the eaves to leave room for the cot and there were new curtains at the end window, more fitting for a nursery.

Aaron straightened, almost hitting his head on the sloping ceiling.

'Careful!' she cried.

He avoided a crack on his skull by a hair's breadth. 'I'm used to rooms like this,' he said. He stood perfectly still and stared at her with pain etched in his features.

'I'm so sorry, Aaron,' she whispered. 'Please don't think ill of me.'

'Give me a reason not to,' he pleaded.

Phyllis shook her head wearily and answered, 'It's a long story.'

One she could not tell. Oh dear Lord, what had she done? It was what she hadn't done that grieved her. She had not told the truth. Why? Because she was so worried about Miss Martha that she had not given a thought what it might do to her own life. Her reputation was tainted for ever. Her mother might understand eventually and she would love the child as her own because she was a good woman. But Aaron, dearest Aaron, could not forgive her. She had betrayed him, not in the way that he believed, but in not being honest with him and telling him the truth. How could she? How could she ruin everything for Martha? And what future was there for Shawna May?

Phyllis faltered as she went on. 'Other people are involved.'

'Lord Melton, you mean? He doesn't know about the baby, does he?' His voice was tight as though he were suppressing his anger and he went on, 'Might he think she is his and lay claim to her if he did? You needn't fret yourself about that. Melton wouldn't be interested in her anyway because she's a girl. Violet had a girl, too, and we all know what happened to her.'

'I don't. What did happen to Violet?'

'He wouldn't have her back at the Hall afterwards.'

'But she said he loved her!'

'Then she was a fool to believe him! Her family didn't want her either. The last anyone heard was that she scrubbing floors in a doss house in Liverpool.'

'Oh. Poor Violet.'

'It was her own doing. Thank God, you have an understanding mother.' He stared at her in silence for a minute then changed the subject. 'This is a pretty bedroom, is it yours?'

She looked around. It was a child's room and she was a woman, old enough to shoulder her own responsibilities. She must live with the consequences of her actions. Her heart ached for the love she had lost but she replied with a smile, 'It's Shawna May's now. Come down for tea before you start on the cot. Mother has made a fruit cake.'

Alone in the motor car as Aaron drove her back to Doncaster, Phyllis reflected on what a wonderful woman her mother was, and on how much she must have tried her when she was at school. Her initial frostiness had melted during tea. Aaron was charming to her mother and Mary was such a sweet innocent girl that Ellen took to her immediately. It was only as she had left, when Mother kissed her at the garden gate that she whispered in her ear, 'Shawna May is an absolute darling, my dear. Her hair and eyes are very dark, though, not like yours at all. Does she take after her father?'

Phyllis mumbled an incoherent response. She was so relieved that Martha had not travelled with them as it would have been perfectly clear to astute Ellen Kimber who was the baby's mother.

Mother had not pressed her and the more Phyllis considered it, the more she realised that Ellen may have guessed the truth. Phyllis frowned to herself, not sure whether to be cross or pleased with the thought. However, when she arrived at the hotel in Doncaster she found Martha was fretting about Shawna May and spent most of the evening reassuring her that all would be well. Phyllis truly wished to believe her own words.

Aaron stopped outside Melton Lodge where George Strayhorne had taken up residence. During his daughter's absence, he had modernised and refurbished the compact dwelling and installed a butler from a York agency to ensure his life ran smoothly. The lodge had four bedrooms, and three attics for servants reached by a back stairs.

'I'm so proud of you, honey,' he said as Miss Martha stepped down from the motor. 'Melton is giving a banquet in your honour tonight. The Earl of Red Fern is here and a Marquess and some Lord Lieutenant guy are coming. You can tell them about your trip. Where is it you went in France?'

'The Brittany coast. The Atlantic air is recommended for health and vitality.'

'Well you sure look better now. Why didn't you write me about your change of plans?'

'I know how you worry and I was quite safe with Smith.'

George Strayhorne followed Miss Martha, Phyllis and Aaron with the luggage upstairs to Miss Martha's bedroom.

'It's lovely, Daddy. I adore the French style! I shall imagine I am Marie Antoinette.'

Miss Martha wandered around her new bedroom and into the ajoining bathroom. Phyllis heard squeals of delight

359

from her as she turned on water taps. 'Hot water, Daddy, just like at the Admiral!'

'Noting is too much trouble for my little baby.'

Phyllis heard Miss Martha give a choked sob. She was busy organising the numerous pieces of luggage that Aaron carried in. She glanced across at her mistress and realised that she was having a difficult time of holding herself together. 'That will be all for now, Wilson,' she said and tossed her head towards the door.

'Not quite,' George added. 'I wanna talk to you about my next phase with the Melton.' He followed Wilson out to the landing.

'Thank you, Smith.' Miss Martha sank onto her gilt and brocade chaise longue. 'I can't do this. I want my baby and I want to go home. I don't like Melton. He's arrogant and selfish and now he has Daddy's money all he's gonna want from me is an heir. She turned her dark eyes towards Phyllis and pleaded, 'I gotta get away from here. Help me, Smith.'

'You have to make a show of your marriage for now, Miss. You'll be going to America on a visit next spring.'

'I can't wait that long. And I want Shawna May with me now.'

'Well, you could . . .' Phyllis hesitated, unsure whether her idea was a good one or not. 'You could visit Lady Redfern at the Abbey. It would be easier for you to go to Chase Cottage from there.'

'Smith, you are a wonder! She will be shortly be my aunt.' Her face brightened. 'I'll go as soon as I can after the wedding. Melton won't mind. He'll be too busy with his automobile works.'

Phyllis wondered what her mother would say. Ellen Kimber was always at pains to keep her away from working at the Abbey. This was different of course. Phyllis had to go where her mistress went and Mother would understand that. But it meant more lies and deception.

She had made such a mess of her life. A trip to America was the answer for her as well as Miss Martha. It would be a chance to get over her attraction for Aaron. She might even stay there. A fresh start in a thriving young country might be just what she needed. But she wondered how her mother would react to such a plan.

George returned several minutes later with a red leather box tooled with gold in the shape of a large oyster. 'I've bought you this gift, honey. Tonight will be a grand occasion so wear one of your Paris gowns.'

'Oh!' Diamonds and rubies sparkled in a silver setting. She picked it up from its red velvet lined case and placed it around her neck. 'It's beautiful, Daddy.'

'Gee, I sure wish those Pittsburgh dames could see you wearing that tonight. I'll show Lord Melton what I'm made of.'

'I thought you already had, Daddy, with the automobile works.'

'That was business. This is personal. He oughtta give you more jewels.'

'He will, Daddy, after our marriage. I'll get the family heirlooms then.'

Phyllis was unpacking valises and hanging garments to air. She was pleased that Miss Martha was distracted by her marriage preparations. It took her mind off Shawna May for a while. Everyone else seemed happy with the arrangements. But Phyllis could not get the child out of her mind because, for her, everything was wrong about the arrangements and she could do nothing to make them right. Quite the opposite, she was a main instigator of the deception and it grieved her. If only she had someone to share her distress. Both her mother and Aaron would surely understand if they knew the truth. But she could not even confide in the two people who might have supported her. Oh, for the luxury of being able to speak the truth to someone!

'Smith. Smith! Did you hear me? Where are you?'

'So sorry. Miss Martha, I'm in your dressing room. Have you decided which gown you will wear for dinner tonight?'

'The dark red that I bought in Paris, with my new rubies and diamonds, don't you think?'

'I do, Miss Martha.'

She looks stunning, Phyllis thought when Miss Martha was ready. She would most likely outshine all the other ladies with her jewels. But that was her privilege as the bride-to-be. Phyllis imagined the dining room at the Hall; the long mahogany table glittering with the silver and crystal, butler and footmen in their best spotless livery, starched white shirt fronts and pristine gloves. Below-stairs would be buzzing with activity and even though the extra work was back-breaking, banquets were fun. When the worst was over the servants would have their own party to celebrate.

Mr Strayhone's motor car crunched on the gravel drive. Phyllis recognised the sound of the engine and moved to the bedroom window. 'Your father's chauffeur is here, Miss,' she said and hovered behind a curtain to observe Aaron as he waited patiently for his passengers. Had he said anything about her to Mr Haddon? She hoped not. Mr Strayhorne's servants were new, so if she stayed at the Lodge no one need know who she was, unless Aaron mentioned her. She wondered if he would be at the servants' party.

Maybe she ought to say something to him, just in case? She hesitated, hovering in front of the window with her hands poised to throw up the sash. But she was too late as a pool of light appeared from the lodge hallway and he stepped forward to open the motor car doors for his passengers. Within minutes the engine was cranked and purring again, the small party was on its way to the Hall and Phyllis returned to inspecting Miss Martha's extensive wardrobe.

She was aware of the other servants moving about in the attics above her head and took several items needing a stitch or button to her room.

'There you are, Smith,' Mr Strayhorne's butler beamed. 'We shall be walking to the Lodge in an hour for the servants' party. We're all invited.'

'Oh. Oh, I didn't know. I really have too much to do after Miss Martha's travelling. Would you be so good as to give my apologies?'

'Lord Melton's servants will be disappointed. They were looking forward to meeting you. You'll be one of them after the wedding.'

'I – I . . .,' she floundered. Phyllis dreaded coping with the questions about where she had been since she left. It was already difficult to handle her deception and she dare not compound it with further lies. Truly, she was beginning to feel the weight of the huge burden of Miss Martha's secret too much for her.

She raised the back of her hand to her brow. 'I am quite tired after the journey and would prefer to meet them when I am at my best. I am sure they will understand.'

Actually, she thought they wouldn't, because any servant worth his or her wages did not pass up the chance to meet and gossip with others whilst eating, drinking and dancing. They would think she was odd. She closed her eyes, her mind exhausted and the butler misread her meaning.

'I hope you're not coming down with something. None of us can afford to be ill with the wedding just around the corner.'

'I'll be fine,' she reassured him, 'just as soon as I have Miss Martha's wardrobe sorted.'

'Very well, Smith. I'll make your excuses.'

Her initial relief was short lived. She had to speak to them sooner or later. She switched on the electric light and concentrated on her sewing. The Lodge servants left and silence settled over the house until she heard an approaching motor car engine and hurriedly tidied her appearance, wondering who was returning so early. She opened the front door and waited.

Aaron came round the side of the Melton but instead

of opening one of the doors he headed straight for her. 'They told me you weren't well,' he said.

'Oh.' She glanced around him. Now her eyes were used to the dark she saw that he had no passengers. 'I'm busy and tired, that's all.'

He held up one of the kitchen shopping baskets. 'I've brought you supper. Mrs Phipps insisted.'

'Have you told them who I am?'

'No. Why should I? But they'll find out soon enough. So will Lord Melton.'

She swallowed and blew out her cheeks.

He went on, 'There's a lot you are not saying but I shan't push you. Shall we eat this in the kitchen?'

She nodded and he followed her through the front hall to the back rooms where the domestic offices were situated. Mr Strayhorne's housekeeper had left her kitchen spotless and Aaron unpacked his basket onto a large deal table. Phyllis opened the damper to draw the range fire and filled a kettle. 'I'll make some tea.'

'Mr Haddon asked me to fetch you, but I guessed you didn't want that. You can't go on like this, you know.'

'Miss Martha is going to stay at Redfern Abbey after the wedding so I may not move in to Melton Hall until we return.'

'Mr Haddon says they are not going away for a honeymoon but taking an extended trip to America next spring when the new Melton prototype will be ready.'

'Are you still living at Melton Halt?'

'Yes. I'm not a servant any more. I manage the

365

workshop and look after Mr Strayhorne's Silver Ghost. Each motor car is built individually according to the customer's specifications, but Mr Strayhorne has asked me to develop a standard model to sell in America. That's the prototype.'

'You're very busy, then.'

'I am. Mr Strayhorne drives himself to and from Melton Halt. When you've got a Silver Ghost, it's a pleasure, not a chore. The Melton Motor is the same.' Aaron paused, then added, 'You won't see me after the wedding until the prototype is ready to ship.'

'Is that what you came here to tell me?'

'I guess so. I expect you'll persuade Her Ladyship to stay at Redfern often so you can visit your baby.'

'Yes,' she said.

This time he didn't kiss her when he left and she was so disappointed she could have cried.

'Gee, my little girl is a viscountess.' George Strayhorne smiled and hugged her. 'Lady Melton. I can't wait to take you back to New York and show you off.'

'I can't wait either. I wanna go home too, Daddy.'

'It's all fixed, honey. Melton wants to go over there with us. We have plans to sell his motor car in New York. I've already told him I'll buy you an apartment near the von Steins as a wedding gift.'

'Daddy! You're wonderful.' Martha kissed her father fondly and pushed Lord Melton and his motor car out of her mind.

He wasn't interested in her as a wife; he only wanted

her father's money. So be it. Her father wanted the status that went with his daughter's title and she – what did she want? Martha did not have to think twice about that. She wanted her child with her and she wanted to go home to America.

Their wedding had been a glittery occasion with a grand reception at Melton Hall. Lord Melton didn't expect much of her as wife but insisted on regular marital relations until she became pregnant. And he was unconcerned about Smith. He said his wife could have who she wanted for her maid and seemed relieved that she was happy with the time he spent at Melton Halt. She was content to visit his aunt alone, leaving him to his motor car workshop. In fact she couldn't wait, for Smith would arrange for her to see Shawna May.

Martha felt no disloyalty towards her husband. They both knew that her father had bought her this husband and his title. Melton had what he wanted and now it was her turn. Before she left for Redfern she asked, 'When do we sail home, Daddy?'

'Next April. The new liner I was telling you about has to have sea trials first but I've got reservations for all of us on her maiden voyage.'

'Oh, I'm so excited to be going home! What's she called?'

'*Titanic*, and she sure is. She's the biggest, fastest liner in the world and we have the best suites. This time when we sail we really will be dining on the captain's table, Lady Melton.'

His swarthy features beamed with pride and he leaned

over to kiss her. Martha's heart swelled. 'We did it Daddy, didn't we?' she smiled.

'We sure did, honey. We sure did.'

Chapter 27

Autumn, 1911

'The Abbey is beautiful, Aunt Amelia.' Martha stood at the dining room window after breakfast gazing at the view. 'Edward tells me he has a fine chase, beyond the village.'

'Indeed he has. Hunting rights were bestowed on the first Earl Redfern for his loyalty to King Henry.'

'May I see it?'

'I am afraid the tracks are not suitable for a motor car.'

'I can explore on horseback, if I may take one of your hunters.'

'Of course you may, my dear. Edward will ride with you.'

Edward was finishing his breakfast coffee at the table. 'It's Thursday, Mama. I am meeting Anne from the railway train to take her to the women's rally in Sheffield.'

'Oh yes, I forgot, dear. I'm so sorry, Martha.'

But Martha had not forgotten that Edward would be busy. 'It seems a shame to waste such a beautiful day, Edward. Would one of your stable staff ride with me as my guide?'

'I don't see why not.' Edward drained his cup and stood up. 'I'll send for my steward right away.' He walked around the table to kiss his mother. 'We shall be in for dinner, Mama. Anne is looking forward to meeting my American cousin.'

When Edward had left, Martha came back to the dining table and said, 'I've given Smith the day off, Aunt Amelia. Apparently, her mother lives on your estate. Isn't that a coincidence?'

'Smith?' A troubled frown crossed Amelia's brow. 'Oh, yes, that's Kimber, isn't it? Was changing her name her idea or yours?'

Martha gave her brightest smile. 'It was mine, Aunt Amelia. I cannot think of calling her anything else.'

Amelia appeared pleased with this response. 'Would you sit a moment, my dear? You are aware of the – the child?'

'The one she left with her mother? Of course I am, Aunt Amelia.'

'In my day a maid would have been dismissed for such conduct. Does your husband know?'

'Good gracious no. I do not speak of such things to him. He has no interest in servants' gossip.'

Amelia took a deep breath. 'He should be told, Martha. Smith was employed at Melton Hall before the birth. It is possible that one of your husband's servants may be the child's father.'

'She has assured me otherwise, Aunt.'

'Do you believe her?'

'I do.'

'Nevertheless, Melton will dismiss her when he finds out about the child.'

'She is my maid and he knows I am happy with her. I'm sure Daddy can persuade Melton I should keep her.' She wanted to add that Melton was more interested in his automobile than her personal maid but realised this would have offended his aunt.

However, Aunt Amelia still shuddered at this response and after a pause said, 'A mother's love is very strong, Martha. Do you not think Smith will be unsettled by being so close to her child? She will surely visit while she is here.'

'It is too late now. We are here.' Martha became restless and anxious to be away from this interview. She jumped to her feet and exclaimed, 'I am wasting this beautiful day!' Then she composed herself and smiled, 'I'm looking forward to meeting dear Anne. Does she ride?'

'She does. But hear me well, Martha. Whatever you do, please do not mention Smith and her baby with Anne.'

'I have no reason to, Aunt. Smith is a servant. Now I must change for my ride.'

Martha's escort from Redfern stables was a charming young fellow who took her for an exhilarating gallop and then on to the village where she directed him to fellow drinkers in the bar so she could take her luncheon in a private room at the Redfern Arms. She could barely contain her excitement as she ate and several times took the note of directions from her pocket to remind herself of the way. Her horse was rested when she remounted but she resisted the urge to gallop along the bridleway. As she approached the edge of the chase she dismounted and led the large hunter carefully along the track. Phyllis was waiting for her at the cottage gate and took the reins.

'How is she?' Martha asked, her eyes sparkling with anticipation.

'Thriving and adorable,' Phyllis replied. 'She is asleep at present but will waken shortly.'

'Does your mother know I am coming?'

Phyllis shook her head. 'She has taken Mary into town for the day. I arrived early so that they could go to the market. It will be dusk before they return.'

'I shall have to be back at the stables before then, or cousin Edward will send out a search party. I told my escort I was visiting people in the village this afternoon.' She stopped talking and her eyes softened as she gazed at her sleeping child. The sparkle melted into tears that rolled down her cheeks. Martha's hands reached out to take Shawna May into her arms, only to be stilled by Phyllis's hand.

'She will waken naturally in a few minutes. Let her sleep until then.'

Martha took off her riding hat and coat, placed them with her gloves and whip on the hall table and returned to the sitting room. She stood motionless by the crib without taking her tearful eyes off Shawna May's angelic sleeping face until her baby snuffled and wriggled and finally awoke. And then her child was in her arms and her velvet skin was against Martha's wet cheeks. Shawna May protested and whimpered at first and then settled quietly in her mother's arms.

'Mother says she is a contented baby. She will need a change,' Smith said.

'I'll do it.'

'Use that chair. Here's a towel.'

Martha sniffed audibly. 'I can't stop crying. My hands are shaking and she is so tiny. You'll have to help me.'

When Shawna May was dry and sweet smelling, Smith took her so that Martha could blow her nose and dry her eyes. Martha tucked away her sodden handkerchief and shook her head slowly. 'I can't do this, Smith. It's breaking my heart to be away from her. I have to have her with me.'

'You know that is impossible. As it is you are lucky that Lord Melton tolerates me.'

'Aunt Amelia is worried too. It was unheard of in her day.'

'In our day too, Miss Martha. Mother says Lady Redfern was scandalised by the fact that you kept me on. She has indulged you because you are American.'

'And I have married her wayward nephew.'

'She hopes you will give him the next Viscount Melton.'

The darkness of her bedroom at Melton Hall flashed in front of Martha's eyes. The nightly alcohol and tobacco perfumed rutting, and the half-truth she had told about the possibility of pregnancy so that he would let her leave for Redfern Abbey. Lord help her, she did not want to go back, not to the Hall, not to Melton and not even to explain to her father!

'What have I done?' she said quietly.

'You have done nothing that many other women have not done before.'

'But I must be with my child. I must.'

Smith shook her head as she tried to think of something to say that would help.

'Look at her,' Martha went on. 'She is so small. She needs me, and I need her too.'

'I can't see a way . . .' Smith began.

'I can. I'm going home with my baby. You'd like to live in America, wouldn't you?' Excitement gripped Martha as she considered this. She went on, 'Yes. That's what I'll do. Melton is such a bore. He talks only of his automobile and he treats me as though I were a baby machine. I shall be glad to be free of him.'

'I doubt that His Lordship will allow you to stay in America so soon after your marriage, my lady,' Phyllis cautioned.

'I don't see why not. America is not so far away with steamships and the telegraph.'

'There will be talk of a rift.'

'I don't care! Don't you understand? I won't be apart from my daughter.'

'You mustn't do this, My Lady. His Lordship will be suspicious.'

'But she will be on board with you and Mary.'

'You really mean this, don't you?'

Martha folded her hands together and clenched them to her breast. 'I am so unhappy here. I can't be separated from my baby like this. I can't.'

Phyllis saw the bleakness in Martha's eyes and recognised the despair. She had seen it before, on the cliffs in Ireland, and it frightened her. 'Please try and be strong, My Lady,' she said.

'I can't,' Martha wailed. 'I'm not like you.'

'But you have to be for Shawna May. You mustn't weep. You will distress her with your tears.'

Martha made an effort to blink back her tears and straighten her spine. 'You're right. Oh, Smith, what would I do without you?'

'You would have to tell your father about your baby.'

'Daddy knows I'm homesick. He's already said he'll buy me an apartment in Manhattan. 'I'll go house-hunting and take Shawna May with me. Then she can be with me all the time. Don't look so worried, Smith. Daddy will talk to Melton.'

It was so hard for Martha to leave. But she consoled herself with the knowledge that the visit could be repeated whenever she was at Redfern. She arranged a day the following week.

But Phyllis remained worried, for Miss Martha's notion of fleeing to America seemed as harebrained as her idea that she could pass Miss Martha's child off as her own. She would have to go with her to live out her lie. Her

375

mother believed that Shawna May was her grandchild and was already attached to her. This cruel deception was tearing Phyllis apart. Phyllis felt that she was caught in a web and the more she struggled to free herself, the more entangled she became. She so desperately wanted to tell the truth.

Ellen Kimber and Mary returned with full shopping baskets and parcels wrapped with brown paper and tied with string. Phyllis had had time to recover from the trauma of Martha's visit and had laid the table for a cooked tea. The kettle bubbled softly on the hob.

Mary dumped her heavy bag on the table. 'That is one of the best markets I have ever seen. So many bargains! Has Shawna May behaved herself?'

'She will need a feed soon. Her milk is warming on the hob and there's hot water in the boiler for you to wash.'

Mary drew a can of steaming water from the brass tap in the range and disappeared upstairs. Ellen flopped into a chair and stretched her legs. 'I haven't enjoyed a trip to town so much since you were a girl. Do you remember how we used to look forward to our days out together?'

Phyllis smiled at the memory. 'We had to walk all the way then. Now you can take the omnibus from the main road. Are you hungry? I've collected eggs for tea.'

'Oh good, I have some flitch bacon from the butcher to go with them.' She levered herself to her feet. 'I'm parched. Would you make a pot of tea while I put away the shopping?'

Shawna May began to whimper in her crib and Ellen went over to check. Phyllis watched her for a moment and pressed her lips together. Mother was really fond of the child and she wondered how she would react to her going to America. She had her back to Phyllis when she spoke. 'She isn't your child, is she?' It was a statement not a question and Phyllis stood stock still with the heavy kettle of boiling water half way to the teapot. Her mother continued, 'Shawna May is not my granddaughter?'

Phyllis put down the heavy kettle. 'What makes you say that?'

'I expect it's because it is the truth. She doesn't look at all like you.'

'She – she takes after her father.'

'Then who is her father?' Ellen came over to her and pleaded. 'Please tell me, dear. I am your *mother*.'

'I – I – can't.' Phyllis could not think of anything useful to add.

'Is it Lord Melton? Tell me dear. I shan't blame you at all. I know how it is in these titled houses.'

'He is not her father. Truly, Mother, I swear he is not.'

'Then who?'

'I – I can't tell you. I wish I could but I promised.' She picked up the kettle again and made the tea. 'I'll put the bacon on while this mashes.'

Her mother went back to her shopping baskets and Phyllis busied herself with cooking bacon and eggs for the three of them. Mary came downstairs in a fresh apron and attended to a fretting Shawna May. The three women

377

concentrated on their tasks in silence until Mary commented, 'Was Lady Melton here today?'

Phyllis blinked at the frying pan. 'Why do you say that?'

'You put on Shawna May's nappy the same way as I do, but her Ladyship does it different.'

Ellen came into the kitchen from the larder. 'Well, was Her Ladyship here?'

'Yes. She – she was out riding and happened by.'

'Happened by? No one comes this way without a purpose. Was Lord Redfern with her?'

'No one, she was alone.'

'Surely not! His Lordship would never have allowed that!'

'She – that is, one of the grooms was with her. But he waited for her in the village. Lady Melton is an expert horsewoman. I'm sure she was quite safe.'

'She must have known where our secluded cottage is.'

Mary's eyes were wide with alarm. 'I didn't mean to cause any trouble, Miss. I'm sorry.'

'It's all right, Mary,' Phyllis said. 'You've done nothing wrong.' She addressed her mother. 'I – I told Lady Melton that I was coming here today and she was in need of refreshment. I – I gave her tea and she nursed the baby for a while.'

Ellen stared at her in silence for a moment then said, 'You are telling me that Lady Melton came here for tea and changed your baby's nappy.'

'Well, yes,' Phyllis shrugged. 'She isn't like Lady Redfern,

Mother. She's American. She's young and modern and does things differently.'

Her mother continued to stare keenly at Phyllis's face until she stumbled on, 'Lady Melton is very fond of Shawna May and she will have one of her own one day – one day very soon, I expect.'

However, her mother was not satisfied with this explanation. 'Her visit was planned, wasn't it?'

Phyllis nodded. 'I didn't think you'd mind.'

'Well I do.' Phyllis was grateful her mother didn't say, 'It would never have happened in my day' even though she must have thought it. Instead Ellen added, 'Please do not encourage Lady Melton to come here. Her cousin might well have been with her.'

'Why shouldn't he call in to one of his tenants' cottages? Lord Redfern's father came here when Father was dying!' Phyllis retaliated.

'That was different.'

'I don't see how.'

'Don't argue with me. You should have told me.'

Phyllis realised that her mother was really very cross with her. Mary was looking increasingly alarmed and suggested she take Shawna May into the parlour.

'No, no, stay where you are. I am at fault and I am sorry, Mother. It won't happen again.' She wanted to tell her about Lady Melton's planned trip to America but thought better of it. She wondered how she could break the news with the least pain. Ellen was very quiet through tea and Phyllis stayed as long as she dared. When they said goodbye at the garden gate, her mother hugged her tightly and whispered in her ear, 'Be honest with me, Phyllis. She isn't your baby, is she?'

Phyllis had to pinch her lips together hard as she shook her head.

'It's all right, my dear.'

'How did you know?'

'I'm your mother. It's my business to know these things.'

'I can't tell you . . .'

'I understand. You don't have to say any more. I'm grateful that you felt you could come to me to look after the child.'

'I – I didn't know what else to do. It's so complicated.'

'Not for the child, my dear. She is well cared for and loved. Her mother – well, her mother is another matter.'

'She wants to go home.'

'Her home is Melton Hall now.'

'Please don't say anything, Mother. Promise me.'

'Of course I promise. But if I can guess the truth, then others will.'

'I – I shall be taking her away quite soon. Lord and Lady Melton and her father are going home – for a visit. I shall go too.'

'To America? How exciting for you. It is what you have always wanted.' Mother leaned forward and kissed her cheek. 'You will be coming back though, won't you?' she whispered.

Phyllis swallowed and nodded. Another lie. Lady Melton was planning to stay in her homeland. For Phyllis, leaving England was one thing, but leaving her mother was another matter entirely. And there was someone else she did not wish to leave. Aaron Wilson was never far from her thoughts. And she believed he harboured affections for her, in spite of his animosity towards her. He was disappointed in her but he did not totally condemn her.

'Of course, I shall come back,' she reassured her mother. 'It is only a week or so away by ocean liner.'

Mother kissed her again on her other cheek and managed a tearful smile. 'I am very proud of you, my dear. I know that you always act in the best interest of others, as you see it. But do not forget to look after yourself. You are all I have left in this world.'

Phyllis's spine was ramrod straight as she walked away. She dare not turn her head and let her mother see the tears streaming down her face. The bond between mother and daughter had been strained but had not broken. She raised an arm to wave but did not look back.

Chapter 28
Spring, 1912

'I have made up my mind, Smith. I'm going to tell Melton about my baby.'

Phyllis was packing Lady Melton's cabin trunk at Melton Hall to send on to Southampton. 'Oh! Is that wise, My Lady?'

'I shall wait until we dock in New York. But I am determined not to be separated from my baby any longer. I shall tell Melton about Shawna May.'

'His Lordship will be furious, My Lady. He will divorce you. He will be obliged to.'

'Exactly, Smith. I win on all fronts. I hate my husband and I love my baby. I'm going to tell Daddy everything once we're on board the *Titanic* and I shall set foot on American soil with Shawna May in my arms.'

Phyllis inhaled slowly. She admired Lady Melton for

her courage, but she couldn't imagine what her husband might do to avoid such an obvious humiliation and scandal. She said, 'Lord Melton can be vindictive, My Lady.'

Lady Melton smiled. 'So can my daddy. He doesn't like to see his little girl unhappy, whatever the reason. He and Melton have business in London before we sail. They are taking the railroad and staying at Redfern House, so Daddy has agreed that we can travel to Southampton by automobile. Wilson will bring Shawna May to the Lodge as soon as they have left. You must write to your mother and tell her.'

Phyllis saw the joy and sparkle in Martha's eyes as she continued, 'Mary will come with her and we shall leave the following day.'

'We'll be in Southampton well before the *Titanic* sails.'

'I want you all aboard before the boat train gets in from London with Daddy. These ocean liners are huge and the *Titanic* is the largest ever built. I remember how confusing it was on the *Lytham Star*.'

'I shall find my way to you in first class, My Lady.'

'But I shan't find you and I have to reach you to see my baby. You have a four berth cabin for the three of you.'

Martha continued talking, excited about her plans. Phyllis shared her enthusiasm, but hers was tempered by the anticipation of the motor car journey with Aaron. She had to keep Her Ladyship's secret until her father knew and then, at last, she could be honest with him, to explain why she had to deceive everyone about Shawna May.

Phyllis had lost all hope that Aaron might fall in love with her as she had done with him, but she did not want him to think ill of her. She wanted, at the very least, to clear the air between them. He would not forgive her but surely, surely, he might understand? She became tense with anticipation about when and how she would unburden herself.

'I have the reservation, Mama! I secured one of the best staterooms. Anne will be delighted, I am sure.' Edward's plans for his honeymoon in early summer were coming together.

'I should hope so. Your father and I went to Italy.' His mother gazed out of her drawing room window over a green expanse of parkland and murmured, 'Tuscany was so romantic.'

'The *Titanic* will be romantic, but in a different way.'

Amelia smiled. 'Everywhere is romantic when you are on honeymoon.'

'Well I'm sure we shall hear all about it from Mel and Martha when they return. Anne is so looking forward to New York.'

'I am told that it can be quite hot over there in the summer. Has Anne definitely decided on Branbury for her marriage ceremony?'

'She has.'

'Well, it's tradition, I suppose. I married your father in the chapel at Melton Hall.'

'Rest assured that when I have a daughter, her marriage will be celebrated at Redfern.'

Amelia suppressed a sigh and frowned.

'What is it, Mama? I've noticed this concern whenever I talk about the wedding. Something is worrying you. You do approve of Anne, don't you?'

'Of course I do. It's just that I — I don't care for the idea of going forward into a marriage with—'

'With what, Mama? Stop frowning at me. You should be happy for me.'

'I am. I am.' She covered her brow with her hand and leaned her elbow on her ormolu desk.

Edward moved closer and bent to encircle her shoulders with his arm. 'What is it, Mama? Is it because Father isn't here to see me marry?'

'Yes, no, oh, I wish he were here to advise me! I wish he had never burdened me with his secret. I promised him I would do the right thing. But I don't know what the right thing is! I don't know!'

'Mama?'

She placed both elbows on her desk and the heels of her hands into her closed eyes. 'You should know! You cannot go into a marriage with such a secret waiting to destroy you!'

'Mama! What are you talking about? What secret is haunting you in this way?'

'I dearly wish your father had not told me, but it burdened him and now it burdens me.'

'Then you must let me share that burden. It cannot be so devastating.'

She moved her hands and he saw the beseeching look in her eyes.

'Can it?' he queried.

'I fear the knowledge will put your marriage in jeopardy.' His mother stood up and walked around her desk. 'Come and sit by the fire and prepare yourself for a shock.'

Edward picked up a fresh log and added it to the flames before taking the seat on the sofa. 'My shoulders are broad and strong,' he said.

She took hold of his hand and began, 'Do you remember a young maid who caught your attention just before you went away to university?'

He gazed at the cracking, sparking wood and did not answer her for a long time. Eventually, he said, 'It was over twenty years ago, Mama.'

'Do you know what happened to her?'

'Father sent her away.'

'What he did was for her best interests. Your . . . actions had ruined her marriage prospects.'

'But *I* loved her, Mama. *I* wanted to marry her.'

'Well that was not an option.'

'She must have believed that I had deserted her.'

'Perhaps. Your father persuaded her that you had a duty to the Redfern name and that it might not recover from the scandal. He introduced her to one of his best workers who became her husband.'

'I hope she found happiness with him. I have often thought of her. Indeed, I still do.' He became pensive then pulled himself together. 'Surely it would not be such a dreadful scandal if people found out about the affair now?'

386

His mother appeared to be holding herself rigid when she replied. 'Yes it would. She had a child, Edward, and the child was yours.'

'Mine! Come now, Mama.' He could not believe this! 'You have just told me that Ellen married.'

'You remember her name?'

'Of course I do! Ellen was my passion. I have not loved a woman in the same way since!' He stopped and stared at his mother, then to excuse his outburst, added, 'Anne is different. I am different. I am older and − and wiser.'

'I am not so sure that age affects the way we love, or that wisdom exerts any influence. But I have wrestled with my decision to tell you. If I was going to, it has to be before your marriage.'

'So that I could inform Anne and prepare her for a possible scandal? How long have you known, Mama?'

'When your father's days were numbered, he told me and made me promise to do the right thing for Ellen and her child. I have kept quiet so far, but this child is my flesh and blood too. Your father has left me with this dilemma. What is the right thing to do, Edward? You have a daughter, a grown woman who is my granddaughter.'

'Has Ellen been to see you about this?'

'No. She is not aware that your father told me. As far as she is concerned, now that your father and her husband are dead she is the only one left who knows the truth.'

'Has she told her daughter?'

'I am certain she has not. I have met her − her daughter − and so have you. She has a position at Melton Hall.'

'She is a servant?'

'She went first to help Nanny Byrne with the children and when Clara was alive she was her maid.'

'I remember her! And she went back when Melton married Martha. Martha calls her Smith.'

'She is your child, Edward. She was brought up as the daughter of your father's groom.'

Edward heart seemed to turn over and his chest felt tight. 'Where is she now, Mama? I must speak with her.'

'Please calm yourself, my dear and do not do anything hasty.'

'Hasty? I have been a father for over twenty years without my knowledge! Mama, is she going to New York with Martha?'

'She is.'

'They are sailing in a few days. Melton and his father-in-law have already left for London to meet up with them in Southampton.'

'Then do not act on this until they come home, my darling. Give yourself time to think of the consequences.'

'No, Mama. Too many years have been wasted already.' He bent to kiss his mother's hair. 'I'll sail with them if I have to.'

'Edward! Please exercise caution. It is too public. You are the Earl of Redfern and – and Phyllis is a servant.'

'She is my daughter.'

'I'm not sure you'll get a passage at this late stage. They are sailing on the *Titanic*. It's her maiden voyage and all the staterooms were reserved weeks ago.'

'Then I'll travel second class. I'll go steerage if I have to.'

'Now you are being ridiculous. Anne will be expecting you to be here when she arrives next week.'

'Anne! Good God, Mother, she doesn't know.'

'You have to talk to Anne first, my dear, before you go chasing across the Atlantic.'

His mother was right and he nodded pensively. 'I'll leave her a letter.'

'You should speak to her, Edward. This news will come as a shock.'

He thought about this but he did not change his mind. 'I am sorry, Mama, but at the moment, being with the daughter I have not known is more important to me. I shall offer to release Anne from our engagement. You must prepare yourself for her decision.'

'No, Edward, please don't do that! Wait for Anne to arrive and discuss it together. She will understand.'

'She will understand very well, Mama. I have humiliated her. If our roles were reversed and it was she who had a secret daughter, she is well aware that I should be obliged to call off the wedding.'

Amelia groaned. 'No, please no. Oh dear Lord, I wish I had not told you.'

'And I wish you – no, not you, Father – had told me years ago. I loved Ellen. I wanted more than anything for her to have my child. Twenty years, Mama! Twenty wasted years!' He pushed the bell at the side of the fireplace. 'I'll telegraph Mel in London and leave immediately.'

His mother shook her head. She had tears in her eyes.

'You are making a mistake, darling. I have a bad feeling about this.'

Edward relented slightly. 'You may be right, Mama, but I have to do it. I have to speak with her.'

'Then take very great care with her feelings, Edward. She does not know that you are her father.'

Again his mother's wisdom made him stop and think. 'Who does know?'

'Ellen, me, and now you. Your father protected you well.'

'Wilson's back, and he has Mary and Shawna May with him. I am so excited to have her with me again!' Lady Melton skipped about the drawing room at Melton Lodge as though the carpet were made of hot coals.

Phyllis was apprehensive about this arrangement, for mother and baby would be separated again as soon as they boarded the ship. She went to the front door, opened it and stood on the threshold as Mary carried the baby past her to the warmth of the entrance hall. Aaron followed with a travel bag. He seemed more relaxed and even managed a smile for her.

'Mr Haddon has all the valises waiting for me in the luggage room at the Hall. Your mother is well. She has sent some things for the journey although where I shall stow them in the motor I do not know.'

He seemed in remarkably good humour considering that he had been driving all day and had to pack everyone's luggage in the Melton before he went to bed.

'Thank you. There's tea and cake in the kitchen.'

'Will you join me?' He removed his gauntlets and hat and glanced at Mary waiting to hand Shawna May to Phyllis. 'Take the baby to Lady Melton. I want to talk to Miss Kimber.'

'I should be with Her Ladyship.' Phyllis took one step but Aaron moved faster and barred her progress and said, 'She will not notice you are missing. Her attention will be diverted for hours.' His good humour had gone and his expression was serious. 'Your mother told me of her doubts – about the child.'

Phyllis realised that he knew the truth. She tried desperately to hide her anxiety but could not and he went on. 'You weren't serious about concealing it for ever, were you?'

'No! Oh I – I don't know. Lady Melton was – very distressed when she had to give up her baby. She wanted to kill herself, and I – I couldn't let that happen.' Her voice cracked in her throat as she added, 'Not again.'

Aaron's voice was soft. 'You blame yourself for the death of Lord Melton's first wife, don't you?'

Her eyes were shiny with tears and she choked on her words.

'His Lordship's servants said that was the real reason you left.' He said, grasping her hand. 'I have misjudged you dreadfully.'

She took comfort from the touch of his skin. 'I didn't know what else to do and I didn't think about the consequences until afterwards. It was too late to go back on my word then.' She inhaled raggedly. She was shaking.

Aaron moved closer and placed his arms around her,

holding her head close to his chest. 'It's all right, Phyllis. The secret is secure with me.'

'Promise me,' she beseeched. 'Lady Melton lives in absolute dread of her father finding out the truth before she has a chance to tell him herself.'

'She needn't. He speaks of no one else when she is away, and in such glowing terms. He will forgive her anything because he loves her. I am not so sure about Lord Melton.'

'Her Ladyship has prepared herself for divorce and she says she doesn't care as long as she has her baby. She has decided to tell Lord Melton the truth. She cannot go on living apart from her baby.'

It was such a relief to be able to share the secret, and to share it with someone she trusted and − and loved. She leaned against him, feeling the cold brass buttons of his livery jacket press into her cheek. He stroked her hair on the back of her head and she felt the pins loosening. 'There'll be an enormous scandal,' she muttered into his chest.

'You'll be with her for support, and I'll be with you for the same.'

'You?'

'I shall be in New York with you.'

She lifted her head. 'Her Ladyship will talk to her father on the *Titanic*.'

'And we shall spend all our spare moments talking to each other.' He gently pushed her face back to his chest. 'I was wrong about you.'

'I was at fault, not you. Oh, it will so liberating to speak freely on so many things.'

'We certainly have plenty to discuss.'

'And so much to look forward to.'

She stayed locked in his gentle embrace until she heard the drawing room door open and Mary's voice calling her. She straightened and glanced in the hallway mirror, instinctively tucking away a few strands of hair. She smiled at his reflection over her shoulder.

He grinned back. 'This is our secret now.'

'For the present,' she nodded.

She hardly dared think of a future with Aaron. She had dreamed of one before and fate had conspired to separate them. This time her once-girlish dreams were about to be fulfilled by a whole week on the biggest most luxurious ship in the world with the man she loved. Her life had suddenly taken on a new meaning and the spring in her step was light.

Chapter 29

'What is it, Fraser?' Amelia had not rung for her butler and she had everything she needed at her breakfast table. But not everyone, she thought. Edward had telegraphed to inform her of his plans. The short message had kept her awake at night.

JOINED MELTON AND PARTY ABOARD TITANIC STOP ALL IS WELL STOP EDWARD.

All was most certainly not well! Anne had returned to her own mother as soon as she had read Edward's letter. Amelia's heart was heavy and she wished, she so desperately wished at times such as this, that she had a daughter of her own.

Fraser coughed again. He had his hands behind his

back and his shoulders sagged. He was clearly distressed. 'I . . . I . . .'

Amelia placed her napkin on the tablecloth and stood up. 'Fraser? Are you unwell?' She pulled out a chair. 'Sit down. Do as I say, my good man.'

He made an attempt to straighten his back. 'It's this, My Lady.' He handed her the newspaper he had been concealing. His hand was shaking. 'I – I understand your nephew and his wife were aboard.'

Amelia saw the headline and snatched it from his grasp. 'Oh dear Heaven, no.' She crumpled in her chair. 'Edward sailed with them.'

'Not His Lordship, too?' He collapsed against the chair and sat down with a bump. 'I do apologise, My Lady.'

'This is no time for ceremony, Fraser.' It couldn't be true. The *Titanic* was unsinkable. Amelia scanned the article underneath a picture of the ocean liner with its distinctive four funnels and the words 'great loss of life' jumped out at her. Her heart began to thump uncontrollably. But there were lifeboats. People escaped in the lifeboats. Survivors were picked up by a passing ship. Dear Lord, how long could you survive the icy Atlantic in an open lifeboat? She must be strong, she must stay positive. Amelia drained her tea and poured another cup, offering it to Fraser.

'Thank you, My Lady.' He took it without a protest and drank. 'What shall I tell the servants, My Lady?'

Her experience of dealing with the aftermath of mining accidents took over. 'Well, we cannot keep the newspapers from them but say nothing about His Lordship until we have more information. They already know that my nephew and his wife are – were – aboard.' She tried to raise a smile, but could not. 'Tell them that no news is good news.'

'Very good, My Lady.'

'Send a telegraph to Miss Branbury at Branbury Manor from me, too. *Edward aboard* Titanic. *Await further news*. Thank goodness that Miss Branbury is with her family for support.'

'Would you like the vicar's wife to call on you, My Lady?'

'That is very thoughtful of you, Fraser, but no. I shall make a visit myself this morning. Would you send the carriage round?'

'Not the motor car, My Lady?'

'No, Fraser. I'll take the small carriage. There will be two for lunch.'

He stood up glad, as she was, of something to do, she guessed. Amelia had been self-sufficient since her husband had passed on but she knew that could not be alone now. Losing James had been such blow but the possibility of losing Edward and Melton as well was too much to bear. 'We must keep ourselves busy, Fraser,' she said, rising to her feet.

'Yes, My Lady.'

Ellen Kimber rose early as usual, lit the range fire, break-fasted on porridge and washed up. She cleaned her cottage then sat down to plan what she would do with the rest of her day. It was only a week since Mary and the baby had been collected by Aaron Wilson and she was already thinking of contacting the vicar's wife about another foster child. She wished that Phyllis had been able to come over with the chauffeur, but understood how busy her daughter was with preparations for Lady Melton's sea crossing. How wonderful that Phyllis was able to travel as she had always wanted. Of course she missed her dreadfully but she was pleased that her daughter had gone back into service and not turned out to be a suffragist after all, especially now that, these days, they were so aggressive in their behaviour.

A ray of sunshine broke through the clouds and lit up her kitchen window. 'I'll sow some flower seeds,' she said out loud, and went through to the outhouse for her gardening apron. The yellow daffodils lining the front path were in full bloom. She tidied the borders around the squares of grass on either side and knelt down on a piece of old carpet to sow nasturtium seeds. A robin hopped about the surrounding privet hedge and she heard a blackbird protesting vociferously about a marauding predator. Then she heard a carriage coming down the lane, the unmistakeable clatter of a horse and carriage. She stood up and shielded her eyes against the bright spring sunshine.

'Lady Redfern? What on earth is she doing here?' she whispered to herself.

As soon as the driver reined in his horse, Her Ladyship opened the monogrammed carriage door herself and climbed down. She was carrying a newspaper.

'Mrs Kimber, may I speak with you?'

Ellen brushed her hands down the front of her jute apron and pushed her hair away from her face. 'Of course, My Lady, please come inside.' She cleaned her boots on the boot-scraper by the front door and led the way into her front room.

Lady Redfern scanned the room and asked, 'Are you alone here, Mrs Kimber?'

'Yes, My Lady.' The fire had been cleaned out and re-laid the day after Mary left with the baby. She bent to put a match to the kindling. 'Please excuse me while I wash. Would you care for some tea? Or coffee? I have coffee.'

'Thank you, coffee is most welcome.'

Ellen's mind was racing. Why had Lady Redfern called in person? If it were a welfare committee matter, the vicar's wife would have called. Perhaps the vicar's wife was ill? She pushed the kettle to the centre of her kitchen range hotplate and went to scrub her hands in the scullery then hurried upstairs for a clean dress and shoes.

The coffee tray was heavy as she pushed open the front room door with her bottom. Lady Redfern was already on her feet and she lifted the heavy coffee pot while Ellen put down the tray. 'Sit down, Mrs Kimber. Will you allow me to pour?'

'Of course, My Lady.' Ellen remembered the kindness shown by Lord Redfern when her own husband had died and a cold hand took hold of her heart. She became aware of the chill in the room although the fire was drawing well. She took the chair opposite the one vacated by Her Ladyship and glanced at the folded newspaper on her side table.

'Has something happened, My Lady?' she asked. 'Is it serious?'

Her Ladyship added cream and sugar to her coffee and handed it to her. 'I am afraid so, Mrs Kimber. There has been the most dreadful disaster. You must read it for yourself.'

As Ellen absorbed the words of the newspaper article they began to blur before her eyes. 'Fifteen hundred feared drowned,' she whispered. 'My Phyllis was on board.'

'Do not give up hope. Just as many lives have been saved by lifeboats.'

Ellen heard the choke in Her Ladyship's voice and realised whom Phyllis was travelling with. 'Oh My Lady, your nephew and his new wife.'

'And my son,' she croaked. 'Edward joined them just before they sailed. I had a telegram saying he was going to New York with them.'

'Oh no. No, no, no, no, no.' The newspaper crumpled as Ellen gripped it. 'But they said it was unsinkable.'

The article reported that there were not enough life-boats for everyone and it was mainly women and children who were saved. It gave Ellen hope for Phyllis but not, alas, for Lord Redfern or Lord Melton.

She said, 'You must believe that your loved ones were in the lifeboats and have been saved. You must keep saying that to yourself.'

'We must repeat it to each other. I should like to ask a favour of you, Mrs Kimber.'

'Anything, My Lady. I'll do anything to help.'

'I have lost loved ones before and suffered grief, and I have comforted the families of others who mourn, but this is not the same.'

'It is the not knowing that is tearing me apart,' Ellen added.

'The waiting,' Her Ladyship went on, 'is more than either of us can bear alone. I – I cannot face the next few days alone. Will you come and stay with me at the Abbey?'

The surprise must have shown in Ellen's face for Her Ladyship faltered.

'I – I should stay home for when Phyllis sends me a telegram.' Ellen's voice rose to a shrill. 'She will. Any time now, she will telegraph to tell me she is alive.'

She saw the alarm in Her Ladyship's eyes and forced herself to calm down. Hysteria was no good to anyone, least of all herself.

Lady Redfern reached across for her hand. 'Fraser will inform the post office of your whereabouts. Please, Mrs Kimber,' Her Ladyship's voice trembled, 'only you can understand how I feel, and—' she inhaled raggedly, 'you are the mother of my granddaughter.'

A half-strangled cry escaped from Ellen's throat and she began to shake. 'You know? Have you always known?'

'I have not. My husband told me not long before he died and I have wrestled with the secret ever since. You see, he never told Edward about your child and, at the end of his life, he regretted it.'

Ellen let go of Her Ladyship's hand and stood up anxiously. 'No, His Lordship did nothing to regret and, eventually, I

400

understood that. Edward's responsibility was to his family name and the future of Redfern. I could not have been a part of that.' She relaxed a little and added, 'We were very young, My Lady, and had no thought for the future.'

'But I believe that my son would have wanted to know about Phyllis.'

'I have often wished that he did. I am very proud of her. Her father was too. I – I mean Mr Kimber, of course.'

'So was His late Lordship, Mrs Kimber. And, like you, I wanted Edward to share that pride. We have more in common than you realise.'

'I can't lose her, not now,' Ellen whispered and the hysteria began to bubble in her throat again. 'She hasn't drowned, has she, My Lady?'

Her Ladyship rose to her feet and took her hand again. 'We have to sit this out together, Ellen. I may call you Ellen, mayn't I?'

Ellen's throat closed and she was unable to speak. She nodded and sniffed back a tear.

'Thank you, Ellen. You may call me Amelia.'

'Oh I couldn't, My Lady. It wouldn't be right.'

'You must try. You will come back to the Abbey as my guest, won't you?'

'Oh I couldn't.'

'Yes you can. Now go and pack a bag. We need each other, Ellen.'

After a moment, Ellen rose to her feet. 'Very well, My Lady.'

As Ellen went out of her front room she heard Lady Redfern add, 'I'll just wash these pots while I wait.'

This is unreal, Ellen thought. *The Countess of Redfern is standing at my scullery sink in a long-sleeved dress with her hands in dishwater.* Well, it wasn't unusual, the vicar's wife had told her, for Her Ladyship to help out miners' wives and widows at difficult times. But her only son and the heir to Redfern may be *dead*. Ellen would not allow herself to even contemplate such a fate for her daughter. Phyllis was alive. She had to be. She had led Mary and the baby to a lifeboat and she had survived. *She had survived.* Ellen repeated this over and over to herself as she took out one of Phyllis's valises and her best clothes and undergarments. If she were to be treated as a guest at Redfern Abbey, then a housemaid would unpack for her. She took extra care with folding her dresses, changed into her Sunday best shoes and carried the valise downstairs to her tiny hall.

Lady Redfern was standing in the kitchen doorway, peeling off sleeve protectors. 'I have damped down the fire.' Ellen was surprised she knew how to. 'Harvey will take your luggage.'

The carriage driver stepped inside her front door, touched the brim of his cap and said, 'Ma'am.'

Ellen knew Harvey by sight. He lived in the village and drank at the Redfern Arms. She managed a smile. 'Thank you, Mr Harvey.' But her mouth lost its optimism as she realised that it would not be long before everyone in the village knew about Lady Redfern's visit and her move to the Abbey. Tongues will wag. Had Her Ladyship spoken to anyone else about Phyllis? She could not bear for her darling daughter to be the butt of village gossip

402

and hesitated. 'I don't think I should go with you, My Lady. People will talk.'

'Your daughter and my son were travelling in the same party, Ellen. Either or both of us may receive the most distressing news and we must be together for the worst.' Her Ladyship's face lifted a little as she added, 'Or the best. We have to believe that our children are safe.'

'Yes. Yes, of course they are. When shall we know for sure, My Lady?'

'Fraser is making enquiries on my behalf. The post office has a telephone and he has contacts in London. He may even have news at the Abbey as we speak. Shall we see?'

Ellen locked up her cottage and followed Her Ladyship to the carriage.

'What on earth has happened to Fraser?' Lady Redfern asked as her head footman announced luncheon.

'He is not back from the village, My Lady. Before he left he asked me to wait on Your Ladyship in the dining room today.'

Ellen was staring out of the drawing room window, hardly noticing the splendid parkland that stretched as far as she could see. 'Why is it taking him so long?' she queried.

Her Ladyship replied, 'He will have to wait for a telephone line. I expect the London exchange is especially busy. Come along, Ellen, you must eat.'

'My stomach is tied in knots, My Lady. I do not think I could eat a thing.'

'The menu is light, I assure you, and you have to keep up your strength.'

She followed Her Ladyship into the grand dining room. It had not changed much since she was a girl except that the ornate chandeliers were now lit by electricity and the walls had been repainted. The same silk damask curtains hung at the huge windows and the woven Turkish carpet looked as good as new. Even the polished rosewood dining table had retained its high gloss. She lapsed into her memories of being young and pretty and experiencing her first love. And her only love, she realised, apart from Phyllis who had made her heartache worthwhile. Jack had taken care of her and she had served him well as a housekeeper but she had not loved him as a wife.

Ellen might have enjoyed the consommé and fish if her mind had not been elsewhere and she was constantly drawn to the window for sight of Fraser on his bicycle. Her Ladyship, too, was similarly distracted but they both agreed that the rice and pear pudding was particularly good.

'He's here, My Lady.' Ellen stood up for a clearer view of the driveway. 'Yes, I'm sure that's Fraser.'

Her Ladyship joined her at the window. 'It is.' She turned to her footman. 'Bring tea to the drawing room and ask Fraser to come straight in.'

Ellen was unable to sit still. She roamed around the comfortable linen upholstered chairs and sofas until Fraser entered the double doors, closing them behind him. He was frowning and her hand automatically clutched her throat.

'Come and sit down, Ellen,' Her Ladyship said.

'I can't, My Lady. I am on tenterhooks.'

'Well, Fraser, what have you found out?'

'I am sorry to say there has been a large loss of life, but many of the first class passengers were saved, especially the women and children. Also, it is known that the managing director of the shipping line and several wealthy passengers were in the first lifeboat.'

'Then we may hope that Edward and Melton are alive! Martha and her father, too.'

'Yes indeed, My Lady.'

'And what is the news of second class passengers?' Ellen asked.

Fraser seemed lost for words at first until she pressed, 'My daughter was travelling as maid to Lady Melton. She had a – a nursemaid and child with her.'

Fraser's frown deepened. 'It appears that there were not enough lifeboats for everyone on board. There – there are reports of people swimming for their lives and – and being pushed away from the lifeboats.'

Ellen suppressed the cry that rose in her throat. Lady Redfern stood up immediately and said, 'But Phyllis would have been attending to Martha. She will have been saved alongside her.'

'When shall I know?' Ellen anguished. 'When shall we all know?'

Fraser tried to calm her. 'There are telegraph messages coming in to London constantly, Mrs Kimber.'

Ellen turned away from them both and stared through the window at the greying sky. A movement in the distance caught her eye and she refocused on the tiny figure at the far end of the drive, pedalling for all he was worth on a bicycle. The telegraph boy from the post office!

'It's a telegram,' she cried. 'Oh My Lady, it's a telegram!'

'Fraser.' He only needed that one word from Her Ladyship to remove himself speedily from the drawing room.

He must have been away for only a few minutes but Ellen's nerves were at breaking point. He returned with the small folded document on a silver tray. 'It is for Her Ladyship,' he said.

Lady Redfern swallowed and picked up the message, opening and unfolding it quickly. She began to breathe heavily as she read and re-read the words. 'Our children are safe,' she announced. 'Ellen, they are safe. Fraser, you may tell the servants that His Lordship is alive and is on his way home.'

'Praise be to God,' Ellen cried. 'And Phyllis is alive, too?'

'Read it for yourself. It appears that Edward and Phyllis were not on board the *Titanic* when she crossed the Atlantic after all.'

Ellen took the small sheet of paper.

DISEMBARKED CHERBOURG WITH PHYLLIS STOP COMING HOME STOP MELTON MARTHA AND GEORGE ON BOARD STOP EDWARD

She read it twice. It was true. Neither Edward nor Phyllis had sailed. She frowned. 'Cherbourg? Why was

Phyllis with His Lordship instead of Lady Melton? I don't understand.'

Lady Refern did not comment but said, 'Fraser, would you bring in some of His Lordship's brandy?'

'My Lady.' He bowed his head and retreated.

'Do not be angry with me, Mrs Kimber. I told Edward about Phyllis. It has taken him a long time to find Anne and I did not wish to risk a future scandal. At least, I wanted him to be prepared.'

'But Phyllis's real father has been a very safe secret since she was born, My Lady.'

'I felt that my son should know the truth before his marriage. It is his decision whether or not he shares it with his future wife.' Lady Redfern appeared to hesitate. 'There is also Phyllis's baby to consider.'

'Oh. You have heard about the child that has been in my care?'

'I – I have heard that Phyllis has had a child whom you are looking after. Did you say *has been* in your care?'

'I did, My Lady. The child is no longer with me.'

'Has Phyllis taken her to America?' Lady Redfern looked frightened. 'She was on board the *Titanic* with her?' She seemed to shrink in her chair. 'No. No, no, no, no, no. The baby is my son's granddaughter and a Redfern.'

Ellen was flustered by the fact that Lady Redfern knew about Phyllis. 'Oh no, My Lady, you are wrong. The child is not my Phyllis's. She is—' Ellen frowned as she realised it did not matter whose child she was if she was in danger, '—she is Lady Melton's daughter.'

Lady Redfern shook her head in disbelief. 'But she

was born before . . . Oh yes I see, my nephew met his future wife on his last trip to America. But that means the baby is my great-niece. I don't understand why she was with you.'

The pain in Ellen's face intensified. All Lady Redfern's family could have been drowned. Her Ladyship needed the truth. She said, 'The baby who was with me was not your nephew's child. But it was Lady Melton's. Phyllis – well, Phyllis foolishly agreed to say the baby was hers so as not to jeopardise Lady Melton's marriage.'

'Did Phyllis tell you this?'

'I guessed most of it and Aaron – that's Wilson, Mr Strayhorne's chauffeur – has confirmed my suspicions. He took the child and her nursemaid to Southampton to board the *Titanic*. They were to travel with Lady Melton and Phyllis.'

Fraser came in with the brandy and poured two glasses. Her Ladyship took hers and drank immediately. 'I must speak with Wilson,' she said. He will have returned to Melton Hall by now. Fraser, would you send a telegram to Haddon at Melton Hall asking him to send Wilson here immediately?'

'Very good, My Lady.'

'He told me he was going to New York with them, My Lady,' Ellen said.

Chapter 30

Lady Redfern guessed that Haddon would be making enquiries just as Fraser had and asked him to telegraph anyway. If only she had a telephone! If only she had not objected to the telegraph poles across the park! Edward had asked her not to be obstinate but had allowed her decision to stand and the telephone company was taking its wires around a much longer route. Instead of feeling that a telephone would be an intrusion into the tranquillity of Abbey life, Lady Redfern was now convinced, as Edward had been, of its value.

A reply came from Melton Hall by return. Amelia was walking in her ornamental garden with Ellen. A chill breeze took the edge off the intermittent sun.

'Shall we sit in the summerhouse before we go back for tea?'

'Yes, why not? This wind is going straight through me.'

'I'll look out a fur for you. You have not experienced a truly warm coat until you have worn a fur.' Amelia was ready for Ellen's objection and went on quickly. 'I lend furs to my guests all the time. The east wind can be treacherous when one is not prepared for it.'

'Thank you, My Lady.'

Amelia smiled to herself, nodded then caught her breath. 'Is that Fraser?'

'It is, My Lady.'

Her butler hurried towards her, his long coat tails flapping in the breeze. Amelia took the document he offered on a silver salver, slit the seal with a silver paper knife and turned her back to the wind to unfold the telegram.

'*Wilson sailed with Melton Motor stop No news yet stop Haddon,*' Amelia read the words aloud. 'Thank you, Fraser. No reply.' Her heart was heavy. Another poor soul from her nephew's household in mortal danger. She twisted around to face Ellen and was shocked to see her eyes brimming with tears. 'Oh, you know Wilson! Is he a friend?'

'He – he came for the baby and her nursemaid and – and we talked about Phyllis. Oh My Lady, it was the way he spoke about her. He – well, he was very concerned about her so I . . .' Ellen inhaled raggedly and swallowed her tears. 'I told him the truth about the baby. He is in love with my Phyllis, I am convinced of it. He is such a kind man too and so perfect for her. I was so happy for them when I knew he was driving the party to

410

Southampton. He told me he and Phyllis had much to talk about.' Ellen shoulders sagged. 'I thought it was wonderful that they were sailing together. Oh My Lady, he would have been in second class!'

Amelia watched her tears spill over. 'Come along, Ellen. We won't go to the summerhouse. We'll go in for tea now and have a little brandy with it. Melton's old nanny used to take a drop in her tea when she came in from particularly bracing walks.' Her own voice cracked when she said his name. Melton. Her nephew Melton. Was he alive? If he was, where was he? She could not tolerate this waiting! 'May I take your arm, Ellen?'

'Of course you may, My Lady.'

'You may lean on me, too. Thank goodness we have each other. I shall ask Fraser to put on records in the music room after dinner tonight. Why did I not think of the gramophone before? We shall have our own private concert.'

'That will be nice, My Lady.'

Within a week, Amelia had received another telegram from her son to say that he was in London and would be on the railway train for Sheffield the following day. But she was not inclined to celebrate until she had word of the others in the party. There was still no news of her nephew and his wife, Lady Melton's baby and her nurse-maid, or of Mr Strayhorne and his chauffeur. Nonetheless, she ordered Edward's favourite roast ribs of beef for dinner and despatched Higgins with the motor car to meet him from the railway station in Sheffield.

Ellen accepted the wisdom of Lady Redfern's decision

for them to wait together until their son and daughter arrived home, except that Redfern Abbey was not Phyllis's home or hers. As well, she wasn't exactly comfortable with her position as guest and continued to put away her clothes at night and make up the fire in her bedroom. She stacked dirty dishes at the dining table and often fetched the silver brush and pan from the sideboard to sweep down crumbs before dessert. If Lady Redfern objected, she did not voice it and Her Ladyship's expression remained passively indifferent.

However, it was not etiquette or manners that worried Ellen. It was her meeting with Edward and the more she thought about it, the more she did not want it to happen. What was there to say to each other after all these years? They had each done what his father had required of them and she had accepted her fate stoically. She had understood. She had loved Edward and understood why she could not be a part of his life. What had happened to that love?

Jack Kimber did not even try to fill the gap and Ellen had grieved during her pregnancy. But when her baby was born, Phyllis had filled every corner of her being and her fragile young heart had healed. It did not matter to her that Jack had not loved her. She had Phyllis. And today? Her love for Phyllis was not diminished. Her passion for Edward had been over twenty years ago and she was a different person now, a mature adult. It was reasonable to assume that Edward had grown up too, yet she was nervous of his return.

'I think I shall go back to Chase Cottage for when

Phyllis arrives,' she suggested at breakfast that day. 'Perhaps you will allow Higgins to bring her and her luggage over?'

'I should like you and Phyllis to stay here, at the Abbey.'

'I am sure that finding out who her real father is will have been a shock for my daughter, My Lady. She will have many questions.'

'Quite so. I should like to give her time to know her father in his home.'

'Well, yes, I see that you would prefer that, but Phyllis may not wish to.'

'True. We shall let her decide. But whatever she does, you belong with your daughter, Ellen.'

Ellen could not argue with that. *Dear me*, she thought, *Phyllis gets her strong will from her grandmother.* 'Perhaps,' she agreed. 'My daughter has a mind of her own. I have known that since she was a little girl when sometimes she tried my patience to the limit. I know she will take a course of action she believes to be the best for everyone.' Ellen took a deep breath. 'My Lady, it is I who do not belong here! I belong where I have always lived, in Chase Cottage on the edge of the estate.'

'Indulge an old lady, Ellen, and allow me one night with my son and granddaughter and her mother under my roof. If Phyllis wishes to leave with you tomorrow, I shall not object.'

'Very well, My Lady.'

That day was interminably long and Ellen fidgeted constantly with not enough to do. She was used to working in her cottage and garden, not reading the

413

newspaper and dealing with estate correspondence as Lady Redfern did. The servants gave her cross looks when she attempted to help them and Fraser had had a word with her about 'getting under their feet interfering with their ways'. She could not wait for the party to arrive, yet dreaded it at the same time. The sight of the motor car from the drawing room window, making its stately progress across the park, caused her heart to thump. She stood, breathing deeply to quell her anxiety, as it approached the front door.

'Come with me, Ellen,' Her Ladyship said. 'All the servants are outside.'

She stood at the bottom of the steps by the side of Lady Redfern. The male servants were standing to attention on her right and the female ones on her left. Higgins stopped the motor car exactly in the middle and got out to open the doors. He was too late. The door nearest the house was opened and Phyllis was running towards her, her shoes crunching on the gravel, before Higgins reached it. Ellen was unaware that she, too, had been hurrying towards the motor, or that tears were streaming down her face.

'Mother!'

'Phyllis! Oh Phyllis, my darling, I thought I had lost you!' She did not know who was hugging whom the hardest. 'You didn't go! You didn't sail!' He voice was muffled by the fur collar on Phyllis's coat.

'His Lordship told me,' Phyllis whispered. 'He pleaded with me not to go to America until he knew me better. Aaron wouldn't sail without me, so he came off at Cherbourg with us.'

414

'Aaron is with you?'

'He's helping Higgins with the luggage.'

Ellen felt a light touch on her arm. 'Shall we go inside?' Her Ladyship was smiling and, beside her, her son stood tall and straight with an unreadable expression on his face; a face more worn and lined than she remembered, and his hair like hers had a touch of grey, but he was unmistakeably Edward, and the Edward she had loved. She was steered away between Phyllis and Her Ladyship.

The party was hungry and welcomed a substantial afternoon tea in the drawing room. But the atmosphere was sombre as Edward brought distressing news from London of many passengers unaccounted for. The survivors were being taken to Canada on board the *Carpathia* and there was still no word from Melton.

Ellen noticed that Aaron wasn't with them in the drawing room and asked after him.

'He'll be in the garages with Higgins,' Phyllis answered. 'I shall walk over there after tea. Will you come with me, Mother?'

Before she could reply, His Lordship interrupted, 'I should like to speak with you, Ellen, if I may.'

Ellen's heart began to thump again. 'If you wish, My Lord.'

There was a short awkward silence before Lady Redfern rose to her feet and said, 'Use the morning room. Would you come and find me afterwards, Edward? Dinner will be at eight tonight. Fraser is serving sherry at seven.'

Ellen allowed His Lordship to escort her to the morning room.

'Please sit down,' he said. He indicated the comfortable chaise longue by the fire.

'Thank you, My Lord,' she answered.

For some inexplicable reason she felt small, physically tiny. It was her surroundings, she realised. She was out of her depth in the Abbey. When his father had come to see her years ago, she had been on her home ground, at least at her lodgings in the village. For the first time in her life, as a mother herself, she wondered if her life would have been different if her parents had not been taken so young. The orphanage had been tolerable and she had been fortunate enough to gain a charitable award for her two years at Lady Maude's. But it wasn't the same as having your own mother and father. She gazed at the lively coals and her mind wandered.

'Will you, Ellen?'

'I – I'm sorry, My Lord, I . . .'

'Will you call me Edward?'

'Oh, I couldn't, My—'

'It would mean so much to Phyllis.'

Ellen spread her hands. 'She is able to adjust more easily than I, My . . .' she stopped, swallowed and added, 'Edward.'

'Oh, Ellen, Ellen, I did not know about her! You could have created such a scandal and you didn't!'

'I loved you. I wanted what was best for you – and for my child. She might have been taken from me and I could not have borne that.'

He came and sat beside her, picking up one of hands. She was inclined to snatch it away but resisted. 'It's gone,

416

Edward. The love has gone. It happened long ago and I have grown up.'

She had told the truth and the relief was evident on his face. 'Me, too. You know how much I loved you then, and I am truly sorry that I caused you so much pain.'

'You suffered more than I. I have had the love and the joy of my beautiful daughter, thanks to your father.' She saw a hurt expression cross his brow and regretted her frankness.

'You ladies understand affairs of the heart better than gentlemen. I pray that Anne will understand and – and forgive me.'

'She will if she loves you, Edward.'

'I sincerely hope so. I have been without my daughter for too long and I shall not disown her. Phyllis is part of our future.' He smiled for the first time and she saw in his face the young Edward she had once loved.

'Go to Anne now, Edward. She needs you.'

'I shall.' He let go of her hand and stood up. 'Thank you, Ellen.'

Ellen thought that Amelia seemed more robust at dinner, as though she had absorbed strength from those around her. She retired early, making a point of kissing each of her guests on the cheek before she left the room. Ellen was the most surprised and least comfortable with this. Aaron and Phyllis were at ease and seemed to take their new family's acceptance in their stride. Their family. *Theirs*. In her mind they were a couple, at least, she prayed they were a couple, for she was certain they loved each other.

417

But they were a twentieth century couple, she thought, ordinary folk with the benefit of education and travel that gave them confidence to move in the highest circles.

Dinner, though delicious, was an exhausting occasion. The emotions of loved ones who had escaped almost certain death by a stroke of fate were influencing everyone's behaviour at the Abbey. Lady Redfern had known that it would, whatever the outcome, and had come to her for support. Ellen had watched her cope so graciously with the trauma of the last few days. She was an old lady, old enough to be Ellen's mother, and Ellen had needed her as much as anyone else at this table.

The discussions continued and Ellen noticed the butler becoming restless. So did Lady Redfern, who rose to her feet a little awkwardly. 'The servants need to clear,' she said. 'Shall we continue our conversations over coffee in the drawing room?'

Ellen got up immediately. 'Edward, your mother is tired. Perhaps Phyllis can pour the coffee? Shall I help you upstairs, Amelia?'

'Thank you, Ellen. That is most kind of you.'

Chapter 31

Christmas, 1912

'Here are the stepladders! Hurrah! Aaron, where do you want them?' Phyllis watched him direct the Redfern electricians to set up a pair of high wooden steps as near to the Christmas tree as possible. It was, she conceded, one of the biggest Christmas trees she had ever seen and it had taken six men with a block and tackle to position it in the marble-floored Great Hall of Redfern Abbey. A tree any smaller would have been dwarfed by the room's lofty proportions. The enormous fireplaces at each end had been banked up and roaring since early morning to take away the chill.

'Do they have to be at the top?' Aaron called as he mounted the steps.

'At the very top, on that upright branch that stands above all the others.' She stood back to get a clearer view and added as an afterthought, 'Like a crown.' A circle made up of the flags of His Majesty's Empire was traditionally the crowning glory for any Christmas tree.

'I don't suppose the children can even see it from down there,' he commented.

'That's not the point. The adults expect it. It's their Christmas as well.'

'Not this afternoon, my love. How many children are coming?'

Phyllis didn't reply. It still caused a thrill to stir in her heart when Aaron called her 'my love', because she knew he meant it. She could not wait for them to be alone. She wondered when that would be this Christmas. After the dreadful news from Canada before the summer, he had been obliged to return to Melton Hall and oversee the motor car workshop until its future was settled. It was Phyllis who had suggested to her father that he invite Aaron to the Abbey for Christmas and New Year.

'Do be careful, Aaron!' she cried as he stretched over to secure the flags.

'Do you want them there or not?' he answered. 'Are they straight?'

'I can't see properly from here.'

'Well, stand over by the door where you can. I'm not coming down until they have your approval.'

Phyllis surveyed the majestic hall from the ornate double doors, opposite the French windows that looked out on to the park. The Christmas tree took pride of place in front of the floor-to-ceiling glass doors so that the children would see it as they came along the drive in traps and farm carts and a horse-drawn omnibus from the village. As soon as Aaron had finished, the estate electrician would take away the steps and switch on the new tree lights.

'It's beautiful,' she called.

'Can I come down now?'

She laughed and he began his descent. Before long more than a hundred children of varying ages would be entertained and fed by Abbey servants and a band of mothers and fathers marshalled by the vicar and his wife. Phyllis knew, because her mother had told her, that most parents were delighted their children were out of the house on Christmas Eve so that they could finish making their presents and prepare Christmas dinner to go in the oven tomorrow.

The Great Hall had been divided by screens brought down from bedrooms to accommodate all the planned activities. The gramophone was carried in from the music room and a list of party games arranged. Phyllis would be reading Christmas stories to the little ones in her own corner that she had furnished with cushions on the floor and a collection of dolls to act out the parts. Aaron would be helping with the magic lantern show in the opposite corner. They had electric light for that too, now. When she had been a child the lantern had used oil lamps and candles.

The biggest attraction by far was tea, laid out on long trestle tables in front of one of the fireplaces with sand-wiches, cakes, jellies and sweeties that the children loved. A kitchen maid walked by her with a plate of lemon curd tarts. They looked delicious but Phyllis grimaced as a voice in her head, one that sounded too much like Nanny Byrne for her comfort, murmured, 'I hope none of them are sick.' She wandered over to the vicar's wife and said, 'Are we using the servants' water closets in the basement?'

'They are the nearest.'

'But even so, some of the very tiny ones . . .'

'Don't worry, Miss Kimber. One of the ante rooms has been furnished with commodes and washstands just in case. The other one is the hat and coat lobby.'

'Yes, of course. You do this every year, don't you?'

'We do indeed,' the vicar's wife smiled and added, 'it is good to have you on board.'

Phyllis smiled back but thought her choice of words was unfortunate, considering the past year's upheavals. She moved away, her mind distracted by that awful event. Even now, she shivered at the thought that she should have been on board the *Titanic* when it hit that fatal iceberg. Aaron too, and they would surely have perished along with most of the other passengers in second class and steerage.

At the very last minute her newfound father had embarked with her. Her real father! The very thought of him made her shiver with excitement. He had filled her heart and mind for days, shutting out all others including her darling Aaron. Now, she thought naturally of Lord Redfern as her father, but she remembered when she had not believed him.

They had talked through the night and it was his need

to return and explain his actions to his beloved Anne that, Phyllis had realised, was tearing her father in two. This dilemma had persuaded him not to sail and, as he did not wish to be parted from Phyllis so soon, he begged her to disembark with him. Although Phyllis had been looking forward to a new beginning for her relationship with Aaron, she agreed and sought out Aaron to tell him. Aaron – again a shiver ran through her as she recalled his decision – Aaron, her dearest, darling Aaron would not cross the Atlantic without her. Love had saved all three of them and she trembled every time she thought of it.

Love had also saved Shawna May and Mary. Lady Melton's love for her baby had made her decide to give up her marriage long before they sailed. As things turned out, Phyllis was sorry that Martha would never return to England. But she understood the traumas Martha had faced during that endless icy cold night in the lifeboat. But their last conversation had been a civil one where Martha had asked Phyllis to join her later in the year. There was no such exchange between Aaron and Mr Strayhorne who had dismissed him on the spot when Aaron had informed him of his decision to disembark.

On that disastrous night when the *Titanic* went down, Lord Melton and Martha's father had met a fellow motor car enthusiast and were dining with him. They had bribed – Martha's own word in her letter to Phyllis – a crew member to allow them into the cargo hold to show off the Melton Motor, chocked and strapped for its journey. They were deep in the bowels of the ship when the iceberg ripped into the ship's hull and must have been amongst the first to perish.

Martha had taken advantage of their distraction and taken dinner in her stateroom. She had insisted that Mary join her with her child. As women in first class and with an infant, they were on one of the first lifeboats to be launched, and spent a freezing night exposed to the North Atlantic weather, distressed, but alive, waiting to be picked up by the *Carpathia*. Phyllis had read later that every child travelling in first class had been saved. Others were not so lucky.

'The children are waiting for you, Miss Kimber.' Phyllis walked across the marble floor to her reading corner for story-time. She glanced over at Aaron keeping a careful eye on the older boys, as directed by the vicar's wife, until it was time for their special ghostly magic lantern show. Phyllis loved acting out stories for the little ones and was sorry when the music for country dancing started. She closed her story book and ushered the children to their places for tea. Afterwards, they played pass the parcel and blind man's buff while their older brothers and sisters devoured a mountain of food that continued to appear from the Abbey kitchens. Phyllis knew that some exhausted parents were being similarly fed in the servants' hall below stairs.

It was dark outside by four o'clock and the electric chandeliers glowed brightly. The little ones were tired and the older children quietened by extended stomachs when the vicar's wife called for silence.

'Hush!' she cried. 'Listen, children!'

The Great Hall became still as the sound of small bells

became louder. Aaron appeared by her side. 'Are they old fashioned horse bells?' she whispered.

'Sleigh bells, I believe,' he answered seriously.

'Really?'

'Wait and see. The estate carpenters have been working on this all day. I fixed the lamps.'

'What's that outside, children?' The vicar and his wife were standing in front of the French windows beside the Christmas tree and someone switched off the electric light. In the gloom through the glass a farm cart drawn by a heavy horse wearing a collar of bells plodded to a standstill. The cart was decorated with holly and ivy, festooned with coloured paper chains and lit by carriage lamps. But it was the driver who riveted the children's attention.

'It's him.'

'He's here.'

'Look, he's outside.' The whispers hissed around the room as a figure in a long red coat and hood edged with white cotton wool climbed down from the cart. He heaved a bulging sack onto his shoulders. The vicar opened one of the French doors. 'Look children, it's Santa Claus and he's brought everyone a present.'

Santa came inside and set down his sack. He was a tall thin gentleman wearing a cotton wool moustache and beard that was supposed to disguise his face. 'Now then, children, boys line up this side and girls over there, little ones at the front.' His put-on Germanic accent made the adults suppress giggles but the children were captivated.

'It's my father,' Phyllis laughed.

'Ssshhh, don't let anyone hear you.' Aaron slid his arm around her waist. 'Are you exhausted? These children take more organising than Lord Melton's daughters.'

Phyllis agreed. She was sad for a moment as she thought of those little orphans. They were her second cousins. 'What will happen to them now that Lady Melton isn't coming back?' she asked.

'Their day-to-day life hasn't changed as they didn't see much of their father anyway. Nanny Byrne has two nursemaids from Lady Maude's, and their mother's brother is their legal guardian.'

'Really? I didn't know the first Lady Melton had a brother. Did he ever visit her?'

'Very rarely. He was in charge of Ashby Shipyards in Scotland so they hardly saw each other. He didn't get on with his sister.'

'She was a difficult lady,' Phyllis commented.

'Her uncle, Mr Ashby's younger brother, is taking over in Scotland so that his son can move back to Yorkshire with his wife. They will look after the children.'

'Poor girls. They'll have to move from Melton Hall.'

'No, certainly not. Ashby Shipyards own it and have done for years.'

Phyllis could hardly believe her ears. 'Who told you that?'

'Mr Ashby's solicitor called a meeting of all the servants and explained. He said the Ashbys were moving in and keeping on all the servants.'

'Including you?'

'Sadly not. I was Mr Strayhorne's chauffeur. But I am

still in charge of the workshop at Melton Halt.' Aaron did not seem very happy about this. 'I spent a year of my life on the prototype that went down with the *Titanic*. It was supposed to secure orders for our future.'

'Our future?'

'Mine and yours. I planned to ask you to marry me when we were in the middle of the ocean. Then His Lordship arrived on board and said he was your father. It was as much a blow to me as it was to you. I have to say you appeared to take it very well. I realise now that your composure was all a cover, wasn't it?'

Phyllis nodded. 'I shook like a jelly every time I thought about it.'

'Me too,' he echoed, 'but for a different reason. Overnight you became Lady Phyllis. Why would the daughter of an earl want to marry the son of a farm labourer?'

'Because she loves him!' She said it without thinking and her raised voice cause a few heads to turn. 'She – I – love you,' she added more quietly.

'Oh my darling Phyllis, I love you too.' He lifted her hand to his lips and kissed it.

Phyllis heard one of the older children choke on a giggle and she pulled away her hand. 'Not here with all these people around us.'

He looked disappointed at first then said, 'I should ask His Lordship's permission first, anyway.'

'You don't have to. I'm over twenty-one and, strictly speaking, not legally his daughter.' She wasn't Lady Phyllis either, for the same reason, and never would be.

427

'Nonetheless, I shall wait a little longer. I'm not taking any chances with your happiness. You are too precious.' His hand crept further round her waist and hugged her closer.

Phyllis could have stayed there in the shadows with her head resting on his chest for ever. But mothers and fathers or older brothers and sisters appeared to collect the children and she was on hat and coat duty. She was thrilled, of course, that Aaron had effectively proposed to her yet his concern for their future worried her. Phyllis intended to marry Aaron. But there was a bigger hurdle to overcome than her father. A huge question mark was hovering over the future of the Melton Motorworks.

Phyllis knew this from Martha's letters and had kept it to herself. The workshop was losing money. If it closed down, Aaron would be without a job. He was a proud Yorkshireman and he would not offer her marriage unless he was in a position to support her. She bit her lip. She should have said something when he mentioned the workshop a moment ago. But it would have spoiled the moment, and, anyway, no one had heard officially from Martha's lawyers yet.

George Strayhorne had owned Melton Lodge and the motor workshop. The extent of his investment was kept secret because the workshop traded on the Melton name. When he perished in the Atlantic, Martha as his next of kin inherited all his wealth. Lord Melton had left his wife nothing except his title, ironically the only thing she and her father had really wanted. All that remained of the

Melton fortune were trust funds for each of his daughters, which were locked up until they reached twenty-five. Martha, more than anxious to sever all connections with the biggest mistake of her life, planned to put the workshop and the Lodge up for sale. Phyllis knew, as Aaron did, that without American orders, the Melton Motor did not have profitable future. She knew, also, that Aaron would not make her a formal offer of marriage without some hope of a future for them both.

They separated reluctantly, she to the children's hat and coat lobby and he to help store away Santa's sleigh safely in the garages for the following year. He was staying at the Abbey but dining with her father's land steward and his wife tonight, so she would not see him again until Christmas Day. Christmas dinner at the Abbey was a larger than normal gathering this year, with the Branburys as well as Ellen, Phyllis and Aaron.

Her father had asked his young cousins with their new family to join them as well. It wouldn't be easy for anyone as Christmas was the time when lost loved ones were most missed. Her father planned to formally remember those they had lost on that tragic night last April. Phyllis acknowledged that it was necessary. He had discussed a prayer with his mother to say when they assembled for Christmas dinner, to be followed by thanks for those who had survived.

Young Mrs Ashby sent everyone her best wishes for the season but declined the invitation. She felt that the children who understood their loss would manage their grief better in their own surroundings. Phyllis agreed with her and, although she had not met the new mistress of Melton Hall, she admired her for that decision.

And there was Anne, wonderful, wise Anne Branbury who, despite her young years was making an excellent Countess of Redfern. The Dowager Countess approved, and more importantly to Phyllis, her own mother agreed. Phyllis valued her mother's opinion above all others. They both wanted her father to be happy and he was. He and Anne had had a quiet September wedding. The new Lady Redfern had not attended the children's party as she was feeling a little out of sorts and Phyllis knew why. Anne was expecting already. Most of the women in His Lordship's household had realised this and they waited patiently for him to make a formal announcement.

Aaron was late for sherry before dinner on Christmas day. Phyllis was feeling unusually nervous. When Aaron was near she wanted to be physically close to him, to love him properly and let him love her in return. He wanted her too, she was sure, so why was he taking so long? She knew he was worried about gaining her father's approval and about his future at Melton Motorworks so she did not press him. But she was tempted! He would crumble, she had no doubt, if she was determined to seduce him. If they didn't seal their love this Christmas when would they next have a chance?

Edward and Anne had not yet appeared. Phyllis was wearing a fashionable dusky pink costume that her mother had made, consisting of a high-waisted skirt with a fish-tail flounce at her ankles. It had a matching short jacket that covered her rather risqué low-necked blouse and she wore a tall feathered hair ornament fixed by a jewelled tortoiseshell comb. Her grandmother had kindly lent this to her for the evening and it finished off her outfit splendidly. When Aaron did arrive he wore a formal black dinner suit with starched white shirt and black bow tie. It was the first time Phyllis had seen him in evening dress and she was momentarily stunned. He smiled broadly, acknowledged the other guests in the room, collected a glass of sherry from the silver tray and walked purposefully towards her.

'You've cut it fine,' Phyllis whispered, 'we'll be going into dinner soon.'

'I've been talking to His Lordship. You look very beautiful tonight, my love.' He leaned forward to kiss her cheek.

Phyllis's eyes darted from side to side. Several pairs of eyes had watched Aaron enter the room and walk over to kiss her on the cheek. Oh well, she supposed everyone knew about their relationship anyway. A few seconds later, Edward and Anne entered the room followed by Fraser who announced that dinner was served.

The dining room shone with polished rosewood, crystal and silver. Red candles in the shining candelabra added a festive touch but the atmosphere was sombre as Edward led his guests in a prayer of remembrance followed by grace. Phyllis glanced at the menu card in its silver holder. Nine courses! And just as many wines! The scullery maids will be washing up at midnight! She smiled inwardly, knowing how much Abbey servants enjoyed their below-stairs life.

Servants stayed at the Abbey because they took pride in their work and they loved it. A factory or shop was not for them. Here they had bed and board, good clothes on their backs, and friends. The servants' hall was their own private club where even her father and grandmother were intruders. The house steward ruled through the butler and housekeeper and everyone knew their place. Her mother had known the value of such an existence but it had been different for Phyllis. She had been out in the wider world and she knew she could never go back to life in service, not even as a lady's maid. It wasn't for her, or, she suspected, for Aaron either.

They were seated together and could speak to each other only at every other course. However, Aaron refused to be drawn on his conversation with her father. 'Wait and see,' he commented.

After fish with mayonnaise, stewed pigeons on toast and tomato farcies it was time for roast turkey followed by a saddle of mutton. Thank goodness she was expected to eat and drink only a small amount at each course. Aaron seemed to have no difficulty with quantity and his eyes lit up when the three tier plum pudding appeared. Then they had fruit from the Abbey's productive glasshouses, made into a salad that Phyllis enjoyed, and French *foie gras* for any of the gentlemen still hungry.

It was after ten when Lord Redfern tapped a glass with his spoon and rose to his feet. His butler stood to attention by his right hand. Edward began by thanking Fraser, asking him to extend his thanks to all the servants for such a wonderful meal. There was a spontaneous and appreciative clapping from the guests and, much to Phyllis's surprise, Fraser's face coloured. He didn't expect to be thanked for doing his duty. When Fraser had left, her father thanked everyone for making this Christmas day the best he and his family could hope for in the circumstance and gave a short speech on looking forward in the twentieth century.

'We have, all of us, been through difficult times, but we have survived them as a family. I pray that, as a family,' he scanned everyone sitting at his table and repeated, 'a family I am immensely proud of, we shall always stand together as we have done this year.'

There was a murmur of supprt. Aaron's hand reached for Phyllis's on her lap. 'He approves,' he whispered.

Phyllis raised her eyebrows.

'Of me as your husband,' Aaron added.

Phyllis wanted to whoop with joy but she was obliged to sit and wait with the widest of smiles on her face for her father to finish his speech.

Edward continued. 'And now for the announcement you have all been waiting for me to make. I am delighted to inform you that my darling Anne is expecting our first child next summer. Please raise your glasses in a toast to the future, to all our futures.'

Everyone stood up, murmured, 'The future' and drank.

'And now, 'the King.' After the toast to King George they remained standing. The servants on duty filed in and they all sang the National Anthem.

It was an exhilarating moment for Phyllis and she sat down feeling that she really was amongst her family and that included Aaron. Three footmen appeared from behind the screens with dessert. They placed the dishes of nuts and grapes at intervals along the long table for guests to help themselves. Fraser served coffee at the table. The formality of the evening was over. Amelia and Lady Branbury went over to Anne, while Phyllis noticed her mother speaking to Edward. She would be saying how pleased she was about the baby, Phyllis thought. Fraser opened the door that linked the dining room with the music room for those who wished for entertainment. She felt a tug on her arm.

'Over here.' Aaron drew her behind one of the high window drapes out of sight of the group around Anne and knelt on one knee. He had a tiny box in his hand that he opened to reveal a small gold ring set with rubies and pearls. 'I love you Phyllis,' he said. 'Will you marry me?'

'Yes,' she nodded. 'Of course I will.'

He slid the ring on her finger.

'It's beautiful.'

'I'm so glad you like it. It was my mother's.' He kissed her briefly on the lips and led her back to the table. She noticed him exchange a brief nod with her father, who tapped his glass again.

'Before you all scatter,' he exclaimed. 'I have a second announcement. My daughter, my lovely Phyllis, has just agreed to marry Mr Aaron Wilson.'

Phyllis beamed and held her left hand high for all to see. Everyone clapped and above the din, she heard her father call, 'Fraser. We'll have the champagne now.'

* * *

Later that night, Phyllis collapsed onto a couch in the music room declaring, 'I can't dance another step, I'm exhausted.'

'Drunk, more like,' Aaron laughed. He had taken off his dinner jacket and his black bow tie was undone.

'Maybe,' she agreed. 'But very, very, very happy.' She looked around. 'We're the last up. Everyone else has gone to bed.'

'They've no stamina, these aristocrats.'

They laughed together. When they had calmed, Aaron said, 'I couldn't wait to ask you to marry me and I had to sit through all that food!'

'You enjoyed it well enough, as I recall. Are we agreed, then? We'll have a winter wedding, here in the village church?'

'Agreed.' He was serious for a moment. 'Your father has been very generous.'

'Mmm.' Phyllis nodded. He had bought Melton Lodge with the motor car workshop from Martha and was giving it to them as a wedding gift.

'I'll have to raise other investment, though, to continue production.'

'You'll get it. You know what you're doing.'

'So do you. Mrs Ashby was very keen for you to be her lady's maid.'

Phyllis was shaking her head. 'I wasn't going to tell anyone that she'd written to me. Anyway I declined. I felt bad but I did offer to find someone for her.' She sat up suddenly. 'That's given me an idea.'

Aaron plonked himself beside her on the couch. 'Yes?'

435

'I could do the same for others. They have agencies in London for placing servants. I could set one up, here in Yorkshire for local folk. I could even train them if they really want—'

He kissed her in mid-sentence, deeply, passionately, with an open mouth and searching tongue and she was the one to crumble, pulling him on top of her and returning his passion with her writhing body.

He sat up and whispered, 'Not here. Fraser is still around.'

'Let's go to my bedroom.'

'I'll carry you.'

'It's a quarter of mile of corridors!'

'Well, maybe half-way then.'

'We'll run, it's quicker.' She stood up and took his hand.

He grasped hers firmly and gave it a squeeze. 'Together,' he said.